D0006476

A PLUME BOOK

THE GARDEN OF RUTH

EVA ETZIONI-HALEVY is professor emeritus of political sociology at Bar-Ilan University in Israel. She has published fourteen academic books and numerous articles. Born in Vienna, she spent World War II as a child in Italy, then moved to Palestine in 1945. She has also lived in the United States and spent time in Australia before taking up her position at Bar-Ilan. Eva lives in Tel Aviv with her husband; she has three grown children.

ALSO BY EVA ETZIONI-HALEVY

The Song of Hannah

THE
GARDEN OF RUTH

Eva Etzioni-Halevy

A PLUME BOOK

PLUME

Published by Penguin Group

Penguin Group (USA) Inc., 375 Hudson Street, New York, New York 10014, U.S.A. · Penguin Group (Canada), 90 Eglinton Avenue East, Suite 700, Toronto, Ontario, Canada M4P 2Y3 (a division of Pearson Penguin Canada Inc.) · Penguin Books Ltd., 80 Strand, London WC2R 0RL, England · Penguin Ireland, 25 St. Stephen's Green, Dublin 2, Ireland (a division of Penguin Books Ltd.) · Penguin Group (Australia), 250 Camberwell Road, Camberwell, Victoria 3124, Australia (a division of Pearson Australia Group Pty. Ltd.) · Penguin Books India Pvt. Ltd., 11 Community Centre, Panchsheel Park, New Delhi – 110 017, India · Penguin Books (NZ), cnr Airborne and Rosedale Roads, Albany, Auckland 1310, New Zealand (a division of Pearson New Zealand Ltd.) · Penguin Books (South Africa) (Pty.) Ltd., 24 Sturdee Avenue, Rosebank, Johannesburg 2196, South Africa

Penguin Books Ltd., Registered Offices: 80 Strand, London WC2R 0RL, England

First published by Plume, a member of Penguin Group (USA) Inc.

First Printing, January 2007

10 9 8 7 6 5 4 3

Ⓡ REGISTERED TRADEMARK—MARCA REGISTRADA

LIBRARY OF CONGRESS CATALOGING-IN-PUBLICATION DATA

Etzioni-Halevy, Eva.

The Garden of Ruth / Eva Etzioni-Halevy.

p. cm.

ISBN 978-0-452-28673-3

1. Women in the Bible—Fiction. I. Title.

PR9510.9.E89G37   2007

823'.92—dc

                         222006019992

Printed in the United States of America

Set in Bodoni-Antiqua and Cochin

Wherever you go, I will go;
where you stay, I will stay.
Your people shall be my people,
and your God my God.
Where you die, I will die,
and there shall I be buried.
I swear a solemn oath
before the Lord your God:
nothing but death
shall pry us apart.

—Ruth 1:16–17

Part One

IN THE FOOTSTEPS
OF RUTH

Chapter One

By the time Osnath entered her chamber, night had fallen over Bethlehem. But the moon shed its silvery light over it, so she had no need to light the oil lamp that stood on the table. She prepared to slip off her shoes and slide into bed when a muffled noise arose from it. Her senses suddenly alert, she inserted the small stick of wood lying on the table into the pan that kept the fire alive. Once the wood caught fire, she lit the lamp and lifted it above her head. When she bent over the bed, she heard the noise more distinctly: a rustle, accompanied by a flicker of movement under the sheet.

She straightened herself and stood motionless, her throat tight and her eyes wide with the quiver of fear that ran through her. Gathering her courage, she lifted the sheet with a swift sharp movement. She was aghast at the sight of a snake, a poisonous brown-and-yellow-patterned viper, writhing before her eyes, until its head buried itself under the cushion, followed by its lengthy wriggling body.

Osnath's mouth opened to a soundless scream. Dropping the sheet, she dashed out to the backyard on which her room opened, with the lamp still in her raised hand. Once she had shut the door behind her, she uttered the strangled cry that had been sitting inside her, and it tore the night's silence.

There was a patter of hastily shod feet, as the relatives with whom she had been visiting for more than two months came tumbling out of the house. At their head was her old kinswoman Hagith, with her headscarf askew. Annoyed at being startled out of her sleep, she admonished Osnath, "What were you about, to scream like that?" But when scrutiny of the girl's face revealed the terror in it, her heart softened and she enfolded her young guest in her arms and whispered soothingly to her.

After Osnath had been prevailed upon to tell what had happened, several lighted lamps were brought into her room. Her bedding was lifted up and closely inspected. The table and the chair that flanked it were moved out of the way, the colorfully woven rug on the floor was folded up, and her belongings were removed from the little wooden case that stood against one of the walls. The entire room from floor to ceiling was searched, but there was nothing. The snake had vanished.

From the dubious looks on her relatives' faces, Osnath knew that they doubted it had ever been there. They knew the fifteen-year-old girl to be given to dreams, on whose wings she soared to bygone times and distant places; and they believed that the viper had been yet another of those dreams. But Osnath was not pacified, and her heart continued to race with wild fears and suspicions.

Her scream and the commotion that followed it also woke the inhabitants of the adjacent house. The father, Jesse, hastily adjusting his garment, followed by his wife and all eight sons spilled into the common backyard of the two houses, bearing flaming torches in their hands.

The firstborn son, Eliab, the tallest of the lot, was the one she suspected, after what had previously transpired between them. She angrily quizzed him with her eyes. The sadness in his as he noticed her suspicion momentarily melted her mistrust. Then she took in his dark looks and overbearing demeanor, and her suspicion reared its head with even greater vigor.

When Eliab saw that her misgivings had not been laid to rest, he stepped forward and told Hagith that it would be well if Osnath were to spend the night with her in her room. The girl pointedly ignored him, but he did not wait for her response. As one accustomed to having others defer to him, he put his hand under her elbow and helped her to that room.

But when all had calmed down, and Hagith, her breath rasping through her open mouth, was sleeping peacefully beside her, sleep would not come to Osnath. Even in the worst of the nightmares that occasionally troubled her at night, she had not conjured up an event of this harrowing nature: that a man to whom she had done no harm would conceal a poisonous snake in her bed. Was it because by digging into the history of his great-grandmother, Ruth the Moabite, she might discover a murky secret that he was determined to keep from her prowling eyes?

Ruth. A name so short, so beautiful. How could such a small name contain such a big mystery? One so devastating that a man was willing to kill to keep it safe?

The next morning, Eliab gave instructions for all cracks in the walls of the two neighboring houses to be filled and plastered over, so that no snakes could lodge in them, and for all low-growing plants in the two families' joint garden to be cut down, so that serpents would no longer be able to find shelter in their foliage. He also ordered any snakes found in the vicinity to be killed and their nests destroyed. But even this did not restore her trust in him.

For a man who could take advantage of a young girl's innocence was capable of any despicable deed.

Osnath had come over from Ramah in the hill country of Efraim to visit Bethlehem in the domain of Judah at the beginning of the tenth month of the year, when the wintry rains had eased off for a few days. At that time nothing was further from her mind than the notion of retracing the past.

The thought had come to her when she caught sight of some curious words on an ancient little scroll. Strangely, it had been Eliab's own invitation that led her to it, an invitation he had issued on the evening of her arrival.

She had come to Bethlehem to escort her mother's mother, Pninah, on a visit to her sister, Hagith. She had moved there many years ago to marry a man from that town and, like Pninah, was now a widow. With them was her uncle, the prophet Samuel, Pninah's deceased husband's son by another wife, who went there to convene with the town's elders.

Pninah was greatly concerned with the welfare of the girl, the youngest of her many grandchildren, the one who was so dreamy and distant from all that surrounded her. And so, too, was Samuel her uncle, who always had kind words for her. Indeed, they were like second parents to her, and she was often in their company.

Thus it came about that when they traveled to Bethlehem, they offered to take her along. She was eager to go with them, as she wished to visit the distant town she had not seen before, and took pleasure in riding in Pninah's carriage.

It was driven by two stablemen, who also served as guards. Pninah and Osnath reclined on the backseat, and Samuel, sitting straight-backed in his mule's saddle, rode at their side. A tall, broad-shouldered man of advanced years, he had wild graying curls, which protruded on all sides from under his head covering, and blew in the wind. The road, which wound across gently sloping green hills and valleys, rolled by under the carriage's wheels. Swaying with its pace, Osnath dozed, her head resting on Pninah's shoulder.

Though weary from the journey, she snapped her eyes open as they reached the outskirts of Bethlehem, where the houses of the two families stood before them. These imposing, spacious structures, built of heavy hewn stones, were spread out in a rambling manner. Their many rooms attested to their owners' wealth and high stature. Beyond their shared backyard stretched their hedged garden, set with fig and almond trees, and lined with shrubs and flowers.

The carriage entered the front yard to the rich, welcoming fragrance of fresh bread baking in the furnace and garlic-spiced red lentil and lamb stew simmering on the cooking stones. As Samuel helped Pninah and Osnath alight, Eliab, who stood close by, saw the girl for the first time.

While words of welcome were spoken, hugs and kisses exchanged, and gifts proffered and lavishly praised, Jesse's eldest regarded her closely. He was entranced by her pretty face and by her blue-gray eyes that seemed too large for it. They proclaimed a bewildered innocence, belied by her incongruously sensuous mouth. He was captivated by her skin—the color of milk with barely a touch of honey in it—and by her untidy mass of dusky curls that spilled onto her flustered cheeks.

And by her round breasts, like those of a woman grown, which even under the coarse gray woolen dress she had selected for traveling were visible on her still-childish, slim body. He found this child-woman strangely alluring. He could not take his eyes off her.

Osnath was far from being enchanted by him. She glanced up at him furtively, and instantly recoiled from his unusual height and breadth. His black eyes and swarthy skin and sinister looks, no less than his brown head covering and his garment of the same color, seemed dark and frightening. Oddly, even the fringe he wore at the edge of his garment, laced by a blue thread at its corners as prescribed by Torah law, seemed ominous to her. She let him unload their bags from the carriage, but the moment she took hold of hers she retreated from him and rushed into her relatives' home.

Undeterred, the young man waited only until the guests had been provided with copper basins to wash their hands and feet. No sooner had they sat down for the evening meal at the oblong table that filled Hagith's front room than he came in.

Hagith, her firstborn son, Uri, whose wife had died the year before, and his daughter, Adah, the only one of her grandchildren who was still unmarried, sat down for the meal with their guests.

Adah was an uncommonly pretty girl, eighteen years of age, with copper-colored curls and dark, almond-shaped eyes; a hearty smile seemed to be permanently glued to her face. Yet Eliab was oblivious to her presence. While hosts and guests were stilling their hunger with the bread and stew set before them, he sat down next to Osnath. He declined the food offered him, feeding instead on the sight of her, the like of which he had never seen in all the twenty-seven years of his life.

Osnath knew that his family was related to Hagith and that she owed him the courtesy due to a kinsman. Yet she kept her head bent, clearly demonstrating that she wished to be left alone. But Eliab ignored her unfriendly demeanor. While the others ate and traded family gossip, he told her about himself and asked her about herself, but she was guarded with her words to him.

When, on his request, Osnath bashfully told him her name, he said, "Your mother has chosen well in naming you after the wife of Joseph, the forefather of your tribe. It is a proud name, well suited for the daughter of a noble family such as yours."

When this flattery elicited nothing but a faint smile from her, Eliab was not in the least discouraged.

Osnath's grandmother and her mother were both scribes, engaged in instructing children in the art of reading and writing and in the Torah tales and laws. Ever since she was seven years old, she had studied with them to become a scribe, too, and she shared their love for the written word. When Eliab learned of this from Samuel, his eyes lit up. "Women scribes are scarcer than rain in summer. And whoever heard of three generations of women scribes in one family? It is wondrous indeed."

Loath to bask in glory that was not her due, Osnath demurred. "Although I can read and write, my proficiency in the Torah has not been deemed sufficient for me to be proclaimed as a scribe."

"But no doubt it will be so soon."

Eliab's renewed effort to ingratiate himself with her called forth no response from her at all. Instead, it elicited one from Hagith's granddaughter, Adah. The meal having been concluded, she rose from her chair. A moment later the door closed silently behind her.

An awkward silence ensued, which left Eliab unperturbed. It was Pninah who broke it, by speaking to him. "Although female scribes are indeed rare, they are not unheard of. Apart from myself and my daughter, there are two more women scribes in the hill country of Efraim, one of whom is also a poetess."

"My great-grandmother, Ruth, was also wont to write poems. This house harbors a scroll room, built by my great-grandfather Boaz, on her whim," Eliab said helpfully. "You, esteemed lady Pninah, and Osnath may come at any time and browse through the many scrolls stored there."

At last he had succeeded in impressing the girl, for scroll rooms were to be found only in the houses of scribes or of the wealthy. Although her grandmother's house also held one, there must surely be a multitude of scrolls here that were not available there. Osnath had a penchant for reading the tales of olden days written down in ancient, crumbling scrolls hiding in remote corners of forgotten shelves. Perhaps Eliab's scroll room contained some of those. The opportunity to read them took strong hold of her mind.

Thus, for the first time, she met his gaze head-on with a smile on her face.

During the next few days, Pninah was engaged with her sister and her nephews and nieces and their children, almost all of whom no longer lived in the house but came to visit on her account. And Osnath was wary of invading Eliab's house on her own.

So, to fill her time, one day she obtained Pninah's permission to go out for a solitary walk in the fields. The sky had been washed clear by the previous day's rain. When the trees that lined the fields were already casting lengthy shadows, but before the sun slid down behind the hills in the west, she followed a bend in the path that rounded itself alongside a small hill. Emerging into an open terrain, she was startled by the sight of arrows flying, then lodging themselves in a large tree a mere twenty paces from her.

Wary of being hit by a stray arrow, she was about to turn on her heels and tread the path around the hill once more, when she heard a voice calling, "Cease!" and saw an unknown young man striding toward her. Some way behind him was a contingent of some fifty youngsters, lowering the bows in their hands.

Catching her unsteady breath, Osnath found herself face-to-face with the young man. He was red-haired, with skin as light as a sunlit day, eyes as dazzlingly blue as the summer sky, and a body as lithe as a deer.

"Who are you?" she gasped in surprise.

"I am David, the youngest son of Jesse and the shepherd of his flock. And you must be Osnath, Hagith's young guest and the niece of the prophet Samuel. How is it that you came this way on your own?" he added sharply.

"I was merely going for a stroll. But what are the strange goings-on here? I cannot see that you are tending any flock," she retorted indignantly.

"I have bestowed it in the sheepfold. And now I am teaching the young men of Judah archery."

"People may inadvertently be hurt."

"All the townspeople know not to approach this spot before apprising me of it. You must not do so, either."

Her indignation now gave way to curiosity. "What is the purpose of this?"

Suddenly his eyes came aglow with a strange light, as if a fire had been lit behind them. "We must study war so that when our enemies attack we may be able to defend ourselves."

"But how can such a small group of youngsters stand up against our vast enemies?"

"Once trained, each one of them goes forth and trains fifty more young men, so that in time we will all be prepared."

As there was a king in Israel, Saul, this seemed odd to her. "Should not the king send out his officers to engage in this task?"

"The king has other matters on his mind," replied David airily.

"Are you not too young to be coaching others?" she persisted.

"I am sixteen years of age," he replied stiffly, as if she had hurt his pride. "I have been practicing archery and battling with a sword and shield and the slinging of stones ever since I was a child; and now I am well versed in all manner of warfare."

Having put his second-in-command in charge of the contingent, he announced, "I will accompany you home."

At first he walked in silence, his gaze straying from the path in front of them to her face. He regarded her intently, his blue eyes delving into her blue-gray ones.

"Why are you looking into my eyes?" she asked shyly.

With a smile lurking in his, he declared, "Because I can see your soul reflected in them, and I like what I see."

"You are funning," she protested.

"Why else would I be looking into your eyes?" he teased her. "You cannot think I am doing it merely because they are so beautiful."

Her cheeks assumed the color of red roses. Noticing the blush on her face, he inclined his head toward her and recited words from a famous love song: "'I am the rose of the valleys.' Imagine a rose of the valleys in the hills of Judah!'"

"You are jesting again."

"No," he contradicted her, the smile vanishing from his eyes. "I am entirely serious."

By that time they had reached the edge of the two houses' common garden. He opened the gate for her to enter. Then he retraced his steps, leaving her to wonder about this young man, so unusual in his coloring and his demeanor. Wondering also whether she had truly found favor in his eyes.

The next day, upon Eliab's return from the fields, he coaxed Osnath to enter the scroll room with him. It was a square chamber, three of whose walls were covered by shelves on which rested a plethora of scrolls arrayed in layers, one on top of the other. Its fourth wall held a stone bench and a window. A blue curtain hung over it to shield the writings on the shelves from the strong sun streaming in, and the light that filtered through the hanging was pleasantly subdued. The scent of parchment and the musty smell of years long past hung in the air.

Eliab made Osnath sit at the table, showed her some of the room's many treasures, and assured her again that she had his permission to come there whenever she was moved to do so. After that, she went there daily and plowed her way through the books, shelf after shelf. She delved into times of old, reading the most wondrous stories about heroes—judges and prophets and leaders—who had brought succor to the people of Israel whenever they were in dire straits, tales that sparked her imagination. They also awakened in her an aspiration to write a tale of her own.

She had a way with words and liked to spin them into yarns of days long gone. At times her daydreams were so powerful they almost seemed real. Even so, she was aware that they were only figments of her imagination. She yearned to write a tale that would record as-yet-undiscovered momentous events that had truly occurred.

A few days later, as her hand moved about on a high shelf in search of another book to read, it came to rest on a tiny scroll. It lay hidden in a dark corner under a much larger one that she had just dislodged. She pulled it out and unrolled the tightly rolled-up parchment and held it up to the light. She began to read:

Hear me, my loved one.
You are red-haired and fair.
As a wild goat in the desert
yearns for a spring of water,
so does my body yearn for you.
Abandon him, who is unworthy of you,
and give your love to me alone.
So speaks the man to whom you are pledged.

Osnath was mystified, a hundred wonders in her heart, a thousand questions in her mind. The missive had without doubt been written by a man to the woman he loved, who was pledged to him, yet preferred another. But who had written it and to whom?

In the flicker of that instant, a bold notion took shape in her mind: to trace the mystery enfolded in the words she had read.

She would be like the spies Moses had sent out to explore the Promised Land. As they had explored the unknown country, so would she trace the life of the unknown woman, and of the two men who had formed part of it. Then she would write a scroll in which their veil of secrecy would be torn off and their story brought to light.

While she stood gazing at the letter, Eliab, who had returned from the fields, came in, recalling her from her reveries. With his eyes even darker than usual, he drew the scroll from her hand without uttering a word, and placed it on the highest shelf. But its contents had already ingrained themselves in her memory.

"Did you write the missive, sir?" she marveled aloud.

He laughed. "Can you not see that the parchment has assumed a brownish color? The letter was written long before my birth. So long ago that I had forgotten its existence."

"Who wrote it?"

"This is part of the saga of my family, which cannot be of any concern to you. There are enough other scrolls for you to peruse."

"Still, it has made me curious. Can you not tell me anything about it?"

"Let the dead rest in peace. Withdraw your hands from them."

His words held a note of finality. Disappointed, she left the room with hunched shoulders, and went to recline against a tree in the garden.

Eliab followed her and tried to distract her by telling her about other members of his family. But she sat with her chin resting on her drawn-up knees, and a churlish look on her face, until he gave up and went to wash away the sweat of the day's labor.

She was not left sitting on her own for long. A short time later, David came back from tending the family's flock on the hill and, after hustling them into the sheepfold, sat down next to her.

Apart from the rare colors of his eyes and hair and skin, the bones of his face were splendidly shaped, like what she imagined the sculpture of a Canaanite god to be. Thus, she did not find it surprising that there were several girls from neighboring houses who looked at him seductively from under their eyelashes. But since he had first encountered Osnath in the fields a few days ago, he'd had eyes for her only. He sought her out in the garden whenever he was not engaged with his flock or with his archery, and now he chatted gaily with her about her life and his.

It occurred to her that since he was red-haired and fair, he might be a descendant of that red-haired fair loved one to whom the words in the scroll had been addressed.

When she inquired if it was so, he concurred. He said that Ruth, the mother of his grandfather, had been red-haired and milk-skinned, and had also had blue eyes like his. She had brought those unusual features with her from the land of the Moabites, where she had lived before she became part of the people of Israel. He also resembled her in that he composed poems, as she had been wont to do.

He had no answer to the question of who might have written Ruth the love poem she discovered. But he recalled some rumors that had been rife in his family that she had been a widely acclaimed beauty and that there had been another man—besides his great-grandfather—who had succumbed to her charm.

Then David, having lost all interest in his great-grandmother, plucked a flower and lightly brushed Osnath's face with it, and told her softly that he preferred her shiny black hair, in which the rays of the setting sun sparkled like diamonds, to that of any other color.

While she was searching for suitable words to voice in response to David's, her eyes alit on Eliab, who was at the window of his sleeping room, watching her keenly. There was an intense look in his face that at first made her feel vaguely uneasy. Then she realized in astonishment that it was not entirely unpalatable to her, and the words she was about to utter withered in her mouth. She took leave of David and returned to Hagith's house. And it was quite a while before the turmoil in her soul subsided.

Chapter Two

Once she had calmed down, Osnath went to look for Pninah and found her sitting with Hagith and Adah in the front room. While the elder women talked, the two girls sat without uttering a word, as befitted the modest number of their years. Then Osnath realized that Hagith, who was of an older generation, might enlighten her about the love letter she had unearthed, more than David had been able to do. So when Pninah retired for the night, she remained behind and prompted Hagith to tell her whatever she knew about Ruth.

Hagith had a shrunken face, with deeply etched lines like those of the parched earth after a drought, and a dwindled body. The strands of her hair, which peeked out from under her headscarf, had been dyed with henna into a brownish red color, which also covered her eyelids. Her almond-shaped eyes often had a vague look in them, but they became surprisingly sharp at Osnath's question.

When she first came to reside in this house, Hagith replied, she saw Ruth and talked to her quite often. Since then, so many years had passed that she could offer only scraps of half-forgotten memories. But as she spoke, they came to life and wore flesh and bones again.

When I first saw Ruth, she recounted, the Moabite was already old. But I was told that in her youth her face had been a sparkle of sunshine framed by a crown of luxurious red hair, with two tiny tresses descending over her temples, and the rest falling in ringlets down her back.

The skin of her face, visible between her plaits, had been light and smooth as ivory and her teeth as flawless and as white as pearls. An aroma of crushed myrrh lodged in her dresses, so that she was always fragrant to the nostrils.

Despite the flaming color of her hair in her youth, she had never been bold and brazen, but modest and friendly and generous. In her old age, she always had a kind word on her lips for me, who was even more of a newcomer to Bethlehem than she.

Since Ruth was so much older than I was, I felt reluctant to ask her prying questions about why she had come over from a distant land to make her home in this town. But in time Ruth warmed to me and told me on her own.

It had begun a long time before, at the time when the land was still ruled by the judges. There was a famine in the land, and a man from Bethlehem, with his wife and two sons, went to the land of Moab to find sustenance. After a while the man died, leaving his wife, Naomi, a widow. Her two sons took Moabite wives, one of them Orpah, the other herself, Ruth. In time the two sons died also, so that Naomi was left with her two daughters-in-law.

When the famine was over, Naomi set out to return to Bethlehem with the two young women. By the time she arrived, though, only Ruth was with her, Orpah having left her on the way. But Ruth never enlightened me as to why this had come about.

Her elbows on the table and her hands supporting her chin, Osnath sat listening attentively to the story. But it left her confounded, for it did not supply an explanation for the missive to Ruth she had discovered. When she asked Hagith about it, her old relative fell silent.

The girl pelted her with a barrage of questions. But Hagith answered only that this message held a tale that would best be left untold. Then she closed up the way a flower shuts its petals at sundown, and Osnath could extract nothing more from her.

After her old relative headed for her room, Osnath was left alone with her granddaughter. As soon as Hagith was out of earshot, Adah, who had never repeated her impolite conduct of the first evening, said, "At times my grandmother's words spill out of her like a spring in winter, but at other times she is as silent as that same spring in the summer, once the water in it has dried out."

Osnath found the old woman's silence incomprehensible. "Why is she so adamantly guarding a secret of so long ago?"

Adah's smile was usually quick to emerge and hardly ever left her face, yet now her countenance darkened. "My grandmother says that some secrets are so vicious, they lash out at those who reveal them even after several generations."

The oil in the lamps on the table and in the niches along the walls was getting low. The lights began flickering and then, one by one, they dimmed and died out, leaving behind darkness.

Suddenly, inexplicably, Osnath felt herself shuddering.

Still, she hoarded Hagith's words in her mind as bees hoard honey. When she reached the room allotted to her, she sat at the table and lit the one oil lamp that stood on it. With only the stillness of the night and an inkwell and iron pen as her companions, she made a record of her kinswoman's words on an empty scroll that Samuel had given her as a gift.

Hagith's sudden silence and Adah's dire warning only made her all the more eager to solve the puzzle contained in the letter to Ruth she had discovered.

Ten days after their arrival in Bethlehem, as they all sat eating their morning meal of bread and olives, Samuel announced that he had accomplished all he had set out to do in the town, and asked Pninah if she were ready to accompany him back to Ramah.

She agreed, but Osnath demurred. "My revered grandmother and uncle," she said, "I have discovered many marvelous books in the neighboring house's scroll room, and if Hagith is willing to put me up for a while longer, I request that I be left behind until I've had time to read them all."

Pninah hesitated, for she suspected that the eight young men in the neighboring house, two of whom had rested their eyes (if not their hands) on the girl already, were the true reason for Osnath's wish to prolong her stay.

But, to Osnath's relief, Samuel supported her. He ran his hand through his unruly hair. Then, with a glimmer in his deep green eyes, he said that her path would not be strewn with roses initially in Bethlehem, but that she would eventually meet her fate there.

Osnath did not know what her uncle's enigmatic remark signified but was grateful for his intervention, for no one in her family ever disputed his judgment. Hagith, who had taken a liking to her sister's granddaughter, added her voice to that of Samuel. Only Adah pursed her full lips until they formed a thin line, which no one paid any heed to. So a messenger was dispatched to her parents, requesting their permission to extend her visit.

A few days later, the messenger returned with their reply. Her father and mother set it as a condition for their consent that Hagith take it upon herself to guard the girl as closely as if she were her own granddaughter. When Hagith good-naturedly agreed, Pninah and Samuel departed.

No sooner had they left than Adah came to Osnath's room. She sat down on the bed and, after hesitating briefly, announced, "Last night I had a dream. A strange dream about our grandmothers, when they were still young women. Your grandmother visited mine, and while she was here, she did all she could to attract her husband's attention.

"Our grandmothers then had a noisy quarrel, with shouts flying back and forth between them, at the end of which Pninah left Bethlehem, never to show her face here again."

Rushing to the defense of her adored grandmother, Osnath exclaimed, "Pninah never endeavored to steal your grandfather's affection. She had, still has, enough love of her own."

"The dream took on a life of its own, and I could not put a halt to it. I will pay no further heed to it."

Yet Osnath thought of how much Adah and herself resembled their grandmothers as they had been in their youth. Hence she did not require Joseph, the forefather of her tribe, the great dreamer and interpreter of dreams, to decipher Adah's dream for her. Adah was set on engaging Eliab's affection and feared that Osnath might deprive her of it. And she hoped devoutly that Osnath would put the greatest possible distance between herself and Bethlehem, as had Pninah.

With her light curls and dark eyes, Adah was undoubtedly the best-looking of the girls in the neighborhood. Besides the beauty of her face, there was something earthy about her. It had not taken Osnath many days to note that the right sleeve of her tightly fitting dress was wont to slip casually off her shoulder, revealing more of her well-formed breast than was seemly, whenever Eliab was present and her grandmother was not. Osnath saw, too, that her rounded thighs swayed seductively whenever she passed by him.

But equally it did not take Osnath long to realize that Adah was wasting her efforts: Eliab showed no more than amused indulgence at her seductive wiles. She had a mind to tell the young seductress that her dream was senseless, for Eliab's affection was not given to her in any case. But she decided to spare Adah's feelings and kept her peace.

Old age was imperceptibly creeping over Hagith, and she became more scatterbrained by the day. She was sorely remiss in fulfilling the duties she had taken upon herself as Osnath's guardian. But the girl made no complaint, for thus did she enjoy more freedom than she ever had before.

This enabled David, whenever his other duties allowed for it, to sit with her in a secluded spot in the garden, where he murmured words of love into her receptive ears. He was more eloquent than she had thought anyone could be; each day he found new and ever more elaborate words in which to express his feelings for her. She was deeply touched, and greatly admired him, but told him that she was not yet ready to respond in kind. This prompted him to assure her that he would wait patiently for the day on which she would reciprocate his love.

Whenever David was not with her, Eliab was. Each day, after coming home from the fields, he hardly let her out of his sight. When she sat in the garden on her own, spinning dreams threaded with the gold of sunshine, as was her custom, he was quick to take up his place at her side. He was more sparing with words than his youngest brother, but his eyes spoke a language of their own, conveying the message that his lips left unspoken. Eliab's powerful body and his dark coloring, which had frightened her at first, no longer had the power to do so. At times, she even found his manly strength reassuring.

Still, of the two young men who were strenuously vying for her, to her mind it was David who was endowed with outstanding gifts that no one else could hope to equal. He was a marvel to her in every way, and there were many others who marveled at him as well.

Shortly after Pninah and Samuel's departure, once at twilight, Osnath heard a noise in the backyard. When she looked out, she saw it filling with a large crowd of young men of all sorts and demeanors, who sat down, evidently waiting for David. When the backyard and the garden beyond it had filled to capacity, he came out to them. As she sat at her window, she heard him deliver an elevating speech.

David fixed his eyes—their deep blue color reflecting the darkening sky—on a point in the distance. With his clear, melodious, yet penetrating voice, he regaled his admirers with a vision: of the land of Israel secure from its enemies, the murderous Philistines, who were threatening its borders. Of a land in which each man sat peacefully under his vine and his fig tree. And of the House of the Lord to be erected on the highest mountain in the mighty city of Jerusalem.

He interspersed his speech with lofty hymns extolling the splendor of the Rock of Israel, whose glory filled the world, who would bring them succor from their foes. He let it be known that with the Almighty's help, he, David, would make the dream turn into life.

Since the vanquishing of enemies on the battlefield, like the training of young men for warfare, was in the king's domain, it was anything but clear to Osnath how David could do so. But the youngsters drank in his words as if they had bubbled out of the fount of wisdom. They caressed him with their eyes and cheered him exuberantly, and he accepted their homage easily, as his due. He mesmerized them as if he were their leader and they, not merely his followers, but his servants to command.

Osnath thought it puzzling that one so young should call forth so much adoration. But she found the answer in the compelling sound of his voice, which seemed to spring forth from the innermost recesses of his soul, in the glow that lit his eyes and the eyes of all who beheld it, and in the magic of his words.

David was unique also in that he had a way with song and with the lyre, which he now took up in his hands. Osnath sat for a long time, listening to his melodies as they sailed into what had become the dark of the night. Her eyes were fixed on the moon hanging heavily over Bethlehem; and in her mind she saw it setting the town's roofs alight with its silvery rays, as David set it alight with his tunes.

When David's admirers dispersed, she went out to him. The air was still, filled with the scent of garden flowers. He spoke to her softly, telling her that her eyes shone more brightly than the stars, and that she was the flame in his heart and the delight of his life.

After a while, she asked him what his followers expected of him. David recalled himself with difficulty from his amorous mood. When he did, he merely said, "Is it not obvious?" and left her perplexed, asking herself what it was that should have been obvious to her.

At times, Osnath continued to delve into the life of her two suitors' great-grandmother. She searched the scroll room for any hint it might yield about her, but for a while she found nothing.

Eliab thoroughly disapproved of her design, yet was drawn to her like an ant to date nectar. With his hungry looks constantly on her, it was as if he was waiting for the right time to lure her into sin. Then one day, at dusk, the opportunity came.

As she was sitting in her usual spot, the sky, overhung with heavy clouds, began to rumble. She could hear the sheep and goats bleating their fear in the distance, and the wail of the wind like jackals in the night as it swept through the trees. Then, flashing swords of fire tore the clouds before they exploded into roars of thunder. Torrents of rain poured down and lashed at her face, soaking her dress, wetting her to the bone.

She ran toward Hagith's house but tripped and fell into the mud, feeling the sharp pain of a stone graze her knee. Eliab, who had been peering at her through the lattice of his window, shuttered it. He wrapped himself in his goatskin cloak and came running toward her and lifted her to her feet. He enfolded her in his cloak and pressed her body, shivering with the cold and the wet, to his dry and warm one and rushed her inside.

When she emerged from his cloak, she found herself in a strange room, evidently his. She turned to leave, but the rain had become a veritable flood.

"Let me dry you," he said, "and when the rain lets off, you may go."

He sat her on a chair and wiped the rain and the mud from her face and hands and legs with a cloth. There was nothing loverlike in his brisk manner, and she felt unexpectedly comfortable under his rough ministrations.

When she was as dry as he could get her, he brought forth a decanter of wine distilled from dark grapes and poured a cup for her. Though sweet, the wine was strong, and Osnath could swallow only a few sips of it. Even so, it soared its way into her stomach, until she warmed up and her teeth ceased chattering. Then Eliab filled a cup for himself and drank deeply.

Emboldened by the wine, he sat on a chair next to hers. He drew her into his lap, sitting her sidewise, with her head resting on his shoulder, and rocked her soothingly. In something of a daze, she nestled in the warm safety of his large body.

The wind was still whistling, and the rain was pounding on the windowsill. But inside, a fire crackled on the hearth, its flames dancing on Osnath's face and striking into the twilight. She was warm from its heat, which mingled with that of the wine she had drunk.

Eliab saw her eyes gleaming with the heat outside and inside her, and thought there was an unspoken promise in them. Aroused beyond bearing by the outlines of her body under her clinging wet dress, and by the feel of her in his arms and by her womanly scent, he turned her around, bit by bit, to face him. But she folded her legs to one side and kept her knees tightly locked and primly covered with her dress.

He lifted it slightly and stroked her thighs gently. An unsought, previously unknown surge of desire raced through her, causing her to tremble anew. It also made her relax her legs, enabling him to bring one to each side of him and thrust into her.

Suddenly, lust gave way to pain and wrath, and a pang of fear shot through her. She mustered all her strength to fend him off, but she was wedged between his arms on her back and his chest on her front. Her exertions had as much effect as if she were attempting to dislodge a heavy oak tree firmly planted in the ground.

His mouth closed over hers, muffling the yells that tried to escape from it, which were drowned out also by the torrential rain and the gusty wind outside. He was dauntless, going on with zest, taking his pleasure, oblivious of her anguish.

When it was over, Osnath staggered to the nearby chair and folded up her knees and buried her face between them, sitting curled up like a babe in its mother's womb, in a languid stupor. Soon she regained her senses, and it was then that she began to feel debased and besmirched. She straightened up and began ripping at him, blaming him loud and long and bitterly for what he had done.

When her litany finally ceased, he said softly, "You did not utter one word that could have led me to believe that what I did was unwelcome."

"My mind was addled by the wine you made me drink," she said feebly.

He looked at her in scornful disbelief. "You hardly touched the wine."

She glared at him. "You lulled me into a sense of safety, then took advantage of it."

"And you tantalized me by quivering with passion in my arms."

She disregarded his words. "You should have asked me."

"Would you have wished for me to elicit your permission in writing?" he mocked her.

"While you were ravishing me, I wailed with pain, yet you did not let off," she persisted on a sob.

"I was not ravishing you, and at times pain and pleasure sound much alike."

"Do women wail with pleasure when you . . . I cannot credit it."

"I hope that some day you will."

Saying which, Eliab arose from the chair and stood, looking out through the cracks in the window's shutter. After a while, he stole a glance at Osnath and saw that her previously flushed face had dulled like the iron gray sky left by the abating storm.

Suddenly, she seemed to him small and fragile. When he gazed down at her dress, he saw that it was smeared with her blood. It was not merely her ruptured hymen. As he belatedly realized, although she was fifteen years old, apart from her large breasts, her body was still uncommonly immature for her age.

She had not repulsed him as she could have, of that he had no doubt. But she had been unripe for the act, and he had injured her delicate maidenly body with his oversize manhood and his vigorous thrusts. The sight sobered him, and he was distraught and deeply repentant.

"I beg your forgiveness, Osnath," he said in a meek, faltering voice, as he knelt next to the chair and covered her body with a blanket, tucking it around her.

The rain had stopped but the roof was still dripping; and the water splattering from it onto the windowsill was the only response to his words.

"I have sinned against you," he continued. "But I love you more than you can imagine. I will make amends for what I have done by taking you to be my wife immediately. Tomorrow morning I will set out for your father's house in Ramah and request that he give you to me. I will pay him a large bride-price for you, as befits the station of your family and mine. Then we will hold a feast, the like of which Bethlehem has never witnessed since Ruth became my great-grandfather Boaz's wife."

With a tremor of fury in her voice, Osnath spat out, "After the manner in which you have dealt with me, I would sooner become the wife of a wild tiger."

"Don't dismiss the offer I am making to you out of hand. For though it comes in the wake of a cursed act, it springs from the depth of my love. I will make you my wife, and we will know happiness together all the days of our lives."

Pninah had explained to Osnath that the act of love was also an act of joy. She wondered silently how they would see happiness together, when—apart for some brief moments beforehand—she had found neither love nor joy in the deed he had perpetrated on her.

She averted her face from him and broke into renewed sobs like the little girl that, at the moment, she felt she still was. He took her in his arms, and when she recoiled, he said, "Have no fear. I will not repeat what I have done," and kissed her streaming eyes and her wet cheeks, and stroked her curls, but she was not placated.

In the following days, Osnath was unable to recuperate from what had befallen her. She took her meals with the family but at all other times remained locked up in her room. At first she lay on the bed, nursing the searing pain in what her mother had told her was the innermost shrine of her body, and in her soul. Nursing also her resentment toward the man, disgustingly unrestrained in his lust, who had inflicted it on her.

Her mother had warned her that if a man knew her before she became his wife, her monthly way of women might cease and she might come to be with child, and thereby bring disgrace on herself and her family. Besides all else, she was now gripped with a horrendous fear that this disaster would overtake her.

She was loath to confess her shame to her relatives. So when Hagith asked her why she was not out in the garden as was her habit, she pleaded an indisposition that made her throat sore and pained her limbs. She was thankful when the old woman did not probe any further.

Eliab came bearing a peace offering of dried grapes and peeled almonds. When he called to her to open the door for him, she saw no reason to do his bidding. He deposited the bowl on her doorstep and left.

One morning he caught up with her when she came back from her meal and entered the chamber in her wake. He closed the door behind him and leaned on it and said, "When Moses pleaded with the Lord, 'Forgive the people's sin in the vastness of your mercy,' what was the Lord's response?"

"'I have forgiven as you say,'" replied Osnath without difficulty.

Fathers were often wont to send their sons, but only rarely their daughters, to teachers to learn the Torah. Hence Eliab had never crossed the path of a girl who was as well versed in this holy book as she seemed to be. Yet, as he knew that praise left her unmoved, he refrained from commenting on this and merely said, "So do I beseech you to forgive me, hoping for the same response."

"I have not the presumption to emulate the Lord. Before you took me to your room, I was a maiden. You defiled me with your lechery, and now I am a maiden no longer."

"Can you not find it in your heart to grant me forgiveness, when I so humbly beg for it?"

She made no reply.

"Then I will atone for my sin by coming before the elders at the town gates and confessing to them what has transpired, letting them impose on me whatever penalty they deem fit."

These words only served to whip up her anger. "The Torah lays down that when a man comes upon a virgin, it is incumbent on him to take her for his wife in a hurry. If you came before the elders, they would merely impose this injunction on you."

"This is indeed the Torah law. Yet the elders may impose a harsher penalty on me of their own accord, and I will bow to their decree."

"I do not strive to unleash vengeance," Osnath replied, "and neither do I want the elders to know how basely I have been dishonored."

"Then what would you have me do to atone for my iniquity? Name your demand," he begged, "and I will do it, no matter what it entails."

"All I demand is that you no longer harass me, so that I may become the wife of . . . of . . . whomever I choose."

Eliab had been looking at her softly, but at these words his face soured. "If it is David you have in mind, I am not keeping you from him. But be aware that he is merely seeking to curry favor with your uncle, for a purpose of his own. Once he has attained his goal, he will cast you off like a worn-out garment," he prophesied darkly, and turned on his heels and left.

After she had languished in her misery for six days, Osnath's monthly flow began. Thus her mind was eased; at least she had been spared the worst of all calamities. Slightly reassured, she decided that she could no longer keep to her room and do nothing but mourn her desecration. So, bit by bit, pushing the memory of what had befallen her into a corner of her soul, she resumed what she had been doing before that fateful evening.

Only now, in her enmity toward Eliab, she was drawn to David with a new strength. And she became even more conscious of his many charms than she had been before. She thought that he differed from his eldest brother as honey differs from vinegar. He was as light-footed as the son of a gazelle, not bulky and heavy-footed as a bear, as was Jesse's firstborn. And he spoke magnificent words of poetry to her, which Eliab could never hope to match, words that were like balm to her ears.

Thus she took up a new custom: following David up the hill where he grazed his flock. There he promised to pluck stars from the sky and string them into a necklace that he would clasp around her neck to betroth her to him, yet they would not be able to outshine her eyes. And he would wield the sunshine into a ring to place on her finger under the canopy, yet its brilliant light would not be stronger than his love for her.

David was also unlike Eliab in that he dealt honorably with her. He would never be so base as to lure her into his room, to defile her. Even when he was alone with her on the hill, he refrained from over-stepping the limit, promising that he would rupture her virginity only on their bridal bed. As Osnath well knew, there was naught left to rupture. Yet she nourished the hope that when the time came, he would overlook this.

Where previously she had felt only admiration, she now felt love for David sprouting inside her as the wild spring flowers began sprouting around them. For the first time, she reciprocated the words of his love for her with some of her own. Upon hearing them, he encircled her in his arms, and in the rapture of his embraces and kisses, she forgot all else that prevailed in the heavens and the earth.

In her newborn love for David and her happiness with him, she became more generous, and with the passing of time almost forgave Eliab for wronging her.

But now, a month after that event, having been terrified to the edge of sanity by the snake burrowing under her pillow, she saw this ghastly viper as nightmare piled upon nightmare. She thought it vindicated her initial fear of Eliab and was further evidence of the evil in his heart. As Hagith lay immersed in slumber at her side, Osnath once again recalled her tormentor's slanderous words about his brother's scraping and groveling before her uncle.

To her mind, Eliab's words revealed little about David but much about Eliab himself, showing that Samuel was much on his mind. The prophet was a seer, one able to divine all that ever was and all that ever would be, if only he set his mind to it.

When once Osnath had asked him where his unfathomable power derived from, he had laughed and said, "I am not like Samson, the hero you have read about in a scroll. Unlike his power, mine is not lodged in my hair."

"Then where is it lodged?"

"In the one who has granted it to me for his own purpose."

Samuel's power was widely renowned, and it occurred to Osnath that the vile one might believe that her uncle harbored some knowledge about Ruth that must not be revealed. If so, the snake could have been a warning to her to refrain from asking Samuel to divulge his knowledge to her.

Still, she made a firm resolution to discover the truth, even if it meant doing precisely what Eliab was set on preventing.

Chapter Three

The thought of finding her way through a welter of events that were lost in the mist of time struck deep roots in Osnath's soul. She had never thought of herself as brave, for in truth she was easily frightened. She imputed movement to inert objects, and when she was alone in the dark, even the faintest noise startled her. At times, her eyes darted back and forth, as if she expected some monstrous creature to leap out of a shady corner. Yet now she gained a previously unknown courage; she was determined not to let Eliab's snake intimidate her into abandoning her aim.

She weighed the possibility of talking to Eliab's father, Jesse, who was Ruth's grandson, and to his wife, Atarah. Both must remember Ruth, and might be willing to tell her more than Hagith had been.

Jesse was a tall man with keen eyes and gray hair, and Atarah was almost as tall, with skin sallow from her advancing years, but black and luminous eyes. She was a woman who saw much but said little, deferring to her husband. But before he spoke he looked at her, as if seeking guidance from her.

Now, as Osnath was about to approach the couple, they seemed remote to her. Although they regarded her kindly, she shrunk from coming forward with her request.

There was another man in the house, though: Jesse's father, Obed, the oldest man of the two families. Of the little she had seen of him, he had struck her as being too old and decrepit to approach. Yet he was Ruth's son and at one time must surely have known more about her than anyone still dwelling on the face of the earth. Perhaps his mind could be rattled into recalling some of his knowledge, and enlighten her. As he was stricken in years, his days were doubtlessly numbered. If she did not speak to him now, he might take whatever memories were stored in his mind to the depth of the grave, the pit of silence, with him.

One morning, she went to Obed's bedchamber. Since the two daughters of the house had married and moved to their husbands' homes, a maid had been put in charge of his care. When Osnath stood on the threshold of the heavily curtained, dark chamber, this serving woman was engaged in tidying up all manner of litter, after which she left.

Only then did Osnath take note of the white-bearded, wrinkled, toothless, and spindly-legged figure reclining on a weathered chair in a corner, dozing peacefully, with his chin sunken on his chest.

"I am Osnath," she proclaimed herself in a loud voice, to awaken him.

Obed slowly opened his bleary eyes and shuffled his feet in confusion, apparently unable to decide how to handle his uninvited young guest. After a lengthy pause, he motioned her to sit down on the only available chair.

When she told him that she had come to hear some stories about his mother, which she intended to write down on a scroll, his crumpled face came to life. In a voice rendered feeble by the fragility of his aged body, he declared himself keen to tell her all he could remember. For his mother had been an outstanding woman, whose memory ought to be kept alive forever.

Pleasantly surprised at the clarity of his mind, Osnath asked in what way she had been outstanding.

Obed shook the crumbs left over from his last meal off his beard. Then he began chewing some of its strands between his toothless gums, an act that seemed to refresh his memory.

Ruth, he replied, was like the father of our people,
Abraham. Like him, she left her homeland and her family
to go to a distant land, which the Lord had shown her.

When Osnath asked why Ruth had seen fit to tear herself away from her home to come to a foreign country, he explained:

After Naomi's sons had died, and the famine no longer plagued her homeland, she decided to return to it. Unwilling to separate from her, her two daughters-in-law set out with her on the road to the land of Israel. On the way, Naomi tried to convince the young women to turn back. Orpah obeyed her mother-in-law, but Ruth clung to her and adopted her God and her land and her people as her own.

After his response, Obed, too exhausted to speak, leaned back mutely on his chair.

Osnath listened raptly, yet she could not fail to notice that he had left unanswered the question that troubled her.

"Why is it," she persisted, "that Orpah was easily convinced to turn back, while Ruth was so determined to brave life in an unfamiliar land?"

Orpah, replied Obed with a sneer in his voice, was an inferior woman. She deserted her mother-in-law in the midst of the wilderness that separates Moab from the land of Israel. Only my mother was of such elevated spirit as to be willing to embrace the Lord.

The girl was unconvinced. The various pieces of the story she had gleaned did not tally. She found Obed's tale of Ruth as a pious woman willing to embrace the Lord incongruous with the image of the woman willing to embrace someone very different from the Lord, as it emerged from the letter she had uncovered before.

"I found a missive," she said, "which proves that a man other than your father, to whom she was pledged, had come into your mother's life. Is there anything you can tell me about him?"

The old man shook a reproachful finger in her face. "You impudent girl!" he snapped. "You are making this up out of your own depraved heart. Once my mother became my father Boaz's wife, she loved him alone and was faithful to him all the days of her life."

Obed's reply was evasive, for it skipped over what had come to pass before Ruth became Boaz's wife. Thus Osnath could not resist one last question. "Could it be," she asked, "that Ruth encountered the other man before she ever came to Bethlehem and crossed your father's path?"

Her seemingly mild question had a powerful effect on Obed. He began muttering inaudibly to himself. Before long, he had whipped himself into a tremendous rage, which lent him renewed strength, as if he had suddenly shed his years.

Trembling in all his limbs, he bent toward her and hissed, "Who gave you leave to vilify my mother, the godliest of women who ever walked on the face of the earth?"

Osnath spoke to him soothingly, assuring him that, at the time she had in mind, Ruth had been a widow, and for a widow to know a man was not prohibited by Torah law and hence was not a sin. But it was to no avail: the old man continued to fume, preparing himself for a new onslaught, while his finger showed her the door.

Since Obed was feeble in his body, though not in his mind, Osnath feared that his overwhelming rage might lead him to succumb to an affliction that could hasten his demise. So she humbly apologized for her error and hurriedly withdrew from his presence.

҉

Osnath went to her customary corner of the garden to sift through what she had just learned. After a spell, she drifted toward the scroll room again, where she searched through numerous scrolls she had not already read. They had not been wiped off for a long time and had accumulated the dust of ages. But none that she could lay her hands on had any bearing on Ruth.

The window curtain flapped in the wind but protected her from prying eyes as she climbed onto a creaking chair. Although alarmed by the noise it made, she did not draw back. She began searching the highest shelf, where Eliab had placed the mysterious little scroll that had first ignited her curiosity about his great-grandmother. If she could manage to retrieve it and look at it more carefully, she thought, it might yield some hints that she had overlooked. Her hand roamed around on the shelf for a long time without locating it. The scroll was gone.

Just as she was about to climb down, her eyes alit on a scrap of parchment that had been uncovered by her dislodging of another scroll. She took it up and scanned it. It was written in a foreign language, which was sufficiently close to Hebrew for her to make out its contents:

Today the Unnamed from
Bethlehem has come to me.
It was from the gods.
It was marvelous in my eyes.

Below these words the parchment was torn; some of the letters in the last line were cut in half, and the words were nearly illegible. But Osnath had read enough for her eyes to widen in amazement. As she gazed at the cryptic passage, she heard a rustle outside the door. Hastily, she jumped off the chair and hid the scrap of parchment in a pocket of her dress.

When the door opened, she was not surprised to see Eliab on the threshold. He had an uncanny ability to trace her at all times and appear precisely when he was not wanted.

He shot her a virulent glance. "I have been called back from the fields because my grandfather was unwell and took to his bed. I should have known that it was your doing. And that I would find you here, probing into what is not for you to see."

This was his scroll room and not hers; but he had invited her to use it freely, so his recriminations seemed grossly unfair. She said nothing but frowned her disapproval.

"You are brazen in your design," he said in utter contempt. "I will not have my great-grandmother's reputation ground to dust. Give me what you have found without delay." With these words he held out his hand imperiously.

To gain a respite, she made a show of straightening her dress and pulling it properly over her legs. Then, as he blocked her way to the door and she saw no route of escape, she dug in her pocket for the torn sheet and reluctantly handed it to him.

He looked at it briefly, and then his voice rose to match his wrath. "Why did you come here to stir up trouble? If you continue to thwart me, I will have you expelled from Hagith's house and sent back to Ramah."

Displaying a confidence she did not feel, her cheeks flushed, she muttered, "You have done worse than that already," and watched him grow pale.

His pallor imbued her with courage, and she continued. "You have sent me a snake to spew out the poison in your heart."

"You cast aspersions on me," he said hotly, "which you well know to be unfounded. I never sent a snake into your bed, and the only poison is in your own heart."

With these words he stepped aside, and she passed by him. She turned back and stood facing him for a moment, then ran off to her quarters.

Eliab had been able to compel Osnath to surrender the scrap of parchment to him, but not to erase it from her mind. Nettled by what had occurred, she sat and wrote down its content, and all else she had learned that day, on her own scroll.

Since the words on the parchment were in a foreign tongue, there was no doubt in her mind that they had been written by Ruth herself, the only foreigner she had heard of who had ever lived in the house. As these words spoke of "the gods," rather than of "God," they must have been written while she still lived in Moab, before she adopted the Lord, who is one.

The Unnamed, the lover from Bethlehem Ruth mentioned, who must have returned to his town after his visit to Sdeh Moab, amply explained her eagerness to follow her mother-in-law there. It also explained Ruth's refusal to turn back even when Naomi beseeched her to do so.

But who was this Unnamed, and why had he come to Moab? Was he merely one of the Israelites who had gone there to escape the famine in the land? This did not seem plausible, for, if so, why did not Ruth refer to him by his name? He must have gone there with another, more devious intent, which made it necessary for him to conceal his name. But what had it been?

Above all, why was Eliab so anxious to prevent her from discovering the truth? Could it be that if it emerged, it would jeopardize his inheritance or even his life? It was all in a jumble in her mind, and she could not set it straight.

It occurred to her that as Ruth was well versed in the art of writing, she might have written a record of her life, as many people of high standing used to do. What she had uncovered might be but a small fragment, accidentally torn off from its main body. So the rest of the record must still be stowed away somewhere in the scroll room. She decided to explore this possibility by searching it more thoroughly. But the next day, when she arrived there, she found the door locked.

She went to her favorite tree, in whose shade she sat straining her brain to devise new ways by which she might decipher the mystery. There Eliab found her when he came home from his day's toils and told her that henceforward she would be allowed to visit the scroll room only in his company. To Osnath, this indicated that there was still much left for her to uncover there.

Whatever it was that he was hiding, he should have known that she simply longed to unravel the events of days past as one unravels a string of wool from a knotted ball. That she was tenacious but not spiteful, and malice was beyond her. No matter what she uncovered, she would not reveal anything that might hurt him or his family.

One morning a few weeks later, Osnath arrayed herself in her best dress, a well-crafted linen one in the palest shade of yellow. It looked as if the rays of the morning sun had been glued to it, and stood in charming contrast to her dusky hair. Around her waist she tied a blue linen sash, which accentuated her narrow waist and her large breasts. Pleased with her reflection in the metal mirror on the table, she climbed up the hill to be with David while he tended the flock, as by now she was used to doing almost daily.

Her love for the young shepherd grew from day to day. He was the answer to every prayer her heart had ever whispered in the dark of the night. He was the one whose words, as sweet as honey, resuscitated her after the bitter ones Eliab constantly hurled at her.

By then, the beginning of the first month, the rainy winter had shaded over into spring. The branches on the trees and the sprigs on the bushes had burst forth into colorful buds. As the earth had been amply watered by the winter's rain, the pastures were thick with juicy grass and covered with a mass of white, red, and pink flowers. The air was filled with the scent of the damp meadow and the blossoms on the trees, pungent yet soft.

The hill she ascended was teeming with goats and sheep, wandering about, halting to nibble here and there, and she felt their warm, soft, woolly bodies rubbing against her legs as she walked by them. The small clouds drifting across the sky looked like woolly sheep, too.

The hill was set aside for Jesse's flock only; so apart from David, there was no one on it. When she reached him, he sat down with her under the branches of an oak tree, in a spot hidden away by thick, leafy bushes from all that surrounded it. There he drew her down and placed her head on his knees, and called her eyes doves, and her breasts, twins of a gazelle.

Drawing a deep sigh of contentment, she asked him from where the beautiful words he mouthed derived.

"I pluck them like flowers from the meadow, my beloved," he replied, "and will weave them into your hair." While he spoke, he picked a few flowers from the grass and lifted his hand to her hair in a dizzying caress, interlacing the flowers with her curls.

Timidly, she put up her hand to touch his face, to caress his fledgling beard of a burnished copper color, and felt it tickling her hand. He closed his hand on hers, and it fluttered in his like a bird in flight. Then his hands strayed to her face and from there to her body, where his touch was as soft and light as his smile, and as welcome to her.

He peeled off her dress and his light brown garment and lay down, and she stretched out against the youthful litheness of his body. He slid into her as easily, as smoothly, as if he had been there many times before.

His breath was short against her ears as his quickening movements brought him release, though none to her, before he drifted into sleep. To her relief, his sleep came too fast for him to notice either her disappointment or the absence of her virginal blood.

When he woke up, he said, "I had hoped to hold out until the night of our wedding, but my love for you has proved to be too strong."

"And also mine for you."

"But it is no great matter, for I will certainly arrange our betrothal, and then our wedding, as quickly as an eagle crosses the sky." Then he repeated what he had done before.

Having no doubt that David would soon redeem the promise he had made to her, Osnath knew no worry of coming to be with child. If she did, there would be no harm in it, for once she and David were married, no one would know that the child had been implanted in her before he had pressed the seal of wedlock on their love.

She felt no more than a flicker of remorse for having committed a grievous sin by Torah precept, and hence in the eyes of the Lord. For she knew the Lord to be a God of justice but also of mercy and forgiveness, especially for a sin that had not been committed callously, but out of the depth of the love overflowing in her heart.

Although Osnath had felt nothing of what her grandmother had once told her a woman ought to feel in the arms of her man, she was nonetheless elated. After she had slipped on her dress, she skipped down the hill as if she were floating on a cloud, borne not on her feet, but on her dream of happiness.

She entered Hagith's front room to find her uncle Samuel sitting there with the old woman, quenching his thirst with a cup of grape juice.

He rose and gathered her up in his arms, and swirled her around, then drew her down to sit on a chair next to him.

Her face was grave and her forehead creased with worry. "My revered uncle, is my grandmother well?" she inquired. "Why did she not come with you to visit her sister?"

"I came for one night only, so there was no occasion for it. I promise you," he added hastily, "that she is entirely well."

"Are my father and mother and sisters also well?"

"They are well, and your mother wants you back in a hurry."

"Did you come on an errand from her, then, to take me home?"

"No, my niece. I came on an errand from one who ranks higher even than your mother," he said playfully, a smile lighting up his green eyes.

Osnath's eyes flew up to his, a mute question in them.

"I will not disclose its nature to you now. But if you step out of this house in a little while, you will see."

Osnath's mind was in a whirl, her eyes bright with wonder. But she knew that there was never any point in pestering her uncle with questions he had no wish to answer, so she refrained.

He continued. "What you are about to see will affect many lives, and most definitely yours. Later in the evening I intend to talk to you about this."

Before long, a delegation of the elders of Bethlehem came into the yard with hasty strides to meet Samuel. Standing at the front room's doorpost, Osnath observed them as they gathered around him and bowed to him and said in unison, "Illustrious prophet, come in peace."

"May the Lord be with you," he responded, bowing to them in return.

One of them said, "You are always welcome to our town. But why are you honoring us with your presence this day?"

"I have come to hold a feast in the town square," replied Samuel. "Pray accompany me to partake of it."

As they spoke to each other, Jesse and most of his sons, who had just returned from the fields, entered the yard, and Samuel conferred on them the distinction of inviting them also.

Osnath trailed the men through Bethlehem. She had not ventured to walk in the town before. And now, as she lifted her eyes, she saw that it sprawled over several hills. The valleys between them were already in shade, but the crests of the hills were still bathed in the golden rays of the setting sun.

In the town's poorer parts, on the lower slopes of the hills and the vales, small huts built of irregular little stones huddled together as if they were whispering secrets to each other. In its wealthier parts, on the upper slopes, the houses were larger and built of massive stones, and some were plastered over with earth-colored clay, or whitewashed. Here the houses were separated from each other by an abundance of fig trees and olive trees and climbing vines and bushes, all in a pleasing disorder. These left only little space for the pebble-strewn streets, which Osnath now crossed in the wake of the men.

When they had reached the huge town square next to the town gates, she stood at its edge, watching from afar. She perceived several set tables in its center. These were flanked by spits with lambs and goats roasting on them, tended by people who worked in Samuel's household. Soon they were concealed from her view, as the square filled up with onlookers.

All of Israel, from Dan to Beersheba, knew that Samuel had been established as a prophet who could invoke the glory of the Eternal One and convey his messages to the people. Word of his arrival in the town square spread like fire in a field of dry brambles, and the square and its surrounding streets filled up. Soon the place was teeming with people who had gathered to hear him speak and to observe what they sensed would be a highly unusual event.

Samuel stood on the highest spot in the square, and a hush fell on the multitudes as he addressed them.

Speaking in a fiery, resounding voice that carried easily from one end of the square to the other and beyond, he declared: "Each man, woman, and child in Israel, and the people as a whole, are God's prized possessions. Yet now one tribe, Judah, and one town, Bethlehem, have been singled out for a special mission."

A loud cheer arose from the crowd, and several men shouted in unison, "Whatever the Lord decrees, we will accept."

One of the elders called out, "Exalted prophet! Tell us the Lord's edict. Reveal to us what the mission laid upon Bethlehem is to be."

But Samuel was in no hurry to disperse the haze he had created. He raised his arms to quiet the people, and said, "Rest assured that it will elevate this town for all the times and generations to come."

After a slight pause, he told them of widespread resentment among the people with the one whom, at the Almighty's behest, he himself had previously anointed, King Saul. The man had proved himself unfit to reign. He failed to heed the Torah commandments and did not conduct the battles against Israel's enemies properly, besides exacting a heavy tribute from the people against their will.

"Hence," he continued fearlessly, "the Lord has repented of having enthroned him, and will rend the kingdom from him and from his seed. The kingdom is the Lord's to bestow as he sees fit. He has now found another man after his own heart, whom he will install as king.

"A branch has sprouted from the tree of Jesse. The spirit of the Lord will rest upon him: the spirit of courage, and wisdom, and the love of Israel."

Osnath climbed on a high rock at the edge of the square, from whose vantage point she gained a better view of the proceeding. She saw that at the conclusion of his speech, at Samuel's request, Jesse paraded his sons before him, with Eliab, the firstborn, at the head of the line.

David had not yet returned from the hill, and even with all her animosity toward Eliab, she had to admit to herself that he was the tallest and the most handsome of the lot. Of all the men in the square, only Samuel, she thought with pride in her uncle, matched him in height and the breadth of his shoulders.

Despite Eliab's stature, Samuel did not favor him. "He is tall and good-looking, but the one who has sent me does not see as man sees; men judge by appearances, but the Lord judges by the heart. He is not the one," he ruled.

Jesse presented the rest of his sons who were there to Samuel. They filed by him one by one, but with each one the prophet declared, "No, the Lord has not chosen this one." Then he looked around and said, "Surely these are not all?"

"There is still the youngest," admitted Jesse, "but he is looking after the sheep."

"Send and fetch him, Jesse," Samuel demanded. "We will not sit down for the meal until he comes."

So Jesse sent for David, and a murmur rose up in the square as the crowd awaited his arrival. Looking at him as he appeared, Osnath thought that he was not as tall or as ruggedly handsome as Eliab. But with his reddish hair and fair skin and bright blue eyes, he was unquestionably the most beautiful of Jesse's eight sons. Besides, he was blessed with an inner radiance and a blithe assurance, and he moved with the same easy confidence that he inspired in those around him.

It struck Osnath that in some inexplicable way he irresistibly drew the eye and would stand out in a crowd of thousands. To her mind, he had the bearing of a prince, a king in the making.

Samuel must have perceived this, too, for he announced in his ringing voice, "The Lord has spoken. He has commanded me, rise and anoint him as king, for this is the man."

Osnath hardly dared to draw a breath. She just watched in awe as, with these words, Samuel took a horn filled with oil he had with him and poured it over his own fingers. Then he spread it over David's forehead and his eyelids and his cheeks, anointing him. This deed was performed in the presence of David's father and his brothers and the town elders, and the masses of Israel. These raised a big shout, cheering noisily at the sight of the king-to-be, to whom they readily transferred their allegiance.

Osnath thought that David's brothers might feel humiliated by having been passed over by Samuel. But apart from Eliab, who had a scowl on his face, they all appeared to be in good cheer. Apparently, they found consolation in the fact that they, too, would be elevated as part of the king's family.

David himself was neither disconcerted nor elated. He took it all in stride as if it were his due, as if he had known since the day of his birth that he was destined to reign.

Then the people surged forward and besieged Samuel and the freshly anointed David, overwhelming them with their worshipful love. The love which, as Osnath had been told, King Saul had never been able to elicit from them.

When the crowd began to disperse, Samuel and the elders and Jesse and his sons sat down to the repast that had been prepared for them. And Osnath knew without a shadow of a doubt that on this day she had witnessed an occurrence whose memory would not be blotted out for as long as the sun shone over the earth. An event of which she would be able to tell her children and her children's children, who, she hoped, would be David's as well.

That evening, Samuel summoned Osnath to the room that Hagith had given him for the night.

He sat and made her sit down on a chair facing him. "My niece," he began, "although I came here for a different purpose, my sister has charged me with bringing you home to her."

With David no less than the still-unsolved mystery of Ruth hovering before her eyes, she retorted, "My uncle, pray let me stay here some more."

"Truly, I would leave you here, because this is where the man who is for you dwells. But you have not guarded yourself, as your mother instructed you to do."

She blurted out impetuously, "I have been assaulted," thus revealing what she had previously resolved to conceal forever.

Samuel was not surprised. "Rape is a dastardly deed, for which only he who commits it bears the guilt. But I doubt that this is what has befallen you. As you well know, the Torah holds a girl who has been tortured in that way blameless, provided she repulses her assailant and calls out for help that fails to materialize."

As he spoke, there was a piercing look in his green eyes that seemed to penetrate her innermost being. It was not a look designed to make her feel at ease, and although he directed it at her for an instant only, she felt disquiet.

For a while she just sat there, her gaze fixed on the ground in deep shame at her lapse at having failed to repulse Eliab.

"I was confused," she retorted in the end, in an attempt to justify herself.

"True. Utterly confused and childishly innocent. You were wickedly seduced, but not raped."

After a pause, he persisted, "You have not heeded yourself with David, either. It behooves me to caution you. The Torah imposes death by stoning on a young woman who, of her own volition, comes to her bridal bed no longer a virgin. This retribution, being so harsh, is not implemented. But it serves as an indication of the gravity with which the Lord considers the sin you have committed. A sin, moreover, which may beget its own punishment. If you find yourself with child without a husband, your life will be burned to ashes."

"I stand in no such danger. My beloved will soon take me to be his wife."

"David is the Lord's anointed, and rightly so, for he is truly out of the common way. He is descended from a noble family, which can trace its origin all the way back to the father of its tribe, Judah. He is by his very nature a hero, a fierce warrior, who will never shun risking his life for the sake of the people. He has a stately bearing and the making of a superior leader of men. He will be a peerless king, and Israel will flourish under his rule. He will also be the father of a glorious dynasty of kings, renowned forever.

"But judging from the peoples around us, superb kings are rarely devoted husbands. If he marries you, you will walk among queens. You will be the wife of a king and perhaps the mother of one. But you will be miserable all the days of your life."

"How can this be, when we love each other so much?"

"Kings have the custom of taking many wives and concubines, and also the means to do so. Before long he will take another wife, and another one, and you will hardly see him for all the women who will surround him. There is jealousy ingrained in your soul. Is this what you pine for in your life?"

She tossed her head defiantly. "David loves me too much to rest his eyes on any other woman."

"I will not argue with you, for it would be useless," he said mildly. "At least promise me one thing, Osnath, and I will allow you to stay: that you will not let him come to you again until he has betrothed you, thereby truly committing himself to take you for his wife."

She promised, and to her relief he told her that she could stay.

The next morning, Osnath rose early, so as to be able to see Samuel before he left. When they sat eating bread and cheese alone together, she told him of her goal to uncover the life story of David's great-grandmother Ruth. She asked him what he knew about it and why everyone was so eager to conceal what had really happened to her.

Her uncle seemed distracted by other concerns and merely said that Ruth's secrets were buried underground. Osnath could not imagine what he had in mind. But just then Hagith came in, and Osnath was unable to question him any further.

As soon as they rose from the table, Samuel and his men set out on their way back to Ramah. And only after the clatter of their mules' hooves had faded from the yard did it occur to Osnath that he had not divulged the name of the man who, he had claimed, was for her.

Chapter Four

After Samuel left, Osnath went to look for David but encountered Eliab instead. She was about to walk by him as if he did not exist, but he halted her by placing his hand on her shoulder.

"Let go of me," she said petulantly.

But he was incapable of it. He was still ensnared by her eyes' shining innocence, which stood in such glaring contrast to her sensuous mouth, all of which he found irresistible.

He cupped her face in his hand. "You are making a grievous error," he said sternly. "Don't scorn my love for you. Your mind is still that of a child, but one day you will learn that love is better than a kingdom, which in any case will not fall into your lap."

"I care nothing for the kingdom, but only for the man who has been chosen to stand at its head, who loves me as I love him," she told him.

Eliab's lips twisted into a mirthless smile, and he gave a snort of incredulity. "David is endowed with the gift of the tongue, but his pompous declarations mask a shallow heart. His love for you is as flighty as the clouds floating in the sky, while mine will last as long as I draw breath on this earth. Even so, like any man, I crave sons and daughters, and I will not wait for you forever."

"You should not wait for me at all, sir," she said determinedly.

"I will heed your words, Osnath," he answered bitterly. "But you will do well to heed mine. Soon he will be so highly placed in his own eyes that you will no longer be sufficiently exalted for him."

Osnath felt nothing but disdain at Eliab's repeatedly reviling his brother. Yet, against her will, she was rattled by his speech. "I am exalted enough. My uncle . . ." There was a tremor in her voice as her words petered off.

The smell of damp moss hung in the air, and the croaking of frogs could be heard from a nearby pond. Eliab continued, "David is a frog that has outgrown the pond in which it was hatched, and is heading for a bigger pond. Before long he will have the impertinence to set his sights higher than you."

Osnath was now thoroughly annoyed. "You are merely grinding flour you have ground before." Disgusted with his entire bearing toward her, she continued, "All I have ever obtained from you are rebukes and degradation and a viper in my bed, which might well have killed me."

"All my reprimands have been just," he retorted earnestly. "I am deeply repentant about coming to you, even though I had your consent. I had no notion of degrading you. I would have taken you for my wife, if only you had let me. As for the snake, you cannot believe this foolishness. If ever I send a serpent into your bed, it will be the one from the Garden of Eden, to seduce you into mine."

His dark face came alight with laughter, but she did not find his jest funny.

After a short pause, Eliab continued: "How is it that you only ask other people about my great-grandmother? I am the one in charge of the scroll room. It should have occurred to you that through the records I have uncovered there, I am more familiar with the tale of her life than anyone. Yet you have never turned to me."

She fixed her eyes on his. "What are those records?"

"The letter and the scrap of parchment you unearthed are not the only ones that have survived. There are more."

"Would you show them to me?" she exclaimed.

"No, but I am willing to tell you as much as I can about Ruth without demeaning her reputation."

Her face crumpled like that of a disappointed child. "Then it will not be the truth."

"Every word will be true. But if you believe you can uncover more without my assistance, do as is good in your eyes." With these words he turned from her.

Osnath had set her mind on whiling away the day with David, wherever he might be keeping himself. But this was an opportunity she could not miss, for Eliab might soon change his mind. She ran after him and touched his arm.

He was about to set out for the fields but turned around and led her to the scroll room instead. And this is the tale he told her, which she later copied into her scroll:

Naomi had an open smile on her face when she left Bethlehem for the land of Moab, but a bitter scowl when she returned; and Ruth's state was even worse.

When she came to Bethlehem, she found herself at a loss, a stranger adrift in an inhospitable land, where people saw her as an intruder. She retreated into herself as a turtle retreats into its shell, and her shoulders were bowed with the weight of her loneliness.

"But there was one man from Bethlehem she knew," interpolated Osnath. "I am sure of it."

"Do you wish me to tell you the tale, or do you prefer to tell it to me?"

"Forgive me."

Naomi had no means of livelihood, so both she and Ruth were bereft of sustenance. She explained to Ruth that the Israelites were not allowed to strip their fields bare, but were obliged by Torah law to abandon what was forgotten or left behind in corners of the fields after the harvest, for strangers and orphans and widows to gather.

So, since it was during the harvest, Ruth went out to gather the grains left by the reapers in the fields.

Now Naomi had a kinsman, a man of great wealth, Boaz, my great-grandfather. He was a widower, thirty-five

years of age. As it chanced, Ruth went to glean barley in
his fields, and kept gathering grain there until the end of
both the barley and the wheat harvests.

As you know, when a widow has borne no son to
her deceased husband, his brother or closest kinsman is
obliged by law and custom to take her for his wife. Yet,
although Boaz was a kinsman of Ruth's husband, he
showed no inclination to fulfill this obligation.

Once, when he stayed in his fields overnight, at
Naomi's behest, Ruth lay down stealthily at his feet.
And when he was startled from his sleep by her unsought
presence, she reminded him of his duty. His response was
that there was one who was more nearly related to her
husband, who was bound to marry her; but if he did not,
Boaz would do what law and custom required.

Osnath had a mind to listen to the rest of Eliab's story, but at hearing
his last words, she could not contain herself. "Are you leading me to
believe that this is all that took place between Boaz and Ruth that
night? Despite my tender years, you cannot think me so gullible as to
believe that."

Eliab made no reply.

"If Boaz was your ancestor," Osnath insisted, "he probably resembled
you in his nature. If so, he must have been as lecherous as you are. I cannot credit that he was impervious to the allure of the attractive young
woman at his feet. She was entirely at his disposal, yet you would have me
believe that he abstained from touching her. He must have taken advantage of the darkness of the night and of her helplessness before him.
Then he offered to marry her, to cover up his infamy."

"You have a lively imagination, Osnath. It is one of the things I love
about you, and I have no wish to eradicate it."

"Yet it is the truth."

"Have it as you will, but don't dare to write a shred of a word about
this in your scroll."

"I will write what is good in my eyes."

Eliab gritted his teeth. "Then I will do to you as is good in *my* eyes."

So far she had spoken with determination, but now a soft, cajoling note invaded her voice. "Ruth must have written a record of her life. I discovered a little piece of it, and you told me yourself that you discovered more. You may even have unearthed her entire book. Pray, sir," she pleaded, "let me see it."

"I have not discovered her entire book."

"Then favor me by letting me see what you have discovered."

"You will sooner see the sun shine at midnight."

This reply revived her animosity. "I will put my hand on it in spite of the obstructions you put in my way."

He tucked one of the stray curls that spilled into her face to the back of her ear. "Why are you always bickering so insensibly, defying me even when I am helping you? It will do you no good to be so headstrong, for the day will come when I will tame you. In time you will submit yourself to me as you should."

"You will sooner see the stars shine at midday."

She glared at him, then stomped out of the room angrily, like a child whose will had been thwarted.

When Osnath had calmed down from her fury, she set out to look for the man she loved.

She expected him to be sitting somewhere in council with the town elders, as befitted a king-to-be. But to her surprise, his mother told her that he had gone up the hill with the flock, as usual.

The rains had previously painted the hill green, and its fresh color still persisted as she climbed it. Once she reached David, he made her sit down at his side, and she said with a smile of admiration in her eyes, "My lover, you must surely be the only king in the world who tends sheep."

"I am not king yet, my beloved. There is still a long way to go. In the meantime, I am not averse to tending the flock, for from this I gain experience on how to tend the people," he said laughingly.

"Will not the yoke of being in charge of their well-being bear heavily on you?"

"Since the Lord has assigned me to reign over his people, he will also lend me the strength to do it properly," David said with calm dignity, astonishing in one so young.

Then he abandoned his regal bearing and assumed that of a lover instead. When she perceived his change of mood, she rose up and darted to the other side of the hill, forcing him to chase after her, until he caught up with her. With their breath short from running, they tumbled onto the grass, where his breath was short again, from his wanting of her.

But when he lay down and attempted to repeat what he had done the day before, Osnath would not allow it. She told him of her promise to her uncle that she would not let David come to her until he had betrothed her to him.

David was supporting his head on his left elbow, while his right hand was caressing her body. But upon hearing these words, he slid his hand from her and rested it on the ground.

The ensuing pause seemed to Osnath to run on for an unbearably long time. While it lasted, she worried that contrary to his previous assurances, David had no true intention of betrothing her, much less of marrying her.

Finally, he spoke. "You cannot renege on your promise to Samuel, so I make you a promise of my own. When I go home today, I will immediately seek out my father and advise him of my wish to take you for my wife. Tomorrow I will ride over to Ramah to visit your father, to gain his permission for our marriage. I will invite him and your mother and your uncle over here for the paying out of the bride-price, and for the ceremony of betrothal, at which the day of our wedding will be set."

Osnath was awash with a deep sense of relief. The prospect of becoming king had not led David to regard her as being beneath him. His impending greatness would not prevent him from loving her, as she would love him, all the days of their lives.

In the face of his renewed promise, she had no doubt that the next few days would see them engaged, after which the wedding would not be delayed for long. Hence she did not feel that she was breaking her commitment to her uncle when, reveling in David's love, she yielded to him again and again.

The setting sun was like a ball of fire, the clouds in the sky reflecting it in a grayish pink, before all colors blended together in the gradually dimming twilight. When the sun had completed its retreat in the sky and was sliding down behind the hills of Judah, David held her hand in his as they descended their own hill together.

But after the flock had been bestowed in the sheepfold and David came before his father, as he had promised to do, Jesse was too busy to listen to him. He was engaged in extending his hospitality to an awe-inspiring guest: an envoy from King Saul's court in Gibeah. Thus the betrothal of his youngest son was as far removed from his mind as is the desert in the east, where the sun rises, from the Great Sea in the west, in which it sets.

Jesse was sitting with his wife and with the official in the sizable front room of his house, in which several candles were already lit for the night. When he saw David approaching, he came to the door and called him in. Osnath's face fell in disappointment. As Jesse perceived this, in his kindness, he ushered her in as well.

It was the first time she had entered these premises. She took stock of her surroundings and was favorably impressed. In the room's center was a brick-shaped table flanked by numerous chairs, and a sideboard and a couch stood against two of the walls. Though old, the furniture was skill-fully carved and brilliantly polished. Dotted about the room's surfaces were bowls of artfully shaped pottery from faraway places. The voices that arose in it were muffled by lush, heavy carpets that lined the floor. The air was stale, but as Osnath sat listening to the extraordinary tale of the emissary, she no longer noticed.

He was a gray-bearded man, whose clothing—a shimmering blue tunic—and entire bearing bespoke his position as a high official in the king's court. He sat sipping the sweet wine that had been set before him and, at Jesse's request, repeated what he had previously recounted to him.

"Lately, King Saul has been seized by an evil spirit, becoming but a shadow of his former self. One of his courtiers said, 'I have seen a son of Jesse of Bethlehem, who is blessed with numerous accomplishments.

Apart from stringing tunes on the lyre, he can sing the glory of the Lord in a thrilling manner that surpasses the angels. He also radiates gaiety and good humor, and the Lord is with him.'

"Saul has therefore sent me to you, respected Jesse, the son of Obed, and I request that you permit David to come with me to the king, to turn the darkness of his soul into light."

Jesse recognized the courtier's speech as the flattery it was. So after exchanging a glance with Atarah, he voiced his polite reluctance to do the king's bidding. But David was eager, and Jesse and Atarah were swayed. No one paid any heed to Osnath as she slipped away, crestfallen.

Later in the evening, as she sat in the garden nursing the sorrow of her impending parting from David, he came to sit next to her. He told her that, having been summoned by the king, he could not refuse. He would have to leave Bethlehem with the envoy at the break of dawn, so there would be no time for their betrothal now.

But he reassured her by adding: "I will yearn for you day and night. As soon as Saul is resuscitated, I will return to you with the speed of an arrow shot from a bow, and take you for my wife."

Chapter Five

A week after David's departure, a runner arrived bearing a letter from him to Osnath. And this was the testimony it contained:

> My beloved, listen to my voice calling to you from the distance. Since coming to the king's castle, my eyes have met with nothing but sumptuous splendor, which yet has not affected my soul. If I am elated, it is because Saul has elevated me—a mere newcomer—above his long-standing trusted servants. Within a few days of my arrival, he bestowed on me the honor of becoming his armor bearer.

Having given vent to his exultation, David reverted to what was between them:

> Hear me further: I will apprise my father of my intention to wed you in one of my next letters. And when I return, I will compensate you for my absence by an even stronger outburst of my love for you, in proof of which we will come together as husband and wife, and we will spend the rest of our lives in each other's arms. So speaks your husband-to-be, David.

Beforehand, Osnath had felt some disquiet over whether the splendor of the castle would not lead David to hold her cheap. But the letter convinced her that her worry had been in vain, and that his love for her was as enduring as life itself.

As she sat under the tree she had come to consider hers, with tears of joy still veiling her eyes, Eliab came by. He sat down at her side and looked at her, then at the letter, a question in his raised eyebrows.

Osnath saw no reason to keep the glad tidings from him. When she told him of her forthcoming marriage to David, his face did not betray his devastation by as much as a flicker of his eyelids. But she could discern the hurt in the tone of his voice as he wished her a long life of happiness with her chosen one, then left her on her own.

David's ardent outpouring of love in his first letter, though, was not followed by a second one. If he wrote to his father and mother, Osnath was not advised of it. Certainly, there was nothing to indicate that he had notified Jesse of his intent to take her for his wife.

One evening Jesse came over to Hagith's house after the evening meal, but it was merely to announce that Saul thought so highly of David that he had sent word asking Jesse to let his son stay in his service for a further spell of time. Jesse admitted that he had felt honored by the king's request, and had acceded to it.

Osnath's heart sank like lead in deep water.

The light that had previously sparkled in her eyes went out of them as of a burned-up oil lamp. Her only consolation was that she had not conceived from David. Apparently, her mother's and her uncle's warnings notwithstanding, a girl did not come to be with child as quickly as she had previously feared. Apart from this one glimmer of light, all around her—the two houses, the entire neighborhood, the entire town—seemed dark and cheerless. As desolate as a deserted dry well, as was her soul.

Eliab was not unmindful of Osnath's consternation, and despite himself he felt a twinge of pity for her. But a new hope for himself also flared up. For all that she had rejected his offer, he resumed seeking her out.

Seeing her in the yard one day at twilight, he stepped up to her and said in a husky voice, "Even though you have spurned my love for you,

Osnath, it is still as sturdy as iron. I still take pleasure in your looks, and in your voice, and in the liveliness of your mind. I want to do all I can to gladden your heart. I am willing to tell you more about the Moabite if it will coax you out of your sulks."

Up until then Osnath had been so deeply entangled in her own grief that Ruth's tortuous life had receded to the nether regions of her mind. But now her curiosity reared its head, and she let Eliab place his arm around her shoulder and lead her into the scroll room.

There he sat down with her at the table and took up his tale where he had left off, and she later recorded it.

After Ruth spent a night at Boaz's feet in the field, he went up to the town gates, where the elders were assembled, and sat there with them. At his request they summoned Ruth's husband's next of kin, whom he had mentioned to her, to appear before them. When he arrived, Boaz reminded him of his duty.

"What was the relative's name?" Osnath interrupted.

"Boaz did not mention his name before the elders, although they probably knew him in any case."

"Why did Boaz refrain from naming him?"

"Unfortunately, we cannot ask him. We know only that he presented the kinsman as Ploni Almoni."

"Which means 'the unnamed.' If so, he must be the Unnamed referred to in the scrap of parchment I discovered."

"I should have known that you were too sharp-witted to miss that."

"So, as Ruth's poem shows, she had met and loved this nameless man in Sdeh Moab, and she must have come to Bethlehem for his sake; that much is clear. But why was his name concealed?"

"I will leave this question unanswered," Eliab said in an offhand manner.

Osnath bit her lips in disappointment, but she did not let off. "Was he whose name must be hidden willing to take Ruth for his wife?" she prodded.

To this last question, at least, I can supply an answer,
he said. He refused outright and suggested that Boaz (who
was her husband's next of kin after him) do so in his stead.

At hearing this, Osnath could hardly rein herself in. "Why is that? It
is very confusing. It does not fit in with the poem, in which Ruth described him as having been sent to her by the gods."

"It is indeed baffling."

"But you are not willing to help me make it less so?"

"I am honor bound to desist. Still, I am willing to tell you the rest of
the story."

"It would have no value; the chain would be broken without this
missing link."

Eliab hesitated, then said, "I am also willing to console you for your
heartbreak in an entirely different manner."

She merely scoffed at him.

Eliab brought his chair close to hers and bent over her, lifting her
face with his hand to meet his. His voice dropped to a whisper, yet he
spoke coarsely. "Since you spread your legs for him, who is faithless, why
not for me who loves you so much?"

She regarded him with a withering glance. "I have found no pleasure
with you."

A shadow crossed Eliab's face. "Did you find pleasure with him?" he
asked skeptically.

Her cheeks were flaming; but being honest, she had to admit that it
was not so.

"There is no delight in it for me at all," she muttered dejectedly, and
rose and walked to the door.

He rose as well, and she left him standing there, looking after her
with a heavy heart and a twisted smile, as she closed the door behind her.

🗡

In the following days, Bethlehem came alive with rumors—as dark as
the night's moonless sky at the time—of David's exploits with girls at

Saul's court. When they were first whispered into Osnath's ear, though her lips trembled, she resolved to disregard them. But they were persistent, like the humming of a bee that precedes its sting. And in time she had a vague foreboding that the sting of those rumors was still to come.

As time passed and no word came from David, her apprehension gave way to a deep oppression of spirits. She had thought him trustworthy, had not suspected him of such duplicity. He must have become much different from the youth with whom she had spun her dreams of happiness.

By then the heat was gathering in the land, the pastures were drying out, and the hills surrounding the town were beginning to assume their yellowish brown summer colors, as if they had been scorched by fire. These shades suited Osnath's mood, and when the heat of the day abated, she began taking solitary strolls on their slopes, with her head bent, her gaze fixed to the ground, as one mourning the life she had not yet lived.

One day Eliab caught up with her and talked to her of the matter weighing on her heart. "You should not have imputed so much weight to his promise to make you his wife," he said lightly. "He has always been honey-tongued, but his sweet words are only rarely matched by deeds."

Her hands, suddenly sweaty from hearing his words, dug deep into the pockets of her dress, whose blue-gray color enhanced that of her eyes. "He has been blinded by the splendor of the court. He has had to face temptations too strong for so young a man to resist," she said in a desperate attempt to shield David from his brother's attack. "I have no doubt that he still loves me."

"Happy is he who believes," retorted Eliab.

Osnath flinched but made no response before walking away in silence.

At twilight, when Osnath entered the yard, she saw Jesse standing there, awaiting her. She bowed to him respectfully, and asked if he was well.

"I am well. It is your affairs, my girl, that I am intent on discussing with you," he replied, and took her to his front room.

She thought that David must have finally notified his father of his intention to marry her, and that Jesse was now bent on making arrangements with her for their approaching nuptials. So she tumbled gleefully into the room. As it was hot there, she wiped the sweat off her face with the sleeve of her dress, sat down on the chair he offered her, and waited expectantly for his words.

"Is it true," he queried, "that my son David has promised to make you his wife?"

"Yes," she assented.

"And that he has promised to notify me of this by letter?"

"Yes," she reiterated.

"He had not even hinted of this before he left," said Jesse, his low voice attesting to his concern, "nor has he mentioned it in his missives. The rumor has reached me in roundabout ways."

Osnath did her best to hide her disappointment, and Jesse continued: "His failing to take me into his confidence is ludicrous. Yet, because of his silence, I am ignorant of what is in his mind. Rest assured that I will not permit him to wrong you. I believe my best course will be to raise the matter with him on his forthcoming visit here."

This was the first Osnath had heard of David's impending visit. His failure to advise her of it spoke more loudly than any words could of what she now recognized as his indifference toward her.

"It is kind of you, sir," she said fervently with tears springing forth in her eyes, "but I have no wish to become the wife of a man who has to be prodded into taking me."

"You are a lovely and exceedingly bright girl, as befits the niece of the prophet Samuel. Your rare skills in reading and writing will do honor to your husband, as they do to your family. David would be very fortunate to have you for his wife. Indeed, he may not be averse to marrying you, once I remind him of his duty; so let us wait and see."

Osnath wrapped herself in the silence of her hurt, and when Jesse saw how deeply injured she was, he attempted to divert her mind from her sorrow. "It has also been called to my attention," he continued, "that you take an interest in my grandmother, Ruth, and that you are writing her tale onto a scroll. I hold fond memories of her from the days of my childhood; and after her death, my father told me much about her. But now he is an old and easily excitable man. Rather than questioning him, you should have come to talk to me."

It occurred to Osnath that in his attempt to take her mind off David's wrongdoings, Jesse might be willing to disclose that which all others had withheld from her. She could not let such a splendid chance pass. So she told Jesse that she was anxious to hear all he had to tell her.

At first he repeated much of what had been told to her already. Then he continued the tale at the point at which Eliab had previously left off.

> After the Unnamed refused to wed her, Boaz had the
> right to do so. When he did and they came together, the
> Lord caused her to conceive and she bore Boaz a son, my
> father, Obed, as well as two daughters.
>
> In due course, Obed grew up and took a wife who gave
> birth to me. And Ruth, my grandmother, became my
> nurse. We loved each other as only grandmother and
> grandson can. And just as she nursed me when I was little,
> so did I nurse her when she was old.

Osnath had been despondent when Jesse had begun his tale, and hearing it did not improve her mood. On the contrary, she sensed that, like all others who had talked to her of Ruth, Jesse was only telling her what he believed it was suitable for her to hear. She was as certain as she was that the heavens were high above the earth that the heart of the tale was still missing. For the second time during her talk with him, she was disappointed. "Is that the entire tale?" she asked in disbelief.

He refrained from answering and continued:

> After Ruth became the wife of Boaz, her life ran on
> still waters and there is nothing much to tell about it. Her
> existence with my grandfather was blessed with profound
> happiness. She lived the full span of her existence and
> more; and she died peacefully, satiated with life. I held her

hand when she crossed over into the world beyond to
dwell there eternally, leaving her blessed memory behind
for us to cherish.

"If that is all, why is everyone reticent in talking to me about the relative who was unwilling to take her for his wife? Surely everyone in the family must be well aware of who he was. Why will no one mention his name?"

Though he was fond of Osnath, Jesse did not welcome her inquisitiveness and waved her to silence. "I have told you a heartrending story, every word of which is the truth. You could write it down on a scroll that would be passed down in our family from generation to generation. Yet you are set on digging deeper, to unearth filth . . . even where none exists," he added hastily. "Your encroaching questions are beyond what is permissible."

It seemed that even such a kindly man as Jesse was set against her, and this deepened Osnath's lethargy even further. She bowed to him and, weary and subdued, she left.

Apart from her persistent curiosity about Ruth, Osnath took but a tepid interest in her surroundings. But as she knew that it would please Hagith, she spent long stretches of time with her. She listened patiently to all her old kinswoman had to tell her about her numerous offspring, all of whom were apparently gifted with the looks and goodness and wisdom of angels.

Once Hagith had run out of praise to lavish on her descendants, Osnath decided to ward off the emptiness inside her by gaining from Adah the knowledge about the Moabite that had eluded her so far. Hagith's granddaughter had previously hinted her away from Ruth's secrets, but since then some time had elapsed, and Osnath decided to try again.

Hagith's family was wealthy, so there were maids to draw water from the well and fry meats and boil stews on the cooking stones. It was also their task to grind flour and knead dough and bake bread in the furnace. And it fell to their lot to do the cleaning of the house and the laundering. Instead of being burdened with these heavy chores, Adah was free to busy herself with spinning and weaving and sewing up her own dresses, as well as concocting ointments to lighten the skin of her face.

Osnath admitted that Adah's dresses were colorful and of a rich texture, and her skin as soft and as light as any maiden could wish for. But as she herself found little to fascinate her in the tasks that absorbed her young relative's attention, she had not, so far, spent much time with her.

Adah had mostly been friendly enough in her bearing toward her guest, but through the dream she had recounted to her, and by failing to seek her out afterward, she conveyed to Osnath the feeling that deep in her soul she resented her presence in her grandmother's house. Thus Osnath knew that talking to Adah now would require an effort on her part.

She found Adah sitting in front of the house, in the shade of a fig tree. In her left hand she was holding a wooden spindle, which she turned rapidly with her fingers as she deftly drew the fibers of wool she was holding in her right hand onto it, thereby fashioning them into an even yarn. A gentle breeze rustled through the tree and fanned its leaves. The broken sunbeams that passed through them painted the grass below a yellowish color, which formed a fitting background to Adah's striking copper hair and her red-and-white-striped dress.

After Osnath sat down facing her, she talked to Adah of family matters, leading up in a roundabout manner to that which was truly on her mind.

When Adah realized that it was Ruth that Osnath was bent on talking about, she was incensed. She laid her spindle and wool fibers down on the grass, and with her hands on her waist, spoke in a menacing voice: "You are erring in being so willful, in delving relentlessly into Ruth's life, even though it has been made plain to you that your inquiry is repugnant to us. Unless you cease, it will not bode well for you."

Osnath's anger flared up as well. "Are you threatening me, Adah?"

"No, Osnath, you misunderstand. I am not threatening but warning you. We share great-grandparents. You are my kin. Even if you were not, I would never lift a finger against you, for it is not in my nature. But there is one who resents what you are doing so much that he might."

These words cooled Osnath's anger. But they revived the suspicion she had previously harbored about Eliab's placing the snake in her bed, which lately had begun to subside. "Is it Eliab whom you have in mind?"

"No, no," replied Adah quickly, too quickly, thereby funneling Osnath's suspicion to an even higher peak.

"Why is he, like your grandmother, so bent on concealing the secret of a long-deceased woman?"

Adah cast down her eyes, thus hooding them. "He, whoever he may be, fears that we would be threatened by its revelation."

"In what manner could such a revelation be threatening?"

"Hagith's family, my family, was somehow involved in it," she replied in a low voice, as if she were whispering a confidence. Then she clapped her hand to her mouth in distress. "Why did you make me mouth words I was determined not to say?" she complained.

Undeterred, Osnath inquired, "Can you not tell me any more?"

"No."

"Have you never discussed this with your father?"

"My father said that it is better not to stir up dirt and spew it forth like a troubled sea. I have obeyed him, and I counsel you to do the same."

"In the course of time, you must have heard some rumors. You must surely know more than what you have told me," Osnath insisted with urgency in her voice.

"I will not chatter unnecessarily. I have said too much already."

"At least tell me why Eliab is so ridden with anxiety. Is it your family, or his own family, or perhaps his vast inheritance that he is fretting about?"

"How could it have any bearing on his inheritance?" Adah mused. "If you suspect that Obed was not Boaz's true son, and hence Eliab is not Boaz's true descendant, banish this thought. There is not a grain of truth in it."

These words made Osnath prick up her ears. Adah would not have denied this ghastly rumor—it would not even have occurred to her—had it not been previously voiced in her presence.

If it was so and Obed was not truly Boaz's son, he had inherited what was his on the force of a deception. And if the property did not rightly belong to Obed, it would never truly belong to Jesse either, or to his sons after him. It was for this very reason, she was now sure, that Eliab was so anxious to fasten shackles of iron on her exploration and prevent her from uncovering the truth. But if so, Ruth must have conceived from another man.

Before she could voice her thought, though, Adah continued, "Leave off your insistent questions, and take your inquisitive mind off the Moabite and what she did or did not do before she met her husband." There was a steadfast note in Adah's voice, and Osnath knew that it would be pointless to daunt her with further questions.

Yet she was too single-minded to abandon her quest for knowledge about the woman whose life seemed to be more inscrutable by the day. Recalling her earlier conjecture that Eliab might have placed the snake in her bed to deter her from consulting her uncle Samuel, she decided to do just that.

She wrote him a letter, in which she reminded him of telling her that Ruth's secrets lay buried in the ground, and entreated him to relate to her all he knew of this. Then she took three silver shekels from the pouch her father had given her. With those in hand, she set out for the town gates, where she sought out a messenger and gave him her letter to deliver to her uncle's house in Ramah.

Before Samuel's answer arrived, David did. His visit was so ominous that it made her forget his great-grandmother for a time.

Chapter Six

David's arrival was preceded by that of a crier from the king's court. He called out with great pomp that the king's favorite young official was on his way and would arrive shortly.

The two families assembled in the front yard to welcome David. Before long, three men flying King Saul's banner came into view, heralding his approach. Then David himself, riding a mule, with an escort of ten royal guards at his heels, appeared.

The rumors of his infidelity at court momentarily laid aside, Osnath was about to rush forward into his embrace. Then, to her dismay, she perceived a luxurious carriage, with a young woman reclining on its backseat. Her retinue of an elderly woman, apparently her nurse, and two maids—all riding donkeys—and a spare donkey weighed down by her belongings trailed the carriage into the yard.

Osnath froze into immobility. The sparkle that had lit her eyes and the rosy color of excitement that had infused her cheeks both faded from her face.

After David dismounted his mule and assisted the young woman in alighting from her carriage, he bowed deeply to his father and mother, greeted them respectfully, and asked if all was well with them.

Then, without the slightest embarrassment, he declared that the girl before them was Michal, the younger daughter of King Saul, and that she was his bride-to-be. The king had not yet consented to their marriage. But his granting her leave to accompany him, to be presented to his family, augured well for this prospect.

As Michal stepped forward, Osnath came face-to-face with her. Flashing a furtive look at her, she beheld the most resplendent lady she had ever seen. The young woman carried herself with her head held regally aloft, as befitted the princess that she was. Osnath's gaze was diverted from her face to her body by the rustle of her elegant dress. Its shining fabric was woven in different shades of purple, the color of royalty and wealth, overlaid with violet; and its waistband was ingeniously embroidered in pink, the color of innocent maidenhood. On her neck there hung a pendant in which gold and silver were interlaced in an elaborate pattern, the likes of which Osnath had never set eyes on before.

Michal was refined in her face, her body, even in her voice, which she now raised in well-rehearsed words of greeting to the family of the one who would soon be her bridegroom. Although her words were gracious, she did not pay the customary obeisance to the man and woman who were to become her father- and mother-in-law, and did not bow to them. It did not take Osnath long to note that she was haughtily aloof, her bearing speaking a pride that even a king's daughter had no right to display.

The princess's gaze rested on Osnath briefly. But she must have felt that the girl merited little of her attention, for her look was blank and soon moved on to other sights. She paid no further heed to her.

Michal evidently had not mastered the skill of ingratiating herself with the family of her husband-to-be. But this did not afford Osnath any consolation. Without uttering a word, holding herself as stiff as a stick to mask the insult she felt, she turned on her heels. Those around her gave her looks of thinly veiled pity, but she ignored them. She headed for her chamber, and as soon as she entered it, she slammed the door and flung herself onto the bed.

There she lay, raving mad with jealousy. Michal had done no wrong; she was probably unaware of Osnath's very existence in David's life. Yet a rush of hatred, as searing as the heat of the sun at midday, welled up inside her.

How was it, she asked herself, that David, whose mirth gushed forth like a cascade, had fallen prey to a woman as icy cold as the frost on the ground on a cold winter night?

Before long, David came in and knelt down at her side. She gave him a quelling look, but he was not abashed by it. "I have not forgotten you,

Osnath. You have been in my heart perpetually," he said silkily, with no trace of hesitation. "I came to sweep away your misgivings. I will still marry you, as I promised."

"I will not share you with another woman," she said bitterly.

David acted as if he had not been remiss in any way. He never lacked for words appropriate to any occasion, in evidence of which he piled them upon each other like grains in a storeroom. "I did not woo Michal," he explained. "It was she who advised me of her desire to become my wife. I demurred and said, 'How can a poor man of no consequence marry the king's daughter?'

"But Saul's courtiers drowned out my objection with a flood of protests. They persuaded me that being the king's son-in-law would put me in an elevated position. With my prospective kingship in mind, I could not refuse. This has nothing to do with you, though. My heart is still yours," he asserted in a convincing tone.

She failed to be moved by his honeyed words. "Your heart holds no love for me. By now you deem yourself to be so highly placed in Israel that I am no longer good enough for you. No lesser woman than a princess can elicit your devotion."

"I feel no love for her. What entrances me is her station as the king's daughter, which will remove the obstacles in my way to becoming king myself. Even though I adore you alone, I cannot let you prevent me from following the destiny that has been carved out for me by the Lord himself."

"So you value your kingship more than you value me."

David waved his hand in the air as if he were shooing away a fly. "You are making a mountain out of a mound. This is a trifling matter that does not warrant the bustle you are creating over it. It will take time before my wedding with Michal is arranged. But as soon as it is over, I will marry you as well."

Her eyes widened. "And take me to Saul's court with you, and flaunt me before your new father-in-law?" she queried, raising a dubious eyebrow at him.

For once, David had no sleek reply ready. For the first time ever, the words did not pour from his mouth as fluently as they usually did.

She laughed in disdain. "You would wed me and then leave me here on my own. You must think very little of me if you would have me be a widow in my husband's lifetime, while you steep yourself in your new-found glory and revel at court with the king's daughter and all the other girls I have been told about."

He hesitated. At last he said, "Even though I cannot take you to court, this should not disturb you unduly. You will always have a place under my parents' roof. You will lack for nothing, and I will come to visit you frequently. I will stay here with you for long stretches of time, with no princesses and other ladies of the court around to encumber us. You will be my favorite wife."

She sniffed her incredulity. "You have been caught in the web of your own empty promises, and now you are attempting to use the smoothness of your tongue to extricate yourself from it."

"I will truly wed you, if you wish for it," he said somberly.

"I no longer wish for it. I would prefer to remain unwed for my entire life."

He threw up his hands as one acknowledging defeat. "It shall be as you decree. But you are too beautiful to remain unwed," he added in an attempt to soothe her; only it had the opposite effect.

She was unable to restrain herself any longer. "Leave these premises instantly," she hissed, "before I burst into screams and alert everyone, and also your lofty princess, to the disgusting manner in which you have treated me."

David spoke not another word. Silently, with his eyes on his intricately laced, elegant shoes, he let himself out of her room.

Osnath, who in David's presence had been halfway to tears of mortification, now felt them hot on her cheeks, overflowing like a spring in a rainy winter, coming forth even from her nose, streaming down her chin, with only the sheet underneath her to dry them.

She was still wiping away the smudges the tears had left on her reddened face when Eliab came in. He looked at her soberly but not unkindly. "You have dismissed my words as unworthy of notice," he said in a voice as calm as a spent storm. "At least admit that I was right."

Osnath nodded her head mutely and shifted her gaze away from him to the floor.

He was about to say more but restrained himself. He merely lifted her chin and kissed her softly on her mouth, still damp with tears, and left.

How had she failed to realize on her own, she thought bitterly, that once David rose to eminence, he would not hesitate to abandon her?

Eliab was by far more trustworthy than his brother. The pain and the humiliation this man had inflicted on her on the night of the storm would always remain ingrained in the innermost recesses of her being. But he had bitterly repented his deed and had done his utmost to expiate for it in the manner prescribed by the Torah, by wedding her. He had also been willing to accept any other penalty the elders would have imposed on him—no matter how severe it might have been—had she let him approach them. At the very least, he had never dealt falsely with her.

Thus, in the following days, as her tears for David dried out also in her soul, she began weighing in her mind whether she had not been too hasty in declining Eliab's offer. Perhaps, following David's perfidy, she should accede to Eliab's entreaty to let him approach her father. Or perhaps she would do well to forget both brothers and return to Ramah to seek her fortune there.

While Osnath was still agonizing over what she should do, a missive from Samuel, borne by a man she recognized as working in his household, was delivered to her. It was the reply to her almost forgotten query, which she had sent to him over a week ago. And this is what it contained:

> Hear me, my treasured niece. When your missive
> arrived, I was away from home, hence my tardy reply. Rest
> assured that my heart is with you in the recent disillusion-
> ment you have suffered. But remember that vicissitudes are
> here to test our endurance and strengthen us. I counsel you

to leave the stage of your life in which you were linked to
David behind you without regret, as one leaves behind a
bad dream. Better things lie in store for you.

In the meantime, I praise you for your efforts to uncover Ruth's tale. Your dauntless diligence in this matter
calls forth my admiration. Hence, and also to take your
mind off your recent trouble, I will help you further it.

Now, to ensure the success of your venture, you must
be careful to follow meticulously the instructions I am
about to give you.

There is a massive terebinth tree that stands between the
house of Hagith and the house of Obed. Ruth planted it as
a sapling with her own hands when she settled in Boaz's
house. Years later, she dug another hole next to it, into
which she sank a clay jar containing the key to her previous
life. With the jar she buried that life, in certainty that it
would not come to haunt her again for as long as she lived.

Yet the tree became her own tree of knowledge: she
hoped that after she left this earth someone would be
made privy to that knowledge by discovering the jar.

Since then the jar has lain undisturbed in the ground,
and if you dig around the tree, you will undoubtedly discover it.

But remember that the tree and the soil that surrounds
it belong to Obed and Hagith and their families. Hence it
is incumbent on you to seek their permission before you
thrust your shovel into the ground. So speaks your uncle
Samuel, who is ever concerned with your welfare.

The letter ignited Osnath's imagination anew. As soon as she read it,
she abandoned all thought of returning to Ramah before she had uncovered that which lay in the ground of Bethlehem.

She recognized her uncle's demand that she seek permission for
what she intended to do as just, and she had no wish to flout his authority. Yet she was certain that she would never gain such permission.

Instead, others would snatch the treasure she was seeking from under her eyes. So she resolved that the deed would have to be done in a clandestine fashion, under the mantle of darkness.

That evening after the meal, Osnath stretched out on her bed but kept herself awake. Once night had descended, and all lay asleep in their beds, she arose from hers. For a while she sat on the threshold of her door, waiting until the last part of the night when, she knew, their sleep would be the deepest. Then she walked as noiselessly as she could to the edge of the garden, opened its gate stealthily, and walked out.

Not far away, at the side of the plot of land that belonged to Hagith's family, there stood a toolshed. Its door was not locked, and Osnath entered it and took hold of a shovel. This she brought back with her and placed at the foot of the terebinth tree.

The crescent moon was but a sliver in the sky, hardly disturbing the dimness of the night. In its faint light, the branches of the tree were like crooked arms reaching out to her, set on strangling her. The shadows created by them were deep and dark and frightening. She stood still for a while, straining her ears for sounds that might herald someone's approach, fearful of the rustle of the leaves in the gentle night breeze.

By now she had deep misgivings about the propriety of her endeavor, and she regretted her rash decision to do her deed in the thick of the night. But she inhaled the fresh air, moist with dew, and it soothed her. Besides, she was staunchly determined to make Ruth's jar relinquish its secrets to her, and there was no other way to achieve this. She was enmeshed in this already and could not draw back. So she warded off her doubts and began digging.

For a while, the shovel overturned clamps of soil, but nothing came to light other than more soil. As time slid by and all she could see were growing mounds of dug-out earth, it struck her that she might be engaged in a backbreaking but futile endeavor.

She did not doubt Samuel's instructions. But the jar she was searching for might be close to the tree, or more distant from it; in a shallow spot, or deep beneath its roots. Even if she continued digging through the night, it was as probable that her labor would bear fruit as hail was in summer. Yet she was unwilling to give up, and stubbornly continued her labor.

Then, to her utter amazement, she heard the clang of the shovel's iron as it hit a hard object. Her heart gave a thud; then she continued hammering feverishly as she went on digging, until a long narrow clay jar, caked with the soil in which it had been encased, stood out from the ground like a watchtower in a city wall.

She bent down and lifted it up with trembling hands. It was closed with a bowl-shaped lid, but with some effort she managed to pry it off the jar. She inserted her hand into its opening and removed from it a lengthy bundle: a rolled-up scroll. It was wrapped up in a cloth and tied with a string.

Attempting to ascertain whether there was anything else in the jar, she peered into its aperture but met with nothing but a deep black hole and a moldy odor. Then she shook it and heard a rattling inside. She turned the jar over and spilled out its remaining contents: an object in the shape of a large ring, which tumbled out, noisily hitting a stone.

In her excitement, she ignored the noise, set the jar down on the ground, and picked up her find. Turning it over in her hand, she noted in delight that it was a seal, artfully crafted of shining lapis, dangling on a half-decayed cord. By that time, the glittering of the stars was gradually being extinguished by the pale light of the rising dawn. Thus, by straining her eyes, she could discern that the ring bore an inscription. At first she could not make it out, but as light slowly subdued darkness, she succeeded in deciphering it:

MISHAEL OF BETHLEHEM

In that flash of a moment she realized what this must signify. Ruth's scroll, and the name of her unidentified lover, which Osnath had been tracing for so long, had finally surfaced. She was elated.

Before she had a chance to fill the hole she had dug, to cover the traces of her deed, a faint, muffled noise reached her ears, making her start. When she looked around, she could discern nothing; but she sensed that someone was watching her, and the sweat of fear began trickling down her back.

All at once she heard another noise from behind. She swung around and was startled by the sight of Eliab almost upon her. She hid her right hand, with the scroll in it, behind her back. And she balled her left hand, which was holding the seal, into a fist, enclosing the gem in it.

She barely had time to press her closed hand into the folds of her dress before he confronted her. He was so close that she could feel his breath on her face. His wrath was evident in his eyes, which, in the dawning day, looked ferocious. She was overwhelmed and shrank back before him.

"What are you doing here, burrowing in the ground like a rat?" he demanded sharply.

Her cheeks were burning in shame, and she was thankful for the dimness of the light that prevented him from perceiving this.

"What have you uncovered, and why are you so secretive about it? Why are you getting up to mischief again?" He plied her with angry questions.

She cast about in her mind for a reply that would appease him, but could think of none. She just stood there, wordless, with her head dipped and her hair tumbling down over her temples, in confusion.

He noticed her right hand behind her back, came even closer until his chest was pressed to hers, and wrested the scroll from her hand. Then he stood back and shoved it under his arm.

Now his gaze came to rest suspiciously on her left hand. He caught sight of a little corner of lapis peeping out at its edge, and his fiery wrath flared up again. "You had no right to plunder our possessions," he fairly shouted at her.

She gave vent to her own rising rancor. "You are a bad-tempered man," she said testily.

"You are quick to find fault, but the fault is yours," he replied irritably.

Recognizing his words as true, she bit her lip. "I have accused you unjustly. I repent my words."

Those were the kindest words she had ever addressed to him, and he laughed out loud in joy.

Then she spoiled their effect by adding, "If I came here in an underhand manner, it is because you have tripped my investigation with your heavy foot every step of the way. Pray, sir," she pleaded urgently, "let me look at the scroll before you stow it away."

He did not favor her with a reply and merely approached once more and squeezed her small trembling hand in his large and firm one, forcing it open and making her surrender her second find to him. He raised it to his eyes and scrutinized it darkly.

"You have overreached yourself this time. Your uncle was without doubt behind this travesty. You would not else have discovered this scroll and this seal, for even I was ignorant of their whereabouts. Did he truly condone your committing such a theft?"

Osnath admitted shamefacedly that Samuel had enjoined her to seek permission before she set out to dig in soil that did not belong to her.

Since she had yielded to him, and had even admitted her transgression, Eliab's wrath dissipated again and his face softened. "No matter. You are nothing but an unruly child," he said indulgently.

With these words, he gazed into her now clearly visible, large bluegray eyes, which were raised to his.

She was glad that he had let her off so lightly and returned his tender gaze with a forlorn smile. He brought his mouth close to hers. But when he was on the verge of kissing her, she became reticent and averted her face from his. Then she turned it back, but the damage had been done: he felt that she had withdrawn from him again. He released her. The tender moment between them faded with the fading stars.

Osnath, feeling the chill from him, looked dejectedly at the dug-out soil at her feet, signaling the wreckage of her hopes.

꒜

After she had helped Eliab to mend her destructive handiwork by filling up the hole, and the earth around the tree had been smoothed out, she returned to her quarters. The sun began to rise behind the hills, so there was no time left to sleep. Instead, she sat on her bed, contemplating her discovery.

Her elation at her success had subsided, and she was downcast again. She was no longer in possession of the scroll or the seal, and Eliab would never let her set eyes on them again. She had ascertained the name engraved on the ring. But she had no idea who Mishael of Bethlehem might have been.

Since seals were used to testify to the truth of important documents, they were used mostly by king's officials or by other men of high standing. So Mishael must have been a man of consequence, probably the ancestor of a well-to-do family still residing in Bethlehem. But there were numerous such families in the town, and she could not divine which one was his.

If Mishael was truly the Unnamed, then he was a relative of Ruth's first husband, and thus of Boaz. But Boaz must have had plenty of relatives, and as he had been wealthy, many of them must have been well-to-do, also. Which one of those might Mishael have been?

When Osnath sat down with Hagith for her morning meal of wheat cakes and olives and milk, she inquired whether she knew of one named Mishael. Hagith spat out the pits of the olives on which she was chewing and pushed the henna-dyed strands of hair that had slipped to her forehead back under her headscarf. She looked at her young relative sternly, her face stiffened, and she wrapped herself in silence.

As she had failed to elicit an answer from Hagith, Osnath sent off an urgent letter to Samuel asking him the same question. But his reply, which was delivered to her a few days later, came in the form of a riddle:

> Mishael was not only Boaz's relative. He was close to
> him in another way as well, yet he was not his friend.

This was the sort of incomprehensible message that her uncle delighted in conveying. Osnath strained her mind for a few days but was unable to make out what it intimated. Yet she knew that one could never make Samuel elucidate his fuzzy messages. Hence she refrained from writing to him again.

Chapter Seven

Two days later, a letter came from David. It was written on behalf of the king, inviting his family for a visit to Saul's castle.

Before they left, Jesse called Osnath to him again. "I am well aware now, my girl, as I was not before David's visit," he said, "that he has dealt dishonorably with you and that you have a just complaint against him. It was stupidly done by him. For with your mind that always thirsts for the unknown, you are superior to Michal in every way. Unlike her, you also show proper respect for your elders, and you are never conceited.

"I cannot overset his promise to marry the princess without giving offense to Saul. The king wields great power, and it is not good for a man to cross his will. But I will not condone David's conduct. When I see him, I will hold him to his word and oblige him to take you for his second wife."

"It is kind of you, sir," she responded, "but I no longer have any desire to become David's wife. I prefer to become the wife of a man who will never be king, but a man who will love me alone as much as I love him, all the days of his life."

Jesse nodded his understanding and fondly patted her cheek.

As soon as Osnath had withdrawn from his presence, Jesse and his wife and family departed, all save Obed, who was too feeble to travel and was left in the care of his maid.

The winter had long passed, and even the spring was petering out; the rains were over and done with. The heat was gathering in the land, but it abated in the late afternoon. On the day after his family's departure, as the sun began its descent in the sky, Obed, leaning on his cane, his shoulders bent like bows, came hobbling out of his sleeping room. He sat in front of it on a chair that had been set up for him.

As he sat, he saw Osnath passing by. Because of the forgetfulness of old age, he failed to recall that he had chased her away wrathfully a few months ago. He called out to her, "Come here, young one."

When she approached, he grumbled, "They have left me on my own. There is no one here, either near or far, but you. You are like a ray of the sun that has been sent by the Lord to brighten my days. Come and talk to me."

She sat down on a stone at his feet.

"Nobody comes to chat with me anymore," he complained. "My father and my mother, my wife and my sisters, and all my friends no longer inhabit this earth. I am like the scarred stump of a tree spared by a forest fire, left entirely on its own amid the scorched earth."

Her heart went out to him in pity. "Surely the memory of your loved ones lives on in your heart and sustains you," she comforted him. "Would you like to tell me about them?"

Though his recollection of what had come to pass recently was dim, his memory of distant events was lucid, as clear as the water that flows down the river Jordan. So she sat for a long time, holding his dry, bony hand, lending her ear to tales of days long past.

Of his father, Boaz, and his success in cultivating his land and extracting abundant crops from it. Of his own skill in coaxing the soil to yield its strength to him. Of his grandmother Naomi and her tenderness for him. Of Boaz's love for his wife, Ruth; and of hers for her husband and for himself, and for her daughters, his sisters, all the days of her life, at the end of which she succumbed to illness after a valiant fight.

Out of her concern for Obed's loneliness, Osnath came to sit with him each day. As she knew that it would bring him solace, she stifled the yawns that threatened to escape her, and listened to the selfsame tale over and over again, until she knew it by heart.

It was a week later, on the fifth day of the third month, and an easterly wind, blowing hot from the desert, was prowling through the yard. In the late afternoon, undeterred by the strong gusts, Obed came out to sit on his chair, to bask in the rays of the setting sun, and to warm his chilled old bones in it.

Once again, Osnath came to lend an ear to his tale. Only this time, when the tale reached its melancholy end, it occurred to her that Obed might be able to shed light on the mystery of who Mishael of Bethlehem had been. So she asked about the friends of his whom he had previously mentioned.

"They all have been gathered to their ancestors. Not one of them has been left behind."

"Not even Mishael?"

Obed seemed shaken. "He has been dead these many years. When he lay down with his fathers, and with his deceased elder brother as well, I was merely a little boy."

"Who was his deceased brother?"

Obed's eyes, which had been gazing hazily into the distance, now narrowed as they came to rest on her. "Why are you asking these prying questions?" he said in a disgruntled tone. "You seem to have a sinister purpose, and it is not good in my eyes."

Osnath was wary of incurring his displeasure again and too late regretted her question. Abruptly, he was overcome with shortness of breath and with a fit of coughing, which made him double over and gasp for air.

In her anxiety for him, she knelt down before him and stroked his knees soothingly. "Esteemed sir," she stammered, "forgive my rash words. I meant no harm. But you seem to be unwell. Pray let me help you to your bed."

Straightening himself with difficulty, he declined her offer with a shake of his head and said testily, "You are no longer the sunshine of my days. Go away from here and never show your face to me again."

As his shortness of breath had ceased and his coughing had subsided, Osnath rose and turned to leave. But not before Eliab, who had entered the yard and slid off his mule, caught sight of her.

Having returned from Saul's court a few strides ahead of the others, he had witnessed the altercation, and he halted her as she was on the way to her room.

"You have been pestering him again," he lashed out at her. He was boiling with wrath, his dark eyes seemed to be shooting poisoned arrows at her, and he was keeping his terse voice down with difficulty so that his grandfather would not overhear him. "You are squeezing the last drops of life from him. If he expires, I will lay his death at your door. I will mete out to you the punishment you deserve: a tooth for a tooth, an eye for an eye, as set out in the Torah."

She winced, yet was not subdued. "And you," she retorted, her voice fuming no less than his, "are determined to accuse me, without reason, of every wrongdoing that ever was."

"What object would I have in doing so?" he asked in astonishment.

"You wish to intimidate me because you are worrying for your inheritance. For some inscrutable reason, you fear that what I may uncover will wrest it from you."

In his anger, he raised his hand to her and almost hit her face. Then, restraining himself with difficulty, he stopped and his hand remained suspended in midair.

She cowered and shielded her face with her arm, and turned from him and scurried to her room. There she sat, attempting to convince herself that he had not truly meant the harsh words he had spoken to her, as she had not meant those she had spoken to him. But she found no peace in her heart.

After a while, she began to ask herself what could have been so abhorrent about Mishael that the mere mention of his name had caused Obed to be overcome with such shortness of breath as might threaten his life. She trembled at the thought that Eliab had been right and that his grandfather might in fact be pushed to his grave by the memory of this long-dead man. Knowing that she would not be allowed into Obed's presence to calm him down, she decided to calm herself down by taking a walk through the windswept fields and the hills beyond.

While she was fumbling with the iron latch that kept the garden gate locked, Eliab, having put the maid who cared for the old man in charge of him, chased her and caught up with her. He inserted his sturdy body between her and the gate, thus blocking her exit.

She feared that Obed's state might have worsened after she had left him, that he might even have died. Recalling the ominous, fierce wrath in Eliab's face, which surpassed anything she had ever seen there, she worried that he might be truly intent on wreaking revenge on her, as he had threatened he would. She decided to flee for her life.

Looking around, Osnath found a hole in the hedge that surrounded the garden. She bolted and squeezed through it. Once on the other side, she scrambled and lurched forward, her feet thudding out her fear.

Eliab opened the gate and plunged into the dusk after her.

For a while, Osnath was unaware of this. When she turned around, the bushes that bordered the fields blotted out her view, and the hissing of the wind blowing through those bushes swallowed up any other sound. She was convinced that he had given up his chase.

She slackened her pace to ease her breathing, but as soon as she did, she heard his heavy footfalls and saw him behind her. He waved to her with his arms and called to her to halt, but this only spurred her on to race faster, as one pursued by a pack of wolves. As she was heading westward, the brisk easterly wind was blowing at her back, pushing her to even greater speed.

Suddenly she found herself in an orchard, its trees heavy with plump fruit, facing a gorge that blocked her escape. It was deep and flanked on both sides by limestone walls that declined steeply into its depth.

Osnath turned southward and continued running along its edge. But a blast of wind, stronger than ever, cut through her dress, blowing her toward the gorge, while it swept her curls into her face, blinding her. Her mouth was dry with dread as she stumbled blindly over a stone. Her legs buckled underneath her, and she was on the verge of toppling over into the abyss.

Eliab, who was close behind, flung himself forward to catch her. He was sweating, his sweat turning into cold drops, sick with sheer terror for her life. His arms encircled her, and he squeezed her to his chest, holding her firmly around the waist.

Her strength ebbed, and she went limp in his arms like a sack of wheat. At first, she could not speak for fear. But when she realized that he had come not to kill but to save her, her stormy face cleared and broke into a thankful smile.

Eliab dragged her away from the chasm, then released her. "What is this stupidity, child?" he asked gruffly. "What were you about, to rush out to this dangerous spot in such a stormy wind? You have been callously unheeding of your safety. You have put yourself, and me, too, in peril of our lives."

As she inhaled the dust the wind was still blowing into her face, the smile on it faded into a frown. "I was fleeing from you," she railed at him. "I feared that your grandfather had died and that you held me culpable for this and had come to carry out your threat to mete out a tooth for a tooth."

"My grandfather has recovered and is well. In any case, how can you be so ridiculously silly? Don't you understand that I was merely speaking in the heat of my wrath? Don't you know how much I love you? That I would give my life to ensure your safety?"

The color that had previously waned from her cheeks rushed back into them. "I am not an infant suckling at its mother's breasts," she said crankily. "I can take care of my own safety."

"You are as reckless as a wild Egyptian mare," he growled. "It is fortunate that I seized you in time, for this place is prone to disaster. Death has prowled here before."

"How is that?"

"Someone has plunged to death in this gorge already. And you were set to be the second one."

His words were odd, and the tone of his voice alerted her, giving rise to a new notion in her mind. "Plunged, or was cast to death?" she asked shrewdly.

"It makes no difference. The main thing is that death has wreaked havoc here before. It must never happen again."

"Who was it that met his end here?"

"It was in days long past and need not worry you. Just keep away from this place."

An odd suspicion overtook her. "Was it to do with Ruth?" she asked in a low voice.

So far as anyone with such a dark skin as his could flush, he did. He made no reply, and she took his silence as a response in its own right.

By then the brisk wind had calmed down, as had her fear of him. As the darkness deepened, she let him lead her out of the orchard to a patch of grass surrounded by bushes, and gently press her shoulders and make her sit down. "My love for you, Osnath, is deeper than the gully in which you nearly lost your life," he declared, the desire clearly audible in the hoarseness of his voice. "Pray let me show it to you."

By that time, her sorrow over David had already been washed away like the dryness of summer by the first autumn rain. And now that Eliab had saved her, she was drunk with gratitude and felt a previously unknown tenderness in her heart for him.

So when he pleaded and panted and covered her lips with his, she did not ward him off. As he thrust his tongue into her mouth in an intrusive kiss, she felt the allure of his manly body against hers. She let him push her down to lie on the grass, and coax and stroke and pet her halfway into compliance. But when he prepared to come to her, she rolled away from under him.

The next day, the sixth day of the third month, was the day of the festival of the wheat harvest. In the old days, when the House of the Lord in Shiloh was still standing proudly erect, multitudes from across the land of Israel would come on a pilgrimage to celebrate the festival there. Now that the Temple had been destroyed by the Philistines, each town celebrated the feast on its own. In Bethlehem, the feast took place after the heat of the day had abated, in one of the fields that had been harvested already, so that no damage would be inflicted on the crops.

The two families left for the festivities together. They were bearing with them the firstfruits of their wheat harvest and the choicest of their animals, goats and ewes and rams, as sacrifices and gifts for the priests, as set out in the Torah.

As they walked, Jesse, who headed the procession, leading a ram on a cord, motioned to Osnath to approach him. When she caught up with him, he told her that he had something of the first order of importance to discuss with her, and instructed her to come to his house after the celebration.

Osnath could hardly contain her eagerness to find out what it was that he wished to talk to her about. Having returned from Saul's castle the day before, he had borne no message for her from her erstwhile lover, nor had she looked for one. But if it was not David, what could it be that Jesse had on his mind? But he refused her request to tell her now, and she forbore to press him.

As she weighed various possibilities in her mind, she began lagging behind; and Eliab, leading a donkey packed with loaves of bread for the priests, took up his father's place at her side. At his sight, the talk with Jesse looming before her faded from her mind. Instead, a new thought flashed through it.

Yesterday, when Eliab had saved her at the risk of his own life from plunging into the gully, he had shown her life to be precious to him. If so, surely he could not have tried to put an end to it by means of a venomous snake, as she had suspected. She confronted him with that realization.

"You cannot truly have credited that I was capable of any such deed," he responded derisively. "I thought you had long been aware that in this, at least, my conduct toward you has been above reproach."

"Then what came to pass that night? Do you believe, as the others do, that I made up the whole incident in my imagination?"

"No, Osnath. The snake was not imaginary. After I led you to Hagith's room, I returned to yours and searched it more thoroughly than it had been searched before. Behind the wooden case that borders your bed, I found a deep crack in the wall. It was there that the viper had taken refuge, and so it had not been noticed before. I pulled it out and killed it. And the next day, as you may recall, I had all the cracks in the walls of both houses filled up, and all snakes in the vicinity destroyed and all low-growing bushes cut down."

"Where did the snake come from?"

"Vipers are occasionally sighted in these parts in the spring and in the summer, when they emerge from their hiding places at nighttime. Each year in the spring we take the precaution of cutting the plants. This year, the snake made its appearance earlier than expected, and we were caught unawares."

"Why did you not tell me this sooner?" she asked in irritation.

"You were in a frenzy of fear already, and there was no sense in making it worse by telling you that these creeping beasts are roaming around freely in our town. I only hope that, now that some months have passed, you will believe me when I say that since we have done what was necessary to eradicate this pest, you are entirely safe."

"My suspicion has been ill founded, then. Forgive me."

"But I have never held it against you; and my love for you has never wavered."

The confusion in Osnath's mind was deeper than ever.

When they arrived at the field designated for the festival, it was already teeming with multitudes, arrayed in their most festive garments and in their most exuberant moods. There were celebrants standing in family groups, or milling around, for as far as the eye could see. In the midst of the field, on an elevated platform of stones smoothed over with soil, an altar had been erected.

A slope led up to the platform, and on it stood a group of priests, whom the celebrants approached one by one. Each man, accompanied by his family, proffered baskets containing the firstfruits of his fields, and the firstfruits of his flock and herd, each in accordance with his means and beyond.

Some of the priests accepted the baskets of bread and bags of wheat that were handed to them, then waved the offerings ceremoniously over their heads before setting them down before the altar. Others took charge of the animals and led them away, some to be slaughtered for the sacrifice or for the meal that was to follow, others to be distributed among the priests for their households.

When the gift-bearing ceremony was completed, the sacrificial lambs were offered up on the altar. And the most eminent priest in Bethlehem, with his richly embroidered white robe flapping in the breeze, and his voice ringing into the distance, invoked blessings:

Oh Lord, God of Israel.
Be blessed for giving

us this land,
a land flowing with
milk and honey.

And all the people bowed down and answered, "Amen."
Adjusting the colorful cap on his head, the priest went on:

And may it please you to
endow our land with
abundant crops so that the
multitudes of Israel may
eat and be satisfied.

Again, all the people bowed down and answered, "Amen."

While the head priest chanted, other priests walked about among the celebrants with bags of wheat in their hands, strewing handfuls of grain over them, as a sign that these blessings were indeed imminent.

Wandering birds of many feathers came by and picked the grains from the ground before flying off into the distance. Occasionally, a gazelle could be sighted on top of one of the surrounding hills, looking down on the proceedings in wide-eyed wonder.

Then the entire congregation sat down and burst into ancient, joyful harvest songs. And the priests turned a deaf ear when they voiced love songs about young men and maidens who met and loved each other in the fields at harvesttime amid the heaps of reaped corn, which never disclosed their secrets. The singing went on for a long time, after which chunks of the meat that had been roasted on spits, and flagons of wine, were brought around.

Osnath participated in the singing and partook of the food absent-mindedly. As she sat with her legs crossed in front of her, feeling the dry rough soil underneath through her thin dress, her thoughts skipped back and forth between her strengthening yet still fuzzy feelings toward Eliab and her curiosity over what her forthcoming talk with Jesse might herald for her.

Little did she know how apt the songs that had been sung would soon become in her own life.

By the time they reached home, Jesse's front room was already occupied by his numerous rowdy offspring, who had returned from the festival before the rest of the two families. They were lounging there, jesting loudly with each other, in what seemed to be a language they alone could understand.

Hence Jesse summoned Osnath to his own quarters, which she understood to be a signal of honor. There she found his wife, sitting on a chair, motioning her with a smile to sit next to her. Then she gave evidence of her reverence for her husband by letting him speak undisturbed.

"My girl," he began, "when I visited David, in accordance with your wishes, I did not raise with him the matter of his taking you to be his wife alongside Michal. But David is not my only son. This morning, Eliab, my firstborn, advised me that since you are now free of your entanglement with David, he is wishful to wed you.

"Let me assure you that you could not do better for yourself than accepting his offer. Both David's mother and I love our youngest deeply, and our souls are linked to his. He is the most devoted of sons; no one in the entire land defers to his father and his mother more than he does. Yet it cannot have escaped you that his attentions are fleeting, that he is like a bee, easily floating from one flower blossom to another. But Eliab's feelings run as deep as the roots of an oak tree, and they are as steady as its trunk.

"Besides, although he will not be king, he is an exceedingly wealthy man. The family's property, of which he is in charge, bears plentiful crops. His skill accounts for much of this, and he will rightly inherit a large share of it from me.

"He is a capable man also in trade. Here, too, he has amassed a fortune with the power of his own mind and the diligence of his own hands. He owns a caravan that periodically bears merchandise of gold from the land of Ophir in the far south, which his men sell at considerable profit for him to jewelers in Bethlehem. With the gold he earns from this trade, he will soon be able to purchase more land, which he will cultivate to bring forth even larger crops from it.

"The Lord has made him prosper in all he has set his hand to undertake. Even at his young age he is a highly regarded dignitary in our tribe, and people are used to mentioning his name with respect. If you marry him, you will be one of the greatest ladies in all the surrounding area."

Osnath was stunned, for she had never heard of Eliab's riches before. She told this to Eliab's parents. This inspired his mother to speak for the first time, which she did in a melodious voice. "He is not a man who brags of his success. You may believe us, though, when we tell you that he is going from strength to strength."

Jesse regarded Osnath with satisfaction, in certainty that she was poised to accept Eliab's offer. But she did not consider Eliab's wealth a sufficient reason to become his wife.

So when Jesse disclosed that he had already composed a letter to her father requesting his youngest daughter for his eldest son, and that he intended to send it off through a messenger immediately, Osnath protested. She begged him in a small voice to postpone the departure of the messenger, for she still wanted to search her heart before she made a decision.

"Although," Jesse replied, "I could approach your father and he would have it in his power to bestow you on my son without consulting you, I will not act against your will."

For the second time Atarah now intervened, saying, "You are still very young, merely on the threshold of your life, yet away from your own mother. Let me offer you my motherly advice, instead. It is that you should not let this opportunity slip away, for you don't know how long it may remain open to you. If you become Eliab's wife now, he will never break faith with you all the days of his life. But if you delay, you may find him led astray to graze in foreign pastures."

Eliab's mother looked at her meaningfully with her gleaming dark eyes, as if she were trying to convey to her a hidden message. Osnath could not fathom what it was, so she merely replied that she would not keep her and Jesse waiting long.

In response, Jesse said, "Osnath, throughout the few months of your sojourn here we have both grown fond of you, and we find you worthier to be our daughter-in-law than any other girl who has crossed our path. I hope that you will make your decision promptly and with wisdom."

With these words he rose to his feet, and when she rose as well, he kissed her on the forehead, thereby gently dismissing her.

Osnath was left with the feeling that she had disappointed them both by failing to give them her answer immediately. But when she reflected on her reply, she knew that she could not have spoken differently, for all inside her was jumbled.

She had misjudged Eliab, failing to recognize that he was not shifty like the clouds on a windy day, as was his youngest brother, and that he had truly cast the mantle of his love over her. Though he had perpetrated a contemptible deed on her, he had also jeopardized his life to save her from death.

If she had found no pleasure in his caresses, neither had she with David. So perhaps she was destined never to find joy with any man, and her act with Eliab was the best she could hope for.

She could not deny to herself that she was strongly drawn to him, to his massive body and manly power, harboring a secret desire to be touched by him, to be engulfed in his strength by feeling his arms around her. At times her heart now fluttered at his sight, or even at the thought of him, as it had not done before. But she did not have the same certitude of her love for him as she had previously had of her love for David. She listened to her wayward heart, but it spoke to her in two voices. She could find no answer to her agonizing doubts.

Five days later, as Osnath sat contemplating her fate, her thoughts reverted to Ruth. Had the young woman, who, like her, had been far removed from her kith and kin, also agonized over whether she should become Boaz's wife?

Osnath reflected that after Ruth did marry Boaz and came to reside in his house, she must have frequented the garden, in which she herself now sat, every day. In her mind, she saw Ruth strolling about in front of her. She was picking fruit from a tree and watering the flowers, humming tunes to herself as she went about her chores. Then Ruth sat down and inhaled the flowers' sweet scent, as she herself was doing now.

Yet Osnath's mind was assailed by doubts about the Moabite. Had her melodies been merry or sad? Had she indeed been happy in her life with her husband, as Jesse insisted that she had been? Or had she yearned for her previous lover who somehow must have been lost to her? Could she have sat on the selfsame patch of grass on which Osnath was sitting now, grieving for him?

Then it dawned on her as suddenly as a tidal wave on a placid sea. Adah had previously raised—and immediately dismissed—the notion that Obed might not have been Boaz's true son, and therefore Eliab was not his true descendant. Adah's quick denial notwithstanding, Osnath believed she now knew what must have transpired as surely as if she had witnessed it with her own eyes.

The Unnamed, Mishael, whose coming to Ruth had been so marvelous in her eyes, must have made her pregnant while he sojourned in Sdeh Moab. Then he must have returned to his own country, abandoning her to her fate, to cope on her own with the trouble into which he had plunged her. And when she followed him to Bethlehem and apprised him of the child she was carrying in her womb, he doubtless refused to assume responsibility for it, as was evident by the fact that he had refused to make her his wife.

Osnath's heart wept for Ruth, who must have been in a pit of despair with no other choice but to become Boaz's wife, and pass off the other man's child in her womb as his.

Even if, as she believed, this was how it happened, she had no evidence to prove it. No one was willing to reveal the truth about Ruth to her, and continuing to chase after it would be like chasing the wind.

While those thoughts crossed her mind, the sun was sliding down behind the hills in preparation for its nightly rest. Osnath was about to return to Hagith's house for the evening meal when her eyes opened to a sight that drove all other thoughts from her mind.

Glaring in disbelief, she beheld Eliab and Adah returning from the freshly reaped fields together. Adah's hand was slung into the crook of his arm, as he stroked her rosy cheeks, the heat between them evident for all to see. Their faces were turned toward each other, and they were engrossed in their own world, as if a transparent curtain separated them from the rest of creation.

At their sight, it seemed to Osnath that the sun halted in its tracks, and the wind ceased blowing and the birds stopped in midflight, as time itself was suspended. She was gripped with a surge of an uncomprehending pain. She had previously imputed evil deeds to Eliab, but faithlessness had not been one of them. Now she blamed herself for having been so stupid as to put her trust in him.

As they passed by, Eliab's face was turned away from her; but Adah's eyes briefly shifted from those of her lover and brushed over her, and she wore what Osnath took to be a smile of triumph on her face. Adah raised her hand in a gesture of greeting and called one out with her mouth as well.

Osnath's hand, though, was as heavy as if it had weights of lead attached to it, and it would not lift in response, and neither would her voice. She just sat upright, stricken into silence, totally inert, with a ghastly smile, such as that on an Egyptian death mask, fixed on her face.

As she had done when David had brought Michal to his father's house, Osnath repaired to the seclusion of her chamber. This time, though, she did not cry. A knot was stuck in her throat, like a ball of rolled-up wool, which would not uncoil itself into tears. She sat gazing blindly out the window, her eyes red but dry.

She realized, as she had not before, how much her well-being depended on Eliab. She did not know exactly when she had come to believe in his love for her and found comfort in it, but she had. In the face of David's perfidy, she had leaned on it as a lame man leans on a crutch, but he had removed its support from under her. He had breached the boundaries of her soul and invaded it; and now he had withdrawn, leaving a gaping hollow behind.

Five days before, his mother had warned her that if she delayed, he would be apt to stray into foreign pastures; but she had not thought that it would happen that soon. This image brought a wan smile to her face, and while it was still sitting there, Eliab came in.

He stood in front of her; but unlike his custom, he did not touch her. "I did not mean to cause you sorrow," he said in a subdued voice.

She wanted to rave and rant at him, but she could not find the words. Her eyes remained averted from him as she swallowed the constriction in her throat. "You professed your love for me, yet you mocked me by having this other woman in secret," she complained despondently.

"It was not a secret. Had you concerned yourself with me, you would have known. Everyone else knew. No one condemned me. There were others before, and no one condemned me because of them, either," he retorted crossly.

After a pause, he added, "Unlike you, Osnath, I am not a child. My loins make their own demands, and I had to heed their voice."

"You advised me and later your parents of wanting me for your wife, yet you did not listen to *my* voice."

"It may have fled your memory, but you never consented to become my wife. And you were hardly ever willing to lie with me. I was entitled to seek elsewhere what you refused to grant me."

"I wanted a short time to think it over, but you were in such haste that you would not grant it to me."

"The time to turn matters over in your mind has passed. You can no longer sit on the fence; you must now make a decision."

"You have preempted my decision. Surely you don't still want me for your wife, or even in your bed, when you have her in tow."

"Odd as it may sound, my love for you is beyond measure, undiminished. But I will not wait for you endlessly, thereby shaming the woman who loves me, as you do not. Else you would not dawdle for so long before you made up your mind. I am tired of your drawn-out hedging. I demand your answer by tomorrow."

Osnath had anticipated that he would be ashamed to face her. But the opposite had occurred. For with these indignant words, he left her angrily, as if it were not he who had wronged her, but she him.

As soon as he was gone, Hagith shuffled in to inquire why she had not come to eat bread with the family, who were assembled at the table waiting for her.

Osnath replied evasively that she was not hungry and begged Hagith's forgiveness for not having advised her of it ahead of time.

Hagith saw that the girl had sunk into a deep oppression of spirits. But all her entreaties to reveal its source were to no avail. Hagith tried to console her with soft words, but Osnath recognized them as empty. The old woman showed her tenderness by stroking and braiding her hair, but Osnath rebuffed her by shifting out of her reach. Hagith left her on her own.

By that time, a moonless night had descended over Bethlehem. Osnath sat, keeping a vigil at the window and contemplating the darkness of the night, which was as deep as that of Egypt during the ninth plague, and of her fate.

Contrary to Jesse's claim, Eliab was a deceitful man. Either that or he had found her too troublesome to cope with. Adah was lighthearted as she herself was not; and neither did she create storms, as Osnath did. She was as lush and ripe as golden grapes, ready to be plucked. Her eyes held the allure of carnal lust and twinkled in mirth, all at the same time. In that, too, she was much unlike Osnath, who was not even woman enough to enjoy the carnal act. With her plump hips, Adah also held the promise of fertility. The fruit of the womb would roll out of her frequently and easily.

Then, too, Hagith's granddaughter was beloved of her kin and friends, unlike herself, who preferred the company of plants to that of human beings. What use could Eliab have for her, who was nothing but a morose stranger in the town?

For a while she agonized over what were still the nagging doubts in her heart. Suddenly homesick, she was overcome with memories of her childhood. Of the many memories that flooded her, she dwelled on those she cherished the most. She thought of Pninah rocking her in her lap, singing lullabies to her, while she inhaled the perfume of apple-scented soap that always wafted from her, until her grandmother's tender voice spun webs of dreams around her.

Of her elder sisters tugging at her toes and announcing that they had pulled out one of them. But when she laboriously counted them, as her mother had taught her to do, the whole lot was still there. Of the tangy taste of the goat milk her mother made her drink each morning, because a healer had told her that it was better for little children than cow's milk.

Of her uncle Samuel accusing her of having stolen the color of his curls, which, because of her base theft, were no longer as dark as they had been in his youth—a jest that made her laugh anew, no matter how many times he repeated it. And later, of her father's trimmed beard tickling her face as she sat on his knee while he inspected little scraps of parchment, on which she had written words, and expressed his pride in her skill.

By the time those memories had washed over her and she scrambled into bed, her decision had been made. She had a home to return to and no need to demean herself by staying in a town that had promised so much and delivered so little. She would leave Bethlehem for good, and her eyes would never alight on it again.

Chapter Eight

As soon as the new day dawned, Osnath wrote a letter to Pninah, requesting that she send her carriage for her.

At sunset, when she saw the men coming from the fields, she went to meet Eliab. She told him that that she would go home to Ramah and never wanted to hear of him or his town again.

That evening, Osnath stayed up late, half hoping that Eliab would come and plead with her to stay. She would not stoop so low as to let him sway her, nor would she scold him again. But it would afford her satisfaction to shame him through utter silence.

She sat at the window listening for his familiar heavy footfalls, peering out, trying to discern his tall and broad-shouldered figure approaching. But time passed without any sign of him.

Osnath reckoned that Pninah's carriage would be arriving for her four days later. So on that day, she awoke from a fitful sleep to a bleak dawn, after which time passed so slowly that she thought the sun would never rise. By the time it did, she had slipped into her coarse light-brown woolen dress—the one she knew could withstand the dust of the road. Her belongings had been packed. She was ready for departure.

Then she went to take leave of all the other members of the two households, except for the faithless one and Adah, who were nowhere to be seen. No doubt exhausted from their amorous nocturnal activities, they were still closeted in his room, immersed in slumber.

Hagith, who was not as sharp-witted as she had been, and her son Uri, who was engrossed in his work in the fields and had little interest to spare for what was going forth in the house, knew nothing of what had occurred between her and Eliab. They were somewhat bemused at her sudden decision to leave. But they bid her a friendly farewell, and Hagith embraced her and enjoined her to come, together with Pninah, to visit again soon.

As Osnath knew that Jesse and Atarah were well-disposed toward her, she took special pains with her leave-taking from them. She slung her arms first around her, then around him. Atarah held her in her arms and hugged her fondly and whispered that she had tarried too long. Then Jesse held her head to his chest, and she shed tears onto it because, as she said mournfully, she would never see him or his wife and family again. Having no comfort to offer, he released her from his embrace helplessly, without a word.

Last, she stood at Obed's doorway. When he called her in, she voiced the hope that he did not bear her a grudge over her intrusiveness. He pinched her cheek and set it as a condition for his forgiveness that she kiss him on his. Then he sent her on her way with a toothless but benign smile, which eased the ache of her departure.

Osnath stepped into the yard just as Pninah's carriage was rolling into it. After greeting the guards—one of them a man and one a woman—she handed them her bag, then took their outstretched hands, and with their aid clambered into the backseat.

At first, as the carriage bowled along, she was jolted in it, rattled by the little stones that paved the streets of Bethlehem. But once it had reached the open country, the ground underneath softened, and she delighted in the carriage's pampering comfort.

It was a strange but elegant vehicle drawn by mules, which Pninah had inherited from a deceased Canaanite friend. Its body was of iron, but the seats and seat backs were upholstered with wool and covered in leather, and it was topped by a roof of the same material. Its color was yellowish brown, thus blending in with the shade of the summery, dried-out pastures around them.

The guards now urged the animals into a canter, and the carriage, which had been moving forward sedately, quickened to a brisk pace. At first, the morning was misty, but after a while the haze cleared. With never a backward glance, Osnath fixed her gaze on the hills that were languishing, as if they had fainted in the scorching heat, and on the brook that ran like a blue vein through the valley on her left. She was greatly discouraged, for she had little to show for her long stay in the town that was fading into the distance behind her.

She had dismally failed in everything she had undertaken. Spokes had been placed in the wheels of her quest to learn of Ruth's life every step of the way. The scraps of the story she had succeeded in piecing together contained only a small part of what had truly come to pass, and not the most important part at that. The two men on whom she had pinned her hopes, one after the other, had found other women in preference to her, proving to be but splintered canes on which she could not lean.

Osnath had always believed that the Lord disclosed all his intentions to Samuel, and that all he foresaw came true without fail. But with his advancing years, his powers must have declined so that he was no longer infallible. True, he had been able to point her to the precise location where Ruth's scroll had lain underground. On the other hand, his powers of premonition must surely have deteriorated. For else he would not have made such a ridiculous mistake as to foresee that she would meet her fate in Bethlehem. Thus her confidence in him deserted her, too.

There was no longer anyone whose strength could nourish her. She felt like a branch torn from the trunk of an apple tree before it had borne fruit.

Before her visit to Bethlehem, Osnath had been used to studying with her mother and even more so with her grandmother.

For when Osnath was born, her mother, Gilah, was almost past the age of childbearing. The years had already imprinted some creases onto her olive-colored skin and colored the hair at her temples gray. Thus her belated pregnancy and delivery were foisted on her against her will, and bore hard on her. Having three daughters already, she had hoped that, at least, her fourth child would be a son. When the midwife announced that this one, too, was a daughter, she felt drained of strength, and caring for the infant was an unwelcome burden for her. She loved her youngest but sighed heavily at the irksome chores she had to perform because of her arrival.

Hence it was a relief to Gilah that her mother, Pninah, though fond of all her grandchildren, felt a special affinity with the youngest one. The one whose blue-gray eyes and sensuous mouth so startlingly resembled those in Pninah's own face, the beauty of which was not marred even at her advanced age by the fine lines that radiated from it. The granddaughter who had also inherited her body, which was still upright and round-breasted but slim.

Only Osnath's hair differed from hers. In her youth, Pninah had been endowed with richly flowing honey-colored hair. As she shunned headscarves, it could be seen that it was now streaked with white ribbons, though not more than was seemly. But the crop of thick, dark curls that framed Osnath's face had come to her from Pninah's husband, Elkanah, who no longer dwelled in the land of the living. This did not prevent Pninah from seeing herself reflected in the young girl, and she devoted much thought and effort to her.

When Osnath came home, Pninah urged her to resume her studies with her, but Osnath felt no inclination for it. Instead, the girl idled away her days, with little to mark them off from each other, and time hung heavy on her hands.

As Osnath only rarely troubled herself to visit Pninah, her grandmother came to her instead. On the first of her visits, Osnath asked her about Ruth. Although she had severed her connections with Ruth's family, she was still curious about her. So as she sat with her grandmother in the shade of an olive tree, she decided to turn her visit to good account by asking her if, when her sister Hagith had been newly married, Ruth had still been alive.

Pninah looked into the distance, as if she could thereby bridge the gap of the years that had passed since then. "She was alive."

"Did you ever see her with your own eyes?"

"Mostly from afar. For by then she was old, and only once did she deign to speak to me."

"What was it that she said?"

"I will not tell you now," replied Pninah obscurely, "but when the time is ripe for you to understand her words."

Osnath was annoyed, but her pleading with Pninah to repeat Ruth's words left the elder woman unmoved.

❧

Samuel, too, came to her home. Osnath thought that he might be anxious to banish the discontent she felt after her disappointments in Bethlehem. Hence he might be willing to enlighten her about Ruth and her lover, by solving the riddle contained in his last letter to her. She reminded him of this letter, in which he had written that the Unnamed, Mishael, had been not only Boaz's relative, but close to him in another way as well, though not his friend.

But Samuel merely quizzed her with his penetrating green eyes and replied, "Surely you are clever enough to solve this little riddle on your own."

And indeed it was as if a light suddenly went on in her mind. "He was close to him because he lived in his vicinity," she said, then bit her lip in shame for not having thought of this exceedingly simple solution before.

Samuel nodded, and she continued, "But in which of the houses that surrounded that of Boaz did he live?"

"Go back to the town you have left prematurely, before your mission in it was completed, and you will know this and more."

"No one there is willing to share his knowledge with me."

He was unperturbed. "My niece, you are sufficiently lovely to storm a man's fortress and make its walls tumble down before you, as the walls of Jericho tumbled down before Joshua."

"If it is Eliab you have in mind," she retorted with tears welling up in her eyes, "you know well that it is rather he who has stormed *my* fortress and demolished the gate that guarded its entrance."

Surprisingly, Samuel took up Eliab's cause. "His taking advantage of your innocence was an uncouth deed. Wildly committed; even more wildly regretted. But Eliab also saved you, at the risk of his own life, from stupidly plunging to your death in the gully. This, together with his love for you, outweighs his lapse."

"There is no love for me in his heart, my uncle. He has proved himself to be as fickle as his brother David."

Samuel ruffled her hair fondly. "You are in error," he contradicted her. "His love for you is still unshaken. Even so, he will not wait for you for long. He needs a wife with whom he can sire sons and daughters to perpetuate his name in Israel."

"Yes," she said grimly, "and it is not necessary for me to be a seer like yourself, to divine who the mother of those sons and daughters is to be," she asserted.

"If you go back to him, in time all will be as you hope."

She regarded these words as a confirmation of her previous conjecture: although Samuel might be knowledgeable in the events of the past, he had indeed lost all powers of foretelling what lay ahead. "I have expelled him from my heart, as he has expelled me from his. I will never go back to him."

"The coming days will tell their own tale," said Samuel, before leaving her alone with her unpalatable thoughts.

At times she wondered idly what the man she had expelled from her heart was doing at that selfsame moment. Then she recalled that they had parted on a quarrel, which had not been of her making; after which he had left her amid the ruins of her life. She decided that she no longer cared what he did.

So it transpired that when, several weeks after her departure from Bethlehem, a letter from him arrived, she did not trouble herself to read it. She took it, still tightly rolled up, with the string that tied it still around it, to the cooking room. There she consigned it to the fire that was burning on the cooking stones, and soon she saw the parchment blackening, the letters on it becoming illegible, before it was consumed and went up in acrid smoke.

Three weeks later, a second note from him went the way of the first.

After that it took over a month before there was another sign of him. It came as she was sitting at the edge of the hill behind her house, immersed in thought. The rains had started early that year, and this had been a rainy day, but the downpour had then stopped. The air still had a humid touch and was suffused with the odor of the glistening wet grass on which she sat. But it was unusually clear and the colors of the hills were fresh, the trees and bushes presenting sharp contrasts of different shades of dark and light green.

When the shadows were lengthening, she looked up and was dumbfounded to see Eliab emerging from amid those shades, holding his mule by the reins. It was as if he had been approaching stealthily and was suddenly confronting her.

While he tethered his animal to a tree, she arose in reluctant welcome and said, "Is Eliab, the son of Jesse, truly in Ramah? Why have you troubled yourself to come here?"

"I came to tell you, my love, that when you left me, you robbed me of the light of my eyes and carried it off with you."

Her heart gave a thump at the sight of him and at his words, yet she could not hold back the bitter ones that now came tumbling from her mouth. "Then why did you postpone your trip for so long?"

"As you would have known had you deigned to read my missives to you, my grandfather's strength began failing after your departure. He was bedridden for some time; I could not leave while he was lying at death's door. He breathed his last breath peacefully in his sleep, and I came as soon as the thirty days of mourning for him were over."

Osnath was shamed into admitting, "I am saddened by my two confrontations with him, for I was truly fond of him. I will mourn him in my heart."

"Strangely, although you were nothing but trouble to him, he was also fond of you. He confessed that he regretted shooing you away the last time you questioned him, and he yearned to have you at his side in his last days.

"This can no longer be. But he was set on easing our and your impending mourning for him. He prevailed on us to believe that his death was a proper sequel to his life: as he had lived in contentment, so did he also die."

"I will cherish his memory for as long as I live."

"He also expressed the hope that you would come back to our house to make it your permanent abode, as my wife. And it was his desire that when you arrived, you would not neglect to visit his grave. I came to fetch you, with both purposes in mind."

"I cannot imagine why you should want me there, sir, when you have one who is beautiful and sensuous, and full of mirth and lust, as a woman should be. One who has willingly given you her heart and body and fulfills all your needs."

"I did not come to summon you only to fulfill my needs, Osnath, but to share my life. Even though your words to me are never loving, your voice is pleasant to my ears, and I yearn to hear it. Although your face always darkens at my sight, it is a feast to my eyes, and I am eager to see it. You have never given yourself to me wholeheartedly, yet I desire you both in body and soul, and you will come back to my house, where you belong."

"Your peremptory commands call forth no response in me," she replied. "I am not a captive of your sword, at your beck and call, like she who ... who ..."

Her words tapered off and he disregarded them. "I have brought you a gift." He fumbled in his pocket and extracted a pouch from it and opened it. It contained a necklace studded with a multitude of sparkling precious stones: huge sapphires and rubies embedded in ornately crafted golden flowers. "This belonged to my great-grandmother," he said, as he clasped it around her neck.

Osnath had never seen anything as dazzling in its beauty. She had no doubt that it was exceedingly expensive and was overwhelmed with his generosity. "This should adorn your mother's neck," she objected.

"My mother prefers one no less stunning in its beauty, which my father has given her," he averred. "She handed this to me to do with as I saw fit."

In her imagination, she inhaled the fragrance of myrrh that reputedly always clung to the woman who wore the necklace before her. Yet she removed it from her neck and handed it back to him. "Then it should rightly belong to your wife. I cannot accept it, no matter how much my heart may yearn for it."

"I have another present for you." Once more he inserted his hand into his pocket. When he brought it forth, it held a little scroll. "I found this hidden on a shelf in the scroll room." He proffered it to her.

She unrolled it and ran her eyes over it as quickly as she could:

Hear me, my lover.
You are dark and handsome and exalted.
Bring me to your chamber.
Let our couch be padded with our passion
and let us rejoice in each other.
So speaks the woman who is pledged to you.

As Osnath saw, the missive had been written with the same delicate womanly touch she had noted before when she had read the little poem about the Unnamed, obviously in Ruth's hand. She must have written it to Boaz in response to his love missive to her, which had been the first thing she had uncovered about Ruth. This time she accepted his gift willingly.

"Will you ever write a poem like this to me?" he asked.

"I do not resemble your great-grandmother either in my looks or in my nature. I could not bring forth a poem from my pen any more than I could make water spring forth from a rock. It is the writing of tales that sustains my soul."

"And will you ever write the tale of our love?"

"I doubt it, for your love is given to another," she said vehemently, with tears glistening in her eyes.

"Your jealousy is as harsh as Sheol, yet I love no one but you."

Her head pounded her indignation. "You have certainly given me proof of that, sir, on the day on which you came back from the fields with her, and you were both like a ram and a ewe in rut."

"My words to you are nevertheless the solid truth, and before this day is out, I will give testimony of it before your father."

When she made no response, he continued, "Besides my love, I have something else to offer you. As my wife, you will be well established, the mistress of a big household. And you will have as many maids as you may require, to do your bidding. You will never have to perform any menial tasks yourself, and you will have finely woven and richly patterned linen and silk dresses to wear."

"I will be satisfied with a poor husband—and coarsely woven wool dresses—if only his love for me is genuine."

"If you are intimating that mine is not, you are making an error that may cost us our happiness. Besides," he added, "I have something even more enticing to offer you."

Her forehead creased as she looked at him gravely.

"If you come back home with me, I will show you the object you yearn to see more than anything in the world, provided you pledge yourself to secrecy."

Osnath's eyes lit up, but only for an instant. "Destiny seems to have decreed that I never set eyes on your great-grandmother's scroll."

His eyes, which had lit up briefly as well, darkened again. "You would do well to read it, though, for you might learn something about love and devotion from her, a lesson that would not go amiss with you."

"Yes, for I could certainly not learn this lesson from you."

"My love for you is deeper and wider than the Great Sea, but you are blinded from perceiving it by your childish notion that a man can live in abstinence."

She understood his words, though not in the manner in which he intended. "You have just convicted yourself out of your own mouth by insinuating that you continue to lie with her even now."

He did not deny her charge, but scowled at her in disappointment. "You are obstinate and stiff-necked," he said at last. "I have offered you my love and all I possess, to no purpose. I have nothing more to offer you."

Since Eliab had traveled from afar for Osnath's sake, good manners prescribed that she invite him to put up at her father's house for the night. She offered hospitality ungraciously; but swallowing his pride, he accepted.

She brought her visitor home and presented him to her mother. Gilah had inherited from Pninah precisely that which Osnath had not. Gilah had richly flowing honey-colored hair, now tinged with gray; but her eyes, having come to her from her father, were dark. Through those she now regarded the unexpected visitor in surprise. As soon as she heard his name, she staked her hope on him on behalf of her daughter.

Once Eliab had settled in the room Gilah had readied for him, he went to seek out Osnath's father, Ithai. When he saw Ithai coming from the fields, Eliab followed him to his own room. Bowing to him, he proclaimed his name and that of his father and requested to speak to him. The startled host made his guest sit on a chair facing the one into which he had eased himself, then inquired about his request of him.

As Eliab noted, the man who, despite all indications to the contrary, he still hoped would be his father-in-law was stout and square-faced, with graying hair. He had passed down to Osnath nothing of his appearance, apart from the manner in which his forehead creased when he concentrated his thoughts. Eliab smiled inwardly at the sight of those creases, which so much resembled those gracing Osnath's otherwise very different face.

He forbore from pronouncing on his looks, and said, "Esteemed sir, I have come with a request and a promise. My request is to gain your consent for my taking your daughter Osnath for my wife. My promise is that, besides the uncommonly large bride-price I will pay to you, I will provide her with the best of all I call mine."

"I am fully conscious of your worth and high standing," replied Ithai thoughtfully, "and I am eager to forge a nuptial tie between our two families. But I will not force my daughter into that which may be distasteful to her. Let us call the girl and ask her."

So Osnath was sent for, and a third chair was pulled out from a corner for her.

When she sat down, her father said in a festive voice, "My daughter, Eliab, the son of Jesse, desires you to be his wife. Will you go with this man?"

Not reason but hurt guiding her, she replied in agitation, "My honored father, he only came here on a call of duty, to redeem a promise he has made to me. In truth, I count for nothing in his eyes. He has found a substitute for me, to supplant me in his affection and to be his wife. If I go with him, I will merely be one of his two women."

Osnath's father turned perplexed eyes to Eliab, awaiting his response.

Had her suitor contradicted her, and affirmed his love for her alone before her father's ears, Osnath would have relented toward him. But he merely gave her a fiery look and closed his mouth, thus strengthening her in her conviction that she had nothing but dejection to hope for in his household. Then, as no one kept him back, the young man arose and bowed himself out of her father's presence, and she was left to stare after him in futile wrath.

Even so, Osnath's mother still cherished some hope of Eliab's wedding her daughter, so for the evening meal, she prepared a veritable feast in his honor: bowls filled with saffron-spiced beef stew, topped with slices of cool, juicy cucumbers, were placed on the table before him. And his cup was filled with wine of a pale golden color, squeezed from the sweetest of grapes.

As Osnath could have told her mother beforehand, the pains she had taken with the food and drink were in vain. For during the meal, the words between her and Eliab were few and strained.

Afterward, as she was about to retire, he halted her by touching her shoulder and took her aside to the edge of the front yard. There he delivered a parting speech. "Have no fear, Osnath. I will no longer scatter my efforts like chaff in the wind in pursuit of you. From now on you may sate yourself on your righteous indignation. I will leave peaceably at first light tomorrow morning and never come back to taunt you again."

Osnath hardly had time to note the grim line of his jaw, let alone say anything in response, before he showed her his back.

The next morning she woke up early, when the chirping of the birds in the treetops had barely begun. As she stretched and turned, she saw Ruth's necklace sparkling next to her head, on her goat-hair pillow. Eliab must have snuck in silently while she was asleep and placed it there.

She rushed out, intent on telling him, "Since we are parting, take your ornament with you."

But he was nowhere to be seen, and a stable boy told her that he had departed before the break of dawn.

Chapter Nine

Although Osnath knew that she would not be able to follow Ruth's traces any longer, the Moabite woman's memory still nagged at her mind. One day when Samuel came to visit, she raised the matter with him again. She told him that she inferred from various scraps of knowledge she had gathered that Ruth had met Mishael from Bethlehem in Sdeh Moab; that he had been her lover there but had subsequently returned to his town.

Samuel made no response.

Osnath persisted. "It puzzles me why he came to Moab."

"Perhaps he was a fugitive from justice," Samuel suggested.

"What crime did he commit? And how is it that he could later return to Bethlehem without fear of being apprehended? Or had he been persecuted unjustly and later his innocence came to light?"

"You must make do with what I have told you, for I will tell you no more. Once again, I advise you to go to Bethlehem. I still believe that the man who is for you awaits you there, and it is he who will help you uncover the truth."

"My exalted uncle, you must have misread the omens about what fate holds in store for me."

"Fate, Osnath, is a wild ram, which you must grasp by the horns and guide to do your bidding."

"My feet will never tread the ground of Bethlehem again," she said with strong conviction.

Samuel's only response was an inscrutable smile.

Having given up hope of gleaning anything further from Samuel, Osnath turned to Pninah. Upon her next visit, she asked her if she knew anything about Mishael, the man who at one time had been Ruth's lover.

To this her grandmother had an astounding reply. "I did know about him. He was none other than Hagith's father-in-law."

Osnath gasped. "Tell me all you know, my grandmother," she urged.

"I remember hazily of Hagith's telling me that he had died long before she married his son. Apparently he had met his end through violence, though I cannot remember how it came about."

If Mishael had been Hagith's father-in-law, there must have been a time when he resided in what was now her house. If so, he was not merely Boaz's neighbor, as she had learned from Samuel. He lived in such close proximity to Boaz, and later also to Ruth, almost as if they had been dwelling in the same house.

How then did the love between them fare: Did it prosper or wilt with the passage of time? And who was it that had brought about Mishael's violent end?

Osnath reflected that the further bits of knowledge that had come her way had merely created more confusion in her mind. She continued to press Pninah. But her valiant exertion notwithstanding, her grandmother's memory could not be jolted into recalling more than she had already told her.

Apart from gathering in the grapes and the olives, which kept the inhabitants of Ramah busy, the following weeks were eventless. The days ran together, swallowing each other up like the gentle waves of a calm sea. Thus Osnath could not name the day when her odd state began.

At first there was nothing tangible. It crept over her by imperceptible degrees, like the coolness of the approaching autumn. At times, she was overtaken with a throbbing ache in her head. At other times, she shuddered as if she were in the throes of a fever. Despite being coaxed to it by her mother, she could hardly swallow a morsel of food. With the passing of the weeks, she became so weak that she had difficulty performing even the lightest of chores, such as setting the table, which her mother assigned to her.

Pninah came, and when she saw how emaciated the girl was, she went to her own home and returned a while later bearing a skin of sustaining lamb broth she had cooked in rare herbs, expressly for her. Then she sat next to her and spooned it into her mouth, as if she were an infant.

When Gilah perceived that Osnath was faring so poorly, she sent for a renowned healer to come by. After examining every part of the girl's body, this woman admitted that she found nothing amiss and could not make out what ailed her. She bade her drink warm milk with honey and nectar of crushed pomegranates. But this advice remained unheeded, for the very sight of those overly sweet liquids made Osnath gag.

Her mother then brewed a nectar of apples and spices for her. But when she brought the hot liquid to her daughter's lips, the girl turned her face sidewise, moving out of reach.

Pninah, who was there and witnessed the scene, tried another approach. "I have recently had a dream that refreshed my memory about days long past. It brought to my mind something I have not told you yet, about the violent death of the Unnamed in Ruth's life, who has so captured your imagination. If you drink the nectar, I will tell it to you."

"Pray tell me now," she demanded.

Pninah shook her head.

Osnath found the prospect of learning more about Mishael enticing, but she recoiled from the murky-looking potion. She declined.

One day Pninah and Samuel came together. Autumn was upon them, the days were cold and rainy, and Osnath had been cooped up indoors. But on that day, although a damp scent arose from the earth, a mild afternoon sun had broken through the clouds. So after Samuel had kissed Gilah, his sister on his father's side, and Pninah had hugged her, they sat down in the yard.

Summoning the remnants of her strength, Osnath came out to sit with the visitors. But she was as pale and almost as translucent as the wispy clouds that drifted across the sunny sky at that moment, and as silent.

After her father had returned from the fields, Gilah spread out a cloth on the ground, and a maid set the evening meal on it.

As the eating commenced, the talk revolved around the year's harvests, and the crops of wheat and barley and olives and grapes they had yielded. The quantities of produce in the clan members' different properties were compared, and the children that had recently been born, swelling its numbers, were counted.

Then, during a lull in the talk, Osnath heard Samuel's ominous words: "As if the countless wars of recent years were not enough, yet another war with the Philistines is looming."

"What is our dispute with them now?" inquired Pninah, in a voice that indicated that she was weary of the slaughter.

"As before, they have nibbled away pieces of our land, from which they must now be expelled by force," Samuel replied.

Osnath, her attention momentarily distracted from her own illness, interjected: "Would we be so callous as to kill live people for the sake of inert land?"

"My daughter," said Ithai, "land is life. It spells fields to grow grain, and vineyards and orchards to grow fruit, and pastures to graze stock and ground to dig wells, hence water to drink. Our people draw their strength from our land; we could not survive without it. We will not give it over to Philistine rule."

"True, my brother-in-law," said Samuel, "hence we stand in dire need of a staunch leader to rid the land from the attackers. Yet the king whom the people have forced me to enthrone is incapable of forging this campaign. We must lift our eyes to the hills of Judah for the one who will save us this time."

Osnath understood that it was David whom her uncle had designated as the savior of Israel in the forthcoming war, and she ridiculed the notion in her heart. David could couch his words in lofty phrases and send off soft melodies into the night. He could even teach youngsters to aim and shoot arrows at trees. But he was still a youngster who had never witnessed a real battle. How could he vanquish time-seasoned Philistine warriors?

Pninah's next words deflected her thoughts from her erstwhile lover: "All the wars you have foretold for the people of Israel have come true, Samuel. Not one has been missing. And now you come with yet more tidings of war."

"Much as I wish that it were otherwise, Pninah, my prophecy will come true this time as well."

"Will we live by the sword forever?"

"Unless people come to know the Lord and call him God of Peace and not God of War, yes."

This was another of those cryptic remarks Samuel was apt to make. Osnath was not sure how to interpret it, though she sensed that it did not bode well for the future.

While she sat with them, the members of her family smiled kindly at her. But when, after the meal, she turned to leave, she could feel the heat of their glances on her back. She imagined them shaking their heads sadly behind her retreating thin figure. Seized with a sudden newfound agility, she slanted forward and made good her escape into the refuge of her chamber.

✄

Thereafter, Osnath hardly spoke to anyone, for she had nothing to say. There was a string of wet wintry days, culminating in a heavy rainfall. As she looked out from her dark room, she saw the raindrops falling steadily, forming a trembling curtain in front of her, clustering together on the windowsill, sliding into dark puddles on the ground.

Her married sisters and aunts and female cousins came by one by one, each with her eyes eloquent with pity, each bringing forth from her bag a fail-safe potion for her to drink to cure her debilitating illness and revive her spirits. At first she submitted, swallowing their reputedly beneficial brews to the last drop. But their foul smell was even worse than their vile taste, and all the effect they had was to bloat her stomach and depress her spirits even more.

Eventually she could bear it no longer, and used a ruse to ward off her well-wishers. She rarely left her room, and whenever she heard anyone approaching, she slid into her bed and feigned sleep, and she did not open her eyes until her visitors were gone.

Outside her window there stood an undersized almond tree, one that had never attained the size of its brethren around it. As soon as the guests left, she sat up. She took hold of the skins filled with the concoctions they had left for her to drink, and poured them out onto the stunted tree in the hope that they would nourish it to growth.

As time wore on, her health deteriorated further. She seemed to shrink like a fire that no longer had any wood to feed it. Her wrists and ankles became fragile, and there came a bitter morning when she could scarcely muster the strength to arise from her bed to face the new day. From that day onward, she kept strictly to her room and spoke to no one save her mother, who brought her food and drink to sustain her, most of which she left untouched in her bowl.

One evening, when her mother came to collect the dishes from Osnath's room and found them still almost completely full, she said to her, "You must make an effort to eat more, my daughter, for you are thinning from night to night, like the moon at the end of the month."

Osnath felt too weak to rise from her chair in her mother's honor, but she replied to her words, trying to make light of them. "Would you rather have me grow thicker and rounder by the night, as does the moon at the beginning of the month?" she teased her.

"It would be a great joy," sighed her mother mournfully, "provided you had a husband to share it with you."

"This will never come to be, my honored mother. I will descend into the grave an unwed woman and never bear the fruit of the womb for any man."

Gilah smiled sadly at the daughter she could never properly understand.

Besides eating little, Osnath also began neglecting herself. Despite her mother's protestations, she took to donning the same drab, shabby tunic day and night, until it became thoroughly crumpled and dirty. She did not trim her fingernails. And her hair, which had seen not soap nor water nor a comb for several weeks, became tangled and knotty and matted.

Pninah called and was aghast to see that Osnath, who was sitting on her bed with her legs tucked underneath her, had become so skinny that the ribs stuck out of her chest. She made no comment on this, but merely sat on a chair facing her and said softly, "I have come to tell you about the man you crave to hear about."

Osnath's heart missed a beat. She straightened herself so that her eyes leveled with those of her grandmother, and looked at her inquiringly with a knit forehead.

"About Mishael, as I promised you I would," Pninah added, and saw her granddaughter slump in disappointment. The girl reminded her forcefully of a house without stone foundations, which crumbles in the wake of a slight earthquake. Pninah drew her own conclusion.

She was somewhat encouraged to note, though, that a remnant of Osnath's previous curiosity about Ruth and her lover still prevailed, for she urged her grandmother to tell her of the memory that had recently surfaced in her mind.

Instead of embarking on her story, Pninah took from the bag she had brought with her a bowl filled with a substance that looked distinctly like food. When Osnath saw it, she felt that her grandmother was tricking her, and she lay down on the bed, with her face to the wall.

"What I have to tell you is of great importance," said Pninah enticingly, "but not a word will cross my lips until you eat this tasty goat milk curd I have strained and spiced for you with my own hands."

"I am not hungry," said Osnath to the wall she was facing. Then she turned to confront Pninah and continued, "And now that you have aroused my curiosity, my revered grandmother, you must tell me in any case."

"There is hardly anything left of you, Osnath. Sit up and open your mouth, and don't argue with me," Pninah insisted, and after a slight hesitation, Osnath caved in and valiantly swallowed the nauseating curd to the end.

Then Pninah spoke in a conspirational whisper. "As Hagith told me, her family was abuzz with rumors that Mishael had been killed by his cousin, one whose name I no longer remember."

Somewhat invigorated by the food that now filled her belly, Osnath voiced her doubt. "Can you imagine a man murdering his own cousin?"

"Not unless he had a very good reason to do it."

"What was his reason?"

"I don't know. According to Hagith, it had something to do with a blood feud and an inheritance, but I can tell you no more than that."

Osnath gave voice to her lingering suspicion. "Was it to do with the inheritance of Boaz, the husband of Ruth, the great-grandfather of Eliab? Did it have a bearing on the patrimony that would one day belong to Eliab?"

"I cannot help you any further. But there is a man who can."

"Yes, one I will never see again."

Pninah disregarded her words. "I also came to convey a message to you from Ruth."

"Has she arisen from the domain of the dead, then, to speak to you?" asked Osnath with a wry smile.

"I am glad that you are still capable of jesting. Her message was delivered while she was still alive, and it has survived her descent into the grave. I did not think it wise to tell it to you before, but I believe that you are now ready to absorb it."

"What was it?"

Pninah went about telling it in a roundabout way, and as she spoke, memories buried deep inside her came to life. "Although by the time Hagith moved to Bethlehem the Moabite was old," she said, "her eyes had not dimmed, and she continued with what I was told was her long-time custom of walking amid the trees in the garden, or sitting in their shade humming softly to herself. But I never took the time to go out and talk to her. For in those days, I was bogged down with my children, who were still little, and with trouble of my own, and so my visits to Hagith were few and brief. And neither did I think that during those infrequent visits Ruth ever took notice of me.

"Yet once Ruth beckoned to me and motioned me to sit down next to her. Even to this day, I can still hear her voice ringing in my ears as she said, 'My child, I am well aware that you are floundering in the valley of the shadow of death.'

"'How is this, when I have never spoken to you before?' I queried.

"'Your face has betrayed you, but no matter. What is important is that you not remain entrapped in hopelessness. Follow the prodding of your heart as I have done, and you will find your way,' and so it was."

Had she not been in so deep a lethargy, Osnath would have beseeched Pninah to tell her about her own life as a young woman. But as it was, she refrained and merely asked, "Did Ruth ever tell you in what way she had followed her heart and found her way?"

"No. For this was the only time she talked to me, and I had not the courage to ask. By the time my children grew up and I had indeed found my way, and also had the leisure for longer visits to Hagith, Ruth had gone the way of all flesh."

For a while, Pninah sank into a reverie, but then she rustled herself up and said: "What Ruth said to me then, I will say to you now: Do not pine away here. Go in the wake of your heart and you will find your path."

"My adored grandmother, the man you urge me to pursue has treated me as if I were the least of the maids in his fields. He asked me to be his wife, then paraded his love for another before his entire family. I will not let him demean me any further by going back to him."

"You are a girl steeped in pride, and rightly so, but pride must be tempered by reason. By considering Eliab only after David had shown you his back, you have inflicted a wound on his dignity deeper than the one he has inflicted on yours by sharing his bed with another. By returning to him, you will not forgo your pride, but display magnanimity by rising above it."

Later that day, Samuel made an appearance as well. "My cherished niece," he said, cupping his hands over hers. "You are wasting away under our eyes. There is a cure for your ailment, but the only one who can administer it has his abode in Bethlehem, not here." This time she admitted his words to be the truth.

It was not her body but her soul that was ailing. She was aching for the one she had previously repulsed, an illness of her own making. It seized her most forcefully during the moments in which she hovered between wakefulness and sleep, when she missed him unbearably and felt a wild desire to seek shelter in his arms. Then his face and his body would float to her through the night, but when her hands reached out to him, they met only the empty space on the sheet beside her.

After Samuel had left, Osnath lay sleepless on her bed, giving free rein to her longing for the one she had previously rebuffed. When the night and her soul alike had assumed the darkness of the inside of a well, she decided to dispel it by taking the horns of her fate into her own hands.

In the morning, Osnath washed herself as she had not done for a long time. Then she took hold of her best dresses and, after folding them, dropped them one by one into a bag. Next she gathered the fragrant soaps, the perfumes, and the scented oils she possessed—with which weapons she hoped to wage the battle for Eliab's heart—and bestowed them in another bag.

Then, as she foresaw that her parents would not permit her to go to Bethlehem on her own, she waited until Pninah came and sought her intervention. Her grandmother spoke on her behalf with her mother and father, assuring them that Hagith would watch over her as she did over the pupils of her own eyes. Then she once again lent Osnath the carriage she owned and appointed the same two people to drive it and guard her on the way.

When the carriage arrived, Osnath's parents placed their hands on her bowed head, blessing her in the triple blessing of the Lord, beseeching the Lord to bless her and keep her, to be gracious and shine his countenance upon her, and to grant her peace.

And Samuel, who had come to see her off, set her on her way with a special blessing of his own: "Go forward, my niece, and spread your wings and soar like an eagle and cut the sky. And do not flag until you find rest for your feet. Until you build your nest, your house in Israel, in the nook of a firm rock."

It sounded easy, but she knew that there were many hurdles to overcome before she could build her house in Israel. Perhaps it would never happen at all.

Chapter Ten

It was almost ten months since Osnath had first come to Bethlehem. Autumn was giving way to winter, and the hills and valleys had donned their winter-green habit. The air was cold and damp with the coming rain when Pninah's carriage deposited her in Hagith's front yard for the second time. Only now she was on her own, and no one stepped out to welcome her.

Pninah had advised her sister of Osnath's visit, but the matter had apparently slipped Hagith's aged mind. For when Osnath found her taking stock of the supplies piled up in her storeroom, she was genuinely surprised to see her.

Hagith kissed her young visitor affectionately and welcomed her to her house with the tidings that she was too late to attend the wedding.

Warily, Osnath asked, "Whose wedding?"

Having made Osnath sit down in her front room and while offering her honeyed water to drink, Hagith replied, "My youngest granddaughter, Adah's, to be sure. She has become a man's wife. The wife of Eliab."

Eliab had warned her of his intention to wed Adah. Still, somewhere in the deep recesses of her turbulent soul, she had nursed the hope that he still loved her too much to tie a lifelong knot with another woman. She had been mistaken. She concealed from her relative how deeply shattered she was by hooding her eyes and quelling her shaking hands.

Unaware of the turmoil in Osnath's heart, Hagith continued, "Has not Pninah conveyed to you the joyous tidings of which I have notified her by courier?"

Pninah had indeed neglected to pass this message on to her, which she found odd. "When did this happy event take place?" she asked in as cheerful a voice as she could muster, to mask her misery.

"A month ago, of course. You should have come then, so as to attend the festivities."

"And when did you dispatch your missive to Pninah?"

"Only yesterday," admitted Hagith, clutching her head with deep remorse. "It was ill done of me, indeed."

"No, no," Osnath reassured her, for she was thankful to have been spared the necessity of sitting as a mourner among the celebrants at the wedding of the man she loved to another woman.

Before long, that same woman came in, and the two young kinswomen dutifully hugged and kissed and asked each other if the other was well. Then Eliab followed his wife in. As custom dictated, Osnath blessed them both by saying, "May you have a long life of health and prosperity with each other."

At Osnath's sight, Eliab's face lit up like a river in the sun, but only briefly, before it darkened like that same river at night. "What went awry?" he said brusquely, disregarding her blessing. "When last I saw you, you were flourishing like a vine in a rainy year. Now you are as haggard as a vine in a drought. What has overcome you in the space of these last few months?"

She could not tell him in Adah and Hagith's presence, and the words she had prepared to recite to him wilted on her tongue. Instead, she let the tears brimming over in her eyes form her reply.

Their eyes locked with each other, wet ones with dry burning ones. He did not press her for an answer. After a while, as if he could not bear her sight any longer, he slung his arm around his wife's shoulders and turned her around. He led her across the yard into his own room, and Osnath's blood boiled with jealousy.

As soon as they left, Jesse and Atarah came in to greet her. There was a broad smile of welcome on Jesse's face, as he said bracingly, "Our eldest and our youngest are now in the toils of other women. But we have six more handsome sons to dispose of, and we are still eager to have you as our daughter-in-law."

When he saw the pallor in Osnath's face, he gathered her in his arms, and as he had done on the day of their parting a few months earlier, he placed her head on his chest soothingly.

Atarah, too, smiled her welcome and hugged her, but her smile was thin and did not reach her eyes. It was as if she had a fair idea of the purpose of Osnath's visit. As if she imputed an evil design to her: that of causing mischief between her eldest son and his new wife.

Oblivious to the significance of what she had just witnessed, Hagith installed Osnath in her old room, whose window faced the backyard. She led her there through the fine drizzle that had begun, and let her settle in before she came to call her to eat the evening meal with her and her son Uri, Adah's father. As that son's sons had moved to a neighboring house, and his daughters had all moved into their husbands' houses, he was now, apart from his mother, the only inhabitant of their house.

On her previous visit, Osnath had paid but scant attention to him, who had hair speckled with gray and was of about the same age as her own father. But now she noted that he regarded her with indulgence and spoke kind words to her. They seemed to paint all she now had to face in brighter colors, and, senselessly, she found comfort in them.

At first, to her chagrin, Osnath spent her days and nights in Bethlehem much as she had done in Ramah: sleeping only intermittently and longing for the man who now belonged to another. But she forced herself to eat more than she had done at home, so that little by little she began to regain the previous shape of her body.

In her need for Eliab, she sat at her window and peered out of it into the backyard. She frequently caught a glimpse of him as he went about his daily tasks. But as he paid no heed to her, this did nothing to bring her joy.

Osnath was aware that during the last months, through her longing for Eliab, she had matured. If ever his love for her was reanimated, he would find that she was no longer the cranky, petulant little girl she had been. But as there was no sign of this coming about, her newly gained even temper was not of much use to her, either.

One morning she gathered courage and tripped along in his wake as he went out into the fields. His father and his brothers had left already, granting the new husband the privilege of spending more time in bed with his young wife before he joined them for the day's labor.

As he heard footsteps behind him, Eliab spun around to face Osnath. "What is it that you want?" he asked crossly.

Instead of answering, she stepped up to him, affording him a view of her drawn face and the sadness in her fine blue-gray eyes.

Placing his hands on her shoulders, he flung her away from him. "I have built a new life for myself. Is there a shortage of men in Ramah that you needed to come back here to torment me?"

"It is you who are tormenting me," she said numbly. "Tormenting my dreams."

"It took you too long to find that out," he said, an unforgiving note in his voice. "You will do well to go back home and shift your dreams to another man."

By now Osnath's exploration of Ruth's life had been buried for such a long time that she had all but given up on it. But now she decided to use it as an excuse to lure Eliab into contact with her.

"You promised that if I came back here you would show me Ruth's scroll. At least open the scroll room for me when you come home from the fields and let me see the book before I go."

Her ruse was not successful. "When you find your new man, you may spy on *his* great-grandmother, rather than mine," he replied unpleasantly.

Osnath tore herself away from him with difficulty, turned on her heel, and walked back slowly, contemplating her next steps.

She was sure that only under Eliab's mantle would she ever find rest for her body and soul, yet he refused to grant it to her. This was the final proof that Samuel had been utterly wrong in his belief that she would build her house in Israel with him. Once again she was deeply disillusioned with his prophetic powers, and even more so with her own dire fate.

Eliab was impregnable to her love. Since his eyes were as blind and his ears as deaf to her distress as those of a Canaanite idol, she knew that she should rightly follow his advice of returning to Ramah. Yet she could not let go. Not yet.

She planned to linger in Bethlehem for another month. If by then she could not sway his heart, at least she would know that she had done all that lay in her power to win him back. Thereafter it would be futile to persist. She would resign herself to her loss, and leave.

As she had little to do during this month, Osnath set out to visit Obed's grave, as he had requested before his death. Having a vague notion of where the family's burial plot was located, she traversed the fields to look for it.

As she walked, it occurred to her that since Mishael had been Hagith's father-in-law, he was most likely laid to rest somewhere at the edge of the property that had once belonged to him and now belonged to Hagith's son. She thought that his grave might reveal some secrets about his life, and decided to search for it first, before she proceeded to seek out Obed's resting place.

After roaming around for a while, she confronted a massive rock with an aperture in it, as if the rock had opened its stony jaws to swallow her up. It led into a cave, evidently Hagith's family's burial ground. There she was engulfed in a stillness that only death can call forth. The ground was covered with moss so that even her steps on it were silent. Several gravestones were fixed into the walls, but in the cave's dim light it was difficult to decipher the inscriptions on them.

She strained her eyes, bringing them close to each stone until, in the deepest recess of the cave, she came across one that read:

MISHAEL THE SON OF YOTHAM
BY HIS DEATH HE HAS ATONED FOR HIS SIN

The name of Mishael's father meant little to Osnath, for she had never heard of him. But her eyes were riveted to the second line of the inscription, which made it plain that Mishael had committed a sin so horrendous that only his descent into the grave could expurgate it. It might have been the one for which he was compelled to escape justice, as Samuel had surmised. The one in retribution for which his cousin had killed him.

Whatever his iniquity, it was clear that Mishael had not been a good man; and if so, his evil spirit might still be hovering over his grave. Suddenly the darkness around her seemed to be invaded by even darker shadows, lurking in hidden corners, ready to pounce on her.

Osnath took fright and groped her way toward the exit. It seemed an eternity until the light at the opening of the cave beckoned to her.

Back in the brazen sunlight, she knew her alarm to have been senseless. She saw yellow wildflowers, those that flourished in the winter, sprouting from amid the cracks in the rocks at the exit of the burial cave. Thus, she thought, does life spring from death, even from the death of a depraved man. Yet she had no wish to rest her eyes on Mishael's grave again. She fled from the burial cave as quickly as her feet would carry her, and took a silent vow never to repeat her visit there.

Neither did she feel any inclination to see Obed's grave just then, and decided to postpone her visit there for another day.

The following two weeks were not eventful. But then one day, as Osnath stood loitering in the backyard, she saw Adah. She followed Adah with her eyes as she passed by with a smile of bliss on her face, and Osnath became conscious of something that had escaped her before. The young woman had grown in girth and was walking ponderously, carrying her newly swollen paunch before her as proudly as if it were filled with precious stones.

Judging by its size, it was clear that Adah's pregnancy had long preceded her wedding. Even so, Osnath could not blame her for her pride, for she well knew that to Eliab, who had long pined for children, what his wife was carrying in her womb was even more valuable than rubies. And all she could do was to swallow her envy.

Whenever Eliab's mother saw Osnath, she scanned her face with narrowed eyes. The kindness she had shown her on her first visit had vanished, for she believed her to be intent on dislodging the one who would soon be the mother of her grandchild from her rightful position.

But it was far from Osnath's intent to usurp Adah's place. She had accepted her fate, which decreed that her young kinswoman would always outrank her in position as Eliab's first wife and as the mother of the one who would probably be his firstborn son. She did not begrudge Adah her happiness any more than she begrudged the almond trees their winter blossoms. She merely wanted some for her hungry soul as well; yet there was none.

The weeks passed, and the day Osnath had set for her departure drew close. She knew that winning Eliab's heart back would be as difficult as rolling a heavy stone up a hill. Yet she resolved not to leave without one last attempt to accomplish the feat.

⁂

One evening, when Adah, exhausted from her pregnancy, had gone to sleep early in her own room, and Eliab was alone in his, Osnath went there under the cover of darkness. She stood briefly in the doorway and took off her cloak, then let herself in.

She had not been in his bedchamber since the night of the storm, almost a year ago. Once again it was raining outside, and the drops falling steadily to the ground were clearly audible through the window. The blaze of the fire in the hearth spread its light and warmth over the room. But this time Eliab was not keen to welcome her.

He arose from the chair on which he had been sitting and approached the door, bent on pushing her back out and closing it on her. Then he halted and asked curtly, "What is your request of me?"

"The last time I was here, sir, you gave me wine to drink to gladden my heart," she reminded him in a low voice.

"It did not fulfill its purpose."

"It may do so now," she said, her voice dropping even lower.

Reluctantly, he filled a cup of wine from a jug he had standing on the table and handed it to her. "Have you any further requests?"

She drained more than half the cup, thus whipping up her courage. "Only that you not cast me away."

"You may not be aware of it, Osnath," he said scathingly, "but I have a wife now."

"I will be your second wife, or your concubine, or whatever you want me to be."

For a while he failed to respond, and the silence was heavy between them.

Osnath had purposely washed herself with the most fragrant of her soaps and rubbed herself with oil scented with the essence of aloe. She had also clad herself in a dress that, in the teeth of her mother's opposition, Pninah had given her before she set out for Bethlehem for the second time. It was scarlet, the color of sin and sweet promises and strong wine, enticingly low-cut and tight. It made her breasts seem ready to burst forth from it like wild beasts chasing their prey. Although it was long, it had deep slits at both sides, which displayed her shapely legs to advantage.

Eliab filled a cup of wine for himself and drank it up in one long gulp. He glared at her breasts, between which the necklace he had given her was dangling, then at her legs. Dizzy with the sight before him and mesmerized by the aroma of her perfume, he abandoned the struggle to fend her off. With a sudden hoarseness to his voice and shortness of breath, he said, "I want you to be at my disposal, so I can lie with you at any time."

"Yes."

"Now."

"Yes."

He advanced purposefully toward her, and she subsided into the hard grip of his arms as he made her lie down on the nearby bed. Impatiently, he ripped off her sinful dress and his own garment, and she knew the exultant pleasure of the heat of his skin against hers, of inhaling the scent of him, the scent of life.

The months of separation had bred shyness in her, but it vanished at his touch, melting into her passion for him, and his for her, which gushed forth like torrents of water long held back by a dam. Yet he was slow and gentle, exploring every secret part of her body, taking special care to arouse her need nearly to a peak before he entered her. His voice was close and warm and moist with his breath when he whispered his love into her ears, while he thrust into her and inside her. She cried out as if in anguish, as a tidal wave of shaking pleasure washed over her, to match his own. She struggled to catch her breath; then a deep sigh of contentment escaped her, and her head nestled against his shoulder.

He had finally known her. Truly known her. Though she had not been a virgin, she had begun the act a child and concluded it a woman. In its course, she had crossed the threshold to womanhood that she had not believed she would ever achieve.

"I had no notion," she said in wonder. "This was really my first time. A miracle."

"One that will continue all the days of our lives." She heard his words, and she marveled at them and thanked the Lord for granting her this miracle.

Then the rain ceased and the clouds dispersed. Through the half-open window, she could see that the night was now full of glittering stars, a quiver of lights, which dispelled its previous dimness.

She molded herself against the length of his naked body, savoring the sheer pleasure of the sense of safety conveyed to her by its large size and muscular build, feeling his hairy chest under her wandering hand. She wanted nothing more. But he was unrelenting in his passion, and soon she was borne on its wings once again.

Afterward, Osnath was overtaken by a gnawing hunger, such as she had not experienced for many a month. She felt as if an enormous gaping hole, as deep as a gully, had opened inside her, and she could not wait to fill it.

When she told this to Eliab, he dressed and went out into the cooking room and came back with a clay bowl filled with tidbits of bread dunked in sweet date nectar. He propped a few cushions under her head and knelt at her side, bringing mouthfuls of dripping bread to her lips with his own hand, until the bowl was empty and her belly full. He made her wash the food down with some more of his sweet wine, then wiped off her mouth and came to her again.

Following their act, Eliab folded a blanket around Osnath and swathed her in it as if she were an infant. Soon she became drowsy and slumber spun its web in her mind; and during what was left of the night, she slept as she had not slept since she had indeed been a baby—the sleep of calm, of satiation, of peace.

And she did not care when, in the morning, several pairs of astounded eyes—Adah's and her mother-in-law's among them—looked at her askance as they followed her progress from Eliab's chamber to her own.

Thereafter, Eliab divided his attention between his wife and the woman who was now his concubine, as he was obliged to do by Torah law. When he was with Osnath, he wanted her without respite, and each time he led her to the peaks of delight that had previously eluded her. It seemed hardly possible that he was the same man who had been so inept with her some months before.

Once, after he had led her to pleasure as soon as he had returned from the fields, she revealed to him her puzzlement over this change.

He lay with his arms crossed under his head and yawned contentedly. "I did not understand then that such an immature child as you needed to be handled cautiously and patiently. Since then, I've had several willing teachers who were prepared to impart this lesson to me."

She had been lying on her back but rolled over on her side to face him, her curls a dark cloud around her face. "And you were not averse to taking lessons with them," she teased.

A grin flicked over his face. "I am not a man given over to the sweetness of stolen water from many wells. I require no more than one woman: you. But what was I to do when you had abandoned me to their mercy? Their love was like balsam on the sore you had inflicted on me. I savored the knowledge that there were those who did not spurn what you had so callously rejected, and even admired the strength in my loins."

"You never gave me reason to doubt your prowess. It was what seemed to be an excess of it that led me to draw back from you initially."

"As you refused me after our first encounter, you never gave me the chance to demonstrate it to you. And since you were left dissatisfied, it behooved me to hone my skills in the art of love."

"Which you have done quite thoroughly."

"I was determined that if ever you came back to me, I would not disappoint you again," he said, stringing her curls through his fingers.

Then all was drowned in the calm of the dusk. The slowly subsiding twitter from the treetops sounded as if even the birds were settling in their nests, at peace with themselves. Even the wintry breeze, audible through the shutters of the window, was soft, as if it were settling down for the calm of the evening, the calm in her heart.

Her thoughts reverted to the months in which, night after night, her heart had called her need for him from the distance; but he had not heeded its call, and eventually her hope had been depleted, worn out by time. Now he had, but the months of her yearning for him had changed the balance of power between them. Previously, he had been in her tow. Now the advantage had shifted to him, and she was content for it to remain so. Although she aspired to better her position in his household by becoming his second wife, she did not urge him, hoping that, in time, he would be the one to offer it.

But her father thought otherwise.

The rumor that the firstborn son of Jesse had deflowered Osnath and continued to come to her morning and night spread all the way to Ramah, as if it had been carried there on birds' wings. When it came to her father's ears, he sent off a stern summons for the young man to appear before him with all possible haste.

Ithai anticipated that now that Eliab had had his way with his daughter, he would have no urge to wed her. He foresaw that he would have to appeal to the young man's sense of what is right and urge him to deal with the girl properly, and that it would not be an easy task. But his fear was unfounded.

For Eliab arrived but a few days later, bearing with him the bride-price, a sizable pouch—not of paltry silver, but of pure gold from Ophir. When he proffered it, and Osnath's father took possession of the gold, it weighed heavy in his hand but lightened his heart, for it formed solid proof of Eliab's intention to marry his daughter. It also proved that when she married him, a man of substance, she would be well provided for all the days of her life.

It was agreed between the two men that as soon as the preparations were completed, Osnath's father and mother were to come to Bethlehem for the betrothal, to be followed a short while later by the arrival of their entire clan for the wedding.

These plans, though, were foiled by others, forged by the one who reigns in the heavens and the earth.

Chapter Eleven

As Osnath's soul was revived, so was her previously flagging eager-ness to learn about Ruth's life. Once again she spent much of her time in the garden that had belonged to Ruth. And her imagination ran rampant with visions of the Moabite in it.

She thought of the time after Ruth's son had been born. Irrespective of whether he had truly been Boaz's son or the son of Mishael, she must have loved him very much. While she strolled through the garden, she might be resting her eyes on the infant Obed, whose cradle she had placed in the shade of a tree. Later on, she might be watching the toddler Obed as his clumsy little hands threw pebbles into the air, or wreaked havoc among the flower beds.

On the day before Eliab was to set out on his visit to her father, she reminded him again of his promise to show her Ruth's scroll. For his part, Eliab admitted ruefully that, contrary to his previous rash words to her, he would not have her pursue the life story of any man's great-grandmother but his own.

Still, when she said that she would like to fill her time with reading Ruth's scroll while he was away, he flatly refused. He said that he would prefer to show it to her upon his return, when they could peruse it together.

Osnath spent the first night after Eliab's visit to her father with him. Early in the morning, while they were still in bed, she heard voices in the yard. She jumped up as one stung by a scorpion, for both she and Eliab had a fair sense of what those voices heralded: the war that had been brewing for some months between Israel and the Philistines must be on the verge of breaking out.

Since Osnath's return from Ramah, she had been so deeply involved in her own life—first in her sorrow and then in her bliss—that Samuel's prophecy of the coming war with the Philistines had been nearly erased from her mind. But this did not prevent the winds of war from gathering force. Now the king's messengers were making the rounds from house to house, to bid the young men of each family to the ranks of the army.

Osnath dressed with shaky hands and followed Eliab into the yard, where the members of the two households were gathered already, to hear the breathless runners' summons.

Jesse was too old to go out with the soldiers, but his three eldest sons, suddenly seized with an unfathomable zeal, lost no time in preparing to follow Saul's call-up to the war. Their mother attempted to dissuade them, but they would not heed her, pointing out that since they were over twenty years old, they were required by Torah precept to be mustered into the army.

When Eliab turned back to fetch the provisions that, unbeknownst to Osnath, he had previously prepared to take with him to the battlefield, she followed at his heels. Once inside his room, she reminded him of the Torah injunction that a man who had newly betrothed a woman was not liable to go to war. As he was pledged to betroth her in any case, she urged him to recite the words "I betroth you to me forever" in front of two witnesses. Thus would he make her his bride immediately, and render it permissible for him to remain at home.

Atarah, who had entered Eliab's room with them, listened to her appeal. For the first time since Osnath's return to Bethlehem, she favored her with a nod of approval, and thereafter regarded her with more kindness than she had bestowed on her for a long time.

But her words fell on deaf ears. Eliab lifted her chin in his hand, as he was wont to do, and said, "Am I to be branded a soft-hearted coward, then? One who hides behind a woman's back at the mere mention of an enemy? I am as able-bodied a man as my two grown-up brothers. It would be disgraceful of me even to weigh your words in my mind. I will betroth you and wed you properly when I return."

She shuddered, for, in truth, she would have vastly preferred him to be a live coward rather than a dead hero, who might never come back to keep his promise to her. But she buried her forebodings of doom in her frightened heart, and kissed him, as did his mother. Then she watched, wordless, as he went to take leave of his father and his younger brothers and his wife, before, flanked by his two next eldest brothers, he rode out of the yard.

No sooner had they left than Jesse's thoughts turned to David. It dawned on him that his youngest son, who was still residing at Saul's court in Gibeah, might be obliged to accompany his master to the battlefield. Thus Jesse might soon have four of his sons in jeopardy of their lives. So, prodded by his wife, he sent word to David, ordering him to come home instantly, giving as an excuse that his help was urgently required to mind his father's flock while his three eldest brothers were away.

Three days later, when David arrived, he bowed low to his father and mother, who stood waiting for him in the yard. After greeting them and asking if all was well with them, he said: "It was incumbent on me to rally to the king when he went out to war, but my duty to do your bidding took precedence over it. Only I must not tarry here for long, and I ardently hope," he added humbly, "that you will release me soon."

When his parents, their faces dark with worry, forbore to reply, he went to his old room. There he cast off the fine shimmering green tunic he had been wearing at court, and donned the coarse woolen shepherd's garment that was still waiting for him. Then he took hold of the shepherd's rod and began guiding the flock up the hill.

Having been absent from the house for a long time, David was ignorant of what had come to pass between Osnath and Eliab. He had banished the incident of Michal's visit to the back of his mind, and he was entirely willing to continue his lovemaking with Osnath where he had left off several months earlier. He was surprised when the girl did not follow him up the hill of her own accord, as she used to do. And when he brought the sheep and the goats back home, he was even more taken aback when she was no longer amenable to his advances.

She was relieved, though not surprised, to note that although her thoughts drifted to the moments of happiness they had shared, she never for even one moment wavered in her resolution that they could never be repeated. She had not thought of David in a long while, so it was only when he confronted her with his proposition that she became aware of not having missed him at all.

David mourned the loss of Osnath's love for as long as it took between the setting of the sun and the rising of the stars. By that time, the house was besieged by a throng of girls who came to welcome him back to Bethlehem. They surrounded him like a swarm of locusts, and soon his eyes were riveted to the prettiest of the lot.

In the next weeks, while her husband was serving as a foot soldier in Saul's army, Adah's belly grew big. By now it no longer looked as if it were filled with precious stones, but with heavy rocks. Its weight came to be such that she could hardly carry it about, and she spent much of her time sitting in front of Jesse's house, stroking it and whispering softly to the infant, who was growing to an enormous size.

Adah would have had to be blind in both eyes, and deaf as well, to be unaware of the fact that Osnath was not merely sharing her husband's bed, but was on the way to becoming her lawful rival. But she had little strength and no thought to spare for anything but her consternation over her child's uncommonly large size, which might herald her own inability to bring its delivery to a safe conclusion.

So, as she sat, she stuck out her full lower lip and pouted and sighed and moaned. And she complained to anyone who was willing to listen to her at not having her husband at her side just when she needed him most.

Even though Osnath knew Adah for her own rival, she shared her anxiety, hoping that the forthcoming delivery of Eliab's firstborn would proceed smoothly. But she reserved her chief worry for that firstborn's father, whose life she imagined to be in jeopardy every moment of the day. Although the travelers who at times came by with reports from the army claimed that the battle with the Philistines had not yet been joined, she was not reassured.

A horrendous fear began smoldering inside her. In her bed at night, she had recurring nightmares of her man being felled at the edge of the sword of one of the murderous Philistines. In her dream, she herself would run toward him to save him. But her feet were heavy, as if weighed down by shoes of heavy bronze, so that when she reached him, it was too late, and she found him wallowing in his own blood.

When she could sustain this torture no longer, she decided to speak to Jesse and spur him on to send out a messenger to the battlefield to inquire if his sons were well. With this purpose in mind, she went out to the fields to meet him. As it was late in the afternoon, she encountered him on his way home, with four of his sons trailing behind him.

To put him in a receptive mood for her proposal, she did not raise the matter with him immediately. Instead, as she turned back to walk at his side, she tried to ingratiate herself with him by talking to him of his deceased father, Obed. She told him that his memory was precious to her. She desired to pay homage to it by visiting his grave, which, as she had been told, he had instructed her to do before he closed his eyes forever.

To her surprise, Jesse was oddly reluctant to accede to her request. He gave her an enigmatic glance, and said, "It will be dark soon, and we shall be groping about like blind men in the cave in which it is located. We will do better to postpone our visit there for another day."

As the sun still had a fair bit to travel before it reached the crest of the hills, she recognized this reply for the lame excuse it was. She quizzed him with her eyes, but he merely returned her gaze with a bland smile.

Jesse's sons, who had grown fond of the girl who was soon to become their sister-in-law, now came helpfully to her rescue. They assured their father that they would happily dislodge the sizable stones that blocked the light from the cave. Thus, as he was left without any further subterfuge, he led Osnath with slow steps into the cave at the edge of his fields, which served for the family's burials.

After a brief walk through a narrow passage, they came upon a hewn stone. In the faint light that penetrated through the opening above it after the rock that blocked it had been rolled off, she saw that it bore this inscription:

OBED, THE SON OF BOAZ
A RIGHTEOUS MAN

Osnath stood before it in reverence, recalling the few times in which she had spoken with him.

After a while, Jesse nudged her elbow, indicating his desire to leave the cave. It occurred to her, though, that the grave of Ruth, Obed's mother, must be nearby. She asked him to show it to her as well.

Jesse regarded her darkly, his look intimating that he had known precisely what her true purpose in coming to his father's grave had been. Then he demurred on the ground that the grave she strove to see stood in the rear of the cave that was shrouded in darkness, where they would be floundering like owls in the daylight.

Eliab's father was clearly intent on keeping Osnath away from his grandmother's grave, and his words alerted her senses to something that, she had no doubt, was very wrong. But with the man she loved at war, she had little interest in pursuing Ruth's life just then. Hence, she was quite willing to follow Jesse's lead out of the cave.

But Jesse's sons had removed the stone that blocked the light from their ancestress's gravestone. Having no choice, he led her down a further passage, at the end of which she stood face-to-face with it. By straining her eyes, she could make out this legend on it:

RUTH, THE WIFE OF BOAZ
A WOMAN OF VIRTUE

At the sight of these words, a spark of her previous enthusiasm about Ruth was rekindled. She remembered the little scraps of parchment she had seen, indicating that although Ruth, having been a widow, had not deviated from Torah law by a hairbreadth, she had not invariably been virtuous. This only made her legend dearer to her, for she knew that no human being was flawless, and only the Lord was perfect in all his ways.

Then her eyes came to rest on a stone tablet perched next to the grave, which bore a poem, apparently engraved on it with Ruth's own hands:

Mourn not for me, for I have lived my life in full.
The first issue of my womb was consigned to the earth,
but the Lord has compensated me threefold.
I have suffered unrequited love,
but my plight was of short duration,
overtaken by a much greater love
and by happiness that will outlast my life.

This poem was yet another riddle, and Osnath stood pondering it for a while. She was about to ask Jesse how it came about that she had never been told that Ruth's firstborn had died. But she perceived his forbidding countenance and decided not to anger him just when she required his assistance in a matter of far greater urgency.

Besides, she was suddenly overtaken by a mindless fear of the dead. So she tucked her hand into Jesse's and urged him to take her out of the cave.

This suited his purpose, so he interlaced his fingers with hers and led her out into the open field, smiling understandingly at her sigh of relief.

Relegating Ruth to the back of her mind, Osnath expressed her worry about Eliab and his brothers, from whom they had heard nothing since they had joined the army nearly two months ago. Then, before giving their father time to reply, she pleaded her cause: "Esteemed sir, pray send one of your servants out into the battlefield to inquire if they are well."

Jesse pondered her words briefly and found them good. So he hugged her slender waist affectionately and took her home. Once there, he called one of his older workmen, who had not gone out to war, and charged him with the task. But David, who had just returned from tending the flock, heard his father's instructions to the old retainer and offered to go out in his stead.

David's mother arrived on the scene, and at first neither she nor Jesse would hear of this. For David was their youngest, the delight of their declining years.

Deviating from her custom of letting her husband voice both their thoughts, her worry for David led Atarah to intervene. "My son," she said adamantly. "Your beard has barely sprouted. You are not of the proper age to go into the battlefield."

But David stood his ground firmly, saying, "My mother, I honor you deeply, wherefore I have done your bidding until now. But your worry for me is unnecessary. The Lord is my shepherd and I have no fear. If I am to be king, I must learn to lead men into battle. And how can I do so if I hide amid the sheep and shy away from even approaching the place where others risk their lives?"

Atarah realized that she could not restrain her youngest any more than she could restrain the wind. So she made no reply, and only her eyes spoke her consternation.

Although Jesse shared her worry, he saw no choice but to give David leave to go. "It is well. Take your brothers ten loaves of bread, then. And take some pieces of cheese to the commanding officer so that he may deal kindly with them. And tell Eliab that the day for his wife to give birth is close and that she requires his support. And bring him back with you immediately."

Early the next morning, David left the old workman in charge of the sheep and set out on his errand. But instead of bringing back his brother as he had been ordered to do, he himself was detained at the front. And neither his father, nor anyone else in the house, had any inkling of where he was and how he and his brothers were faring.

Chapter Twelve

Five days after David's departure, the time came for Adah to give birth. On the morning on which her labor pangs began, her married sisters and her sisters-in-law came to stay in Hagith's house so as to share with her the burden of her first delivery.

Osnath emerged from her room to the sight of a gray sky heavy with watery clouds. One of Adah's sisters expressed her opinion that the darkness of the sky was a bad omen, auguring disaster for the forthcoming event. She was angrily hushed by her kinswomen, who were determined to show the mother-to-be nothing but brightly smiling faces.

The most renowned midwife in Bethlehem having been called for, all the women entered Adah's bedroom in Jesse's house. Only Osnath was kept away from it by being put in charge of the cooking room, to oversee the preparation of the food that would be needed to feed the many hungry mouths.

As Osnath entered the cooking room, she noted that the maids, whose noisy chatter usually bore into the distance, for once were subdued into silence. They were kneeling before the hot furnace or bent over the cooking stones, stirring the contents of the pots that were simmering, immersed in their tasks as if the lives of the mother-to-be and her infant depended on the food they were preparing.

Osnath found the cooking room as oppressive as a mourner's house. In the face of the anxiety that was rife around her, there was no demand for the food that was being prepared under her lax supervision. Once it was ready, it sat untouched on the cooking room table.

Conscious of the futility of her task, Osnath grew restive and abandoned her post. Approaching the room in which the birthing was taking place, she put an anxious ear to the door, straining to hear the sounds from inside.

She had previously wished that she, too, were carrying Eliab's child in her womb. But this desire vanished at once as she heard Adah's intermittent screams, followed by a pause, then renewed yells.

So far she had been deemed too young to lend a hand at a delivery, so she did not know whether those shrieks boded well for the mother and the infant. In the end, as she could not stand her exclusion from the birthing any longer, she opened the door a crack and peeked in. When no one blocked her way, she slipped in, and the sight that met her eyes robbed her of breath.

The room was slovenly, cluttered with all manner of bowls filled to the rim with outlandish liquids and surrounded by soiled garments strewn around. Disregarding the filth and disorder around them, the women were sitting on the floor, lining the walls, their hands shielding their mouths as they muttered darkly to each other.

Adah was squatting on the birthing stones that stood in the center, almost invisible behind her huge belly. Hagith was kneeling behind her, with Adah's weight on her knees. Atarah was sitting on the floor at her right side, holding her hand, while the midwife crouched before her opened thighs. She was rubbing an oily unguent onto her belly with gentle hands, and speaking soothingly to her whenever her screams subsided long enough for her to listen.

But this happened less and less frequently, until the heartrending wails went on almost without respite. In her agony, with her face contorted from her searing pain, and with her sweat running down it, Adah tore at her mother-in-law's hand and demanded that she call for Eliab to be with her in her time of woe.

The midwife bade her to push to expel the child, as thereby she would also expel her own suffering. Adah pushed and pushed, until her eyes bulged and the veins in her temples stood out and almost burst open. But the opening to her womb, where the child's head should have appeared, remained dark. Time went by, and there was more desperate screaming and pushing, but all for naught.

After a while the midwife took heart and said what all the women had surmised already: that the infant was overly large. Besides, its head, which had previously approached the opening, had unexpectedly retracted into the rear of the womb, so that it was not turned downward as it should have been.

She pressed several spots on Adah's abdomen to make the infant turn around, but the baby did not comply. She tried to push her hand in to pull it out; but its rear part, the part that faced the opening, was so big that she could not dislodge it sufficiently for her hand to move in. Although she was renowned for her skill, it was clear for all to see that she was incapable of coping with what was facing her now.

Even in her ignorance about the birthing of infants, Osnath understood that this one was not progressing well, having turned into a struggle for both the mother's and the infant's lives. She stood there, trying to block out from her ears Adah's piteous howls, such as those of a she-wolf.

Hagith, who was still supporting her granddaughter on her knees, leaned the laboring woman against her chest, thus disentangling her own hands. She then raised her hands heavenward in supplication, while she recited a singularly appropriate psalm:

I raise my eyes onto the mountains.
From whence comes my help?
My help comes from the Lord
The maker of the Heavens and the Earth . . .

All the women raised their hands and joined her in prayer; it even gave Adah pause, though only briefly, before she resumed her howls with even greater strength.

Osnath was the only one who was standing. She felt awkward, like a forgotten tree in a long-cleared forest, until one of Adah's sisters pulled her down to sit on the floor at her side. She whispered in Osnath's ear that she had heard of another midwife, a Jerusalemite now residing in

Bethlehem, who had brought with her exceptional skills in the craft of midwifery from the walled city. She had saved women in labor, when all else had failed.

Osnath looked around her and saw several heads nodding in agreement, but also many eyebrows knit in disapproval. The Jerusalemite evidently had some supporters, while others doubted her capabilities. She arose with the intention of consulting Hagith.

But her old relative, having overheard the whisper, preempted her words. "This woman is not a midwife but a butchering scoundrel," she shrieked. "She has been known to slash women open with her knife, and only through a miracle did they survive. I will not have her near my granddaughter."

Osnath looked at Atarah, who spoke measured words. "The Jerusalemite has been known to do some good, but even more evil. We must defer to Adah's grandmother's judgment."

Osnath had found it intriguing that none of the young women sitting around the wall had gone forth to summon the midwife from Jerusalem for Adah. Now she had the answer: Hagith had overruled them, subduing them into a docile acceptance of her decree.

She turned the matter over in her mind. If she called in the Jerusalemite in the teeth of Hagith's objection, and Adah died, Eliab would blame her bitterly. But if she sat with her hands crossed on her chest, doing nothing, and Adah died, she would be no less prone to face his recriminations.

The young woman's wails had become feeble, as life was visibly draining from her. Osnath decided that things had gone awry to such an extent that there was nothing to lose.

So she tarried no more and rose from the floor and stood up to Adah's grandmother, as she knew that *her* grandmother would have expected her to do. "Your granddaughter is about to die, and her infant with her," she called out bluntly. "Will you not grant her this last chance of clinging to life?"

"The Jerusalemite will swoop over her like a seagull over a fish and rupture her entrails and cause her death by bleeding."

Osnath did not know where her strength sprang from, but suddenly she had the audacity to say, "You know this to be untrue."

"It is the plain truth. She will gash her womb. I will have none of her."

In the face of this overwrought response, Osnath concluded that Hagith must be deranged by old age; she turned to Atarah instead. But the wife of Jesse seemed to have given up the struggle for her daughter-in-law's life, for she now sat with her eyes averted from the sufferer.

Osnath crouched down until her mouth was level with her ear. "I entreat you," she pleaded. "Let me assist your daughter-in-law by bringing the Jerusalemite to her."

But Atarah took no account of her and just sat rocking back and forth wildly, in a pit of agony and despair.

Wary of taking too much upon herself by acting without any authority, Osnath darted over to the front room, to look for Adah's father. By this time, the day was drawing to its end and those men of the two families who were not out at war had drifted into that room, there to await the delivery of Eliab's son, which had failed to materialize.

When Osnath came in, they regarded her disapprovingly. For it was the proper way for the women to gather in the birthing room. Penetrating the stronghold of the men, who were deliberately keeping themselves apart, was a severe breach of good manners.

Paying no heed to the men's disgruntled gazes upon her, she knelt down at Adah's father's feet. In a low voice, she told him of what had come to pass and reiterated her request that she be given leave to call in the Jerusalemite midwife, then sat back on her heels to await his response. He was in such deep shock that he could not utter a word. He merely emitted a groan, which Osnath took to be his assent for what she intended to do.

As she came out, one of Adah's sisters gave her directions on how to reach the midwife's home, which stood not far off.

The sky had darkened even further as heavy clouds amassed. It rumbled and grumbled, burst into flames, and broke into loud thunderbolts, as if in the throes of the wrath of the Lord. Then it released torrents of rain interspersed with icy-cold flakes of damp snow.

Osnath grabbed her goatskin cloak from her room and rushed out into the rain. The wind swept the street, and the trees that lined it on both sides were creaking and their branches were lashing at each other as she ran between them. Her shoes were soaked with water, and her feet almost slipped in the mud; but she regained her footing and continued running, her heart thumping with her effort. The hood of her cloak slid from her head, a gust of wind blew the rain into her face, and she let the water that gushed down it rinse away her sweat and exhaustion.

She found the Jerusalemite at home. But she was loath to leave the cosy warmth of her own hearth to go out into the cold and the wind and the rain, when another midwife was already in charge of the birthing.

But Osnath, struggling to catch her breath, explained that the lives of a woman and her unborn infant were hanging on a thread. If she failed to come, their deaths would be on her head. She tugged at her sleeve insistently, and at last the midwife allowed herself to be pulled to her feet. She took hold of her bag and followed Osnath into the storm and the darkening night.

Chapter Thirteen

When Osnath, with the Jerusalemite at her side, approached the birthing room, they were greeted by an eerie stillness, which, her heart thumping with fright, she took to herald Adah's death.

She tore the door open. When she entered the room, she saw that the young woman, who had been carried to her bed, had only fainted. But her face was as gray as the sheet underneath her, and it was evident that the shadow of death was hanging heavily over her.

The local midwife was attempting to revive her, and Osnath worried that this woman of high standing would feel insulted at being displaced by another. But she merely breathed deeply with relief at being released from a burden that was too heavy for her to shoulder.

After examining Adah's belly on all sides with her probing fingers and with her ear, the newcomer declared, "The infant is not positioned as it should be, and it is too big to make its way through the passage in the regular way, or to be taken out by hand. I must use my knife to enlarge the doorway."

Her announcement was greeted with blank faces, but this did not deter her. She removed from her bag a knife whose blade had been polished to a fine sheen, so that it was glittering in the light of the many oil lamps that stood in the room. She brought the knife to the mouth of Adah's womb with a steady hand.

At its sight, Hagith, who was crazed with panic for her granddaughter, sprang forward to grab it from her. She looked frenzied, a strange flame blazing in her eyes, as if she was set to run the Jerusalemite through with the woman's own knife.

But two of her granddaughters, imbued with newfound courage, jumped up from the floor and restrained her, and she subsided in their arms.

The cut between Adah's thighs caused her blood to wash out over her legs and the sheet underneath her. But since her inundation in blood was soon followed by the emergence of the baby's backside, which the Jerusalemite guided out of the passage with deft hands, no one protested. As they all realized, although the infant's emergence had to be bought at the price of some of its mother's blood, she had not been mortally wounded.

The midwife called out proudly that the bloodied little creature in her hands was male, but this aroused no response. For the infant was as silent as the grave, and it could be seen that under the blood that covered him, his lips were blue. The Jerusalemite severed the cord that bound him to his mother. Then, holding him by his feet, she suspended him upside-down in the air and briskly spanked his bottom.

The women held their breath, but for a while nothing happened. Then the infant expelled the lusty scream they had all been waiting for, and it was greeted with cheers of joy.

The new mother briefly regained her senses, and her grandmother raised her head so that she could see her son. But, with her face still bloodless, Adah fell back on her pillow and sank into nothingness again, only now it was the nothingness of relief.

Hagith ran out and shouted the glad tidings to the men in the front room, and howled it at the moon, which at that precise moment emerged amid the clouds with a smiling face.

Once the birthing was safely over, Osnath's apprehension reverted to Eliab. She often stood in front of the house, plagued by ghastly visions of doom, her eyes on the road leading into Bethlehem, straining to see into the distance, but Eliab was nowhere in sight.

With all the worry for the absent men, the family decided to forgo the festivities that usually accompanied a newborn boy's circumcision. On the eighth day after the birth of Eliab's son, a priest was called in to perform the ceremony, but no more.

Osnath was not left to wallow in her anxiety for too long, though, for Adah often wanted her at her side. The young woman, who was still suffering from the aftermath of her ordeal, was healing slowly. Still laid low by weakness, she was confined to her bed. There she lay, either giving suck to her infant or holding him as he dozed in her arms. Her inevitable jealousy of the one who was to become her rival temporarily laid aside, and conscious that she was indebted to Osnath for her life, she felt most comfortable when the girl was tending her needs. Thus it came about that Osnath was engaged in this very task when Eliab came in.

Ten days after the delivery, Osnath came to bring Adah her midday meal, a gruel of fine flour cooked in a mix of olive oil and honey. She found the young mother propped up on several cushions, the sleeping infant beside her.

Osnath had carefully placed the infant in the cradle that stood next to the bed, and handed Adah the bowl of her food, when her heart leapt to her throat. She heard the heavy footfalls she had come to love, as the door creaked open and Eliab stood on the threshold.

Osnath's eyes sparkled with tears of joy at his safe return, and her hands went out to welcome him, a gesture he failed to notice.

She re-collected herself, painfully aware that it was his wife and not her whom he had come to see. She quickly retrieved the bowl she had handed Adah and whisked it out of the way, and beheld him approaching the bed. With hardly a look to spare for Osnath, he bent down and hugged his wife and softly kissed her mouth.

Standing back against the wall, Osnath watched this scene wistfully. She felt devastated, yet also exulted in the knowledge that it was as it should be. The woman who had nearly given her life to give Eliab his firstborn would always hold first place in his heart. She did not hold this against him, admitting to herself that she had no right to hope for anything else.

Eliab now lifted his son from the cradle and rocked him in his arms. As he did so, he reproached the infant gently for having made such a violent entry into the world as almost to tear his mother apart.

The baby, overawed by his father's deep voice, broke into loud wails. Eliab cooed to him and reassured him by saying that he was only funning, that in truth he held him entirely blameless of all that had come to pass. Although he murmured softly into his ears, the baby continued to wail until Adah held out her arms and Eliab laid him at her breast.

Only then did he take notice of Osnath. He barely had time to greet her, holding her hands briefly in his, when the door flew open once more. Eliab's two brothers, who had gone to war with him, urged ahead by all the other members of the two families, barged in.

Eliab shooed them away from his weary wife, so they spilled back into the yard. There, pandemonium reigned as the homecomers had to endure tears from their mother, and embraces and shouts of welcome from their father and from their siblings, who all clamored for their attention and demanded to hear an account of the battle.

In the light of the sunshine streaming through the leaves of the trees, it could be seen that the returned warriors were ragged and filthy, caked with dry mud and blood. Copper tubs were prepared for them in their rooms, and water warmed in huge kettles on the cooking stones was brought there for their bath.

By the time that was completed, the midday meal had been placed on Jesse's front room table for them. Adah, with the infant suckling at her breast, was helped to a couch that stood against one of the walls. A hush fell over all those assembled as they sat around waiting for the soldiers' ravenous hunger to be stilled.

It is only then that Osnath noted that David was not with them. Since all were in a joyous mood, those who were not in battle must have been told already that he was well. Still, she was mystified as to what had kept him from coming home with his brothers. When she asked about this, she was told that he had been detained by the king but would be arriving shortly. Before she could ask more, the honor of telling the story was bestowed on the firstborn, and the words came rushing from Eliab's mouth.

"It came about that the Philistines drew up their forces and camped between Soccoh and Azekah in the domain of Judah. King Saul amassed our makeshift army, stationing it near Elah. The Philistines were occupying a position on one hill and we on another, with a valley between us.

"Each side had marshaled a sizable army, and our commanders had laid careful plans for battle, but they never came to fruition. For the two forces were evenly balanced, and each was afraid to wage war against the other in a head-on collision.

"Early one morning the sentries standing guard over the Israelite camp sounded the alarm. We woke up to the sight of a mighty warrior, a man named Goliath, coming from the Philistine ranks, with his shield bearer marching at his side.

"He was a mountain of a man, and it was a sheer wonder that one of such a gigantic size could have emerged from a mere woman's womb. With the bronze helmet on his head, and the heavy armor of bronze scales he wore on his body, he was a fortress in his own right. He held an iron dagger in one hand and a spear of iron in the other.

"The warrior stood in the valley and shouted to the ranks of Israel, 'Why should you all do battle against us? Choose one of your men to fight me. If he can kill me in fair fight, we will become your slaves. But if I prove too strong for him and kill him, you shall serve us. I defy you: send your man against me.'

"We all heard what the Philistine said, and each of us knew him for a menace to his own life. We were shaken and dismayed. Not one of us, including me," admitted Eliab ruefully, "had the courage to stand up to the brutish Philistine. Morning and evening, for forty days, the Philistine came forward and repeated his challenge, gloating at his own ability to keep us in fear of our lives.

"One morning, to my utter surprise, I caught sight of David, who was searching for us among the masses of soldiers. He approached the lines just as the army was going out to take up its position, and as we waved to him, he ran up to us to greet us. While we were talking, Goliath came out from the Philistine ranks and once more provoked us by parading his armored body before us, and shouting out the same words as before.

"In response to David's inquiry, the men around us explained, 'The king is to give a rich reward to the man who kills him, and has also promised to give him his daughter.'

"David turned to the speakers and said, 'Who is he, a crude, uncircumcised rascal, to defy the army of the living God?'

"I was anything but pleased to see the youngster. Although I held a poor opinion of his flowery speeches, he is still my little brother, and I hold him in deep affection. So, as I overheard him talking with the men in our vicinity and gathered what he intended to do, I grew anxious for his life.

"I gave vent to my anxiety with anger. 'What are you doing here,' I said, 'and who did you leave to look after the flock at home? You are an impudent youngster. You have come to see the fighting as if it were some diverting spectacle.'

"David protested vigorously. 'What have I done now? I only asked a question,' he said with an edge to his voice and turned away. He paid no further heed to me and to his other brothers and walked over to another part of the camp.

"Later we were told that what David had said in denigration of Goliath was reported to Saul, who sent a servant to summon him.

" 'Do not lose heart, sir,' David reportedly adjured him. 'I will go and fight this Philistine.'

"Saul was stunned, for how could a mere boy stand up to such a mighty warrior? It took a while before he collected his wits and said, 'You cannot fight him, David, for you are only a young man who knows nothing of warfare, while he has been a hardened fighting man all his life.'

"David did not give up. 'My Lord the King, I have long been the shepherd of my father's flock. When a lion or a bear comes and mauls and carries off a sheep, I go after him and rescue the victim from his jaws and batter him to death. This fiend will fare no better at my hands,' he assured Saul. 'The Lord who saved me from the beasts of prey will save me from the Philistine.'

"When these words were repeated to me, I reckoned that David had invented the tale, for I had never heard of any wild animals coming within the distance of an arrow's shot of our flock, let alone attacking it.

"Yet the king apparently accepted his words as true, for, as we were told, he said, 'Go forward then, and may the Lord be with you.'

"He invested David with his own tunic and girded him with his own sash. He placed a bronze helmet on his head and gave him a coat of armor to wear. Then he fastened his sword on the boy's thigh.

"But David said to Saul, 'I cannot go with these because I am not used to them,' and he took them off. He picked up a stick, chose five smooth stones from a nearby brook, and put them in his shepherd's bag.

"Then he took an oath: 'I lift my hand to heaven and swear: I will deliver victory to you, as a bride is brought to her bridegroom.' He motioned the men who surrounded them aside and walked out to meet the Philistine, with his sling dangling at his side.

"I and my brothers and all of Israel, who watched him marching forth, were gripped with dread. For the boy could no more penetrate his adversary's armor with those small stones from his sling than he could fly in the air.

"The Philistine came toward David, with his shield bearer marching ahead. He looked David up and down, and he had nothing but contempt for him.

"As we were close to the front of our lines, we heard him snigger and saw him stick out his enormous middle finger in an uncouth gesture. Then he called to David, 'Am I a dog that you come out against me with a stick? If you approach me, I will give your flesh to the birds of the sky and the beasts of the field.'

"This hideous threat did not intimidate my young brother. 'You come against me with sword and spear and dagger,' David called back to him, 'but I come against you in the name of the Lord of hosts, whom you have defied. The battle is the Lord's and he will put you into our power this day, so that all the world will know that there is a God in Israel.'

"The Philistine moved toward him with his spear stuck out, but David retreated and swerved aside and eluded him. Then the boy took his life in his hands and stepped forward to engage his foe. He reached his hand into his bag, brought forth a stone, and slung it.

"It found its mark and hit the Philistine on his forehead. The stone sank in, and Goliath fell flat with his face to the ground, where he lay screaming like a bereaved bear, his blood spurting from him. David ran to him and drew the Philistine's sword from its hilt and ran him through with it.

"By slaying their hero, David dealt the Philistines a mortal blow. When they realized that he had been worsted by an Israelite, they were dispirited, afraid to join battle against us.

"Our commanders now raised the war cry. Spurred on by the blowing of the ram horns and the sounding of the trumpets, we rose up as one man and attacked the enemies. They put up but a scant resistance, and soon they panicked until they did not know their right hands from their left.

"We put them to flight and chased them back to their land. On the way we felled many of them at the edges of our swords, so that the air was pierced with the screams of their mortal agony, and the road was strewn with their dead. And in our pursuit of the vanquished Philistines into their own land, our men lost all restraint and plundered it and laid it to waste."

For a while Eliab sat in thoughtful silence as his family waited. Then he shook his head in grudging admiration. "Our victory would not have come about were it not for David's heroic deed. I have always believed that he was all clouds and wind but no rain. I was utterly wrong. The boy is of noble spirit. I have to concede to my shame that he outshone me, us, in courage and made a name for himself in all of Israel."

The other two brothers squirmed uncomfortably in their chairs but nodded in agreement. Eliab continued, "He has earned the throne that will one day be his in good faith. He truly deserves to be the father of a dynasty of kings, and to be remembered in the entire world from generation to generation."

When the tale came to its end, all those present lifted their voices and wept with relief, and gave thanks to the Lord; and Osnath's tears mingled with those of the others. She was glad, though, that Eliab did not match David's heroism. The man she loved had done his duty and had come home safely, and that sufficed for her.

Then Eliab brought his wife, with his little son in her arms, back to her room and stayed with her until nightfall. But later he came to Osnath. He made love to her more tenderly than he had ever done before, as if in gratitude for what she had done for him by saving his wife and his son. And having been absent for so long, he came to her time after time, with only brief intervals for sleep.

This went on until the light of dawn began filtering through the window's shutters, when he fell into a heavy sleep of exhaustion. And Osnath, invigorated by his love, arose as fresh as an amply watered garden flower to face the new day.

The two families now awaited David's arrival, but he did not make an appearance until a week later, and only then did they find out what had truly delayed him for so long.

As they were told later, at the homecoming of the army, Saul in his exultation sent out couriers. They were to proclaim in all parts of the land the joyous tidings that the Lord had delivered Israel from its enemies.

The messengers were followed by Saul and David themselves, who swept through the towns with their entourage. The women streamed into the streets with tambourines and singing and dancing. So it went on until they reached Saul's castle in Gibeah, where the king, having tired, remained. David continued to make the rounds of the various towns on his own, until it was the turn of Bethlehem to greet the victor.

As they had been apprised of his approach, Osnath positioned herself in Hagith's front window embrasure. From there she had a glimpse of him as he came into view, flanked by three warriors on each side and many more at his heels.

She was overcome with awe and her heart fluttered in pride, though not in love, at his sight. She was hard-pressed not to call out to him in exuberance. But she felt no more than she ought toward her widely admired brother-in-law, as he was soon to be.

As David passed his father's and Hagith's houses, his brothers fell in behind him, and Osnath followed them. He strode through the town in triumph as the streets filled with people in their multitudes, all jostling and shoving each other to gain a glimpse of the young hero, while the king's men ran and called "make way" before him.

They all squeezed into the town square, where more people, clad in their finest attire, rallied to acclaim him. Then hundreds of women, their flowing white robes swaying like waves in the Great Sea, broke into dance and song.

Shielded from the burning sun by Eliab, Osnath watched the dancers and listened to their song. A song that had made the rounds of hosts of other towns before it reached Bethlehem, as if it had grown wings and traveled on its own accord:

Saul has slain thousands
And David tens of thousands.

In response, David waved to the masses and chanted a hymn of thanksgiving:

This is the day the Lord has made,
let us exult and rejoice in it.

When David left the square and the crowd began to thin, Eliab took hold of Osnath's arm possessively and led her back to the yard of his house. There they all sat in a solemn hush to await David's arrival.

After the young hero had refreshed himself and washed and changed his garments, he came out to sit with them. But if they thought that he would enlighten them further as to his battle with Goliath, they were disappointed. "You have probably heard of my confrontation with the Philistine from my brothers, so there is nothing left to be said about this. Instead, I will apprise you of the joyous tidings in my own life. Yesterday, the king consented to give me his daughter Michal as my wife in exchange for the paltry bride-price of a mere hundred foreskins of Philistines, by way of further vengeance on our enemies."

Osnath was deeply shocked, for she thought the king's demand showed him to be as bloodthirsty as a leech.

"He has already promised to give his daughter to the man who slew Goliath, as you have done, David, yet he has not kept his word," objected his mother, her face furrowed with worry.

"My honored mother, the king's promises are as durable as inscriptions engraved in sand," replied David.

"Now he is counting on the princess to be the bait that lures you to your death at the hand of the Philistines. Why is he so keen for your blood?" interpolated his father.

David's face was wreathed in a radiant smile. "Because, revered father, the women singing our praise in all the towns we entered attributed to me tens of thousands of the enemy's casualties, and to him only thousands. They accorded me the welcome that he considered as his due."

"Is that a sufficient reason for him to seek your life?" Atarah further protested.

"The singers' words galled the king. When I came with him for a brief spell to his castle and played the lyre to him as I had done before, he hurled his spear at me, meaning to pin me to the wall, so that twice I had to swerve aside. Saul, who was previously attached to me as if I were his own son, now regards me as a tangible threat to his reign. He is in dread, lest I plot against him. Of course, I will never raise my hand against the Lord's anointed to overthrow him, but instead I will succeed him. Yet he seems to be in a frenzy of fear that the God of Israel has forsaken him in my favor."

"Surely you will not fall into his trap like a bird darting into a snare!" exclaimed Eliab. "By going out to battle the Philistines again, you will cause your father and mother and us dire aggravation for worry of you."

David was unperturbed. "The king is indeed playing a base trick on me. He is not even trying to disguise the fact that he is exacting this new bride-price because he is anxious to be rid of me. But I will make his ruse turn back on him."

He added confidently, "He who is the Guardian of Israel will also be the Shield of David. He will foil Saul's plan by delivering the Philistines into my hand. I will gather around me a group of fierce young warriors from among my admirers, the rough and tough of the earth. When I go out with them in tow, it will not be a great effort to accomplish the task the king has set for me. We will all return safely to pile up the foreskins in a neat pile at his feet. Then I will collect my reward and wed his daughter, just to spite him."

On this, as on everything else, David's words fell easily from his mouth. Yet Osnath could no longer contain herself. "Would you raise your hand to take the lives of human beings, who have been created in the image of God, for such a callow reason?"

He jerked around to face her. "I have no qualms, for unlike the king, I have no intention of killing the uncircumcised. I will merely capture them, and once my mission is fulfilled, I will let them go."

But Osnath thought of the humiliation to which the Philistines would be subjected. She was persuaded that, since David had inflicted such a devastating defeat on them already, it would be better if he now left them alone.

Yet, as no one else objected, there was nothing left to be said, and silence reigned in the yard.

Once David had left, life resumed its orderly pace. As Osnath was to become part of Ruth's family, her thoughts reverted once more to the woman who had fascinated her so much before. Doubts about her, and thus about Eliab's inheritance, began nagging at her anew.

The preparations for her betrothal and nuptials began. But as they were made by Jesse's and Atarah's capable servants, there was little for her to do, so she decided to resume her quest.

Three days after David's departure, when Eliab came home from his work, she intercepted him and recalled the matter to his mind.

"Right now," he replied evasively, "I have more urgent matters to deal with, foremost among them providing accommodation for the numerous members of your clan while they sojourn here for the wedding. But I will weigh your request in my mind."

"You promised to show me Ruth's scroll, sir," she reminded him. "It is not necessary for you to sit down and read it with me, as you had intended to do. All that I ask of you is to unlock the scroll room and tell me where it is located."

"I wish that promise of mine had been washed away by the rain."

"The Moabite hovers before my eyes as if she were standing alive before me. Her memory can never be washed away, not even by a flood."

"Then you will also remember that I promised to show you her scroll only if you made a solemn commitment not to divulge its contents to anyone."

"I sense that Ruth would have wanted me to make her tale known for all time," she objected. "I can almost see her eyes smiling at me, her head nodding her approval, whenever I succeed in tracing some of her footsteps."

"I will make a concession. I will permit you to peruse the scroll, and to write a scroll of your own about Ruth's life. But on condition that it not include the parts of her life that had better sink into oblivion."

"Then there were indeed parts of her life that must be kept hidden," she exclaimed.

"I reckoned you had guessed that already."

"Yes, but this was the first time that you openly admitted it."

"And now that I did, I demand that you write not a word in your scroll until we decide together what it will contain."

"If you insist that I pass over stretches of her life, there is no sense in writing anything at all."

"You will do well to stop haggling with me, for you will not rest your eyes on Ruth's book unless you agree to my terms."

There was much that Osnath wanted to say, but she knew that it would be useless. So she merely bowed her head to signal acceptance of his ruling.

Eliab took Osnath to the scroll room and placed the long-coveted scroll before her.

"Be careful of the parchment," he warned her. "It is ancient and therefore fragile. Besides, it was torn and has been glued together in several places."

"How is that?"

"You remember that you found a scrap of it. As I told you, I located several more myself. Once I had the entire scroll in my hand, I located the spots into which they fitted. These places were glued together, but I cut them with my razor and fitted the deleted scraps in, gluing them in place, except for the one I gave you for a present. You may bring it to me now, and I will insert it into its proper place, after which I will give you the entire scroll for a gift."

While Eliab was gluing the last piece of parchment in its place, she asked, "How did it come about that all those pieces were severed from the scroll, which was then pieced together without them?"

"I am not sure, but I asked my grandfather about it shortly before his death, and he thought that it was Naomi's doing. When Ruth finished writing the scroll, she left it unguarded in the scroll room. He had a hazy childhood memory of coming in and tampering with it while she was elsewhere. He admitted that he had been a little vandal and must have torn it in several places.

"He also remembered vaguely that Naomi, who was caring for him, came upon him while he was engaged in his destructive deed. She probably took care not to reveal his pranks to his mother, so as not to incur her wrath. Since Naomi could not read, she could not have known how to fit the torn pieces back where they belonged. So she must have glued the scroll together as best she could. Then she must have rolled it up tightly so that Ruth would not notice that anything was amiss. She evidently hid the scraps that were left over under other scrolls, and this is how we laid our hands on them.

"But I have now repaired the damage, and the scroll is as one whole piece again. No part of it is missing. See for yourself," he said, entrusting her with the book.

When, after so much searching and guessing and wondering, Osnath finally held the scroll in her hands, they shook so much that she could hardly unroll it.

But once her eyes ran down its rows of letters, there was a delighted gleam in her eyes. In her mind, she saw Ruth and heard her and sensed her, following every ripple of her initially tortured soul, as if it were her own.

Part Two

THE TALE OF RUTH

Chapter One

My life was beset by horrendous tribulations. But the Lord, the God of Israel, has not abandoned me. He has raised me from the abyss, to make me dwell among the most exalted of his people, granting me happiness far beyond my dreams.

All this might easily be forgotten, like the wind once it has blown away. I do not want it to be so. I wish to retain the memory of all that has come to pass, both evil and good. And when I am gone from this earth, I would like others to remember.

For I have been aggrieved, but have wronged no one in return. My honor has been unjustly trodden on, like dirt on the ground, for no fault of my own; but also I have been redeemed from my affliction. And although I did not aspire to such a cruel redemption, I was avenged.

I do not want my memory to be blotted out. I want my voice to be heard throughout the generations, even if it is only the voice of the written words. For sometimes those speak louder, and they are certainly preserved for longer than those proclaimed with a great shout in the marketplace.

Above everything, I don't want my tale to be garbled by my kinsmen and kinswomen, who may do so without intending to. Besides, there is more to be told than they will ever know, or be willing to reveal.

A web of lies has been woven around me. Lies that were as sweet as honey and more palatable than the bitter truth, yet lies still. I am determined to retrace my days and let the truth speak in its own voice.

So I am writing the tale of my life. And I am thankful that my father, the king's official and representative in Sdeh Moab, taught me to read and write, making me the only woman in that town who had mastered those skills. And I am grateful to my husband, Boaz, who, many years later, taught me to convert my writing skills into the Hebrew tongue. For it is he who has made it possible for me to record the events of my life in the language in which I want them to be remembered.

I will bury the record I am about to write and stow it away beneath the ground, where it will remain concealed from prying eyes all the days of my life. But I feel in my bones that a day will come when it will be discovered and retrieved. And if my memory has been besmirched, or even unjustly hallowed, it will be reinstated to its rightful position.

At the sight of those words, Osnath was overjoyed that she, with Samuel's aid, had been the one to unearth Ruth's scroll and make her tale available for posterity. Eliab was resolute that Ruth's tale not be laid bare in its entirety. But if Ruth herself wished it to be so, what right had he to foil her will? All that would remain for Osnath to do would be to copy the Moabite's scroll several times over, so that as many people as possible would be able to read it. When she challenged Eliab about this, he merely said, "Read on, and you will know," then left her on her own.

Where shall I begin?

I will not burden you with the memories of my childhood. For, other than being orphaned from my father before I attained womanhood, I did not have a life that stood out from those of other girls.

Instead, I will begin with the tale of Naomi, an Israelite woman from Bethlehem, my mother-in-law, whose life was intertwined with mine. I loved her on sight and my love for her never wavered, because her brown eyes were as good as the brown earth after it had been watered by rain. When I first met her, she was advanced in years, but the eyes in her elongated face had not faded in color, and there was always a light dancing in them.

As she told me repeatedly over the years, she had come to Moab because the rains in her land had been poor for three years in a row, and became sparser by the year. At first the crops were meager, then they failed. The soil brought forth nothing but thin, shriveled ears of wheat. The fields were left to lie fallow, and the pastures dried out. Where there had been green meadows, there were only strips of dried grass left, as yellow as straw; and the flocks and herds became gaunt and lean. There was an outcry in the land, but the Lord did not lend an ear to it.

Elimelech, Naomi's husband, had filled his storerooms with the grain and lentils of the previous years, and at first his family did not want for food. But when the dry spell lasted for a third year, the stocked produce ran out, and the family could no longer sustain itself.

Having no choice, he did what many others who were left to starve did: he took his wife and his two sons and went down to Moab, intending to stay there only for the duration of the drought. It was the first month of the year, the one in which the children of Israel had been redeemed from their slavery in Egypt many years before, an auspicious month for new beginnings. And indeed, at the outset, all looked bright.

As they headed toward the rising sun, they encountered sheer wasteland, with little but strangling weeds on it, stretching into the distance for as far as the eye could see. But this did not deter them. For as they knew, further along there flowed the Jordan River, where they could replenish their supply of water.

Having crossed the river, they camped for the night. And when the sun, ascending the sky in a yellow blaze, announced another day, they saw Moab spread out before them. One part of it was a gently rolling tableland, cut into small segments by gorges that filled up with the blessing of rainwater in the winter, and another part was mountainous. Through this land the Arnon River ran, flanked on both banks with lush pastures. On these, they saw flocks grazing contentedly in the gathering heat of the day, with many of the fluffy-fleeced ewes heavy with lamb.

Beyond the river they perceived the dark green color of shady woods against the light of the sky. There they rested, sheltered from the midday sun, before making their way southward to what they had been told was the hospitable town of Sdeh Moab.

They knew that the Moabites were engaged in idol worship, which was an abomination before the Lord. Yet they found the people of the land to be friendly and indulgent, allowing them to worship their own God, without interference. As the Moabites' tongue resembled the Hebrew one, they had no difficulty speaking to them and making their home in their midst.

At first, they dwelled in tents and eked out a meager living by hiring themselves out as field hands on other people's properties. But although they had intended to return to the land of Israel as soon as possible, the days turned into months, and the months into years.

With the passage of those years, little by little, they succeeded in improving their position through diligence and thrift. Elimelech's pouch was opened frequently to deposit silver in it, but only rarely to abstract any from it. In time he saved up enough to buy some sheep and goats, and also a simple dilapidated hut, which he and his sons enlarged and refurbished and turned into a comfortable home.

Then Elimelech died suddenly: in the flash of an instant his heart gave out, so that Naomi was left with her two sons. In her yearning for grandchildren to bring her comfort, Naomi urged her sons to take wives. This is how I came to be her daughter-in-law. And so also Orpah, whose hair was as straight and black as mine was curly and red, and whose eyes matched her hair. Orpah always had a surprised look on her face, and she had a talent for wearing the daintiest of dresses, one I tried to emulate.

My mother—from whom I had inherited my flaming curls and blue eyes—strenuously opposed the marriage. She pointed out that the young Israelite who was set to take me was a simple shepherd, little better than a hewer of wood or a drawer of water. "With your uncommon colors and your high, sculptured, cheekbones," she said, "you are comely enough to deserve better. Besides, the bride-price he can afford to offer for you is paltry; you have suitors who offer an amount of silver far above his means."

I did not yearn for riches, though, but for the meeting of minds and hearts. Oddly, only he, though a stranger to the land, could offer me that, as well as the arousal of my senses.

This did not weigh with my mother. She also counseled me against becoming the wife of one who worshipped an alien god, a god so weird that no other gods remotely resembled him.

"A god," she added in a plaintive voice, "who has issued a host of unfathomable commandments. He commanded that his people fasten plaques with ancient inscriptions on them to their doorposts so as to fend off evil spirits. But I fear that they may have the opposite effect.

"The incantation on the doorpost of the man you want to marry marks his house off from all the others around it, and may attract precisely those pernicious spirits it is designed to repel."

How ignorant, thought Osnath, were those people. They actually believed that the excerpts from the Torah that the Israelites had been commanded to set upon their doorposts in affirmation of their faith had anything to do with evil spirits. When she next saw her uncle, she would tell him about this, and they would laugh about it together.

"The God of the man whose wife you are set to become," my mother warned me, "is also cruel. He goes so far as to demand that all males of his people have their foreskins cut off as a sign of a covenant with him." She further cautioned me that if I became the Israelite's wife, I would find him disabled in bed. But when she relented, and I did marry him, and I lay with him, he was not incapacitated at all.

My mother also thought it unwise of me to marry a man who bowed down to a God who was faceless, whom therefore I would never be able to worship properly. But Naomi later explained this to me. She said that Israel was a people set apart from all other nations. Although its God was indeed invisible, he had the heavens and the earth at his command, and his mighty arm was clearly visible in the history of his people.

In the evenings, when we gathered to eat bread together, she told us about this God. How, several generations ago, he had brought the children of Israel forth from slavery to Pharaoh in Egypt. How he had made them wander in the desert for forty years and given them the land of Canaan for their own. And thereafter he had intervened again and again to bring them succor from their merciless enemies.

We all lived peacefully together in the same house. From the outset, Naomi excelled in all she did. We spent most of our days in the roofed inner courtyard that served for the preparation of food. There she displayed her ability to grind even the coarsest of grain into flour as thin as dust, and to turn that into the crispest bread. She could season food so as to transform the plainest meat into the tastiest of dishes. She also kept our premises spotless. Neither Orpah nor I could ever hope to match her skills in the various tasks in the house, but she never lost patience with us.

She always wafted the rich, motherly smell of dough that had soured in preparation for baking. While her capable hands were busy kneading it, and baking the flat bread we all favored in the furnace, and frying savory meat and onion on the cooking stones, I, together with Orpah, worked alongside her. As our hands were moving, so, too, were our lips. And her ears were ever attentive to us, even to the voices of our hearts. She had fallen into the habit of addressing both of us as "my daughters," and in time she came to be closer to me than any other woman in the world, closer even than my mother.

But then all went awry, as the family was hit by stroke after stroke of bad fortune, as if a curse had been laid on our house, just as my mother had anticipated.

Both Orpah and I failed to bear children. Even when I had been barren for several years, my husband never blamed me, as other husbands of barren women were wont to do. He even joked, saying that he had not purchased me as one buys a fertile ewe expressly for breeding. And I basked in his smile, though it was wan and I knew that in his heart he did not feel like jesting at all.

I made a habit of frequenting the town's temple to plead for the fruit of the womb. There I paid homage to the goddesses whose huge copper statues were perched up flanking those of the gods, headed by Chemosh. For I was sure that only female deities could truly feel for a barren woman and would be inclined to extend a helping hand to her.

My mother-in-law had previously declared that the Lord had commanded the people of Israel to worship him alone, forbidding them to bow down to any other deities. But unbeknownst to her, I had little graven images of our goddesses—the goddesses of passion and pleasure and the fullness of the womb—tucked away in a hidden corner of my room. Naomi was strict in keeping the commandments, and on no account would she have tolerated the idols in her home. Had she discovered them, she would have hacked them down without mercy. But I set them up in secret, and as she never inspected my room, it was easy to keep them out of her sight.

Unlike Naomi, my husband was lax in his observance of the Lord's commandments, and he was lenient with me, too. So, in my wretchedness, I took the clay statuettes from their corner and set them up on the sideboard under his very eyes; I bowed down to them each time before and after he came to me. I poured out my soul before them, beseeching them to bless my womb, to fulfill my longtime craving for a child.

But it was to no avail: my prayers remained unanswered. My womb remained closed as if it had been locked and bolted with shafts of iron. The goddesses with whom I pleaded evidently did not have the key to unlock it.

When both my womb and my sister-in-law's had lain fallow, like the land of Israel during those same years, the prospect loomed larger and larger that we would remain barren, unable to give our husbands and Naomi their hearts' desires. Then the ewes in the family's small flock began aborting their lambs, thereby causing us a heavy loss in wool and meat. Finally, both of Naomi's sons fell prey to a mortal illness.

They sickened within days of each other. Both were beset by a lingering cough that rattled them like leaves in the wind, which none of the healers' cures could chase away. All the many herbs and potions that were administered to them, and the numerous unguents that were rubbed onto their chests, proved useless. With the passing of the months, their coughing led them to spit out blood-streaked bile onto the ground, at which the healers merely shook their heads sadly, to indicate that it was just as they had expected.

As I lay at my husband's side from dusk to dawn, he was always in the throes of a fever, bathed in sweat even in the cold of the winter. Gradually the illness sucked out the strength from his and his brother's bodies so that they could not take our diminishing flock out to pasture. Later they could hardly walk about.

They reclined on couches that had been set up for them in the front room. Yet they were overcome with shortness of breath, as if they were climbing a mountain while carrying heavy weights on their backs. We could only watch them helplessly, as their trembling lips almost ceased to utter words. They thinned to the bone, and as they did, their black eyes seemed huge in their gaunt faces. They became unearthily pale, their faces the color of the snow in the north.

My mother said that the malevolent spirits she had been so anxious about had indeed overrun our house. There were those in the town who agreed with her, adding that it was all caused by one particular demon, who had cast his spell over us.

Naomi did not shiver before the power of spirits and demons, and had nothing but disdain for such outlandish beliefs. She herself was gripped with fear that the evil that had befallen our family was in retribution from the Lord. His hand was heavy on us because, at her behest, her two sons had transgressed the Torah commandment that sets the Israelites apart. They had breached the injunction laid upon them not to intermarry with the peoples around them, particularly with Moabites.

She believed that it could not be otherwise, yet she deemed the punishment that had been meted out to us excessively harsh. As her sons neared death, in her bitterness, she renamed her first son—my husband—Mahlon, which means "the diseased one," and the second Chilion, which means "the one who is doomed to extinction."

Chapter Two

Our men had been ill for some four years. As dawn brightened to another day, it was evident that death was flapping its wings over them. Even their mother had given up hope. She and Orpah sat on the ground in the yard, rocking forward and backward, as if the men's impending doom were ordained from heaven, like a drought or a flood. Then they took to chanting lamentations, as if our men were already gone.

Unlike them, I was unwilling to sit idle with my hands folded in my lap and whine helplessly. Hence, I left the sick men in their charge. And, like one on the verge of drowning in deep water, I grasped at the only reed of hope left to me. I went to summon to their side yet another healer, whose skills had but recently been extolled to me, on top of the many who had visited them already.

On the way to the healer's house there stood the town's temple, and I could not pass it without offering prayers there. Its sanctuary stood empty, and I had it for myself alone.

Previously, when I had come there, I had directed my prayers at the goddesses and paid only scant attention to the male deities. But now, since I was about to pray for the health of men, I decided to invoke their names instead.

I entered the sanctuary and prostrated myself before the huge bronze statue of the chief god, Chemosh, and before the smaller images of the lesser gods that flanked him. Then I raised my hands in supplication. I pleaded with them to send salvation to my husband and my brother-in-law, and to keep them from the pit of darkness, wherefrom they would never return.

When I reached the healer's house, I found him to be a stout man with a stooping back. He was sitting with a guest under a palm tree whose branches fanned out into a shady canopy. My eyes were immediately riveted on the visitor, who was evidently a stranger in the land, as his garment was much different from those of Moabite men. In truth, it was like those of my husband and his brother, for it had a fringe laced with a blue thread at its corners, as the Torah has made it incumbent on Israelite men to wear. Hence I was not surprised when, after I had bowed to the two men, the healer proclaimed his guest to be a man from Bethlehem in Judah, my husband's town.

Having been married to an Israelite for so long, I had learned to speak the Hebrew language. So I told him my name, and that I was married to a man from Bethlehem, and asked him for his name.

He retorted laughingly, "I am known as the Unnamed."

Osnath read those words three times before they sank in. This was the man she had been attempting to trace for so long, and this is how Ruth had first come to cross his path.

I looked at him inquiringly.

"Ploni Almoni," he said by way of explanation, "which in the language of my people means 'the one who is not named.'"

This seemed odd to me. Each man has a name to single him out and set him apart from others, so why was this man averse to having his name known?

If, as Samuel believed, Mishael had gone to Sdeh Moab as a fugitive from justice, Osnath thought, this might be the reason for his unwillingness to have his name proclaimed abroad. He must have concealed it, lest rumors of his sojourn in Sdeh Moab reached Bethlehem and someone came after him, to visit on him whatever act of justice he deserved.

But it was not the right time to delay for the purpose of asking questions. So I told the healer my errand and requested that he accompany me to my husband's and his brother's side immediately, for their state was rapidly deteriorating and there was little time left.

The corners of the healer's mouth drooped in displeasure. He muttered something almost inaudible about my having had to seek him out earlier, rather than now, when it was evidently too late and his efforts would be in vain. But as he saw me wringing my hands, and the pleading look in my tearful eyes, he bowed his apology to the Israelite, took hold of the bag in which he kept his potions, and set out with me toward our house.

It was only as we were on our way that the image of the Unnamed rose more clearly before my eyes. Previously I had taken stock only of his clothing. Now, as I conjured him up before me, I contemplated his face, his large dark eyes, his delicate long nose, the creases between his brows, and his dark, trimmed beard. In some vague manner, like his garment, his features, too, reminded me of my husband's; and the man was good in my eyes. As I walked at the healer's side, I wondered vaguely if I would ever see him again, before my anxious thoughts reverted to the men hovering on the verge of death.

But when we reached the house, Naomi's torn clothing and the ashes on her head announced what had come to pass. They told me more clearly even than the wails that went up from her, and the blood her nails had drawn from her chest, that both Mahlon and Chilion were no longer on the verge of death but beyond it, beyond the salvation of any healer's tonics. Having been married for eight years, I was a widow at the age of twenty-five.

I broke into choking sobs, and Naomi, despite her own sorrow, attempted to console me. She said that during the last months both our loved ones had suffered more than any human being should, and that the last breaths they had drawn had been sighs of relief.

The healer left the yard unheeded. All that was left for me to do was to act in accordance with the Israelite custom, as I knew my husband would have wished me to do. I rent my clothing and strewed ashes on my head and wore sackcloth. Once we had interred our dead in the plot in which my deceased father-in-law was also laid to rest, I took off my shoes and together with Naomi and Orpah I sat on the ground, and we mourned our men for thirty days.

By the time the thirty days were over, the Unnamed from Bethlehem had slipped my mind, and it did not occur to me even to ask myself if he was still in Sdeh Moab. It was not until two months later that he surfaced again.

During those months, although the official period of our mourning was over, I was in deep sorrow. Bemoaning not only the life of my husband, but also my own, desolate at such a young age. Whenever I was not busy with the household chores, I sat with my mother-in-law and my sister-in-law in a silence broken only by occasional groans, and we hardly stirred out of the house.

Then one day, Naomi charged me with going to the market to buy some aromatic herbs, which were said to have a beneficial effect on aching knees, as were hers. Relieved to escape the house in which the shadow of affliction was still lurking in dark corners, I left quickly, before she could change her mind.

I pushed through the numerous colorful stalls. They were all filled to capacity with wooden and clay bowls and lamps, and colorful tunics, and balsam and myrrh and hyssop that a caravan had brought in from Gilead, and rare spices — saffron and cinnamon and cumin — carried in by another caravan from the east, and a welter of other fine wares. The vendors were stationed in front of them, shouting the praise of their merchandise and its unheard-of low prices, enticing the masses of shoppers into buying from them.

I went on until I neared the stall that had the designated herbs on prominent display, and the air around it was suffused with their poignant scent. There I stood among all the restless people — shoving others with their elbows or wrangling with vendors over the prices — waiting my turn.

As I came close, I saw that the owner of the stall was the Unnamed from Bethlehem. He evidently recognized me, for, leaving another man in charge, he waved me aside and handed me my purchase.

"You are the wife of the Israelite from Bethlehem," he stated.

"No longer his wife, sir, but his widow," I replied, and as I turned to go, he began walking at my side.

"It was the Lord's decree," he said with a note of sadness in his voice.

"If so," I gave as my opinion, "he was in league with the other gods. They all have the blood of a righteous man on their hands."

"Whoever ordained it did so unjustly."

"True, for my husband was indeed the best of men."

"He must have been, for he had the best of women for his wife."

Disregarding this obvious flattery, I said, "The gods have been known to strike down good men in the prime of life."

In some unfathomable way my words seemed to embarrass him, and for a few moments he remained silent, as if he was immersed in some unpalatable memory of his own.

Then, as if he was shaking off his unwelcome reminiscence, the Israelite went on talking. I bowed my head as he invoked the volatility of fate, the shortness of life on this earth, the irrevocability of its end. He was well-spoken; his voice was beautifully modulated. He seemed to feel for me in my bereavement as no one else did, and his words, though somber, were sweet to my ears.

As he had done on my first meeting with him at the healer's house, in some indistinct manner he once again reminded me of my deceased husband. This time he did so not only in his apparel and his features, but also in his bearing. As my husband had been, so, too, was he nobly refined; and he bore the same mysterious air of a faraway country that had first drawn me to my mourned one.

After we walked aimlessly for a while, the Unnamed said, "I will accompany you and carry your parcel for you," and I ceded it to him.

On the way, I asked him what had brought him to Moab.

Whether, like my husband's family, he had come to flee the drought in his own land.

"I was not chased here by the drought," he replied. "When it first overtook us, my assets were few. But unlike many of my townsmen, I did not sit helplessly bemoaning my fate. Instead, I pulled up my sleeves and set myself up as a merchant, trading with whatever I could lay my hands on. I was frugal and hoarded my silver, so that whenever I sold out my merchandise, I could buy new goods to sell; and so I built my fortune bit by bit with my own hands. And now I have come to pursue my trading in the land of the Moabites."

When we came close to my house, I retrieved my parcel and requested that he retrace his steps, for I could not risk being seen by Naomi and Orpah in the company of a man a mere three months after my husband's demise.

Before taking leave of me, the Unnamed said, "Come back to my stall at the market tomorrow, and I will have a special brew ready for you, one that brings comfort in sorrow and revives a flagging zest for life."

I held out for an entire week, and when at last I went to collect the brew, he said that by now it had spoiled and had to be discarded. But once again he walked with me almost to my home, and urged me to come back no later than tomorrow, when the beneficial posset would be awaiting me.

And the next day found me once again on the way to his stall.

Before I reached it, a wild-haired female, a soothsayer whose dark eyes seemed to be fixed on a sight in the distance visible to her alone, suddenly shifted them to me and halted me. She was sitting on the ground, with a small cloth in front of her, on which stood a bowl of clay filled with pebbles of different sizes and shapes and colors.

She tugged at the seam of my dress. "Come here," she said, pointing to the empty spot across the cloth. "Sit down facing me, and I will conjure up your past and foretell your future free of charge."

Suddenly I felt lighthearted and eager and hopeful. I sat down opposite her. She rattled the little stones in her bowl, then spilled them out on the cloth. After regarding them for a while with a deep frown on her face, she lifted her eyes to mine and said in a muffled voice that made the words in her mouth sound as if they were shrouded in mystery, "Young woman, you have recently been widowed, and the sorrow for your deceased husband still weighs heavy on your heart."

I hardly had leisure to wonder what singular powers had enabled her to read the portents in the pebbles so accurately, when her voice became clear and she proclaimed in a festive tone: "But fear nothing, for better days lie ahead. All the omens are auspicious; I cannot have misread them. The wheel of your fortune is about to turn. You are about to meet a man. A man of good looks and manly build. A foreigner. He will unlock the secrets of love for you, and lead you to joy and happiness."

Then she hooded her eyes and said no more.

I was amazed at the soothsayer's prophecy. And, indeed, it seemed to come true instantly, for I turned around to see the Unnamed confronting me.

I saw the gleam of silver changing hands. And when he led me away, he admitted, his shoulders shaking in laughter, having coached the diviner ahead of time to foretell what lay ahead. "But I have incurred no guilt for this little ruse," he said, "for I am sure that I have not erred, and that the love I have made her prophesy is indeed about to flourish between us."

Although I was too shy to admit it, I felt that the soothsayer's prophecy also reflected that in my own heart.

I held out to him the silver pieces for the purchase of the brew he had promised me. He took them and shoved them, together with a skin containing the concoction he had prepared, into a bag. After handing it to me, he put his workman in charge of his stall and for the third time began accompanying me. This time he led me out of the town through a roundabout path that wound its way around it to my home.

Once again he talked profusely. Inexplicably, I found comfort in his words and in his presence. I felt an odd affinity to him, a stranger, as if he were a relative or a close friend. My senses were soothed, yet aroused at the same time, as they had been by my man before he fell ill.

My attraction to him seemed to mirror his to me, for all this time he devoured me with his eyes. Yet when he touched me, I recoiled, saying that my heart had been sunk in the ground with my husband.

When we approached my house, with his eyes riveted to mine, he said, "I have another brew, Ruth, one that ignites love and joy in the act that celebrates it. I will prepare it anew every day and have it ready for you whenever you come."

I cast my eyes to the ground in embarrassment at the lewdness of his words, for I had never heard any man save my husband mention the act of love. I made no reply and hastened my steps and left him behind looking after me as I entered the yard.

In the seclusion of the chamber that now housed only me, I consumed the brew he had given me. Its taste was that of bitterness and sweetness intermingling, as they did in my thoughts. I don't know whether it had any effect on me, but after drinking it I stretched out on my bed and conjured up the appearance of the Unnamed, and let it hover before my eyes.

This time my memory fastened on his stature, taller and broader than Mahlon's had been. I thought that besides being handsome, he was lively and delightful. He was light of tongue, bubbling over with words that rolled easily from his mouth. In this he was much unlike my husband, who had been grim and sullen and brooding during the last years of his declining life. I felt that I had seen this stranger before, many times, in my dreams, which had now come to life.

After that, I battled with myself for I don't know how long. Perhaps ten days. Perhaps two weeks. I was tormented, vacillating between my conscience and a new, unsought flame burning in my loins. I was reluctant yet tempted; recoiling but lured; determined to cast the Unnamed out of my mind as I thought of him incessantly. Conscience wrestling with passion; conscience vanquished.

While Osnath was reading, dusk had slowly been creeping in. Strange noises, seemingly arising out of nothing, began penetrating her ears. In her eagerness to find out how Ruth's misgivings had been overcome by passion, she decided to disregard them. But when she heard the sounds of trumpets blowing, she could no longer shut them out.

She opened the door to the sight of no less a man than David, flanked by two trumpeters, and a contingent of his followers at his heels, descending from his mule. His face radiant, he lost no time in announcing to all those who had assembled in the yard in his honor that the king had now definitely agreed to his wedding with Michal. He had come to invite them all to it.

It was to take place in a week's time, before Saul, who was given over to moods that soared and ebbed like the high and low tides in the Sea of Reeds, might exact a new price in return for his daughter.

After David acknowledged the blessings of his kin and of all other well-wishers who had come in to greet him, they sat down for the evening meal. When it was over, David found a moment to call Osnath aside and murmur to her under his breath, "You, Osnath, were the love of my youth. No matter how many wives and concubines I take, you will always retain a place of honor in my heart. I am joyous that although you refused to become my wife, you will still be of my family."

Osnath knew to take his flowery words lightly. She smiled at him brilliantly and whispered, "So am I delighted that although you will not be my children's father, you will be their uncle."

David's prospective wedding to another caused not the slightest pang of jealousy in her heart. They parted in perfect amity, with no bitterness on either side.

The next day's rising sun found David lingering, with the members of the two families who were gathered around him still chatting with him. But partway through the morning, when David and his men had been waved on their way and the men of the houses had gone out to the fields, Osnath resumed her reading of Ruth's tale.

Chapter Three

Thus it came about that, at the end of some two weeks, I made my way among the stalls again, until I reached his. It was twilight and the shoppers had thinned, so the Unnamed saw me from a distance and came forward to meet me. Suddenly wildly impetuous, I reminded him of the brew that encouraged love, which he had promised to have ready for me.

He glared at me and said, "I do indeed have it. But I would not dream of giving it to you here, where it might ignite your passion for any stray passerby. Come with me to my house, and we will rejoice in it there, together."

A mute voice from the grave called upon me to spurn his proposition. But every fiber of my being urged me to respond to it with a smile and a demure bow of my head, as indeed I did. Still retaining some reticence, I said that if I came to his home, his neighbors might spot me and take me for a woman of easy virtue. But I would like to go for a stroll with him again.

This suggestion found favor in his eyes. He immediately left his workman to shut up his stall, and before long we found ourselves in a forest.

There he revealed his true name, Mishael, to me. He warned me never to mention him to other people except as the Unnamed. He was unwilling to explain the reason for this as yet, but he promised that the day would come when he would lay his life bare before me.

As we strolled among the trees, he talked as I had not thought that anyone could. He said that I was a bright star in the sky of his life. That I was the queen of heaven and the queen of his heart at the same time. That my breasts rounded under my dress like clusters of grapes. That the act that would give voice to our love would be better than a ring on my finger under a canopy: it would be our glue, joining us together to become one flesh forever.

His words were magic to my ears. They were so persuasive, they could convince a leopard to shed his spots. Even without the love brew he had promised, they convinced me to shed my dress, as soon as he yanked at it.

We lay down on the grass in a small clearing amid the trees. There he guided me through the steps of the ancient ritual of the way of a man with a woman. Although I had performed it countless times with my husband before he fell ill, that had been so long ago that now it was as new to me. I thirsted for it, for him, as the parched earth after a drought thirsts for rain.

His tongue pressed softly on mine, and I felt and tasted it at the same time. He explored my body with tantalizing slowness, like a stranger in a foreign land, as indeed he was. Then we melted into each other as my need, which had found no fulfillment for a long time, tensed and then broke into shattering release, followed by my sigh, deep and content.

When I was back at home, I reflected that it was as Mishael had said. When he had come to me, no priest had recited any blessings. There had been no feast, no tables laden with festive foods. No wine had flowed into the goblets of invited guests; no flutes had played and no drums had been beaten. Yet I felt wedded to him in my overflowing heart.

Thus, for the first time in my life, I was moved to write a poem of praise to the gods.

At this point there were two tiny mended rifts in the scroll. Osnath scanned the parchment carefully by holding it up to the light, and noticed that it had been torn in two places and glued together with skillful

hands, apparently Eliab's. In between the mends were the words she
had previously discovered on the scrap of parchment, which Eliab had
subsequently wrought from her hand:

> Today the Unnamed from
> Bethlehem has come to me.
> It was from the gods.
> It was marvelous in my eyes.

The words were still branded in Osnath's memory, and the evidence
they contained of Ruth's fiery passion for the Unnamed made her
all the more eager to discover what had subsequently gone awry between them.

We met again the next evening. Mishael convinced me that we
could not confine ourselves to the woods forever. For, even if we lay
in the thicket of bushes, someone might come upon us unawares to
witness our rite of love. So I gave in and came to his house.

When I arrived, he took me straight to his bedchamber and left
me there on my own. But he soon returned with a decanter filled
with a hot brew of sweet wine and cinnamon with an unknown
herb mixed into it. It aroused my need for the joy of love, as he
had said it would. Before many moments had elapsed, we were in
his bed. And this time there was no hesitation; we foraged each
other's bodies like a man and a woman starved for love, as indeed
we were.

There followed a string of starlit nights, which ran over into
sunny days, hot and still and filled with our sweat, and I could
hardly tell them apart. My sole regret during those months of the
pleasure of the flesh was that they flew by so quickly.

Since my husband had died less than four months earlier, I
knew I ought to be secretive about my meetings with Mishael. Yet
I became reckless, heedless of my reputation, leaving our house

immediately after sunset, returning only shortly before sunrise, and sometimes only at the dawn of the following day. Then I would walk in splendid solitude through the still-sleeping town, with only the birds' song in the treetops accompanying me, giving voice to the happiness in my heart.

Naomi was not oblivious to my nocturnal disappearances from the house that often ran over into the next day and night. But she did not judge me harshly.

For she knew that I had been unfailingly faithful to her son in his lifetime and had devotedly nursed him through the four years of his prolonged illness. That I had kept faith with him even when his disease had sapped his manly power, which had dwindled like that of an old man; when all he had been capable of doing in bed was to hug me convulsively in fit after fit of worsening despair.

And that if I had meticulously abstained from straying, it was not for lack of opportunity, for I was well-favored and never lacked admirers. And that now my heart was hungry and wanton and desiring.

Reciprocating my wantonness, Mishael could hardly let me out of his sight. Our closeness to each other set us aflame. But it was not merely the tug of our loins. We spent days and nights together, eating and drinking and sleeping snuggled up in each other's arms, immersed in our mutual love.

In the late summer nights, when it was stifling hot inside the house, we would go outside to seek the cool breeze. There, no matter whether the moon was slender in the sky or round and heavy like ripe fruit, we would laugh in the sheer joy of our togetherness, and our laughter was another wordless covenant between us.

Gradually we began to tell each other of ourselves. Haltingly and intermittently at first. But as we became used to each other, the words that had been hoarded inside us rushed out of our mouths more rapidly, until they were running over like the Arnon River in a rainy winter.

Only of my deceased husband and his family was I reticent to speak. Senselessly, I feared that even mentioning his name would cast an evil spell on our love, and Mishael did not press me. But there was much else that we had to tell each other.

I told him of my father. A man who had been born into a humble family, but whose superior mind and uncommon skill with the pen (imparted to him free of charge by a scribe who took a liking to him) had earned him his post of high standing as the king's official. A man who, like my husband, had descended into the grave long before his time. I told him of my mother, whose womb was torn to shreds by my violent exit, after which she was unable to bring forth any more children from it. And of my elder sister, whose lack of beauty was made up for by her ever-ready smile and the goodness of her heart.

Mishael told me of his childhood. Of how the other boys had always been aligned against him. Of how his elder brother had never lent him his protection against their fiendish designs, so that he'd had to stand up for himself. Of how at times his brother had even sided with them to connive against him.

He talked of the property he would inherit in Bethlehem from his recently deceased father, and of his mother, who had died a mere two weeks after her husband's descent into the grave.

Only when I asked about his brother, and what he was doing now, did his eyebrows furrow. He made a futile gesture with his hand and remained wordless. After a while he said, "My brother and I were like the father of our people, Abraham, and his nephew, Lot. The land was not big enough to hold us both. We had to go our separate ways and put some distance between each other."

I presumed that, having had a dispute with his sibling, he had fallen out with him to such an extent that they could no longer speak peaceably with each other. Perhaps that had been the true reason for Mishael's leaving his land to come to Moab. I wanted to ask him, but the forbidding expression on his face told me that it would be pointless.

So I let the matter drift out of my mind, especially as he diverted me by deeds and words of love. He pledged himself to love me always, and I put my trust in his words. For my love for him was as steadfast as the earth under our feet, and why should it not be so for him?

The months passed, the stars followed their courses in the sky, and the moon waxed and waned much as usual. But one night, when the autumn clouds had dispersed and the full moon shone bright in the sky, heralding the time of my monthly blood, I remained dry between my thighs.

I still padded my cleft with rags, thinking that the bleeding would start belatedly, but a week passed and there was nothing. My breasts were hard and sore and swollen. I retched but was unable to vomit. I could no longer deny to myself what had befallen me.

That which I had prayed for, and had eluded me for so many years while my husband was alive, had overtaken me now, when I was a widow. The goddesses had bestowed the blessing of the womb on me, but they had chosen an inauspicious time for it.

Yet, all might still be well. For although I had no husband, as custom prescribed that I should, I had a lover who was better than ten husbands for me. In my imagination I saw the smile of bliss on his face when I imparted to him the glad tidings of his impending fatherhood.

The next time we met I was about to do so, but some unfathomable fear, a vague premonition of evil, halted me. I decided to hold off until our act of love was completed before making my announcement.

After we had come together, Mishael wound my hair around his finger. And he did not flinch when he told me that he was forced to go back to his own land, and much as it pained him, we would have to part. He added without a blink of an eyelid that, although we would dwell at a distance from each other, the bond between us would continue from afar and would last forever.

His voice sounded unfamiliar, like the voice of a stranger. It was as if I were frozen in a nightmare, and his words rang like the sound of doom. I could hardly credit what my ears had heard.

Could there have been any warning signs before, which I had

missed? Nothing came to mind. I had surmised that one day my lover would return to his own land. But I had presumed as a matter of course that he would take me with him. It had never occurred to me that he would leave me behind.

It was only now that the magnitude of his betrayal emerged, as I realized that he had made a mockery of my love for him. I had merely been a vessel into which to pour his seed; it had not been his object to have it sprout inside me. So I stifled the words I had been about to utter. My announcement would never be made.

When Mishael saw me looking at him in amazement, he did not seem concerned over the undeserved pain he was inflicting on me. He offered an intricate explanation for his hasty departure, no part of which I could properly understand. Then he added as an afterthought that perhaps a day would come when we would embrace each other again. But he showed no inclination to bring about that day.

At this, we both understood that there was no point in drawing out the leave-taking, and he made it abrupt and cursory. He said that he wanted to give me a parting gift, by which I would always retain him in my memory. Unaware that he had already given me a reminder by which I would constantly remember him, he now bestowed on me his lapis seal and the cord on which it was hung.

He enjoined me to carry it on my heart, and pledged that he would always carry my memory as a seal on his heart. These smug words rankled with me more than any he had spoken that night, for their falsehood, the lie enfolded in them, would have been plain even to an infant in a cradle.

I felt a strong urge to hurl the seal, together with some coarse insults, into his face. But I bit back my words of outrage and merely gritted my teeth and forced my quaking hands to keep still at my sides.

Although I was furious, my heart went out to my lover. "Don't desert me, Mishael. If you must leave, take me with you."

The words were uttered inside me, but I did not have the

strength to bring them forth from my mouth. Like the tidings about the child I was carrying in my womb, these words, too, would never see the light of day.

When the tears were falling from my eyes, he had already put on his clothes and turned from me.

I was crestfallen. My world had come apart. More than I blamed Mishael, I blamed myself for not having foreseen what he had held in store for me. Yet I could not cease loving him. He had imprisoned my heart like a fly in a spiderweb, and notwithstanding the base manner in which he had dealt with me, I could not disentangle myself from him.

Even at night when I lay sleeping, my heart was awake with yearning for him, and my dreams were shaped by my longing. In those dreams, my lover came by my window and peered in through the lattice, engulfed in the light of the rising dawn. But when I arose to open the door for him, he was no longer there. I ran after him, but he had disappeared from sight.

In the daytime, when I thought more soberly, I could find no explanation for the manner in which he had treated me. I had pleased his body; there was no doubt of that. And his heart, I was sure, had not remained untouched, either. I could not fathom what he had later found objectionable in me.

I foresaw that this would remain a mystery to me. Yet I decided that at least I would find out what had prompted Mishael to leave in such haste. Since he had been friendly with the healer in whose house I had first met him, I went to visit that man and asked him about his friend's abrupt departure.

The healer said that it had followed the arrival of another Israelite from Bethlehem, advising him that someone there had unexpectedly died, so that he could now resume his residence in that town.

When I asked how this man's death was connected to Mishael's return to Bethlehem, he would only say mysteriously that he who knows too much suffers the most.

Downcast, I begged him not to withhold his knowledge from

me, but he merely stood back to let me pass, thus indicating that my visit with him had come to an end. My hope of comprehending what had come upon Mishael drifted away like the clouds in the sky after they have been emptied by the winter rains.

It occurred to me that the man recently deceased in Bethlehem might have previously dealt with Mishael in an underhand manner. He must have been plotting against him. And now that he was dead, it was urgent for Mishael to go back to reclaim his inheritance there with all possible speed, lest he forfeit it.

With this possibility in mind, I half forgave my lover his desertion of me, and the pain of my separation from him was eased.

Nonetheless, being abandoned to face my pregnancy on my own was a calamity for me, the like of which had never befallen any other woman I knew. I was now forced to confront it squarely, and my heart gave a pang of fear.

My husband had died six months before, and my pregnancy could not be attributed to him. As soon as it became evident for all to see, I would be regarded as a widow who had committed an outrage. One who had failed to pay tribute to her husband's memory, taking a lover even before the earth had settled properly over his grave.

I yearned to be the carefree, frivolous young girl I had once been. Yet I was conscious that the gods never turned life backward, only forward. There was no one from whom I could seek help. For I knew that even my own mother would condemn me with bitter words for having brought shame on the family. To survive, I would have to save myself on my own. The pain in my heart notwithstanding, I decided that there was no choice but to be rid of the infant inside me.

The sun having reached the middle of the sky, Atarah came to summon Osnath for the midday meal in the front room, where Adah was already at the table. During the meal, the older woman spoke of the forthcoming trip to the king's castle for David's wedding. Since they would have to spend two days on the way, and as they were wishful to reach their destination well ahead of time so as to enjoy a full measure of the king's hospitality, they planned to start out on the following morning. Clearly, she said, Adah could not bring the infant along, nor could she leave him behind. She would have to remain at home.

"Since the journey is to last for ten days," she continued, "we cannot leave Adah to her own devices. Her grandmother is prevented from traveling by her old age. Her mind is getting hazier by the day, and it would be too cruel to leave Adah in her sole company. Another woman will have to stay at her side. Since I cannot fail to attend my son's wedding, it must fall to your lot, Osnath, to be Adah's companion."

At first, Atarah's announcement was met with silence. Adah was still deeply indebted to Osnath, but she was no longer as comfortable with her as she had been before. Now this discomfort kept her usually talkative lips tightly sealed.

Although Osnath had looked forward to attending the festivities in Saul's castle, after giving the matter some thought, she saw no choice but to acquiesce to Atarah's wish and respond to it with proper docility, by saying, "Revered lady, I will do whatever is right in your eyes."

She consoled herself with the thought that, by staying behind, she would gain the peace that would enable her to give Ruth's tale her undivided attention. She made her way back to the scroll room, where she sat detached from all that surrounded her, as yet unaware that peace would be as far removed from her as righteousness was from the wicked.

Chapter Four

O nce the notion of releasing myself from my pregnancy had taken hold of my mind, I lost no time. On that same day I sought out a midwife, one who also saw to the aches and pains that beset women.

This was a woman whose face was lined with her compassion for the countless women whose sore bodies and souls had been brought to her attention. A woman whose straightforward look into my eyes spoke to her honesty.

When I confided my trouble to her and begged her to release me from it, she said: "I could dig into your womb and scrape out your child; but I might mutilate you, and you would be barren all the days of your life. I could give you a potion with ingredients known only to myself to drink, and it would bring forth your blood and wash away your baby. But the bleeding might be so strong that it would drain you entirely of this life-giving liquid."

"Is there anything else that you could do?"

"I could cast spells and chant incantations over your naked navel, but they would be as much use to you as abundant rain to a felled tree."

"Have you no other remedy at hand to offer me?"

"I have advice to offer you. Get the man who made you pregnant to take you for his wife."

"He is an Israelite and has returned to his own land, abandoning me to my fate."

"If so, entice another man to marry you before your belly begins to protrude, and no one will be any the wiser. You are fair of face, and your body is still curvaceous. It should not be difficult."

"I could not deal falsely with the man who would be my husband."

"It would not be unheard-of. Ever since human beings began roaming on the face of the earth, there have been women who have had secrets embedded in their wombs, which they shared only with their goddesses."

"I could not be of their number."

"Then follow your lover to his land and hold him to account for the hurt he has inflicted on you."

Mishael did not seem to be the kind of man who would easily be held answerable for anything. But I thanked the midwife and weighed silver into her hand, and assured her that I would give her advice some thought.

A rude reality now stared me in the face: my child would stubbornly cling to my womb until the end of its term. When it came forth into the world, it would have no one, no father, not even a mother, who truly welcomed it.

As the months passed and my belly began bulging against my dress, the town was overtaken with a babble of vile gossip, buzzing with hateful malice. Not even my home was a haven for me. For although Naomi showed me tender pity, my sister-in-law had nothing but scorn for me.

Orpah was never garrulous and spoke no nasty words in my ears. Instead, her face, which had always borne a look of surprise, now seemed more surprised than ever. She regarded me frostily and shook her head disapprovingly, and the black mane of her long hair shook with it. Even when she perceived that I was in despair, she offered me not so much as a word of comfort. The stones on the walls had more compassion for me than she did, as they appeared to cry out my sorrow.

Yet I could not hold Orpah's condemnation of me against her, for even my own mother disowned me. When I went to seek counsel of her, she had nothing but derogatory words for me.

As I stood amid the ruins of my life, I reckoned that the gods had now perpetrated their worst atrocities, and that there was no further damage that they could wreak on me. I was wrong.

The next blow fell that same evening. Naomi, now bereft of her two sons as well as her husband, declared that she could not bear to live in the house in which she had seen so much happiness with them, and where their memory haunted her day and night.

It had come to her ears that the Lord had relented. The rains in the land of Israel had resumed, and its inhabitants once again enjoyed the fullness of the earth. Hence she planned to return there from her exile.

"My daughters," she continued, "the time has come for me to leave the land of the Arnon River for the land of the Jordan River. My hometown beckons to me from across the wilderness that separates me from it, and I will heed its call."

I was stunned. My husband and my lover and my mother, each in their turn, had deserted me. The prospect of being abandoned by Naomi, too, weighed as heavily on my breast as a massive stone at the opening of a well, impossible to dislodge. All was bleak, and I began to nurse even deeper fears about my future.

Then the midwife's words came to my mind. Perhaps I should accompany Naomi, thereby following my lover, whom I still missed sorely. Contrary to that woman's advice, I would not approach him while the child was still in my belly. Even afterward I would say nothing about it, until our love had been firmly reestablished.

There was no assurance that Mishael would be willing to receive me into his house. But I would still be better off in Bethlehem than I was in Sdeh Moab, no matter what. For there no one knew precisely when my husband had died. So no one would be able to tell whether the child in my womb was begotten from him or from another.

Yet my predicament was such that for a while I could not see my way clearly before me. It was as if I were walking in a dark cave. I saw the light at its exit, but whenever I approached, it moved out of reach. At last, I resolved that the land in which I had opened my eyes for the first time would not be the one in which I closed them for the last time.

When I told my intention to my mother-in-law, she was not keen to have me accompany her. "This man who calls himself the Unnamed," she said, "must surely have a very good reason for disguising his name. There must be some unsavory deed that he prefers people to know nothing about.

"Besides, this Ploni Almoni is an odious, devious liar. Craftily taking advantage of the purity of your devotion for him and leading you astray, then casting you off as if you were a rag to be used to wipe off his shoes. Even if he finds that you carry his child, he will repudiate your claim on him with both hands and deny that he had anything to do with it."

Although I had no intention of making any claims on Mishael, I was chilled at her words as she continued: "He will shake you off as a fly from his sleeve. Discard him from your mind, my daughter, as he has discarded you. He is not worthy of being followed across the town, let alone across the desert."

"But you, my adored mother-in-law, are worthy of being followed to the four edges of the earth."

Naomi was not swayed. "Although I yearn to have you at my side, I must warn you. If you come with me, you will be uprooted from your homeland and separated from your family, a stranger in an alien land, where you will feel like a bramble among roses."

The place toward which Naomi would be heading was indeed her homeland, not mine. I did not relish the prospect of being a foreigner among its inhabitants; it even filled me with dread. Yet fate had not decreed that I remain one forever. "I will become part of your people, the people of Israel. In time, no one will remember that I was once a Moabite."

She looked doubtful. "Apart from everything else, the journey through the rugged desert that must be crossed will be long and arduous and fraught with danger, for we may run out of water and bread on the way. And how will you have the strength to cope with its hardships, with the child inside you weighing you down?"

I brushed aside her concerns. "I will cope with everything. I swear that I will not be a hindrance to you on the way; only do not leave me behind to weather adversity without your support."

"You have your mother's protection."

I stood firm. "I have become but an unwelcome burden to her. My whole dependence is on you. Even though I did not come out of your womb, if you leave, I will be as a newborn lamb left on its own by its mother," and these words softened her heart.

Orpah assured Naomi that her fate, too, was linked to hers, and she would not be left behind. So our mother-in-law acquiesced in our wish to accompany her, and said no more.

彡

Once Naomi had made the decision to return to her own land, she was in a rush to be gone. She sold what was left of our meager flock and our house, and we prepared for our travel.

As part of the preparations, I visited the temple of my gods and goddesses. I poured a libation of olive oil scented with myrrh over the altar in front of them. I burned holy incense in the incense burner until a soothing odor, pleasing to their nostrils, filled the air. While its scent spread throughout the sanctuary, I bowed down before them so that my forehead touched the ground. I recited a prayer, the prayer of the traveler who is about to embark on a perilous journey. I besought Chemosh and the other gods and goddesses to move heaven and earth and do all that lay in their power to pave our way with success.

When I raised my head from the ground and looked at them, I gained the distinct impression that they smiled at me benignly out of their kindly eyes. I counted this as a blessing that augured well for the new life I was about to begin.

My last visit was to my mother, to take leave of her. She was grouchy and not kindly disposed toward me. Only with great difficulty was I able to convince her that, although I had fallen headlong into disrepute, I was still her child. It took much pleading before I prevailed on her to bestow her blessing on me, her errant daughter, to set me on my way.

I knelt with my head bent before her. As I did not leave her much choice, she did bless me with these words:

My daughter.
May you always walk in a garden among flowers,
and may your life blossom as they do.
And may you inhale their sweet scent,
the scent of happiness, all the days of your life.

Even then she still held herself stiffly aloof, every part of her face and her body speaking her disappointment in me. Yet at the last moment before I left her presence, we fell into each other's arms and mingled our tears in sadness over our looming separation, for we were sure that we would never set eyes on each other again.

And only in the years to come did I realize how apt my mother's blessing had been.

The day Naomi had selected for our departure was the first day of the first month, the same month in which she had arrived in Moab. A time when the spring was blossoming but had not yet reached its peak.

On that day we arose even before the night paled into dawn. The noise we made in preparing for the trip must have disturbed the birds from their slumber, for they darted sprightly from limb to limb and seemed to chirp a twitter of farewell for us.

The night before, we had piled up our provisions in a cart. They consisted of bread and water, one blanket for each of us, and a tent and fodder for the animals we would take with us. These bare necessities filled the cart to capacity, so we were forced to hang the bags with our clothing on hooks attached to our donkeys' saddles.

Since those animals would have to bear us as well, and in fear of overloading them, we took only tiny bundles of clothing with us. As we thought it a shame to leave our best clothing behind, we decided to wear it. Instead of arraying ourselves in faded, threadbare, old tunics suitable for travel, we clad ourselves in our finest apparel and shod our feet in our best shoes, even though they might be ruined on the way.

Then we hitched our ox to the cart to draw it. We saddled our donkeys and mounted them, and, just as the first rays of the rising sun began dancing between the leaves, Naomi signaled us to start. We rode on either side of her, with the cart and the ox, which we led by a cord, bringing up the rear.

I had previously thought that I would leave the land of my birth and my childhood without regret. Yet, when the distance between us and the town of Sdeh Moab increased, my eyes and those of my traveling companions were red with the clinging memories of the beloved we had left in its soil.

Naomi wanted to close the lid to her previous life, not little by little, but in one irrevocable slap. Hence she refused to look back. As she explained half in laughter but (as I suspected) half seriously, it was for fear of turning into a pillar of salt, unable to move. For this was precisely what had overcome Lot's wife when, in defiance of the Lord's commandment, she had looked back with longing on the town of Sodom, where she had spent so many happy years of her life, going up in flames behind her.

We advanced as quickly as we could, and so it was not long before we came up against a ridge of mountains that stood in our way. By that time the sun had risen behind our backs, the heat was gathering strength, and the singing of the birds in the treetops was subsiding. Since the hill before us had no road on it and was strewn with rocks, we had to ascend it on a tortuous, winding path that had not been smoothed out for us by others.

We clambered up its steep incline without incident, but after we had crossed the summit and began our descent on the other side, we met with our first mishap: the ox drawing the cart tripped over the protruding root of a long-felled tree. The animal staggered forward, and before it recovered its footing, the cart was overturned. Its contents spilled to the ground, and one of its wheels creakingly came off the hinge. The ox, too, collapsed to the ground. Its forelegs were hanging from it at an awkward angle and it bellowed in pain.

All our attempts to minister to the animal and make it rise on its bruised and evidently broken legs were in vain, as were our attempts to repair the cart. We rummaged through the cart's contents and salvaged whatever loaves of bread and flagons of water we could load onto the saddlebags that weighed down our donkeys. Cruel as it was, we had no choice but to leave the wounded beast and all the rest behind.

Afterward, we followed a desolate path that few had previously trodden, which led us down into an arid valley. For a while we talked among the three of us, but little by little, our chatter ceased. Our shadows, which earlier had been stretching into the distance before us, shortened and then disappeared as the sun reached midsky. The heat of the day bore down on our heads with its full might. All became still with the silence of the desert in which we now found ourselves—broken only by the occasional rustle of a lizard, surprised by the noise of our donkeys' hooves, scuttling to shelter in a juniper bush.

Naomi, who was still riding between Orpah and myself, had fallen into deep brooding, her forehead knotted like the parched earth under our donkeys' hooves. Suddenly, without warning, she halted her donkey, forcing us to stop as well.

Then she rode a few steps ahead, turned around to face us, and said: "Go back, both of you, to your mothers' homes. May the

Lord keep faith with you as you have kept faith with the dead and with me; and may he grant each of you peace in the home of a new husband."

Her words came as an utter surprise to me, as thunder on a clear day. Surely, as far as they pertained to me, they were empty. For Naomi knew well that, with my belly the size of a heap of grains, as it was by then, it would be impossible for me to find a new husband even had I set my mind to do so.

This did not deter her: she kissed us both and wept aloud. I suffered myself to be kissed, but as soon as Naomi took her lips from my face, I inquired, "Is it because the God of Israel cannot accept a woman such as myself who has dishonored her husband's memory into his flock?"

Naomi reassured me. "Although the Lord is a God of justice, he is also a God of mercy. Anyone can find shelter under his wings."

As my mother-in-law now elucidated, there was an entirely different reason for her determination to send us back home. "Turn back, my daughters. Why should you go with me? Since you have not borne children to your dead husbands, you would be entitled by the laws and customs of our people to marry their brothers. But they have no brothers. And at my age, am I likely to bear any more sons to be husbands for you? Even if I were to become a man's wife this night," she reasoned, "and if I were to bear sons, would you then abstain from marrying and wait until they grew up?" Having spoken, she wept again.

Her words seemed to suit Orpah's purpose. Even though we had begun our journey that same morning, she was already worn out by our travail and seemed scared of the vast, arid terrain stretching out in front of us. Her resolution slackened, and I saw fear pass on her face like the gray shadow of a cloud. Her eyes darted back and forth in uncertainty between Naomi and me. Still, she said dutifully, "We will both of us accompany you on this journey of return to your people."

I murmured my agreement, though I sensed that Orpah's words had been spoken haltingly and that her heart was not in them.

Naomi, shading her eyes against the sun, looked at her searchingly. After hedging for a while, and following a perfunctory show of tears, Orpah kissed her mother-in-law, gave me a thin smile, rubbed her cheek briefly against mine, and turned her donkey around to face Sdeh Moab. It was the last we ever saw of her.

"You see, Ruth," said Naomi, still facing me. "Your sister-in-law is going back to her people and her gods; it is not too late yet. You can still catch up with her."

But I stood my ground. "Do not force me to desert you," I pleaded.

"I am not forcing you," she asserted with sadness in her voice, "but counseling you, and counseling you well."

There was a pause, and suddenly words came spilling out of me, and I heard myself reciting a speech I did not know had been inside me:

My revered mother-in-law.
Wherever you go, I will go;
where you stay, I will stay.
Your people shall be my people,
and your God my God.
Where you die, I will die,
and there shall I be buried.
I swear a solemn oath
before the Lord your God:
nothing but death
shall pry us apart.

Once my words had been spoken, I knew that I had couched them in fancy terms so as to curry favor from the one whom I had now pledged myself to worship. But they struck a chord also with Naomi. As she saw my determination to go with her, she kept her lips pressed to each other and raised no further objections.

As Naomi was familiar with the sorry events in my life, there was no point in hiding my eagerness for my lover from her. Yet, since she knew me like the palm of her hand, she was also aware that my words to her were sincere, the unvarnished truth in my soul. For a reason I could not fathom myself, I was no less keen to join her people and embrace her God than I was to join and embrace my lover.

There was nothing more to be said. After a brief pause for rest and refreshment, we continued. We were a lone party, with no other travelers in sight. And we were unaware that the hardships we had braved already were nothing compared to the ones that still awaited us along the way.

Although the sun had traveled some way from the middle of the sky, the searing heat of the day had not abated, and there were only low dusty shrubs to break the monotony of the landscape. We continued until after sunset, when we spotted the encampment of a caravan of traders on its way from Moab to Egypt. We halted near it, dismounted our donkeys and fed them, and watered them with water we drew from a nearby well. As we'd had to leave our tent behind, the traders offered us hospitality in one of theirs, which they pitched for us.

It was made of light goatskins sewn to each other at their edges. We tied its flaps open so as to gorge ourselves on the night air. And we sat on our blankets as we stilled our ferocious hunger by each consuming a piece of the flat dry bread we had brought with us.

As we ate in the light of the moon, it seemed to me that the blanket underneath me was dotted with tiny drops of an indistinct brown color. I was too tired to examine them more closely, and I immediately lay back and my eyelids shut themselves of their own accord. When I awoke and sat up in the morning, I saw that the little spots of the previous night had dried and paled; they looked like little more than specks of dirt, and I paid no further attention to them.

For that entire day we traveled with the dust thick under us and around us. There was nothing to be seen but more and more dry bushes and puny trees, which covered even the distant hills, where the sky met the earth. Above us there were only a few long, slim clouds, running like white veins through the heavens, until the rays of the sun burned through them and made them shade over into the blue of the sky.

At nightfall, we tethered our donkeys to the trunk of a shrunken tree. We had hoped to discover a well from which we could draw water for them, as we had done the evening before, but there was nothing in sight. We had only a small amount of water in the skins we had brought along, to quench our own thirst; we could not spare any of it for the animals. All we could do was to let them munch on some dry leaves, which we plucked for them from the emaciated trees and tamarisk shrubs in the vicinity.

Our belongings had filled with dust; I even felt its grittiness between my teeth as, once again, we ate from the provisions we had carried with us. Having no tents, we slept under the light of the stars. Even so, I slept the deep sleep of the weary and did not stir all night long.

In the morning, when I went to retrieve our donkeys, I found mine toppled over, lying inert on its side, with its legs stretched out stiffly before it. I could not discern the signs of any disease on its body. It had been old, and under the heavy load it had been forced to shoulder, and the paucity of water to drink, its strength had simply given out. It had left the world as silently and uncomplainingly as it had lived.

A foul smell began emanating from it. So we were eager to push on without delay, even though we had only the one donkey between the two of us. Since Naomi was old, I insisted that she ride it, while I walked at her side, carrying the five-month-old swelling in my belly before me.

We had loaded all we owned on a hook attached to the one remaining animal's saddle, until the tame, submissive creature seemed lopsided, and we were afraid that it would collapse under the heavy weight. Yet, as the day wore on, we were forced to rush our steps, so as to find the shelter of trees before the sun began to bear down on us with all its strength.

We rested for a while. But when we resumed our journey, I was so feeble that I stumbled over my own feet, which buckled under me. After Naomi helped raise me, she supported me as I lifted myself heavily onto the donkey's saddle, leaving her to walk at my side.

Soon the sight of the old woman treading the ground as I was riding became unbearable to me. I slid off the donkey and helped her mount it. I overcame my weakness and walked until the sun approached the crest of the hills before us.

Once again we lay down for the night under the naked sky. The darkness closed in first over the distant hills, then over the dust-whitened shrubs around us and then over my mind, as I shut my eyes to a dreamless sleep of utter exhaustion.

I awoke with the rising of the sun, sitting up to the sight of a steadily spreading stain on the blanket under me and a growing discomfort in my belly. Naomi, who had also arisen, stared at me in wide-eyed horror.

The evening having fallen, Eliab came to take Osnath to the meal and to bed. When the bustle of the families' departure the next morning had ceased, Osnath made her way to the scroll room again. But she'd hardly had time to unroll the scroll to the passage where she had left off the day before when the door opened behind her.

Adah, who, unable to read, had always kept at a distance of a stone's throw from the scroll room, now entered it. Following her grandmother's edict, her shiny copper curls were severely wound out of sight under a new head covering, and her face held the expression of one who had swallowed sour wine.

After Adah's eyes swept briefly over the unfamiliar, scroll-filled shelves, she sat down at the table. Osnath waited for her to speak, but when she did not, spoke first.

"Pray remove this kerchief from your head. It is of a colorful pattern, but your hair forms a much prettier frame for your face, and don't listen to your grandmother if she tells you otherwise." Saying this, she tugged at Adah's head covering until it came off and her curls ran riot again.

Then Osnath took Adah's hands in hers and spoke to her softly about the matter that was weighing heavily on both their hearts. "Adah," she said, "I am well aware that you have been burdened with me against your will and that you wish I had never come to Bethlehem for the first time, let alone the second time."

"No, how could I wish this? I would not else be alive today."

"Don't give this matter another thought; it is over and done with."

"It will never be erased from my memory."

"Then you should also remember that at no time did I have any intention of deposing you from your rightful, honorable position as Eliab's first wife and the mother of his firstborn son. Fate has led us both to love the same man. Neither of us will give him up for the sake of the other. We must learn to live together without eating out our hearts."

With vinegar and honey now battling in her features, Adah extricated her hands from those of Osnath. "This is your notion. It is not mine."

With these words, she arose abruptly from her chair and stalked out of the room, leaving Osnath to wonder what was on her mind, totally baffled.

She resumed reading the tale of Ruth, but it was quite a while before she could concentrate her thoughts on it.

Chapter Five

A cramp sent my hands forward to clutch my abdomen. It was so strong that I doubled over; then I lay down sideways with my knees drawn up, my hands clasping them to my chin. I felt warm moisture between my thighs. And when I looked down, I saw my blood, clotted and dark at first, then liquid and red, coating the blanket, soaking through it into the soil. Before long it was streaming copiously, creating a veritable bloodbath underneath me, and I felt something sliding out of me: my blood had washed the infant out of my womb, some four months ahead of its time.

I gained a glimpse of it and vaguely discerned the bare traces of a face. My stomach turned as Naomi took hold of it and whisked it away. When I raised myself on my elbows, my gaze following her, I saw her rolling my lifeless infant up in her blanket. Then, with a stick she found lying on the ground, aided by her bare hands, she dug a shallow hole in which she buried the parcel, before she covered it with the earth she had dug out.

Previously I had wanted to be rid of the child, to eschew disrepute. And I would have preferred to begin my life in a new land unencumbered by a fatherless child. But since then it had grown, and I had felt the stirring of its life, like the flutter of birds' wings, inside me. In my imagination I had seen its eyes, and felt it in my arms suckling at my breasts, and inhaled the scent of its little body into my nostrils.

Now the child was gone, and all I had was a gaping hole in my womb, as deep and dark as a cave. I was distraught, and I mourned for the child as if it had actually seen the light of day before it died. But my grief remained unspoken, unwept, and I never gave voice or tears to it, either then or later.

I struggled to sit up but was overcome with dizziness and had to lie down again. Naomi sat at my side and whispered soft words into my ear, which sent me back to sleep.

When I awoke, the sun was high in the sky. My head was throbbing with pain, and I was gripped with fever. My eyes were heavy, my speech was slurred, and I was freezing and burning all at the same time, my skin full of pimples such as those of a plucked fowl. I craved nothing except more sleep, but Naomi rattled my arm, restoring me to wakefulness.

She said that even though we had taken care to drink only sparingly from the water we had brought with us, we had hardly any of it left, and our food had nearly run out. We could not afford any further rest, for we were still a long way short of our destination, and if we did not advance quickly, we might die of thirst. There was nothing to be done, she said, but move on until we came upon a settlement with an adjacent well, where we could drink and use some of the silver in her pouch to purchase food.

In the absence of a tent, there was no need to dismantle anything. We just abandoned the blood-drenched, evil-smelling blanket on which I had been lying, Naomi pushed me onto the back of our donkey, and we set out. The elegant dress I wore, the only one I still had with me, was of a muted red color. Thus, the blood that was streaming onto it, which the strips of a torn garment I had placed between my thighs could not stanch, was hardly visible.

Not that it mattered, for we met no one on the way. We saw several piles of charred wood on the ground, giving evidence of people having camped there before. But although we poked through the ashes underneath them, they gave off no smell. So we knew that those who had lit the fires had left some time ago. Morning came, then evening, and I scanned the horizon, and still we seemed to be as far from any human settlement as ever. We had to stop again for the night without any hope for more water or food.

When the blackness of the night was overtaken by the brightening dawn, Naomi once more woke me up. But I was so weak, I had not the strength to take even one more step.

She did her best to encourage me. "We have overcome Pharaoh in Egypt and forty years of wandering through the desert. We can overcome this small trip in it as well."

I certainly had never come forth from under the yoke of the Egyptian Pharaoh, nor had I been plodding through the desert before. But such was the esteem in which I held her that I would not contradict her. I let her pull me to my feet and even swung onto the donkey's saddle by myself.

Midway through the morning, we confronted a magnificent sight that took my breath away. As the town of Sdeh Moab was located in the south of the country, we had taken a southern route; now, as we advanced toward the west, a vast stretch of water, the Sea of Salt, came into view on our right.

It was calm and smooth, and its water lapped sleepily against the shore, caressing it gently. The cloudless blue sky was like an endless tent pitched over it; the sun, an enormous lamp dangling from its ceiling. And its brazen rays were reflected in the lake as in a gigantic shimmering metal mirror, thus increasing the heat of the sultry day tenfold. A dense sulfurous vapor rose up from the water, as if the sea were exhaling its breath. The vapor was as hot as fumes from a furnace, and we were nearly consumed by the heat it unleashed. But it cast no mist over the landscape, for it was immediately dried out by the sun.

We were nowhere near the end of our journey; yet we had drunk the last of our water a while before, and we had not so much as one drop of it left. Though there was an enormous amount of water close by, we could not bring any of it to our mouths. The lake was so salty that no life could survive in it, so we knew that we could not survive after drinking it, either. The scent of salt was heavy even in the air. We drew it into our nostrils and could feel its tang in our mouths, and this aggravated our thirst even more.

We would gladly have exchanged all the silver in Naomi's pouch for a few drops of sweet water to drink, but there was none. Apart from that in the sea, the only liquid in our vicinity was my own blood. It continued to trickle from between my legs, leaving a thin red trail behind me, until I was afraid that my life was pouring out with it. Naomi was helpless to stem the tide. But she began muttering, and repeated over and over what she explained was an ancient saying among her people, "In your blood may you live," in the hope that it would ease my worry.

But even Naomi had not the ability to imbue me with strength. The wheel had turned, and it was she who began lagging behind and after a while lacked the vitality to proceed. In her exhaustion, she reclined under a bush and urged me to continue on my own. I lowered our water skin from the donkey in the hope that miraculously there would be a sip left in it for her, but it was empty. There was no other way but once again to take turns riding, and in this manner we walked through the thirsty soil until we had crossed over to the far side of the salty lake.

Not having eaten for so long, I should have been famished. But I felt no hunger at all. I only felt so weak with the heat outside, and the thirst, and the fatigue of the way, and the fever inside me that I nearly fainted. As I had never walked such long distances before, my feet were covered with water-filled blisters and rough open sores. I could not take even one more step on them, and collapsed into a heap on the ground. Naomi relinquished her place on the donkey to me, but she could hardly move forward herself, her progress being as slow as if she were wading through the water of the Sea of Salt.

Yet, just as I was overcome with certainty that we were dragging ourselves to our inevitable end, we came upon what was nothing short of a miracle.

Naomi, her face toward the setting sun, pointed her finger to a bunch of tents amid a group of palm trees. Those trees, no more than an arrow's shot from us, were blooming as if they were planted in rich soil. I stared at them in disbelief, for I could have sworn that they had not been there a moment ago. They seemed to have sprung up out of the bare soil before my sun-blinded eyes.

I stood rooted to the ground as I perceived, right behind them, a rocky hill. On its slope was a spring from which live water was bubbling out, gurgling cheerfully, before making its way down the cliffs into a little pool, and from it into the sea.

Gathering the last vestiges of our strength, we shuffled in the wake of the animal, holding on to its backside, lest we fail so close to deliverance. When we stood at the pond, we—all three of us— bent forward and drank copiously, and we were revived. Naomi and I scooped up water in our cupped hands and splashed it onto our overheated faces and bodies, and we were refreshed.

Then the tent dwellers, nomad Midianite shepherds, took pity on us. They offered us shelter in their midst, vacating one of their tents for us. They fed us gruel of oats followed by pieces of lamb that had been simmering in water seasoned with the salt of the sea, on hastily assembled cooking stones. Perceiving how sick I was, the Midianites measured out to me a brew of dried mint and coriander, which, they assured me, fosters recovery. I was never more grateful to anyone for help extended to me.

Even so, as I lay on the ground in the tent, I was in desolation. The Midianites' ewes grazing behind our tent, so many of which carried lambs in their bellies, with their teats swollen, seemed to be bleating the joy of motherhood. And they formed living reminders of my bereavement. But my eyes were dry, and the drops of blood still coming forth from me formed the only tears of my sorrow.

My eyelids drooped and I was lulled beyond the edge of consciousness by the sound of the rush of water from the spring. I remained as one in a deep faint until the morning, when the light of the sun and the smell of freshly baked bread filling the air awakened me.

During the next two weeks I continued to bleed, and my fever raged. It was scalding hot in the tent even at night, and the air was so windless that its raised flaps did not stir. But this did not hinder my sweat-covered body from shivering under the cloth that covered me. I languished in a blurry haze, in the nether region between sleep and wakefulness. All the colors of the rainbow were skipping before my closed eyes, as Naomi applied cool damp towels to my forehead to make my fever sink.

When the burning in my body eventually cooled, I was no longer sure whether my miscarriage had truly happened, or whether I had concocted it all in my feverish brain. My breasts, though, were witnesses to what had come to pass. They were hot, and I felt the milk leaking out of them, mingling with my sweat, wetting my garment, with no infant to suckle them dry.

At night my lids opened and shut themselves in rapid succession, and my head rolled this way and that on my pillow. This went on until my eyes closed to a fitful, dream-haunted sleep. In it, my aborted infant stared at me accusingly out of tear-studded eyes for having failed to breathe into his nostrils the breath of life.

I made a slow recovery, but it was steady. Contrary to my fears, once I had regained my strength, no ill effects lingered. When I was up on my feet, we knew that our time had come to leave. As soon as the next day's light filtered into the tent, we blessed our Midianite hosts and hostesses over and over for their charitable hospitality; then we proceeded on our way.

Osnath lifted her head from the scroll with relief. Though she commiserated with Ruth for the loss of her child, she was jubilant that, contrary to what she had suspected, Ruth had not passed Mishael's child off as that of Boaz. Obed had indeed been Boaz's son, and Eliab was Boaz's genuine descendant, rightfully entitled to inherit his share of his ancestor's property. This made it all the more puzzling why he previously had been so steadfast in refusing to let her peruse Ruth's scroll. She resolved to ask him about this at the first opportunity after his return, then bent her head to the scroll again.

Chapter Six

We arrived at our destination a day later, the time of the beginning of the barley harvest. Naomi said that in Sdeh Moab she had always sat down and wept when she remembered her land, and that being back in it was like walking in a dream. My eyes and ears and nose opened, taking in the new sights and sounds and smells that heralded the future, those that would accompany me the rest of my life.

I let my eyes sweep over the fig trees and the climbing vines and olive trees, which, as the winter had been rainy, grew in much greater profusion than they did in our parts. I inhaled the fresh aroma of the trees and plants, which the rains had imbued with new life, and among which bees were buzzing their persistent tunes.

Viewed from a distance, the houses resembled our own; but when we came close, I gaped at the doorposts. All of them boasted a tablet with an inscription from the Torah, which I had previously seen on that of our house only. And I heard words being spoken in the Hebrew tongue, which I knew, but which yet sounded foreign to me.

There were many of those words to listen to, for when we walked through the streets, leading our donkey in tow, Naomi's hometown was in an uproar about her. Her suffering, no less than the passing of the years, had taken their toll on her, and she had deep furrows in her face, running from her eyes to her nose to her chin, like those in a ploughed field ready for sowing.

Thus, at first, the women who poured out into the streets at her sight could hardly recognize her and asked each other, "Is this truly Naomi?"

"No," she told them with strong conviction. "I am a different woman altogether. Do not call me Naomi, but call me Bitterness, for the Lord has embittered my life. I was as full as a pomegranate when I left here, and now I return as empty as a gully in a drought."

Nevertheless, once their doubts as to who she was were dispelled, the women did call her Naomi and enfolded her in loving arms and shed tears of joy at her return.

But in the commotion, no one paid any heed to me. I was unnoticed, as transparent as clear water. I was acutely conscious that I was a woman with no homeland, with no welcome among a previously unknown people.

Naomi's home had been uninhabited during her absence. It had not decayed, but it was covered with ten years' accumulation of dust and cobwebs, and it was infested with mice and all manner of vermin and crawling insects. The neighbors, who came in bearing welcoming gifts of bread and olives and almonds and dried grapes, also helped with the cleaning. Then they kissed Naomi's wrinkled cheeks, which had assumed a pink color of excitement, and left us to ourselves.

My mother-in-law did all she could to welcome me into her home. But without intending to do so, she made me feel as if there was no place for me in it. For she flatly refused to put me to work, to let me draw water from the nearby well, as the town's girls were used to doing, or to perform the household chores together with her, as I had always done in Sdeh Moab.

When I offered to share her chores, she would not hear of it. In Bethlehem, she said, it would be unthinkable for me, her guest, to bring shame on her family, which was highly esteemed in the town, by performing menial tasks. As she could not afford to hire a maid, she tried to cope with all the work herself. And whenever I sent out my hands to help, she shook a rebuking finger at me and shooed me away.

I could not stand by, though, and watch her drudgery. I would not eat the bread of idleness in her house while she broke her old back bending over the grindstones and the cooking stones, working her fingers bare, as if she were still a Hebrew slave in Egypt. Indeed, as the weeks went by, it became too much for her, and she gave me leave to fetch and carry for her. So I fell to work thankfully, doing whatever needed to be done.

Even so, there were times when my hands were not busy, and I was free to go out and explore the town. Once I strolled up the hills that bordered it. As I gazed at the cloudless blue sky and at the mountains of Moab visible in the distance, my thoughts flew back to my own land. It struck me that I had not offered up prayers or burned sacrifices or poured libations to that country's gods since I had left it a few weeks before.

I had vowed to adopt the God of Naomi, the God of Israel; but I had not sworn to cast away my own gods. Yet they seemed to have forsaken me. From the vantage point of the hills of Judah, they seemed distant, powerless, oblivious to my fate.

Having undertaken to serve the Lord, I had every intention of hallowing his name. But to my astonishment I discovered that there was no temple in Bethlehem, no consecrated ground on which I could worship. All that the town boasted was a paltry shrine and a miserly altar for sacrificial offerings in its square.

Naomi said that the House of the Lord had been established in the distant town of Shiloh, and all of Israel went on pilgrimages to offer sacrifices and worship there three times a year. Yet, surely, such a mighty God as the Lord deserved to have a temple constructed for him in every town, so that he might dwell among his people.

The Lord's image was not even engraved in a statue, before which I could bow down to recite my prayers. Years ago, Naomi had explained to me that the Lord had forbidden his people to carve graven images of gods, nor even an image of himself. Yet now, when my heart had opened to him, I asked myself how I could worship a God when I had not the faintest notion of what he looked like.

But when I told my thoughts to Naomi, she was incited to retort: "The Moabite gods are nothing but pieces of clay and wood and copper. Their very existence is merely a tale blown by the wind into people's hearts, to bring them comfort, to stave off their fears."

Perhaps she was right. But at least the Moabite gods and goddesses had always been vivid before my eyes. Yet the Lord was so unbending in his prohibition against setting up his image that I could not even conjure him up in my imagination. I was sure I would never be able to reach out to him.

Naomi's acquaintances all called me "the Moabite." Even so, I was no longer a Moabite, nor yet was I an Israelite. I was nothing. An exile from my country. A lone, wandering bird that had flown into a previously unseen land and was unable to find a foothold there.

I had declared myself to be part of the people of Israel, but I was acutely conscious that those people did all they could to prevent me from doing so. They did not abuse me but found more subtle ways to show me that I was an outcast in their midst.

Whenever I walked on the streets, I tried to link myself to the people with friendly looks and hearty smiles. But they did not return my smiles. When I encountered neighbors, the greetings I called out to them were like a voice calling in the wilderness: they scarcely responded, muttering inaudible replies.

When I bent down to children playing on the ground, intending to feed them pieces of the honeyed barley cakes I always carried with me in my pouch for this purpose, their mothers frowned in disapproval. They snatched up their little ones and walked off, shunning me as if I had white spots on my face, as one cursed with leprosy. All that was left for me to do was hide my mortification.

I was taunted by loneliness, which lay heavy on my heart. I shrunk into my own misery and became homesick as I had never thought I would be. The distant mountains of Moab suddenly held a new allure for me. For even the malicious gossip I'd had to weather there was preferable to being shunned by all. Although spring was drawing to its end, the sky was hardly ever blue but mostly as dull as my life.

What kept me alive in my loneliness was my persisting love for Mishael. My heart still went out to him, and in my longing for him, I was distracted from my other sorrows. It had taken time, but by now my body had regained its shape, and my breasts, their previous soft curves. It was a good time to search for him.

Thus I was set on running errands for Naomi, hoping that while doing so I might encounter him on the street by chance, but there was no trace of him.

Once, when Naomi was away from home, I went to visit a neighbor, one who had dealt more kindly with me than the others, one with whom I had even struck up a friendship. He was an old man who no longer went out to work in the fields, and when I arrived he was at home by himself. I told him that I was searching for a man named Mishael and asked whether he knew of his whereabouts.

The neighbor, who was stooped by old age, tugged thoughtfully at his white beard, as wispy as that of a he-goat. "Bethlehem is a sizable town," he mused. "I know three men here who bear that name, and there may be more. What is his father's name?"

Only then did it occur to me that Mishael had not divulged his father's name. As I had not deemed it important, I had never asked for it.

"Is he Mishael the son of Yuval?" continued the neighbor. "Or might he be Mishael the son of Ehud? Or is it Mishael the son of Menahem who you are looking for?"

I had to admit that I did not know, but I told him that he was a young, handsome man.

An understanding smile slid from the neighbor's eyes into the wisps of his beard. "It could hardly be otherwise. If so, it might be either the son of Yuval or the son of Menahem, for the third one is neither young nor handsome."

He directed me to their houses, and I went to the first one at sunset, when I knew that the men of the town were coming home from the fields. I encountered him just as he entered his yard. As I came close, his startled eyes peered at me reproachfully out of a stranger's face.

The next day I went to look up the second Mishael. I confronted a young man whose beard was as profuse as his head was bald. He was comely enough, but he was shortsighted and had a slight squint in his eyes; he resembled my Mishael as an eagle resembled a horse. And his fat, flabby wife regarded me narrowly from under her headscarf. All that was left for me to do was to apologize for my intrusion into their home, and withdraw as speedily as I had come.

The day after, I consulted a female neighbor, but she was stingy with words and told me that she only knew the same three Mishaels whose names had already been mentioned to me.

Thereafter, I took to walking through the length and breadth of the town, in the hope that I might come upon the man I was yearning for, but still there was no sign of him. As if he were a stalk of grass that had been swallowed up into a meadow, leaving no traces behind.

Then I happened upon the old neighbor with the wispy beard on the street.

"Ruth, the Moabite," he said. "Another Mishael has just come to my mind. He is the son of Yotham. He is indeed young and tall and of a striking appearance, but there are some unsavory rumors about him, and you should have no dealings with such a one."

My heart missed a beat as I asked him what those rumors were.

He gave me an intent gaze. "They are of a nature of which an innocent young woman such as yourself should be ignorant."

My repeated requests for him to disclose them merely led him to shake his head from side to side. I could not make him budge from his refusal any more than I could make the sun move backward in the sky.

I besought him at least to direct me to Mishael's dwelling place. He pleaded ignorance, but his eyes told me eloquently that he was not speaking the truth.

Once back at home, I sat huddled in a corner, my elbows resting on my knees and my chin on my hands, as I weighed in my mind what I should do. The rumors about Mishael were greatly disturbing to me. They were apparently widespread if they had come to my neighbor's ears. And they were without doubt nasty if he was unwilling to repeat them.

That did not mean, though, that they were true. They could have started with some negligible deed, growing each time they were passed from mouth to ear, until they became an enormous ugly monster.

Mishael had, to be sure, proved to be unworthy of my trust. He had trifled with my love for him. But this was the manner in which many men dealt with the women who trusted them. It did not indicate that he was capable of a horrendous act, as the old neighbor had implied.

I decided not to give up my efforts to find him, and cudgeled my brain for a different way to continue my search. But spring had given way before early summer, and still nothing had come to my mind.

Then Naomi approached me with a matter in which she needed my urgent assistance. So my search for my erstwhile lover had to be temporarily abandoned.

When Osnath had finished reading about Naomi's request for Ruth's assistance, it put her in mind of Atarah's request for her own help. She knew that Eliab's mother wished for her to keep Adah company. So she rolled up the scroll and went to sit with Adah and her grandmother, and watched them fuss over the infant and listened to their incessant chatter, interrupted only briefly by the midday and evening meals, until it was time to go to sleep.

In the morning, when Osnath was about to approach the scroll room, Adah caught up with her. "I must go out," she said briefly. "I have left the infant in the charge of a maid, but I cannot entirely depend on her to do what is right for him. Pray favor me by keeping the door and your ears open; and if you hear him cry, go and see to him."

"Much as I would like to do so, I know nothing about the care of infants."

"But I trust you."

"What shall I do if he cries?"

"See if the maid has replaced the cloth that swaddles him with a clean one. Then hold him in your arms and dunk a corner of another clean cloth in the bowl of goat milk you will find on the table in my room, and push it into his little mouth and let him suck on it. Do it again and again until he calms down. This should tide him over until I come back to nurse him."

"I will do as you say," Osnath reassured her. "But where are you going?"

"To visit some neighbors."

"For what purpose?"

"I want to learn from them how to prepare unguents to soothe my little one's skin when it is sore, and lullabies to sing to him to put him to sleep when he frets at night."

"Go in peace," said Osnath.

"May the Lord be with you," replied Adah and left.

Osnath had no doubt that Adah was more highly skilled in concocting ointments than any other woman who had crossed her way. And that Hagith, who had raised so many children and seen to throngs of grandchildren in her day, could teach her more lullabies than all the women in the neighborhood put together. Hence she found Adah's subterfuge singularly unconvincing.

She began reading, but she felt that while the mysteries in the Moabite's life were unraveling themselves before her eyes, a new one was coiling itself into a knot in her own life.

Chapter Seven

naomi admitted that the food with which her well-wishers had regaled her on her arrival, and what little silver she had brought over from Sdeh Moab, had alike run out. Her pouch was as empty as if it were riddled with holes. Elimelech's fields had neither been sown nor reaped for many years. His property would have to be sold. But this was not a simple matter. Until it was accomplished, she had no means to purchase any food. To our misfortune, we were left without any sources of livelihood.

The harvest was still going on, and all that was left for us to do to sustain ourselves, she said, was for one of us to glean in the fields of others, which, by Torah law, the poor and widows and strangers were entitled to do. As she was too old to do it herself, I understood her words to mean that it fell to me to perform the humiliating task.

How had the mighty fallen! At first Naomi had not even let me perform household duties in her home, and now she was forced to hint me out into the fields of others, to collect alms there like a beggar. I never thought I would be reduced to such penury and be so debased.

But there was hunger in the offing. And having helped eat Naomi's storeroom bare, I now had an obligation to stave it off from her as well as from myself. This forced me to bury my pride deep inside me and venture out early the next morning. Fortunately, there were other needy men and women out there already, engaged in the work on which I was about to embark; and this made it easier for me to resign myself to my poverty. I stepped into one of the fields, where I walked behind the reapers, and bent down and gathered up into my bag all they had left on the ground.

Later in the day, as I was crouching to collect some ears of wheat, I felt a commotion in my vicinity. I lifted my eyes bit by bit to see a pair of big shoes with a slight upward turn at the toes, to bare, dark-haired legs and thighs corded with muscles, and from there to the obligatory fringe at the edges of a well-crafted light-brown garment.

In my embarrassment, I did not dare lift my eyes any farther than that. For I had no doubt that the man clad in this apparel was the owner of the fields, and I was deeply embarrassed.

I heard him greet his workmen in a deep voice, saying: "The Lord be with you."

They replied, "The Lord bless you."

I could not remain with my eyes glued to his fringe forever, so I raised them hesitantly to gain a better view of him. I perceived that he was head and shoulders taller than most men and that he had piercing dark eyes, to match his dark hair and skin. There was something bearlike about his massive shoulders and arms, which made me feel as small as a grasshopper before him.

Upon reading these lines, Osnath could not keep herself from smiling at the uncanny resemblance between Eliab and his ancestor. She wondered how Boaz's powerful build had passed over two generations to emerge anew in his eldest great-grandson.

His gaze alit on me, but brushed me only briefly. "Who is this girl?" he asked the man in charge of his reapers.

I thought no one knew who I was, but the retainer must have made some inquiries, for he answered, "She is a Moabite, who has come back with Naomi, the widow of Elimelech, from Moab. She has been on her feet with hardly a moment's rest from daybreak till now."

My story had evidently come to the ears of the fields' owner before, for there was a light of recollection in his eyes as he ran them over me again. Then he turned to me. "Hear me, young woman. I am Boaz, a kinsman of your husband's, hence of yours. You are welcome to my land. Don't go any farther afield, but stay here, close to my maids. I will see to it that my men do not molest you. If you are tired, sit in the shade of a tree and rest. And if you are thirsty, drink from the jars the servants have filled."

I now recalled Naomi telling me of this kinsman of ours, named Boaz, and that by law he had an obligation to marry me, in order to sire a son to perpetuate my dead husband's name. She had also told me that he was a widower, a man of high standing and noble descent, who could trace the origin of his family back to Judah, the father of his tribe. As I now perceived, he had a commanding bearing, which, together with his sizable fields, spoke of the riches he possessed. Thus, it was even more odious to me than before that I was so destitute as to be forced to collect remnants in his fields.

The color flamed in my cheeks, as in my hair. I bowed to him and said humbly, as befitted my lowly position, "Why are you so kind as to take notice of me, sir, when I am only a poor woman and a foreigner?"

"I have been told of all you have done for your mother-in-law, how you left your father and mother and your homeland," he explained gently, though his eyes remained inscrutable, "and how brave you have been in coming to live amid a people that was unknown to you. May the God of Israel, under whose wings you have come to take refuge, reward your deed and give you all you deserve."

Rumor had slightly misled Boaz, for it was my father who had left me, together with the land of the living, long ago. But his words attested to his goodwill.

"Indeed, you have eased my mind by speaking so kindly to me," I said with my head still bent before him, though my mind was far from easy.

Shamefacedly, I resumed my work, but when mealtime came, Boaz said to me, "Sit here and eat with us."

So I sat next to the reapers, who had formed a circle around a gray cloth that was spread on the ground, on which food was laid out. Boaz broke bread off the loaf for me, and I dipped it in a bowl of sour wine that stood before us, and I ate all I wanted and still had some left over.

As the day wore on and the bag in which I had collected barley was still only half full, I heard Boaz order his men in a low voice to pull out some barley from the bundles they had tied, as if it had fallen out unintentionally, and leave it on the ground for me to take up. At his words, the blood once again flooded my cheeks, which came to be suffused with as pink a color as the setting sun, as it was at that moment.

Having no other choice, I collected barley until the darkness of the evening made it impossible, and when I beat out what I had taken up, it came to about a bushel. I brought it home to my mother-in-law and told her of all that had come to pass that day.

When I mentioned the name of the man in whose fields I had been, Naomi reiterated that he was related and obligated to us; then she added with a voice of satisfaction, "He has a reputation for generosity. I'd had a mind to send you to his fields, but feared that you would find it shameful. Blessed be the Lord, who has kept faith with the living and the dead by directing you there anyway, for all will be bright for us now."

For a while, though, it seemed that she had erred in her prediction.

At Naomi's behest, I returned to Boaz's fields day after day. He always showed me the courtesy owed to a kinswoman by summoning me to partake of food with him at noontime. At those times he would speak inviting words to me and spread a cloth on the ground at his side for me to sit on, and give me bread to eat and grape juice to drink.

Yet, although he dealt kindly with me, he was not smitten with me and his heart did not warm toward me. I was merely a poor relative, whose welfare had been laid at his door. He bestowed on me the charity due to me, and no more.

As for me, since my heart was given to another, the power that radiated from Boaz led me to stand in awe of him, but did not lead me to fall under his spell.

Because my kinsman was a widower, we were bound by a different bond: that of a common thread of sorrow for our deceased ones, with whom our souls had been linked. So in spite of himself, as it seemed to me, Boaz fell into the habit of talking to me at length. He told me of his wife, who had perished in childbirth, and the infant, who was to be his firstborn son, with her. I reciprocated by telling him of the lingering, debilitating disease of my husband, which made his body deteriorate slowly, from which he did not recover. We shared our sorrow, and occasionally our tears, and so we brought comfort to each other. But I did not reveal to Boaz that the loss of my husband was not the only sorrow tugging at my heart.

At that time the barley harvest was near completion, and the wheat harvest was in full swing. One day, as I collected ripe ears of wheat in the fields, the girls who worked at my side warned me that I had overstepped the boundaries of the property belonging to Boaz and was in his neighbor's field. Its owner, they said, might not take kindly to my invasion of his land without permission.

I had been at the end of my hope of finding the one for whom my soul craved; I had begun to resign myself to my lot, that of making a life for myself without him. But just as I was about to step back into Boaz's domain, I caught a glimpse of his familiar figure as he walked by.

Oddly, my strenuous search for him had not borne fruit, yet now he appeared before my eyes of his own accord. My heart leaped. But I could not well run after him in plain sight of Boaz's maids, and before long he faded into the distance.

Later, when the girls' eyes were not on me, I slipped away and began roaming Mishael's land. When I spotted him walking toward me, it was as if I were being carried into his open arms on the wings of my love. The instant he touched me, my desire for him, which had been dormant inside me for so long, welled up in me and sprang to life, as did his for me.

"Ruth," he exclaimed, "are you truly here? I can hardly believe it. All this time my body has been aching sorely for yours."

I withheld from him that I had conceived his child and lost it, a tale I was not sure it would cause him joy to hear. "Take me to your home, then," I said instead, "and let us renew our love."

But he could not wait that long.

His threshing floor, which had tucked away at its corner a secluded shed for the storing of ploughshares, stood close by. Wasting no time on useless words, he pulled me into it and pushed me down. Neither of us spoke anymore, and soon we were rolling on the ground together.

There was no need to tell Naomi what had come to pass. She recognized the signs on me: my burning cheeks and shining eyes, and the paucity of the barley I had collected.

Still, as we met in the fields during the following days, I sensed that in some subtle way my lover had changed. He took me with the same passion as he had shown me before, but in all else he seemed to be remote, as if the desert between Moab and the land of Israel still separated us from each other. He was stingy with words, as if each were worth its weight in gold. And when I requested that he take me to his home, he concocted various excuses to refrain from doing so. Still, as if seized by a demon, a demon of love, I came back to him day after day.

Naomi watched, and sighed in disapproval, but her groans had not the power to recall me to the path of righteousness. She knew well that if she rebuked me, it would have as much effect as talking to the trees and the stones. So she kept her inevitable thoughts to herself.

Eventually these thoughts, confined deeply inside her, were like a bird's egg that hatched a chick: they led her to devise a devious plan designed to detach me from my lover, and establish me in life in the manner that she saw fit, at one and the same time.

One day, as she was provoked by what she considered my disgraceful conduct, she said to me, "My daughter, unless you let go of that loathsome man, your life will be riddled with disappointments as numerous as the holes in a copper sieve. I want to see you happily settled, so this is what you must do:

"It has come to my ears that tonight our kinsman, Boaz, is winnowing barley at his threshing floor and taking stock of his crop. As this work continues until after nightfall, he is apt to remain in his fields overnight. Wash and anoint yourself with scented oils and perfumes. Put on your cloak over your head and go down to the threshing floor, but do not make yourself known to anyone.

"When he settles down to sleep, turn down the covering and lie at his feet. When he discovers you there, demand his protection. He will tell you what to do."

Her intention was not difficult to understand. So far, I had made no headway with Boaz. Although as my husband's kinsman he should have offered to take me for his wife, he had shown no willingness to do so. Nor had I given him any reason to believe that I wished for it. Naomi's notion was that if I lay close to him that night and showed him subservience, this would arouse him to lie with me. Thereafter, he would have a double obligation toward me: both as a kinsman and as one who had taken advantage of my presumed innocence.

I spent the day in uncertainty. I had no wish to humiliate myself before Boaz more than I had done already. Yet I had to face the truth about Mishael: during our months of separation, his partiality for me had waned like heat in winter. Despite his initial words of welcome to me, thereafter his deeds of passion had never been accompanied by loving words. I feared that attempting to entice him into love for me was as futile as storing flour in the sieve that Naomi had mentioned.

Above all else, I knew that it was my responsibility to provide not only for myself but also for her, to sustain her in her old age. I had to find a husband for her sake no less than for mine. So in the end, I could not but see the wisdom of her plan.

At dusk, before I went to Boaz, I bathed in a tub Naomi had prepared for me, and scrubbed myself briskly with soap until my skin shone pink. Then I dried and covered myself with oil scented with myrtle and laurel and citron leaves, until my body was fragrant with it. I took up the ivory comb Naomi had laid out for me. I combed my curls to a sheen. Then I slipped into a new dress, blue like a cloudless sky, which unbeknownst to me she had sewn up in advance, in secret preparation for that night.

She had purposely cut it so that it fitted my form more tightly than was seemly, making my breasts protrude in an uncouth manner. She had done so for a clear goal, and I put on the dress and smoothed it out around my breasts as her eyes spoke her hope that it would serve that purpose well.

Naomi tied a sash around my waist, one she had been diligently embroidering for weeks, only she had never told me that it was meant for me. Although, in the dark of night, Boaz would hardly be able to discern its colors, she had designed it so that it would convey a message to him. As she now told me, she had overlaid it with a pattern of red and yellow and violet to signify that I was as fresh as the wildflowers of those same colors that covered the pastures in the spring, and that Boaz would do well to pluck me.

Then, with a nudge from Naomi's elbow and a suggestive wink of her eye, and what I was sure was her smile of encouragement on my back, I went out to the fields. I waited until the last trace of light had been drained by the night, then came down to Boaz's threshing floor. Once there, I did exactly as she had instructed me.

After Boaz had eaten and drunk, he seemed to feel at peace with himself and went to lie down for the night. As Naomi had expected, he chose a spot that lay at some distance from his workingmen and women, at the far end of the field, shielded from their view also by a heap of hay. I contrived to remain hidden from his sight, seated behind some bushes, until I was sure that he had fallen asleep. Then I approached on the tips of my toes, turned back the covering over his feet, and lay down next to it.

I let my dress slide off partway to bare that which should have been covered, but I did not alert him to my presence. At about midnight a rustling sound I made by shifting my body disturbed his sleep. He turned over, and to his amazement he found me lying at his feet. He stared at me, the darkness of his eyes blending with the darkness around us. His vision was blurred from sleep, and he did not immediately recognize me.

"Who are you?" he whispered.

"I am Ruth," I murmured back.

The question he did not voice, of what my request of him was, hung heavy in the air. The answer gathered in my mouth, yet it took time before I gained the strength to bring it forth from my lips.

At length, I spoke the words that served Naomi's desire that, I knew, must also be mine: "Now, sir, spread the mantle of your protection over me, for you are my next of kin."

I held my breath for his reply, but he lay so still that I wondered whether he had heard me or had slept through my petition. I peeked at him, and in the dark his face was like a sealed scroll, his thoughts impossible to decipher.

I waited.

His words were long in coming, but at length he murmured, "You have done well, Ruth, to turn to me rather than to any young man, rich or poor. Set your mind at rest. If I am your next of kin, I will do what I am required to do by law and custom. But are you sure that it is so? I believe there is one even more closely related to you through your husband than I am."

When I asked for his name, he said on a jarring note that he would call him the Unnamed for the time being.

I felt my heart pound inside me like a hammer, and my thoughts chased and overtook each other rapidly. For I'd had no notion that my lover was related to my husband by ties of kinship. No wonder that, as I had perceived from the outset, he resembled him. It irked me that it had not occurred to me at the time that, being from Bethlehem, he might be a kinsman of his.

But I did not intimate by as much as a twitch of my lips that I had an inkling of who the Unnamed was.

"I will approach him and apprise him of his family ties with you. If he is willing to honor his obligation to you as your closest kinsman, well and good; but if he is not willing, I will do so. I swear it. Now lie down until morning and then I will deal with this."

Boaz's words were kind, but the tone of his voice was guarded, and I did not draw comfort from it. Clearly, he had no confidence in his ability to persuade Mishael to take me for his wife, nor was he elated at the prospect of having me foisted onto himself.

As I was about to turn from him in disappointment, suddenly, without prior warning, he reached down to me and gathered me into his arms. Naomi's sly intention notwithstanding, I knew that it behooved me to stave him off.

During the past weeks, I had thought that I was impermeable to his manly allure. Only now did I realize that it had been far otherwise. Without my being aware of it, lust for him had been simmering inside me; and now I felt it suddenly erupt, making me yield to his. I inhaled the scent of his large body and was dizzy with his closeness to me. I clung to him, felt his heat in the darkness inside me, then tenderness, then intensity of pleasure melting into shudders, then the whole over again.

I was the first to speak. "Do not let what we have done this night sway your decision, sir," I felt myself compelled to say.

"You may be in good cheer," he reassured me, caressing my cheek. "All will be as it should."

Then I lay facedown, snatching brief spells of sleep, while he slept heavily. But we both stirred at the first bluish light that heralds the dawn. He kissed my curls, still damp with the dew of the night, and my lips, which opened for his kiss.

Boaz urged me to leave before the light made it possible for one man to recognize another, so no one would be aware of my having shared his cover that night. When I arose, my dress was crumpled, but I shook it out and made it look presentable. He picked out the stray stalks of straw that had lodged in my hair, and straightened out its tangles by combing it with his fingers.

Before he sent me off, he gestured for me to hold out my cloak, and he put six measures of the barley stocked up nearby in it, and lifted it on my back and spoke no more. I slipped away and was back at Naomi's house even before the night's chill had dispersed and before the dew had dried on the ground.

She was awake already, and when she saw me she asked, "How did it go with you, my daughter?"

I told her all that the man had said and done to me. I concluded by saying, "He would not let me come home to you with my hands empty," and turned over to her the offering he had sent.

Naomi's eyes sparkled with joy, and spoke her understanding, and bestowed her wordless blessing on the acts we had performed. Then she took hold of the barley and said confidently, "Wait, my daughter, until you see what will come of it. He will not rest until he has settled the matter."

In spite of my night of lust with Boaz, my love for Mishael had not waned. And I nourished a vague, senseless hope that somehow Boaz, who had no urge to wed me himself, would be able to convince this lover-kinsman of mine to accept me, as was incumbent on him to do.

Everything was shrouded in doubt. Hence, as there was little for me to do, I stood most of that day peering out of my window, wondering what lay ahead.

At that point, Osnath, too, went to peer out of the window. For, little by little, the baby's whimpers had penetrated her consciousness. When she leaned out, she could hear that they had turned into wails.

She hastily rolled up the scroll and rushed into Adah's room. There she spent the rest of the day feeding Eliab's son his goat milk, thinking fondly of how much he resembled his father in the darkness of his eyes and hair and skin, and rocking him in her arms whenever he fretted. She even sang scraps of half-forgotten lullabies to him, dug out from the storeroom of her childhood memories.

The sun advanced steadily in the sky. It rose to its midpoint, then began its descent, then hid behind the hills, painting the clouds above it a grayish pink, and still Adah was nowhere in sight.

It was only after dusk came in that Adah slipped in as well. She took the child from Osnath's arms, but offered no apologies for keeping her occupied with him for the better part of the day.

Thereafter, Adah put Osnath in charge of her son day after day, until the girl became quite proficient in caring for him. This, Osnath hoped, would stand her in good stead when her own children came along. But each evening, Osnath left Adah's room with her eyebrows creased in worry.

There was only a little time left over for reading. It had to be done by the light of oil lamps, a feat that strained Osnath's eyes. Progress was slow, yet she did not let off entirely; she continued following Ruth's life, if only for a short spell each night.

Chapter Eight

It was only on the morning after that Boaz came to Naomi's house to apprise us of his intention: he would bring up the matter with the relative in the presence of the town elders, who gathered at the town gates every day.

Then he immediately made his way there, unaware (as I thought) that he was about to intercede with Mishael not only in order to be spared the necessity of taking me for his wife, but also on behalf of the furtive longing in my heart.

All now depended on the outcome of Boaz's mission. My life hung in the balance, and I awaited his return in apprehension, which I took pains to mask by a show of keeping busy with household tasks. When there was nothing left to do, I sat with my knees trembling and my face resting on my arms on the table, willing Boaz to make haste, straining to hear his approach.

As I heard the door creak open and his hasty steps across the stone floor, I rose to meet him, my face wreathed in a smile of gratitude. Then I raised an inquiring eyebrow at him, but his face revealed nothing.

I had not the courage to urge him to relay what had come to pass, but as he saw my trepidation, he did so without delay. "When I arrived at the town gates," he began, "the elders had assembled already, as is their custom. At my request, they summoned your kinsman, he who is known as Ploni Almoni, the Unnamed, to appear before them.

"When he came, I called him and said, 'Here, come and sit down.'

"Reluctantly, he took his place opposite me. Then, as befitted both his and my station, I asked the ten highest ranking of the elders to sit there with us, and they did so.

"I said to the Unnamed, 'You will remember the strip of field that belonged to our relative Elimelech. Naomi has returned from the Moabite country and is selling it. I promised to raise the matter with you, to ask you, in the presence of the elders of our people, to acquire it. If you are going to do your duty as next of kin and redeem this parcel of land, then do it, but if not, tell me so I shall know, for I am the closest relative after you.'

"'I will fulfill my obligation,' your next of kin responded."

As I heard Boaz's account, I was jubilant, though I did my best to hide my joy.

Then Boaz continued: "Once the kinsman had spoken, I added, 'Be aware that on the day on which you become the owner of Naomi's fields, you also acquire Ruth the Moabite, the widow of Naomi's son Mahlon, so as to perpetuate the dead man's name. You will erect a memorial for him by begetting a son who will be known as his, and who will inherit his property, as is our law and custom.'

"Thereupon the kinsman said with a sharp edge to his voice, 'I am unable to act in this manner, for I would risk losing my own patrimony. You must take over my duty and lay claim to Elimelech's inheritance yourself.'

"So I declared to the elders and all the people that had gathered at the gates, 'You are witnesses today that I am acquiring from Naomi all that belonged to her husband, Elimelech, and all that belonged to Mahlon and Chilion; and further that I am also about to take Ruth the Moabite, wife of Mahlon, to perpetuate the name of the deceased, so that it may not be obliterated in Israel.'

"When I finished my speech, the elders nodded and a murmur of approval rose from all those gathered around us."

As Boaz's tale progressed, the smile with which I had welcomed him, and my initial jubilation alike, faded. I clenched my hands so hard over each other that they nearly broke each other's knuckles. But I let the rest of his account wash over me until it reached its end.

It was as if I did not only hear it but tasted it as well, and it was like bitter poison in my mouth. Afterward I still waited, hoping against hope that there was more to come, but there was nothing.

Only Boaz's eyes continued speaking. They looked into mine, voicing a mute question. Trying to ascertain how deeply I had been hurt by Mishael's refusal to take me for his wife.

But I did not want my eyes to supply the answer, and I hid them, together with the rest of my face, in my hands. My shoulders sagged and I locked my teeth to imprison my tongue, straining to keep myself from voicing my anguish.

On top of my shaming humiliation at Mishael's hand, there was something else that perturbed me. It now dawned on me that I had underestimated Boaz. Contrary to what I had previously believed, he had a fair notion of my grief and what it stemmed from. I could not imagine how he had come by this knowledge, but there was no doubt in my mind that he possessed it.

He raised his hand to touch my face, but I stepped back from him and it fell to his side. "Forgive me," he apologized, as if he, and not Mishael, had been the one to harm me. "I did not mean to give offense."

He did not plague me with an interrogation he knew I would be loath to undergo, and I cherished his thoughtful reticence more than anything else he had done for me.

Still, unable to brave my disappointment any longer, I wanted to storm out of the room so as to be alone with my pain.

Once I reached the doorway, though, I realized that by stalking out of Boaz's presence like an unruly child, I would be dealing with him disgracefully. I composed myself and came back. I expected him to speak to me tersely, but it was not so.

As I stood before him, my mouth twisted into the semblance of an apologetic smile, he stepped forward and took my hair into both his hands and tied it into a knot and said: "The rays of the sun are dancing in myriad dots of light in your shining red hair."

It was the first time he had spoken tender words to me. I felt moved and chastened at one and the same time; and the tears veiling my eyes, which I had been holding back, gushed forth from me. He enfolded me in his arms in a hug, as awkward as that of a bear, and Naomi slipped away through the back door.

He took hold of a fold of his garment and dried my tears with it, and murmured, "Take heart, Ruth, for he is a brutish man of no merit. He is not deserving of even one of the tears from your lovely blue eyes."

❧

I knew Boaz's words to be true, and that I would do well not to waste one further breath on Mishael. Yet, no matter how much I had suffered at his hands, he still held my heart captive, and even then I would not give up. I could not keep from puzzling about him. For his conduct toward me had been not only reprehensible, but incomprehensible.

There was no doubt in my mind that he had been keen on me in Sdeh Moab, as evident from the words of love he had constantly poured into my ears, before he had suddenly decided to leave. Yet, when he first encountered me in his fields in Bethlehem, his manhood welcomed me, but not his soul. My presence in his town, my very existence, had been tiresome to him. And now he had given final proof of this before the elders.

But why? Why had he decided to abandon me back in Sdeh Moab, and what had happened in the space of the months in which we had been apart that had further estranged him from me?

Somewhere in the deepest recesses of my soul, I nursed the unreasonable hope that if only I could understand this — his fateful words to the elders notwithstanding — he would still take me for his wife. Surely there could be no harm in seeking an explanation from him, and nothing more.

Thus, in spite of myself, my love for him led me to seek him out. The next day I went out to Boaz's fields, and from there, I once again made my way to Mishael's land, as I had done many times before. Only, as soon as I crossed its border, I also crossed the borderline of my sanity.

When I saw him, my desire overwhelmed my reticence and quickly eroded my previous resolution of confining him to an account of what had transpired before the elders. I let him lead me, wordlessly, to his shed and make me lie down next to him. As I lay on the ground facing him, I spoke hot words to him, trying to love him back into love for me. But they were like drops of water spilled into the Great Sea: they left no mark.

I heard more words coming out of my mouth, as if of their own volition. "Spin strings of sunshine for me, Mishael. Fill my life with illusions. Make me believe that you love me, that happiness beckons to us from the horizon."

Yet still he refrained from speech. Only his hands roving over me, and his manhood against my thigh, spoke the tongue of passion.

Suddenly I was seized by a new compulsion. The demon that had previously driven me to him had turned the other way and made me halt his mouth as it approached my breasts. Keeping his face at bay from me with both hands, I looked at him expectantly.

This gave him pause. His hands and face withdrew from me, and his lips pressed into a thin line. "I will not play rough-and-tumble with you anymore, but speak frankly. Though I delight in your body, Ruth, my heart is given to another. My wife."

It was the first I had ever heard of his having a wife, and it was a while before I could overcome my agony. "How is it that you never told me of her before?" I managed to ask.

He shrugged.

He had treated me as if I were nothing but a menial maid, whom he had used out of sheer boredom and discarded when he had no further use for her. I cringed before him, but I knew that it would be pointless to remonstrate with him. With his ominous words still ringing in my ears, I rose from his side. I turned my back to him and left him lying on the ground. Before he could get himself to his feet, I walked out of his shed, out of his sight, out of his life.

Yet love was not something that could be extinguished at will like a candle at nighttime, so my heart was still divided. Only later did I realize that, through his vile deeds and words and shrugs, Mishael had redeemed me from my bondage to him and set me free.

❧

Although Boaz had pledged himself before the elders to take me, he made no move to honor his promise. I sat at home with Naomi, deserted as if I were his widow before I had even become his wife.

When two weeks had passed and still he did not come to claim me, Naomi became profoundly worried. She knew Boaz to be a man who never failed to honor his obligations, and why he should not do so this time was unfathomable to her. She urged me to go out into his fields under some pretext, in order to discover what was holding him back.

I hesitated. If Boaz did not want me, I had no intention of forcing myself upon him. Besides, as the barley and wheat harvests were both over, and the unrelenting summer sun all but set the earth on fire, I no longer gleaned in his fields. So I could think of no excuse for visiting them.

But Naomi said that the threshing of the wheat had not been completed, so I could claim that I had come to collect whatever the threshers would leave behind on the threshing floor. As she was pressing me hard, I did as she bid me. I went to Boaz's property and was just in time to share his midday meal.

The moment he saw me approaching, he waved me to his side and made me sit down. He broke off bread for me, and this time he dunked it into olive oil before he gave it to me to eat.

Then he handed me a cup. When I took hold of it, he said, "Your cup is empty, Ruth. Let me fill it for you."

"It has been so for a long time," I retorted with a sad smile.

The meaning of my words was not lost on him, as was evident from his response, "I will make it flow over," saying which he took the jug of grape juice that stood close by and filled my cup and more, until it spilled over the rim. As he did, he smiled into my eyes. His smile seemed to contain a promise, and having pushed Mishael to the back of my mind, I smiled my own promise back at him.

All this time we were sitting amid his workingmen and -women. So far, I had paid them only scant attention. But now I saw that their eyes were on us, particularly one pair of eyes.

They were black and graced the face of a pretty girl whose hair was plaited into one thick tress, as black as a raven to match her eyes. These seemed to shoot arrows of fire, of passion or jealousy — I was not sure which — at him.

I sat motionless, struck dumb by my own stupidity. The young woman had been there before, but she had merely been one of many, and only now did my memory single her out from among them. I must have been as blind as a bat at daytime to have missed the greedy looks, alluding to the way of a man with a woman, that I now saw passing back and forth between her and Boaz.

Although I had no right to it, I felt jealousy rising like bile into my mouth. I averted my eyes from the unpleasant spectacle and finished my meal. Then I thanked my host, and having forgotten the pretext for my visit — to collect grains from the threshing floor — I rose to leave as if a snake had bitten my heel.

Boaz rose to accompany me, but I walked at his side with my lips pursed.

At first he looked at me mildly, but as I continued to sulk, the air came to be brittle with his indignation. "You can hardly reprove me when you have been straying down a sinful path yourself, never shunning the arms of your ignoble lover."

I halted, and my astonished eyes flew to his. For although Boaz had left me in no doubt that he knew of my attachment to Mishael, I had not suspected that he had also been aware of my misdeeds with him.

He glared at me long and hard, with a look that was as icy as the frost on the ground on a cold winter night. When he saw the question in my eyes, he said, "It was not necessary for me to practice divination. It did not escape my attention that you often crossed over to his domain and that considerable time elapsed before you came back, and did so even on the day after I convened with him and the elders.

"I would have thought that after he had declined to take you for his wife, and I had promised to take you for mine, you would have let off seeing him. But your devotion for him is evidently boundless. It is for that reason that I have not visited you to make arrangements for our betrothal and wedding. On this last occasion, two weeks ago, your disheveled dress and hair and the dejection in your eyes told their own tale. He must have lain with you before he apprised you of his wife."

"In this, at least, you are mistaken," I said hotly.

He smiled in contemptuous disbelief.

This smile, more than his words, left me hoping that the earth would open its mouth and swallow me into its depths. At last, I gained enough courage to reply wildly, "You resemble him, sir. What you said before about causing my cup to flow over led me to believe that you had a kindness for me. Yet now it transpires that it is otherwise."

The coldness of his scorn was replaced by the heat of his wrath. He rounded on me and gave me a scalding glance. "You condemn me unjustly. I have been a widower for three years. Surely you cannot have expected me to live in abstinence in anticipation of your appearance."

"Not one word of condemnation has crossed my lips," I said miserably, my shoulders stiff with hurt. "But you cannot hold the stick on both ends. Since you already have a woman, you cannot wish for me as your wife. Nor do I pine for you as my husband."

Far from putting him off, these words were like oil poured onto a bonfire. He flew into an even stronger rage. He had been holding a sprig of myrtle in his hand, and now he poured out his wrath on it. He ripped off its leaves and tore them to shreds. Then his fingers tightened around it, and he broke it into little pieces, which he scattered about him.

Having destroyed the innocent little branch, he grabbed both my arms in his large hands, and knives seemed to be gleaming in his eyes. "A few weeks ago, you seduced me and asked me in utter humility to take you for my wife. It was at your request that I went to speak to the elders. I committed myself to make you my own, in plain sight of all of Israel. Even if you have no desire for it, you are now pledged to me. There is no way back."

I felt his fingers, like tongs of iron, on my arms; on my soul. "Yet you have not spoken the words that would irrevocably have betrothed me to you in front of two witnesses, as my husband had done before he wed me," I said. "So nothing has been firmly decided. If I had a father, he would have the right to give me to you against my will. But as I have not, there is no one to force me into your house and your bed."

Abruptly, he released me. "Except hunger," he said in disdain. I spun away from him, and he turned on his heels and retraced his steps. And he left me with no doubt as to the arms in which he would be spending the night.

Chapter Nine

Thereafter I heard nothing of Boaz for several weeks. All I could do was to toss and turn in my bed in disappointment, until the sheet underneath me was as crumpled as Naomi's reproachful face.

During those weeks, Naomi and I ate our way through the grain I had collected in Boaz's fields. In the same measure as the grain diminished, so did the grudge she held against me increase. When the produce dwindled to almost nothing, she began openly to blame me for my conduct toward Boaz. Not with words, for that was not her way, but with a surly look on her face that spoke louder than the blowing of trumpets. Her look indicated that, because of my callousness, famine was staring us in the face again.

While she was in ever deeper worry about hunger, I was increasingly disconcerted about Boaz. I could not skirt the fact that whatever warmth toward me he might have harbored before had cooled. It could not have been otherwise, when, after he had pledged himself to wed me, he had seen me coming back, disheveled and seemingly uncouth, from my previous lover as if I were a common whore. He had merely sneered at my assertion that nothing had happened between Mishael and me on that day.

There was no way in which I could recapture Boaz's regard for me. The cleft that had opened between us robbed me of sleep at nighttime. And Naomi's grumpy face did not lift my spirits during the day.

I all but despaired of winning Boaz's heart. Yet, early one morning, when the days had cooled and the harvest of the grain had given way to the ingathering of the last grapes, a messenger arrived. The youngster bore a little scroll with a missive from him, and these were its words:

> Hear me, my loved one.
> You are red-haired and fair.
> As a wild goat in the desert
> yearns for a spring of water,
> so does my body yearn for you.
> Abandon him, who is unworthy of you,
> and give your love to me alone.
> So speaks the man to whom you are pledged.

Naomi came in at that very moment, so I hid it in the sleeve of my dress. But the words were as sweet as ripe dates to my palate. They indicated that Boaz was now willing to overlook my previous infidelity. I treasured the beauty of his words no less than their sincerity, and I vowed to keep the little scroll on which they were recorded all the days of my life.

When later I pondered Boaz's words in solitude, I knew that my body, too, had yearned for him. I had relived the lust we had experienced together that night at the threshing floor many times over. I had felt it swelling inside me, surging to greater heights from one lonely night to another. I saw no reason to be ashamed of it, so I sat down and composed a poem of my own:

> Hear me, my lover.
> You are dark and handsome and exalted.
> Bring me to your chamber.
> Let our couch be padded with our passion
> and let us rejoice in each other.
> So speaks the woman who is pledged to you.

I had no silver to pay a messenger to dispatch my poem. But Naomi, who was well regarded in the neighborhood, found a young boy who delivered it to Boaz without recompense.

On that same day, at twilight, he came to Naomi's house to take me to his.

Boaz seemed to be aware of Naomi's fear of approaching hunger, for he bore with him a cake of barley meal and crushed dates, which his maids had baked expressly for her, as a gift. She devoured it with her eyes before, quite devoid of shame, she began to devour it with her hungry mouth in his presence. While she ate, he did not look at me, but instead looked at her. An unspoken message passed between them, after which she nodded her permission. And so also on the following days.

Upon reaching Boaz's house, he fed me well at his table, before leading me to feast in his bed. He said only, "My blood courses in my veins at your touch." I said nothing at all, and before long our blood was coursing together.

Yet, on the next morning, when I returned to Naomi's house, I realized that my blood had been racing ahead of my heart. Although my body was in raptures for being conquered by Boaz, my soul was still a fortress to which he had laid siege, but which he was slow to storm, doing it only piecemeal.

❧

When we came to his house the next evening and sat down to the evening meal, we talked of a matter that still lay heavy between us: Mishael.

"You said that he was unworthy of me," I reminded him. "Yet he is Naomi's and my husband's next of kin. And since you are most nearly related to them after him, sir, he must be your relative as well."

While he ate his succulent roast of lamb, Boaz regarded me pensively. "Although we are bound by blood, happily our kinship is remote."

This seemed a good opportunity to obtain an answer to the question that had been nagging at me for so long. "In what way is he unworthy?"

Boaz's face broke into a grim smile. "Mishael is not lowborn. His family is of high standing and well thought of in Bethlehem. But honesty and generosity are traits that have not been passed down to him."

This answer seemed to me overly evasive, and I prompted Boaz to continue.

"'A good name is preferable to good oil,'" he recited. "So says the proverb and rightly so. Yet he has forsaken his name, and his reputation has been torn to shreds."

I surmised that Boaz believed Mishael to be nothing but a fiendish scoundrel. "How has it come about?" I queried.

"I will tell you in good time."

"Now is a good time."

"Not in my eyes. The opportune moment is yet to come; it is not too far removed, I hope."

"How is it that you know so much about him?"

He laughed, regretfully, as I thought. "How could I not, when he is not merely my kinsman but also my closest neighbor?" He pointed with his finger out the window, toward a nearby house, which, because of the darkness outside, was not clearly visible.

If ever I became Boaz's wife (which was by no means sure as yet), I would be living close to my onetime lover, and I did not cherish the prospect. But I decided not to dwell on this just then, as I continued to prod. "Why did you call him the Unnamed, when surely you must have known his name since childhood?"

"It came to my ears that when he sojourned in Sdeh Moab, he insisted on being called so, rather than by his name, and for a good reason. When he returned here, the rumor of this spread, and 'the Unnamed' came to be a derogatory epitaph for him. I thought it suited him well, so I used it also."

By now, there was no question in my mind but that Mishael

must have perpetrated some foul deed too dreadful to contemplate, although I did not know what it was.

This gave rise to my anger, not toward Mishael but toward Boaz. Knowing Mishael for an evil man, Boaz had nevertheless called upon him, before the elders, to acquire me as his wife. I found this intolerable. "If he is as contemptible as you make him out to be, how could you have given me up to his mercy?" I berated Boaz.

A cloud crossed his face. "Since he is your nearest relative, I was bound by law and custom to give him precedence. But it was merely a show of honoring the custom for the benefit of the elders. I was determined to thwart any purpose he may have had of marrying you. So I met him beforehand to instruct him in what he was to say before the elders.

"At first, he was not inclined to lend an ear to me and turned to leave. But I called him by his name and the name of his father, voicing his brother's name as well, hurling those names at his back like arrows, which stung him."

It was unfathomable to me why his father's and his brother's names should be like arrows in Mishael's back, but before I had time to ponder this, Boaz continued, "As he turned back to face me, I spewed out my scorn at him. I declared you to be my woman and that I would no longer let him defile you. I made it plain to him that I would not suffer him to take possession of Elimelech's property, let alone of you.

"I ordered him to pretend that he was willing to take charge of the patrimony. But of course he could not, unless he received you into his house as well. So I threatened that if he as much as lifted one finger in front of the elders to indicate his willingness to take you, and despite the scandal it would cause for our family, I would bring forth evidence . . ." Here he let his words trail off.

"At that," he continued after a while, "Mishael made a threatening motion, bringing his right hand to his left thigh as if he were about to draw a nonexistent sword from its hilt there. But he recognized the necessity of doing my bidding. He croaked some indistinguishable reply in a queer voice and grudgingly nodded his acquiescence."

I was both dumbfounded and appeased. So, at Boaz's behest, Mishael had dissembled. All that had transpired before the elders had been feigned, except for Boaz's expressed aim to wed me, which, as I now believed, had been genuine.

Would Mishael have agreed to have me had Boaz not threatened him? Probably not. But I felt reassured to the depth of my soul in the knowledge that Boaz had not granted him that opportunity.

Boaz did not disclose the nature of the evidence at his disposal, which he had threatened to lay before the elders. Equally, he did not remove the shroud of mist from Mishael's iniquity until much later, by which time my love for this infamous man had become but a dim memory, erased by the rhythm of passing time and the rising tide of my love for Boaz.

When once I asked Boaz why he had kept Mishael's wrongdoing from me for so long, he replied, "Because I wanted you to repudiate him in your heart before you rejected him in your mind," and so it was.

⁂

There was another matter, as tangible as a wall, still separating us from each other: the black-haired girl with the fierce look in her eyes, who had shared Boaz's bed before me.

One night, a few weeks later, as we lay in his bed, I broached this topic and asked, "Since she was your woman, why did she not become your wife?"

He smiled ruefully. "The truth is that she was not the only one. There were others, too, and until you came along, I hesitated, not even sure that I wanted any one of them."

"Are you also vacillating about me?"

"I did when I first saw you, but no longer. Had you not delayed us with your escapades to your previous lover, we could have been married twice over by now."

"I cannot imagine why you should wish to confer on me the distinction of making me your wife. Is it merely your obligation toward me and the commitment you have made before the elders?"

He shook his head. "Unless I truly wanted you, I would have found a way to eschew my obligation, and I would not have made any commitment before the elders."

Boaz was a man of formidable stature and wealth, and he had all the maids working in his fields and many other well-shaped girls of well-to-do families in the town at his disposal. And why his fancy should have, albeit belatedly, alit on me was unfathomable.

"Why have you chosen me from among the many, and why have I found favor in your eyes?"

"Because your beauty and wisdom, Ruth, exceed those of all others. You are without flaw from the soles of your feet to the crown of your head, and in your soul as well."

I gave voice to my doubts. "You did not take to me at first."

"When I first encountered you, your love for another was written on your face, as plainly as if it had been engraved there with a chisel. Though you were not conscious of it, you always rebuffed me by your looks. Besides, in my heart I was still mourning my wife with all the might of my soul."

"Have I now brought solace to it?"

He stroked my curls gently. "And an even mightier love."

Although Boaz had spoken soft words to me before, he had never voiced the word *love* in my ears, and I could only hope that he had not now taken its name in vain.

Yet how could this be? Could he have erased from his memory that I had allowed myself to be desecrated by another? My voice was choked with tears of contrition. "I wish I had come to you still intact, whole, unblemished."

He cradled me in his arms like an infant. "Being a widow is not a blemish."

As he well knew, it was not my widowhood that I felt guilty of. Yet, when I shamefacedly reminded him of my misdeeds, he preferred to make light even of these, for my sake. He consoled me with the softest words he could muster. "My love has cleansed you from your previous impurity."

I was greatly moved, as he added mildly, "Have no fear, my loved one, and let not the wound of the depraved one's memory fester inside you. I do not hold what you have done against you. For I know well that the void left by the loss of a beloved may lead one to fill it prematurely, before the ability to tell the full grain from the empty straw has been restored."

"How can you be aware of this?" I asked in a faint, failing voice.

"Because," he replied complacently, "more than once, it was so for me."

From that day onward, Boaz always whispered lovingly into my ears, and this soothed me like a drink of warm milk and honey. In his love I came to life. He comforted me also with the warmth of his large body, the way one calms a frightened child, until I felt that I had found safe haven in his strength. His patience, as he bided his time, waiting for my love for him to take root, cured my troubled soul. And in time this soul came to be like a well-watered garden, in which my love for him blossomed in all the colors of the rainbow.

My lust for Boaz, which had lain dormant inside me for quite a while and had sprung to life during the first night in which he knew me in the field, had preceded my love for him. But it was only when my love was in pace with it, and bolstered it up, that I experienced the ultimate in pleasure with him. What I had done with Mishael paled before our act now, which, night after night, exceeded anything I had ever known.

But the villain would not have it so. Having wrecked my life once, he was bent on accomplishing the feat again.

It was the day before the families were due to return. During the evening meal, to which the two young women sat down alone, Adah turned to Osnath and said, "Remove the scowl from your face; it does not suit you. And set your righteous mind at rest. I have not committed adultery, as you seem to suspect. My knowledge of the Torah is sparse; even so, I am well aware of the injunction that imposes the death penalty on an adulteress and on the man who is joined with her in sin."

"I doubt that it has ever been implemented. My uncle Samuel says that punishments like these have been set out in order to indicate the abhorrence with which the Lord holds such deeds."

"I have made myself liable neither to the punishment nor to the revulsion."

"Then what did your mysterious disappearances from the house signify?"

"I gave free range to my heart." Osnath regarded Adah with puzzled eyes, which prompted her to continue. "By Torah law, the innermost shrine of my body is the sole property of my husband. But as for my heart, that is an entirely different matter. It is mine alone, to dispose of as I will."

Osnath did not ask Adah to elucidate her statement, nor did Adah do so of her own accord. They both sat, eating their lentil stew silently for a while, then Osnath asked, "What shall I tell Eliab if he asks about your whereabouts during his absence?"

"Tell him that I went to visit neighbors, which will be the unvarnished truth."

On the next day, on which Eliab's return was expected, Adah did not go out. And Osnath, thankful to be relieved of her duty as the child's nurse, yet deeply troubled by what Adah's words of the night before insinuated, went back to reading what was still left of Ruth's tale.

Chapter Ten

It was my custom to come to Boaz's house after dark. He was the one who insisted on this, to safeguard my reputation; for even though he had pledged himself to me, I was not betrothed to him yet in the manner that custom demanded. But one day, as I strove to familiarize myself with the surroundings of the house I hoped would soon be mine as well, I strolled by before the sinking sun met the hills. Boaz, just coming home from the fields, invited me to inspect his garden.

It was then that I noted, to my chagrin, how close Mishael's house was to his. I had seen his house many times before, but only in the dark. So I had not been aware that his and Boaz's side windows had only some twenty strides separating them from each other.

As fate would have it, Mishael was peering out of one of those side windows when Boaz and I walked by. He came out and intercepted us, and my stomach tightened at his sight.

The degradation he had suffered at Boaz's hands, when Boaz had ordered him to relinquish his right to me, apparently rankled with him. Now he saw his way clear before him to salvage his honor by exacting revenge for it.

After greeting me, Mishael turned to Boaz in a jeering voice. "You will shortly be taking for your wife Ruth"—he now favored my husband-to-be with an insolent smirk—"with whom I have been very closely acquainted."

If Mishael thought that this would lessen me in Boaz's eyes, he had made a grievous error. But it did diminish me in my own eyes. I had not expected my former lover to extol my virtue; but neither had I thought that he was out to demean me in such a low fashion, and my head dropped in shame.

Boaz was well aware of how disgracefully I had let Mishael trample my honor under his feet, but he stood staunchly by me. In his assurance that my love for him was wholehearted, he could afford to be generous toward his erstwhile rival.

"She once gave her life into your keeping," he retorted promptly. "But you repaid good with evil, for you had nothing to offer her but the torture of unrequited devotion. Now remove your claws from the woman I love, for it is no longer in your power to subject her to humiliation."

Boaz had declared his love for me in my former lover's ears, and I stood as tall as a cedar in Lebanon. My head was touching the clouds even as, with a sneer, Mishael replied: "Since you are willing to content yourself with what I have left over, let it be as you wish."

Boaz would not let Mishael abuse me any further with foul words. He warned him in a voice of exasperation, "Unless you put a barrier to your mouth at once, there soon will not be much left over of *you*."

These words chased the derisive look from Mishael's face. With his eyes fixed on Boaz's massive shoulders and muscular arms, he said, "It is not worth kicking up a quarrel over a woman, so I will hold my peace."

My husband-to-be had no mind to prolong the quarrel any further. As soon as the man who faced him had promised to cease his hostile tirade, Boaz was bent on placating him. "We are destined to remain not only relatives but also neighbors, and our children and children's children after us," he said mildly. "Let there be no bad blood between our houses. Let not the ill will between us linger to mar our lives and those of our offspring."

There was nothing left for Mishael to say. With his mouth closed as tightly as if it were filled with water, he turned and reentered his house. And I entered Boaz's house with my face sheltered in his neck, his large hand resting on my hair, and his soft words of love in my ears.

Once inside, I began to harbor a host of new thoughts about Mishael. How is it, I asked myself, that I had been so deceived by him? How did it come about that I had never noticed that his nose was huge and bent like a hawk's beak? That in the months since he left Sdeh Moab, he had grown stocky, and his face was now fleshy like that of an overfed ewe? That the smile on his lips had always been sly? And that he had used it deliberately when he had been bent on ingratiating himself with me? How had I failed to realize what an abominable man he was?

Still, I was glad that the incident had ended so tamely. For in spite of the disgraceful manner in which the vicious one had dealt with me, I had much cause to be grateful to him. Although he had not intended it to be so, sweetness had emerged from bitterness. Had I not encountered him and followed him to his homeland, I would never have met Boaz, with whom my destiny would henceforward be linked; and that would have been unthinkable.

After Boaz had fallen asleep, I lay in his arms, gazing through the window at the moon that was more than halfway to fullness, as was my heart. And in my certainty of this, I gave myself over to the peace of Boaz's even breathing, which now lulled me to sleep.

The next day, Boaz came to Naomi's house at sunset, and after consuming the offering he had brought her, she left us on our own.

Then Boaz said to me, "I once journeyed north to the sea of Kinereth and found it to be blue and deep and beautiful; but it pales before the depth and beauty of your eyes."

I could not think of any response to make, so he reached his hand into the pocket of his garment and brought forth a pouch, from which a necklace spilled into his hand. He had selected the finest precious stones he could lay his hands on, no less than twenty in all, and had them embedded in golden flowers, and they were cool on my neck as he placed the jewels there. They were also smooth to my touch as I fingered them.

Boaz told me that he had chosen the sparkling sapphires to match the blue of my Kinereth eyes, and the rubies to form a contrast to them. But that even these precious stones could not outshine my beauty and were there merely to announce it.

I told Boaz that much as I adored him, I was destitute and had nothing to give him in return for his costly present.

"You have great riches in your soul. You have enriched me as no one before you, not even my wife, has been able to do."

I could not think what these riches might be. He must have conjured them up in his imagination to alleviate my shame at having come to him with hands as empty as Naomi's storerooms.

Then two of Boaz's kinsmen, who had been waiting outside, entered the room, and in their hearing he declared, "With this necklace I betroth you to me forever."

By then, Naomi had also imperceptibly slid in, and she greeted the tidings of our betrothal and approaching nuptials with kisses all over my tearstained face.

My own gods no longer cared for me, nor I for them, but the Lord had gathered me into his fold. Though he was faceless and formless and invisible, I had called on him from the depths, and he had heard my voice.

At the sight of those words, Osnath thought that Ruth had traveled a distance by far greater than the one between the land of Moab and the land of Israel. Ruth had crossed a great divide in her soul to come closer to the God of Israel than she herself, an Israelite by birth, had been able to come.

I was resigned to my wedding taking place without the comforting presence of my own family. But Boaz had a different thought. He assembled a caravan of two carts drawn by mules, and ten guards riding donkeys, and he rode out to Sdeh Moab at its head.

There he sought out my mother, and since my father was no longer alive, he paid her a handsome bride-price for me. I was no longer a maiden but a widow, who did not deserve to have a hefty price meted out for her. Nonetheless, what he weighed into my mother's hand was sufficiently large to reconcile her to the fact that, for the second time, her daughter was about to ally herself in marriage to an Israelite.

He promised her that he would guard me like a precious jewel, and this, too, softened her heart. Thus she was swayed, and together with my sister and her husband, she mounted one of the carts Boaz had brought, and they suffered themselves to be transported to Bethlehem.

When they arrived, the gulf between us, created by our separation, dissolved in the flicker of an instant like honey in hot water. I rushed into their arms. We lifted our voices and wept loudly on each other's necks, for we had never hoped to see one another again.

My sister, whose husband was a carpenter who earned his bread at the sweat of his brow, was duly impressed with what, whispering into my ear, she dubbed "the enormous fish you have caught in your net."

On the day of the wedding, Naomi's house was in a flurry of excitement.

In the afternoon, my mother came to my room and helped me to slip on the many-colored, richly embroidered wedding dress of my mother-in-law's family, and to clasp to my neck and ears and arms and ankles the host of sparkling gold and silver ornaments, armlets, bracelets, earrings, and pendants that had been lent to me by Naomi's many kinswomen.

One of the women came in and smoothed scented oil onto my face, then painted it with practiced hands. She spread my red curls loosely over my back and covered them with shining little slivers of a gold color.

Naomi assured me that I was no less beautiful this day than I had been on the day of my wedding to her son. More of her kinswomen came in and declared that I was truly the most beautiful bride they had ever seen. And although with one part of my mind I knew that they were used to saying the same to all the brides in their family, with another part of my mind I almost believed them.

The wedding was to take place in the front yard of my bridegroom's house, and a wooden litter, painted in a dark brown color, held up by his male relatives, carried me there. While I was being borne through the streets of Bethlehem, my mother walked beside me on my right and Naomi on my left, trailed by my sister and brother-in-law.

The members of both Naomi's and Boaz's families beat drums and played flutes and, lavishly spraying wine and perfumes around me, skip-danced before me with all their might and sang hymns in praise of my alleged beauty. And people lined the streets to wish me a long and happy life with my man in his home, which we were now entering.

My bridegroom came out to meet me, and my mother assured me that he was as handsome as I was beautiful, and that we were as well suited to each other as were a deer and a gazelle skipping on the mountains together.

As I descended from the litter, a young girl approached me and proffered a bunch of mandrakes, as a sign that I would soon be blessed with plentiful fruit of the womb. Then Boaz held my hand as we strode toward the wedding canopy together.

The priest who performed the ceremony had little bells fastened to the seam of his robe, and they tingled cheerfully with each step he took. My mother stood under the canopy at my side, and her eyes shone with the pride of a bird whose chick was flying out of the nest for the first time.

Naomi stood under the canopy at Boaz's side, and when she saw how lovingly he kissed me after he had placed the ring on my finger, she embraced us both and burst into sobs of joy, sharing in our happiness as if it were her own.

After the ceremony was over, the two hundred guests, preening in their most festive garments, lined up to bless Boaz with these words:

> May the Lord make this woman who is coming to your home like Rachel and Leah, who built up the house of Israel.
>
> May you do great things in Bethlehem, and may your house be like the house of Perez, whom Tamar bore to Judah, through the offspring the Lord will give you by this girl.

Then began the feast, a banquet fit for a king. The tables, which were set up all around the front yard, were weighed down lavishly with rare delicacies: roasted quails, choice chunks of veal delicately spiced and baked in cumin, baked fish from the Great Sea basted in honey, dried figs dunked in cinnamon topped with sweet juicy kernels of pomegranates, and raisin cakes fried in oil. And both crimson and golden wines and strong spirits.

The celebrants ate and drank and became merry. Their voices lifted as they burst into song, chanting moving love songs to incite me and my bridegroom to the feats of love that awaited us in the approaching night. My mother and my sister and brother-in-law ate and drank, and their cheeks were flushed; and there was laughter on their lips and song on their tongues.

The women among the guests rose and began swaying and dancing, whirling around and around to the sound of their own singing and to the rhythm of their own drums. The voices and sights around me melted into a hazy hum as I immersed myself in my bliss.

When the feast was over and I heard the clatter of the last donkeys' hooves leave the yard, I knew that I was no longer deemed a stranger in Bethlehem. I had struck deep roots in what were now my own land and my own people.

As Boaz and I came together as husband and wife for the first time, it began raining gently, the first rain of the year, its delicious scent wafting into our nostrils. And even the earth, which was gratefully soaking up the drops of water landing on it, was at peace with itself.

🜃

A few days after the wedding, my family returned to their own land. Naomi returned to her own house, where Boaz kept her supplied with provender, and my husband and I were left on our own.

As we lived together, there was a new sweetness to the love between us, evident in the gleam in our eyes whenever they rested on each other. I feared that our previous declarations of love for one another notwithstanding, the habits of the years in which we had lived among different peoples and worshipped different gods would be bound to come between us.

So I decided from the outset that if there was friction, I would let my husband prevail. For he was entitled to do so by Torah law, which laid down that "he shall rule you." Also, this would ensure that any disagreement between us would never turn into a quarrel.

In truth, there was almost perfect harmony in the manner in which we arranged our days. On the rare occasions on which there was discord, I deferred to Boaz. But there were times when he deferred to me.

For he said that as one of the few females he knew who could read and write, and the only one who had the ability to compose poems, no other woman could measure up to me. When I opened my mouth, it was always with wisdom; thus he could not disregard my notions, as so many husbands did with their wives.

So it came about that, shortly after I moved into Boaz's house, he honored me by asking if I found it to my satisfaction.

"It is well enough, sir," I replied with feigned arrogance, "except that it lacks a scroll room, such as there was in my father's house." I meant these words merely for a jest, for Boaz's house was spacious and well-appointed and exceeded all my aspirations. But he weighed them in all seriousness and found them good.

"I will not have you live in a house that is inferior to the one from your childhood," he said. "Besides, a scroll room in our house will pay tribute to your father's scholarship, and form a suitable memorial for him."

Despite my protestations, his words were followed by deeds. Soon the builders brought in hewn stones and plaster on their oxen-drawn carts. And no more than a month later, the new room stood on its solid foundations. Initially, its shelves were as bare as the shorn heads of Moabite priests. But Boaz said that they would fill up over the years, and in the course of time, they did.

I was wary of how our lives would be affected by Mishael's close proximity. Boaz was not afraid that my love for him would be reanimated, and indeed there was no fear of it: by that time he held no more attraction for me than one of the sheep in our flock.

Yet he was now my kinsman and my neighbor. So I thought I would do well to stand in his good graces, and more so, even, in those of his wife. When I was married, she was pregnant already, and I hoped to be so in the near future. I foresaw that we would share the delights and worries of motherhood with each other, as neighbors were wont to do.

One morning, after our husbands had gone out into the fields, I stepped over to visit her, bearing with me as a gift a jar of honey to sweeten her day. But her face was as sour as the fruit of the cit-ron tree growing in her yard, and there was vinegar in her mouth.

She was not aware of what had transpired between her hus-band and me beforehand. Even so, she could not abide my pres-ence in her home; and she did nothing to hide her distaste of me.

When I proffered my gift, she would not stretch out her hand to receive it, saying that she wanted neither my honey nor my sting. She called me a worshipper of idols, a transgressor of the Lord's commandments—which I no longer was—and snarled at me as if she were a dog guarding a flock I was about to ravage. I swallowed my insult and held my peace, and thereafter avoided her and spent my days mostly on my own.

Fortunately, I took pleasure in our garden and made it my abode. I remembered my mother's blessing when I took leave of her in Sdeh Moab, in which she expressed the hope that I would always walk in a garden among flowers and inhale their scent of happiness. I knew that in many ways her blessing had come true. My favorite task was weeding, for I felt vaguely that by pulling out the weeds from among the flower beds, I was also eradicating the noxious weeds of my past life.

I also took to strolling in the garden or sitting under a tree, humming a tune. I learned to listen to the whisper of the leaves on the trees in the breeze and to the voiceless language of the flowers around me. Thus did the dark shadows of the past give way to the light of the present. On clear days the Mountains of Moab were visible in the distance, but by now I was indifferent to them.

I spent so much time in the garden that Boaz, in the words of a renowned love song, dubbed me "She Who Sits in the Garden." He even said laughingly that I must have been born from the trunk of a tree.

Although I loved the garden and the days I spent in it, as the months wore on, a new anxiety began to weigh heavily on me: the fear that my miscarriage had damaged my womb so that I would not be able to bear a child and give Boaz the son his soul, and mine, craved.

It was at this point of her reading that the homecomers entered the yard. Osnath went out to greet them in trepidation, for she was wary of the interrogation about Adah's escapades, which she expected that she would have to undergo at Eliab's hands. In the event, though, it was not Eliab but Atarah who questioned her.

At first, the travelers' mouths spilled over with accounts of the elegance of the royal castle, and of the enormous hall, hung with violet curtains fastened with silver rings, in which the wedding was held. Of the tables lit with the flickering light of a myriad of candles in elaborate silver candlesticks, and set with multitudes of pottery bowls burnished to a red sheen. Of the sumptuous dishes, too numerous to count, that were served. Of the elaborately carved silver goblets, into which endless quantities of wine flowed. And of the king's being in his most gracious mood, pouring wine into the guests' goblets with his own royal hand, and much more.

But once there was nothing left to tell, Atarah summoned Osnath to her room. The girl bowed to her and waited to hear what she had to say.

Atarah had initially resented Osnath's return to Bethlehem, suspecting her of intending to cause mischief between Eliab and his wife. But after the girl's part in the birthing of her grandson, her enmity had subsided. Now that Osnath had uncomplainingly obeyed her order to stay behind with Adah, this had raised her even higher in Atarah's esteem. So she did not hesitate to share her concerns with her.

Atarah's voice was usually melodious, but there was no melody in it as she said rather harshly, "In this house the walls have ears, and the windows have eyes, and the maids have mouths. I had barely entered the house when I heard the most disquieting rumors about my daughter-in-law's conduct. What was she about while we were away?"

"Revered lady, what is it that you fear?" replied Osnath with a question of her own, although she had a fair notion of what those fears must be.

"I fear that she has been following a design that is evil in the eyes of the Lord. I will say no more until I am certain that I am standing on solid ground. I was hoping that you might be able to enlighten me."

"She did not fully confide in me. But there is one thing I can assert with certainty: she did not fall into sin."

"You are bound to stand up for her."

"I am standing up for the truth, and it is that she did not transgress any commandments."

"Not yet," said Atarah, an uncommonly grave expression on her face.

Being released from her responsibility for Adah now, Osnath dismissed the matter of her conduct from her thoughts. On the next morning, she resumed reading the final part of Ruth's tale with more peace of mind than she had enjoyed for almost two weeks.

Chapter Eleven

Then it happened. It was some six months after our wedding when, for the second time in my life, my monthly blood failed to flow when it was due. This time, though, the signs of the life growing inside me brought exultation. I rejoiced in the gathering heaviness of my belly and my breasts.

When I admitted Naomi into the circle of those who knew of my pregnancy, a circle so small that it had included only Boaz and myself, the tears spilled from her eyes like a waterfall. When they were spent, her eyes shone as I had never seen them shine before.

She let her bony fingers hover over my belly and stroke it. Then she stated in a festive voice, "From this day onward, you are no longer my daughter-in-law, but my daughter. Though I have called you daughter before, it is only this day that you are truly my own flesh and blood. Through you, I will have the grandchild that has been denied to me for so long. It will warm my brittle bones and keep alive my and my sons' memories, and ensure that our names will not be erased in Israel forever."

Early the next morning, Naomi arrived at our house as sprightly as a young woman, with a donkey laden with her belongings. Her wrinkled countenance was placid, a picture of serenity. Boaz, who no longer had a mother of his own, smiled to see her settle into our home as a matter of course, as if it were hers.

When later we were alone in his bedchamber, I apologized to him for her intrusion. But he said that he had known all along that

Naomi would be the dowry I would bring with me to his house, and that he was glad to accept her. He also looked on indulgently as she established her benevolent rule over us.

She oversaw the maids who waited on us, becoming a kindly but exacting mistress to them, an art I had been slow to learn. Under her capable supervision, our house was set to right and the floors scrubbed clean every day. Both the house and yard were suffused with the clatter of dishes emanating from the cooking room, and the air was always thick with the smell of bread and cakes baking in the furnace, and of meat frying in the pans. She also cut and sewed up my dresses and Boaz's garments, which took shape easily in her hands.

Yet our household was taunted with apprehension. The loss of my previous child, of which I had told Boaz some time ago, haunted Naomi; and the disaster that had befallen his first wife during childbirth haunted him. In their anxiety, between the two of them, they never let me out of their sight.

They were accomplices, in league with each other in hardly allowing me to lift a finger or stir from my place. They anticipated every one of my needs and fulfilled it instantly. Since they deemed my miscarriage to have come about as a result of the hardships I had faced during our journey from Moab, they now forced me to rest even when I would much rather have strolled about. They treated me as if I were the most delicate of flowers, one that might wilt at any moment if not watered constantly, which I well knew I was not.

Besides all else, Naomi made me sit and bathe my feet in warm water, with a sprinkling of scented oil, in a little tub that she placed before me. She assured me that it was exceedingly beneficial, for it would soothe me, even though I was already as calm as I could be. I reflected that it was she and not I who needed the footbath. But in deference to her advanced years, I kept my thoughts locked up in myself, and my feet in the water, until they became white and soft and wrinkled like hers. For this I was rewarded with her nod of approval.

Though both she and Boaz wore my patience thin by pampering me past bearing, I was basking in their joy, which reflected my own. I was blooming like the trees in our yard at springtime, as it then was.

Yet when my belly swelled, my face came to be puffed up as well. It was pudgy and dotted with pimples, the likes of which I had never had before. When I looked into the mirror, I could not but notice that I had become uglier than I had ever been.

Before my pregnancy, Boaz had paid tribute to what he called my peerless beauty, and taken a mindless pride in it. I feared that he would now be mortified by my appearance. But in his jubilation at the prospective birth of his child, he pronounced my beauty to be undiminished, unrivaled in the entire town of Bethlehem. And I shed tears in his arms, thankful for the kindness of his lie.

As my pregnancy advanced, both he and Naomi grew restive in an ever-growing trepidation that, having lost an infant once, I would be prone to abort again. As my time to give birth drew near, Boaz no longer went out into the fields. Since there was nothing for him to do in the house, he just sat with his eyes darting around aimlessly.

When the days dragged on and nothing happened, Boaz's state worsened. He became as taciturn as a stone, yet as fidgety as a poisoned mouse. He was unable to sit still, shifting all utensils he found lying around in the garden out of his way so that he could stride hither and thither or pace around and around in circles. He battered the bushes and beat down the grass and the flowers with his heavy feet, nearly eradicating all that lay in his way, almost driving me out of my mind.

Boaz knew that during the delivery he would not be permitted in my room. But when my labor began, in the teeth of the midwife's strenuous objections, he insisted that the door be left open a crack so that he would be able to hear more clearly what was going forth inside.

Then he sat on a stool in front of the door. I could hear him reciting prayers. From my vantage point on the birthing stones, I could see him dripping with sweat, almost out of his senses with dread, his face contorting every time he heard me moaning. In my worry for him, I did all I could to restrain myself. Though my breath was labored, I bit my lower lip until I drew blood, to stifle my wails, rather than giving voice to them, as was my right to do.

Naomi knelt behind me, making me lean on her knees, saying as little as possible, lest her shaking voice give vent to her own anxiety.

But their fear was in vain, for my miscarried infant had eased the passage for my live one. It took only from sunrise to noon until my child slid out of my womb easily and comfortably. Almost as soon as the midwife announced that I had given birth to a boy, and wiped the blood off his little body, he began searching blindly for my nipple to suck from it.

During my pregnancy, I had asked Boaz if he would mind having a red-haired son or daughter.

"I positively demand to have one whose head always looks as if it were on fire, like yours," he had said.

But when our son emerged from my womb, he was dark of hair and of skin and of eyes, and resembled Boaz as one drop of water resembles another. So later, when the child became restless, his father rocked him in his arms and reassured him, saying that although he was deeply disappointed that his coloring resembled his own rather than his mother's, he would nevertheless keep him. Then he breathed soft endearments into his ears, and so the fretting infant was calmed.

In truth, we both agreed that our little one was flawless in every one of his small but artfully shaped features and limbs, the ones that had been crafted by the Lord himself. So it came as unwanted tidings to me when Boaz declared that he would now have to be circumcised. I knew that it was the law, but I saw nothing amiss with the baby as he was, and thought the removal of his foreskin entirely superfluous. It was cruel, even, to mutilate him in such a manner. At the very least, I strove to bend the law by postponing the event until he grew strong enough to withstand the ordeal.

Although Boaz was beaming with happiness at the birth of his son, he would not hear of holding off the ceremony for even as much as one day. For he said that the Torah commandment was for all males among the Israelites to be circumcised on the eighth day after their births, not one day before and not one day after. "Thus is the everlasting covenant between Israel and the Lord marked in our flesh, and it would be unthinkable to breach it."

In my gratitude to the Lord, I submitted to this decree.

In a playful show of generosity, my husband made a concession to me: he permitted me to select our son's name, which, by custom, was my prerogative in any case. But I wanted to choose a name that he, and Naomi, and our neighbors would also like.

When I consulted with them, they proposed that I call our son Obed, which means "worker." I approved of their suggestion, for I said that happy is he who eats the fruit of his labor.

Boaz invited as many guests to the circumcision as he had for the wedding. As if our newborn son were a bridegroom, and only the bride was missing. And indeed his father and the guests were as joyous as they had been during the wedding, and only I trembled in trepidation.

On the day of the ceremony, our house was gripped with excitement. Not only the maids but all the women in the neighborhood, who came in to help, were set to the task of cooking and baking and salting and spicing the food, while their husbands ran out to summon the guests, then borrowed tables and chairs from all the surrounding houses and set them up in the yard. All around was in tumult, with maids and guests alike scurrying back and forth in their rush to complete the preparations for the feast.

Soon the guests assembled, to be greeted by the mouthwatering, steamy aroma of goat meat spiced with cumin simmering in enormous pots, and salted fowls roasting on spits. And by the sight of the decanters of wine and the cups and bowls awaiting them on the tables.

It was of the utmost importance that the circumcision be performed in the proper fashion on the eighth day after the infant's birth. Thus it had to be completed before the sun rested on the crests of the hills of Judah, even before the meal was served.

The priest who performed the ceremony was evidently practiced in the task, so that my previous anxiety turned out to have been superfluous. It was not long before the infant, who had been yawning in sleepy contentment, broke into heartrending, piteous, but brief whimpers, which I calmed by dunking a cloth in sweet wine and thrusting it into his little mouth. After sucking up the liquid, the little sufferer became oblivious of what must have been the strong pain tugging at him, and he fell into a deep slumber in my arms.

Then the priest called out that the name in Israel of the boy who had been born to Boaz and Ruth would be Obed. All those gathered for the celebration broke into loud cheers, which drowned out Naomi's sobs of joy. And they clapped their hands to welcome my son, the son of one who used to be a Moabite, into the congregation of Israel.

Next they rose to their feet, and filed by and blessed us, saying:

May your seed prosper and inherit a kingdom,
and may you become the ancestors of kings.

I joined Boaz in blessing our guests in return by saying in the proper, time-honored manner: "Those who bless us, we bless."

Then the women among the guests blessed Naomi, her face as radiant as if she were our son's grandmother, as by law and custom she truly was. One of them, whom they had appointed to speak in their name, called out,

Blessed be the Lord today, who has not left you without comfort.

The child will give you new life and cherish you in your old age; for your daughter-in-law who loves you, who has proved better to you than seven sons, has borne him.

And I knew the woman to have voiced the truth in my heart.

After the delivery, my fingers, still swollen from my pregnancy, did not regain their suppleness. For the first few weeks they remained clumsy and useless. But Naomi's, though bony and weathered, were deft and nimble. So, mostly, she was the one to tend to little Obed. She also cuddled him in her arms and sang lullabies to him.

I truly believe that she would have preferred to suckle him herself, had she been able to do it. And only because her sagging breasts were as empty as a drunkard's pouch of silver did she lay him reluctantly to mine. Later, he spoke her name before he spoke mine or his father's.

She never fussed over the child, or cooed to him, as so many doting grandmothers did. But she was endlessly patient with him. Even when he first toddled to the table and reached his little hand up and pushed the bowls that were placed on it so that they crashed to the floor, she did not scold him. When she had him in the copper bathtub and he thoughtlessly splashed water in her face, she did not demur. And when he ransacked her room, she merely rearranged her belongings.

Naomi was unceasing in her labors for his sake. When he grew into boyhood and wandered off to wrestle with other boys and came home with scraped elbows and knees, she tended to them with salves she kept in her chest for him alone. And when he tumbled in the mud with the other children and came home with filthy torn garments, smelling of earth and sweat, she took them off and replaced them with clean ones. All his garments were her own handiwork, yet she did not complain when he soiled or tore them.

She merely laundered them and mended them without uttering one word of reproof.

She cared for him from dawn to dusk, but nothing that pertained to him was ever an effort for her, and she was never fatigued.

Boaz was meticulous in observing the Torah injunctions and never turned right or left from them. Always remembering the Sabbath to keep it holy, he laid fodder and prepared water in the troughs for all our animals before it descended. He never went out to sow or reap in the fields, and he was adamant that all the people who worked for us, and even our animals, rest on that day. We enjoyed the peace of that holy day together, and so also the tranquillity of our evenings.

During cold, long winter nights, when silence fell over Bethlehem, we sat companionably before the hearth in our front room. When all dwellers of the town were safely ensconced in their homes and only the moon traveled undisturbed through the night, or when the clouds hung heavy over the roofs and rain battered the ground, the heat and the soft glow of the flickering flames and candles perched in niches in the walls made the room warm and cozy.

While Boaz and I sat on a snug, cushioned dais with our thighs stealthily pressed against each other, little Obed would find his way to Naomi. She would draw him into her lap and bestow absentminded caresses on him, and he snuggled up to her as she spilled into his ears the thrilling tales of his people, of our people, with which I liked to fill my ears as well. And so it went on until her words ebbed, and he drifted into sleep in her embrace.

At times the neighbors would come in and rejoice in Naomi's joy, which was also ours. Her battered old cheeks were aglow in the rosy light of the hearth's fire as she basked in the love by which she was surrounded.

The neighbors who came to her also became my friends. Their warmth engulfed me like the soft woolen cloths in which I swaddled my infant. They said that although I had not been born an Israelite, I was now blood of their blood, and in their love I was born anew.

They declared me fit to make my home in their midst, my seed to become part of the Lord's people forever. And I knew that so it would be.

Even Mishael's wife relented and mended the rift between us. I did not take her previous conduct toward me amiss, and we were reconciled. A day came when her husband met his end at the hand of a killer. Thereafter we adopted her as our sister, her son and mine played together, and our two families became as one.

After that, our lives were good. The rains came in season so that the fields were inundated and the springs in the hills gushed with freshwater. The crops were plentiful and there were rich pastures for our flock and cattle, and we lived off the fat of the land. Our garden was blooming, and the scent of the flowers spread into the distance, and the trees gave their fruit.

Obed thrived, as did we. We were like trees planted on a gentle brook. There was laughter in our hearts, and we rejoiced in the fullness of our days, filled with love for each other and for our son.

The Lord had wounded me, but he also healed me. He had given me the capacity to wrestle with my fate, the way Jacob, the third father of our people, had wrestled with an angel in the dark of the night, and, like him, I had won. Each morning and each evening I gave thanks to the Lord for all that with which he had endowed me, by reciting the Shima prayer.

Boaz said that the choicest of wines were those that matured slowly and mellowed with age, and so also with love. And he was right, for as we matured, our love matured with us, and it was sweeter than the most select of wines from our vineyards.

After Obed, I gave birth to two daughters. Although the Lord then sealed my womb and we were never blessed with more sons, my cup was flowing over and I wanted nothing more. So speaks Ruth the Israelite, the wife of Boaz.

Osnath lifted her eyes from Ruth's scroll, delighting in her happiness. And when she searched her heart, she found it as full as Ruth's.

The tears sparkled in her eyes as Ruth's joy and her own intermingled, until she could hardly tell them apart.

A while before, when Osnath had barely become engrossed in Ruth's tale, Adah whispered into Eliab's ears. As he was about to set out to the fields with his father and his brothers, she asked to speak to him in his room.

Eliab knew that Adah's holding the elevated position of being his first wife did not chafe Osnath. For she was aware that she had brought this down on her own head by rebuffing him when she could have had him for herself alone. So far, he had believed that Adah, too, had resigned herself to the dour fate of having a rival in her home, whom he loved as he did not love her.

Now he learned to his surprise that matters stood far otherwise. "I will not croak with jealousy, nor grunt with enmity, nor fall into despair because of Osnath's usurpation of my place in your bed and soul," Adah announced with a toss of her pretty head. "I was told that I came out of my mother's womb with a smile on my face, which remained there all through my childhood. I was born for love and gaiety and laughter. I will not remain a morose, unloved wife when there is another man who is offering me his undivided heart and home."

Taken aback, Eliab asked, "Who is he who is willing to provide this unalloyed happiness to you?"

"Ohad, the son of Machir."

This man's home was situated but a few houses away from theirs. Eliab had known him well ever since, as little boys, they had shared filched carobs, and traded bawdy secrets about their parents' deeds at night, and pulled girls' plaits together. Ohad had always seemed to have more eyes on Adah than he had in his head, but she had held her nose high in the air and her eyes fixed on Eliab. Now their direction had changed.

He would not have thought himself so easily replaceable in her affection, so in his hurt he spoke sternly to her. "It is not done in Israel for a woman to leave her husband; it is only the husband who can send his wife away from his home of his own volition. And so it is also by Torah law."

"Then let it be you, sir, who sends me away, and no one will dare to stick out his tongue at us."

Adah had dealt his manly pride a painful blow. Yet Eliab could not entirely blame her for looking elsewhere for the love he was unable to give her. He decided, therefore, to deal kindly with her. "Are you asking me to give you a book of divorcement?"

"That, and your consent to my taking our infant son with me to my new home. It is close by and I will bring him to visit you whenever you like. Other than that, I will take nothing from you, not even a thread or a shoestring."

"I understand you, Adah. But equally I hope that you will understand me when I say that what you request is of great moment in my life, and I can neither accede to it nor reject it immediately. I must turn it over in my mind."

In fact, he mulled it over for four restless days and four sleepless nights, during which he kept his own counsel.

Chapter Twelve

As Eliab did not make Osnath privy to Adah's request to be released from her marriage, Ruth's tale remained uppermost in her mind.

Even after reading it in its entirety, some parts of it remained as nebulous to Osnath as a landscape covered with early-morning fog. It still was not clear why Mishael had come to Sdeh Moab. Samuel had raised the possibility that he had gone there to flee from justice, and the rumors about him mentioned by Ruth seemed to vindicate this view. But her book had not yielded as much as a sliver of knowledge of what the crime was that he had committed and that had compelled him to seek shelter there. Neither did it elucidate what had occurred afterward to cause him to return to his own land so abruptly. Least of all did it provide any glimpse of the reason why Mishael's cousin had killed him, as Pninah had told her.

When she spoke to Eliab of her puzzlement, he admitted, "Indeed, Ruth's scroll does not shed light on what has been baffling you for so long. I have in my possession another one that provides the solution to the mystery. It is a long letter written by Mishael to his only son, who later became Hagith's husband. Mishael wrote and sealed it shortly before his death, and gave it into his wife's keeping, instructing her to give it to her son, but stipulating that she do so only when he had grown to manhood. Apparently, he had a foreboding that when that time came, he himself would no longer be able to do so.

"After the death of Mishael's son, Hagith showed it to me. With her permission I made a copy of it before she gave it to her eldest son, Uri, Adah's father, for safekeeping."

He drew it out from its hiding place, on a high shelf well above Osnath's reach. In her eagerness to learn the truth that had eluded her for so long, she almost tore it from his hand.

He prevented her from doing so by holding it behind his back. "I will show it to you but on pain of dire punishment if as much as one word of what you will see ever crosses your lips."

She ducked in mock apprehension. "What will you do to me?"

"I will banish you from my bed for . . . for . . . an entire month," he threatened.

"It is indeed a frightening prospect," she admitted. There was laughter in her eyes but sincerity in her words, for she'd had her fill of longing for him at night and wanted no more of it.

"Then promise that you will not make it necessary for me to mete out this severe punishment to you."

"My lips will remain sealed," she promised impatiently, holding out her hand for the letter.

She had not promised that her pen would remain sealed as well, but she did not give voice to this thought, and he put the parchment into her hand and sat down next to her.

She unrolled it, and its contents were displayed before her incredulous eyes.

Hear me, my son. You have only recently been born, but I am recording the most fateful events of my life for your knowledge. For, like any human being, I have no way of telling what destiny awaits me, and whether, when you grow up, I will still be at your side. So I am conveying my message to you now, using the written word that outlasts life, as the spoken word does not.

Now, while you are still a little one, you look up to me as if I were the Almighty himself. But as time goes by, you may hear your father maligned. You may be exposed to a plethora of pernicious rumors about a crime I have committed. You may also hear about a woman. One whom, by law and custom, I was obliged to marry, yet I refused, thus putting a further blot on my reputation.

Some of these rumors are true, some of them half true, some of them outright lies. You may even harbor suspicions of your own. Hence I prefer to lay bare the entire, unpalatable truth before you.

Perhaps when you read it, you will find it in your heart to forgive my sin. For, like the Lord who is a God of mercy and forgiveness, I hope that you will be forgiving as well. And if you find that, unlike the Lord, you are unable to forgive, know that I will still love you from the depth of my heart, and after my death, from the depth of my grave.

Since my early days, even though I had never done anything to deserve it, I was a man of many quarrels. I did not chase them, but they chased me. Although I yearned for nothing but peace, I was of a hot temper and every man's hand was against me; so, naturally, my hand was against everyone. In my youth I was at odds with all my kinsmen, and, through no fault of mine, I was involved in several brawls.

My father's hand, too, was heavy on me. This came about because, as you will know by the time you read this, your grandfather, Yotham, took two wives. One he cherished as if she were the lily of Sharon; the other was but a bramble to him. My elder brother, Hananel, was the son of the wife he loved, and some of our father's sentiments for his mother were passed down to him, who resembled her closely. I was the son of the despised wife. Because of having closed his heart to her, my father had not a scrap of affection to spare for me, either.

As a firstborn, Hananel was entitled by the rule set out in the Torah to inherit twice as much of our father's property as I was. Nonetheless, I was entitled to a fair-sized share of it as well, and our father had no right to cut me off. Yet this is what he did. He fobbed me off with puny presents, a mere pittance, during his lifetime; and he arranged matters so that after he was gathered to his people, I would inherit nothing of what was his. It was not surprising therefore that I fell out with him and we hardly ever spoke to each other.

When he died, Hananel took charge of the family home and land according to our father's provision, while I was reduced to penury. I sent out my hands to deal with trade, but most of what I earned went from my hand to my mouth. As I had hardly any silver with which to buy merchandise, there was little that I could sell. I was no spendthrift, and in time I put a little silver by, but I did not prosper.

I was wallowing in resentment at being robbed of what was rightly mine. I was also sorely indignant that my brother, who was well-off, was unwilling to lift even one of his gold-ringed fingers to assist me. My discontent ploughed two deep furrows between my eyebrows. I never saw them, for only women are frivolous enough to regard themselves in mirrors. But I felt them deepening, so that my eyebrows were drawing closer to each other by the day.

There was also the matter of your mother. She was an enchanting woman of many graces, and I had set my heart on making her my wife. But her father declined my suit because I had no suitable bride-price to offer for her.

Hananel wished for her as well. His offer was by far the more enticing, and her father gave her to him instead. Thus would your uncle make off not only with my share of our father's patrimony, but also with my woman. This was not only a bruise to my heart, but yet another slight on my honor.

A few days before the wedding was to take place, I strolled through my brother's property. My head was bent to the soil that had been tilled in preparation for sowing, and I was immersed in wistful thoughts about this patch of land and the woman, both of which should have belonged to me. As I raised my head, I saw my brother surveying some fledgling fruit trees he had planted of late near a gorge that also belonged to him.

At the mention of the gorge, Osnath, who had been slouching in her chair, suddenly sat upright, totally alert. When she looked at Eliab, a question in her eyes, he nodded his assent.

Hananel saw me and called me to him. When I approached he said that, as he knew that I lived in want, he deemed it proper to come to my aid. He proposed that I tend the new orchard for him in exchange for generous wages.

Although I could have made good use of the silver he promised me, I made it plain to him that I would not be his day laborer on the property that should have been mine.

Then I touched on what was a sore point with me. "You have cheated me of my rightful place in every way," I said in a shrill voice. "Was it not enough that with your greedy hands you appropriated my birthright? Need you have debased me even further by stealing my woman?" I hissed at him.

Your uncle did not hesitate to show his low regard for me. "You are a swindler yourself, and a liar in accusing me of theft," he barked, though his face remained impassive. "I did not steal her. She came to me of her own accord. She said that you were a worthless ruffian, a disgusting louse, and that she could not abide you."

His words were as a sharp dagger in my heart. I did not believe that my chosen one had piled dirt on me in this manner. Hananel had, without doubt, made the tirade up himself before he let it roll off his filthy tongue. At that, the withering wrath that had been festering inside me for months flared up and spilled over, as boiling water flows from an overly full kettle.

I saw him coming toward me with glazed eyes, and I charged at him like a bull. I balled my hands into fists and pounded his face savagely until it bled profusely. Then I struck him a blow that sent him staggering backward and sprawling on the ground.

As he hit the ground with a thud, he squealed like a woman in labor. But I kicked him without mercy, and he went over the brink of the gorge. His hands clawed at the rock nearest him, but lost their hold and slipped off it. His fingers grasping nothing but empty space, he rolled down the steep slope until he reached the bottom. Where he fell, there he lay, and screamed no more.

Had I merely wanted to show him that he who walks on embers will have his feet burned? Or had I intended to extinguish his life, thus making me guilty of his murder?

I am not sure. When I dealt him his mortal blow with my foot, I acted on the spur of the moment, in a blind fury. When my reflections are cast back to that fateful moment, my mind becomes blank. I remember my deed, but the memory of my thoughts has been erased forever.

The heavens and the earth are my witnesses, though, that when it was over, I felt remorse over the offense I had committed, as deep as the abyss into which I had kicked my brother. But my despicable deed could not be undone, and my self-reproach could not bring him salvation. All that was left for me to do was to extricate myself as best I could from the consequences of what I had done, my drive to survive being as desperate as that of a wounded animal.

Osnath could barely keep her eyes on the scroll, for shock. She was appalled, and shuddered to think of the fate that had befallen Mishael's brother, Hananel. Yet she was stirred to tears of compassion, for, to her mind, Mishael's father, and even more so his brother, had dealt with him atrociously.

But Eliab assured her that Mishael's accusations against his father were vastly exaggerated, for the gifts he had bestowed on him had been far from contemptible. He had distorted the truth in order to place himself in a favorable light in the eyes of his son.

After a while, with Eliab still patiently waiting, Osnath read the rest of the letter.

On that day, the sun and the moon had joined forces to conspire against me, and even the stars in their courses seemed to battle me.

For no sooner did I see my brother lying motionless at the bottom of the gorge than I turned around to the sight of my uncle and his eldest son, my cousin, coming home from their fields, which bordered ours.

By Torah law, expiation for bloodshed cannot be made, except by spilling the blood of the man who has shed it. But a murderer cannot be submitted to punishment based on the testimony of a single witness; only the evidence given by two witnesses is considered reliable enough for that.

To my misfortune, there were indeed two such witnesses, who had caught me at my deed. Besides, as they were my brother's closest kinsmen after me, they were in honor bound to avenge his blood by giving me up to justice, or, if they were unable to do so, by killing me with their own hands.

I saw them running toward me. By now they were so close, they could not have been too far away when I assaulted my brother. They could not have failed to see in minute detail all that had transpired.

In a frenzy of terror, I pushed aside the thorny bushes that stood in the way of my flight and ran as fast as my feet would carry me. Mercifully, after I turned a corner, the witnesses, who had been lagging behind, disappeared from view.

My hands and my garment were stained with my brother's blood and, once in the small hut in which I lived, I stripped them off and changed into another garment. For a few moments I sat helpless, with my head in my hands, contemplating my next steps. The previous sight of the witnesses almost upon me made it clear that I had little time left to plan what next I must do. If I did not contrive to slip away instantly, they would have easy access to me.

Without further loss of time, I crammed a few belongings into a cloth bag and took hold of whatever silver I had saved up. I harnessed my donkey and fled from the town of my birth, thinking never to set foot in it again.

I had no clear notion of where I should head, until my eyes caught sight of a caravan of Midianite traders making their way eastward, toward Moab. The chance of joining them fell into my lap like ripe fruit. I hoped that I could lose myself in their midst, so that if anyone came in pursuit of me, he would not be able to single me out among them.

The Midianites were willing to share their simple fare with me, and even to come to my rescue and connive with me. But they were as crafty as foxes, bent on making a hefty profit from the sword lying at my throat. For an exorbitant price of silver I weighed into their hands, they sold me a black-and-white-striped headscarf such as the ones they themselves wore. They charged me an even more lucrative price for their willingness to remain as mute as the fish in the Great Sea in the face of my possible persecutors.

In the meantime, my uncle and my cousin must have raised the alarm, for before long a contingent of some twenty men came in pursuit of me. I concealed my fringes—which branded me as an Israelite—under my cloak and wrapped my head in the Midianite's headscarf, which still bore the offensive odor of its previous owner.

No sooner had I completed my disguise than I perceived my persecutors scanning the area, searching avidly behind every tree and bush, approaching the caravan. Since my face was half veiled with my scarf, and as they did not inspect me closely, my disguise fooled them. Thus it was not long before I saw them fade into the descending darkness.

I accompanied the Midianites all the way to the town of Sdeh Moab, to lie low. I did not disclose my name to anyone, lest the rumor of my sojourn there be carried back to Bethlehem, and the witnesses or their servants come to bring me home to face justice. I proclaimed myself the Unnamed, in the hope that no one in the land of Israel would know what had become of the man Mishael.

I sustained myself by trading in healing herbs. A local healer skilled in herbs befriended me. Upon making an oath of secrecy, and in return for no more than a reasonable fee, he taught me how to scour the nooks and crannies in the hills for substances that surpassed the balm from Gilead in their healing powers.

In his house I met a woman, her hair the color of rust, the wife of an Israelite from Bethlehem. Her husband, whose name she did not mention, had been riddled with disease for a long time and his death had been slow in coming. So when he died she was starved for a man; I was for her as God-sent as manna from heaven.

She was mine to take; she even thrust herself at me. She took the polished words about our eternal love, which I prattled in her ear, as seriously as if they were the Ten Commandments handed down to Moses on Mount Sinai. She nearly prevailed on me to take her for my wife and sire a child upon her. But although I succumbed to her body, in my heart I kept faith with your mother.

Even so, I might have settled contentedly enough in the land where the hospitality extended to me included the warm lap of a woman. But a few months later, unforeseen tidings reached me from across the Sea of Salt. It came to my ears that my uncle, overcome by a sudden illness, had died. One of the witnesses to my deed was no more. I knew that I could no longer be brought to trial or, if I was, I would be acquitted.

Thus the sword hanging over me had been blunted. I was now at liberty to return to Bethlehem.

There was still my cousin, who, as my dead brother's eldest next of kin after me, was obliged to follow the ancient custom of blood vengeance and kill me. But as he was still a youngster, I was confident of my ability to defend myself from his possible onslaught.

So I made some hasty preparations for my return to Bethlehem and set out on my way.

When I arrived home, I found that rumors of my escape to Sdeh Moab had reached the town through other Bethlehemites who had taken refuge there from the drought. It transpired that my epitaph in the Moabite country, the Unnamed, now clung to me in my hometown as a derogatory name. But I cared little for that, for with the threat my uncle had posed to me safely underground, my way was now clear to reestablish myself in my rightful position in Israel.

That uncle had been a thorn in my eye in every way. Not only had he been one of the two witnesses to the killing of my brother, but he had also laid claim to my brother's property. As Hananel had not yet sired sons, I, as his brother, was entitled to inherit it. But my uncle had brought his suit before the elders, disputing my right to it in accordance with the rule that a murderer may not inherit that which belonged to the man he had murdered. Therefore, as the man most closely related to my brother after me, he laid claim to his property himself.

Since this uncle was now interred in a burial loft, my star was shining bright in the sky. As there was no second witness to my deed, I was not only exempt from being made answerable for my brother's murder but, also, I could no longer be barred from inheriting his patrimony. So neither the elders nor anyone else demurred when I took hold of it as a matter of course.

Shortly afterward, your mother approached me with honey under her tongue. She cast herself at my feet, and kissed my hand and begged forgiveness for having preferred Hananel to me.

She claimed she had never vilified me in his ears, nor had she loved him. She had merely bowed to her father's decree, which she deeply regretted. She affirmed her love for me and acclaimed my superiority to my brother in every way. Her devotion to me passed all bounds, and as I loved her, I forgave her previous infidelity. I took her for my wife, and knew her, and so it came about that you were born.

Little did I know that the widow from Sdeh Moab was not only still hungry for me, but also obtuse. So obtuse that she failed to realize that, had I wanted to bind her to me permanently, I would have taken her with me to my homeland.

She failed to comprehend that when I left her town, it was also with the intention of disentangling myself from her. She pursued me all the way to Bethlehem, and hunted me down and all but offered herself to me in the fields. I was once again beguiled by her, though only briefly.

To my utter surprise, it was called to my attention that I was her deceased husband's next of kin. Since she had been left childless, it was my duty to take her for my wife.

Fortunately, another kinsman of her husband—our neighbor Boaz—was captivated by her. He came to visit me and declared that he had it in his power to destroy me. He had the effrontery to claim that he had at his disposal evidence against me. I knew nothing of the nature of this evidence. It might have been a hitherto unknown witness to my crime, one so shy that he would not come forward except at Boaz's command. But it could also have been nothing but a ruse.

Whatever it was, he thundered at me, threatening that if I stiffened my neck and as much as hinted at thwarting him, he would bring the evidence to light and lay it bare before the elders.

I thought to myself: let it not be said to my shame that I stood in the way of another man's happiness. Then, too, why should I put my life at risk for a woman who was not to my taste, and whom I would not have taken for my wife in any case for all the riches of the earth? So I readily gave her up to him.

I gladly appeared before the elders. There I declared that I refused to wed the widow, thus opening the way for Boaz to take her for his own.

So she became his wife and my neighbor. But although she paraded herself before me by strolling in the garden every day, she had lost all attraction for me. We were as strangers to each other, and I never laid hands on her again.

Thereafter, my life looked bright. All that now remains to encumber me is my guilt and the worry of how my deeds will be reflected in your eyes.

My son, I have laid myself bare to your gaze, condemning myself with my own pen. I cannot wash my hands in innocence and declare that they have not shed blood, for there was blood on the hand that now holds this pen. I will be weighed down with this burden and bear the mark of my guilt, as Cain bore his, on my forehead for the rest of my days.

But I am not totally without merit. There is love in my heart for your mother and for you. It is as firm as iron and will last for as long as I walk on this earth, and beyond. So my soul is not all evil.

Judge me as you will, but know the truth. So speaks your father, Mishael the son of Yotham.

Having read the letter to the end, Osnath continued sitting on her chair, immersed in thought. At long last she mused, "Of course Ruth was aware of these events. Why did she not relate them in her scroll?"

"She knew their gist," Eliab concurred. "As you may remember from her book, Boaz revealed the horrendous truth to her later on. As Obed once told me, on hearing it she was rattled to the core, even though by that time she had already cast him out of her heart.

"Yet she guarded her tongue and her pen. She would not cast stones into the well from which she had been drinking. She would not revile her former lover by baring the worst of his iniquities in her scroll. Naturally, she could not have known that he would do it himself, in a letter to his son."

"What was the evidence against Mishael held by Boaz?"

"He did not reveal this to anyone, so we shall never know. I suspect that he possessed no evidence at all, and that he merely prevaricated to intimidate Mishael into yielding Ruth to him."

"But we have no certitude of this."

"No, but it is very likely that it was so. For if he had any evidence, such as another witness who would have stepped forward at his behest, his conscience would have prompted him to bring him before the elders in any case."

"What became of Mishael? Was he indeed murdered by his cousin?"

Eliab hesitated, then said, "I have heeded your insistent voice and entrusted all our secrets into your keeping. I will tell you the rest, too.

But it is late, and I have an insistent voice of my own, tugging at my loins, calling you to bed with me."

Osnath did not dare defy him, lest the tugging lead him to call his wife to him, instead of her.

So it was not until the next day that she heard the end of the tale, which, as Eliab told her, had been passed from ear to mouth in his family for a long time.

Chapter Thirteen

In the course of time, Mishael's crime overtook him. When he murdered his brother, his cousin, the son of the uncle who had witnessed the murder together with him, was still of tender years. He was no more than sixteen and still unsure of himself. But when he matured, he gained in assurance and assumed a blood feud against Mishael.

He told the son of Yotham that he held him responsible for his brother Hananel's murder, even though he did not have it in his power to bring him to trial. And he reiterated his claim that as his brother's murderer, he was not entitled to inherit his patrimony. Since Mishael's uncle, his own father, was also dead, he and his younger brothers were next in line for the inheritance, and the land and the house now properly belonged to them.

Mishael scoffed at the young man's claim that he had snatched away what should have been theirs. He bridled at his suggestion that he atone for his wrongdoing by turning over part of his riches to them. He did not believe that he would come to harm through his young relative, whom he held cheap. In his misplaced confidence, he did not recognize the threat this young man posed to him.

He was stingy and closefisted, unwilling to open his hand to let him and his brothers share his bounty. All he was prepared to do to appease him was to send him some of his livestock, a few paltry cows and oxen of his herd, as a peace offering. These his cousin, affronted by Mishael's audacity, sent back to him scornfully. After that, Mishael was unwilling to offer his cousin anything more by way of compensation, and he took as much notice of him as if he were dust under his feet.

The cousin was far from being mollified. As he saw his dream of gaining at least a share of the family's riches crumble, he was consumed with envy. In the course of time, he could contain himself no longer, and turned against Mishael.

"How long will the wicked prosper?" he complained to his neighbors and friends.

But all they could do in response was to throw up their hands helplessly.

In the end, in his claim for justice, the cousin did unto Mishael as Mishael had done unto Hananel. According to the tale passed down in the family, he, whom Mishael had so callously scorned, was as a fox and a lion all at the same time. He waylaid his foe on the way to the fields and lured him by some ruse to a distant olive grove. There he struck him down with a shepherd's staff and smashed in his head. Then he cast his lifeless body into the depth of a nearby well, in which the water, having almost run out, had become so murky that it had been deserted for years.

This well became Mishael's watery grave until his decayed body was discovered floating in it. It was drawn out feet first; and then, shrouded in white, it was brought to burial according to the laws and customs of Israel. By the time his son was old enough to read the letter his father had written to him, it had become but a whisper from the grave.

As there were no witnesses to testify to the cousin's deed before the elders, he was not brought to justice, either then or later. Yet he did not profit from his villainy. For it was Mishael's son, who later became Hagith's husband, rather than the cousin, who inherited the coveted house and land.

"Did no one avenge Mishael's blood by killing his cousin?" Osnath asked.

"No, for his son, who should have been the avenger, said that he who spills blood will have his own blood spilled, and he chose life over death. Besides, his father's memory had become but a curse in the family, so he saw no reason to pay homage to it. Instead, he brought the blood feud to a blessed end."

"But the memory of all that has come to pass cannot be blotted out."

"Not entirely," admitted Eliab. "All this remains a taint on our two families. But contrary to your longtime suspicion, as I had known all along and as Ruth's scroll showed, Obed was conceived from Boaz's seed, hence all this has nothing to do with my father's and my inheritance. Instead, it has a bearing on that which comprises the portion belonging to Hagith's son Uri, Adah's father."

"Then why were you so set on keeping it from me?"

"Hagith had put her trust in me by showing me Mishael's scroll. I was bound to protect her and Adah and their family's inheritance. And I could not see its reputation cast to the ground and trampled underfoot."

"To be sure. But how is it that you did not put your trust in me, in my ability to keep the secret?"

"When you first came to Bethlehem, you were fifteen years old, but in your soul you were still a child, Osnath, barely at the threshold of womanhood. And children are wont to blabber of what they don't understand."

"My tongue would have cleaved to my palate. Never would I have breathed a word that could have harmed anyone."

"You would never have spoken intentionally. But your mind was always wandering in distant domains, and your feet did not seem to be planted firmly in the ground. You might have blurted out the secret without intending to do so. You needed to become a woman first."

"You are the one who has accomplished this feat," she said mischievously. "You have turned me into a woman in every way."

"Into *my* woman."

"Yes."

"As you have turned me into your man."

Osnath thought that with these words the tale of the Unnamed had come to its end. But there was a sequel to it, which had to do with Adah.

⅏

Four days after Adah had voiced her wish to be divorced from Eliab, he called her to his room.

The thoughts that passed through his mind in those days were not happy ones. He had no fear of losing his son if he divorced Adah, for he would still be close by. But he worried that when it became known that he had sent away his wife at her own request, this would rebound unfavorably on his reputation.

Yet he had no doubt that the rumor of Adah's petition would spread in any case. Hence, it made no sense to keep in his house a disgruntled wife; one who, as everyone would know, preferred another man. Moreover, if he kept her against her will while her heart was given to another, she would be bound to stray, thus dishonoring him—and herself—even further.

Besides, he had no doubt that Osnath would be joyous to have him for herself alone, without Adah being any the worse for it. His mother, too, who of late seemed to be deeply perturbed by Adah's odd conduct, would sigh with relief.

Even so, there was one concern that kept him from pressing his seal of approval on Adah's request. Although he was wary of wounding her soul, he could not desist from cautioning her. When she came in, he said bluntly, "Ohad, the man you wish to marry, is the great-grandson of the man who murdered your great-grandfather."

Adah had a glib reply ready, which she must have rehearsed beforehand. "Ohad's great-grandfather merely administered to my great-grandfather the death penalty he deserved."

"This deed was committed a long time ago and does not weigh with me," Eliab replied. "But will not your father demur if you marry a descendant of the man who killed his grandfather?"

"No, for as he explained to me, the sins of ancestors are not visited on their descendants. And although Ohad is not as wealthy as you are, over time his family has accumulated assets, and they are far from negligible.

"Besides, my father told me that a murderer is not entitled to inherit the property of the man he has murdered. Therefore, Mishael should not have inherited his brother's property. It should have gone to his uncle instead, and thereafter to that uncle's descendants, and thus, in due course, some of it should have gone to Ohad. When I become Ohad's wife, it will allow my father to allay his own conscience by turning over to my new husband a part of our family's patrimony—which, as he well knows, rightly belongs to his family rather than to ours— yet without admitting that any wrong had been done."

Eliab found Adah's reply satisfactory enough to announce, "I will give you a book of divorcement in accordance with your demand, but under two conditions. When our son reaches the proper age, I will send him to a teacher of my choosing. And when the time comes, he will go out with me each day to work in our fields—part of which will one day be his—rather than in those of your new husband."

Adah readily agreed.

When Eliab recounted to Osnath what had transpired between him and Adah, he added: "So justice will emerge, and the saga of the Un-named, and with it that of Ruth, will come to a just conclusion at last."

Osnath was uplifted by this thought, and said, "At last, Ruth will be able to rest in peace."

Once Adah had been handed her book of divorcement and had re-turned to Hagith's house in preparation for her second wedding, Eliab made a suggestion: "Now that Adah is no longer with us, we may do as is good in our eyes. We have the means to separate from the large family that resides in this house and purchase a house of our own. Would you wish for us to do so, Osnath, my love? I am willing to be guided by you."

It did not take long for Osnath to consider the proposal. What was now Jesse's house had initially been constructed as a four-room house, with the front room running across the three behind it, as was the cus-tom. But more and more rooms had been added to it piecemeal over the years, until by now it was spread out like a little hamlet. It was certainly large enough to accommodate Jesse's and what she hoped would be Eliab's and her growing family.

Hence she said, "No, for I do not believe that it is what you want. If your mother and father will have me, I will be content to live with you in your ancestral home, amid your family, which will soon be mine also."

"My parents have already bestowed their blessing on your residing in our home. Ruth, too, would have blessed you for this, as I do."

"It will please me to live here also because she has pressed her stamp on the house and the garden. Because her memory still hovers over every stone of the house, and over the trees and the blossoms and the flowers of the garden, which she loved so much."

Eliab smiled into her eyes. "Although with your black curls you look so different from my red-haired great-grandmother, you resemble her in many ways."

"Like her, I have sowed my field with tears, but reaped it with joy."

"You are worthy in every way of inheriting her position as She Who Sits in the Garden, as Boaz used to call her. I am as sure as I am of the beauty of her soul that she would have wanted you to do so."

"So do I wish for it, for although I have never seen her, I will always love her, and her memory will always remain alive in my heart."

EPILOGUE

After Osnath had read Ruth's description of her wedding celebration, she proposed to Eliab that theirs should emulate it in every detail. He humored her by arranging it so to the best of his ability. As Boaz had traveled to Sdeh Moab to bring Ruth's family, so did Eliab travel to Ramah to bring Osnath's clan. Thus, giddy with delight and with great fanfare, Osnath became Eliab's second, though sole, wife.

As before the wedding, so afterward, Eliab was insatiable. As Osnath was always willing to assuage his desire, she was soon with child. Her firstborn was a daughter, and thereafter she was blessed with plentiful fruit of the womb, bearing her husband six sons and one more daughter, who followed each other at short intervals.

Like Ruth's cup after she married Boaz, Osnath's, too, was brimming over. Only one matter remained to mar her happiness: she could not reach agreement with her husband on the scroll she intended to write about Ruth.

One morning shortly after the wedding festivities were over, she brought Eliab to the scroll room. There she showed him a table full of tightly written pieces of parchment. "I have all these little scraps I have written down about Ruth, and also her scroll and the copy of Mishael's letter," she told him. "I seek your permission, sir, to use them to write a scroll of my own, laying bare the entire tale of Ruth's life. I cannot stand by and let her memory be swallowed up by darkness."

"You may write the scroll," said Eliab magnanimously, and Osnath was elated. Then he added, "But it will contain only what I permit you to write. There must be no mention of Ruth's connection with the Unnamed, or of the child she conceived from him or her subsequent miscarriage. Since he was Hagith's father-in-law, there must be not one word about the murder he committed, or of his having been murdered under such murky circumstances himself. There must not be even the shadow of a hint that Boaz knew Ruth before they were married."

"Then there is nothing left for me to write."

"You can still write a beautiful, true story that will warm the heart of anyone who sets eyes on it."

She felt her success melting away, and her face assumed an obdurate expression.

Eliab looked ferocious. "There is a rebellious streak in you that no husband would put up with. You will defer to me with good grace."

"I will not let you trample me under your heavy feet."

He tugged at the curls at the rear of her head, to make her raise her face to his. "I am not crushing you, Osnath, but ruling you, as set out in the Torah. But I am doing it gently, while pampering you with the best of all I have. You have every reason to be satisfied with your lot."

"I am not merely satisfied, but in bliss, as you well know."

"So you will cease to harass me about your scroll?"

But she could not, for she knew that nothing she did in her life would be as lasting as this scroll. Without it, her life would be but a passing shadow. So she persisted, saying, "Pray let me keep Ruth's memory alive, as she would have wanted me to do. Do not stifle her voice, which calls to me from across the generations."

Then she sat down at the table with an empty sheet of parchment before her, set to begin writing.

He erupted into a roaring voice. "Give me your scroll. I will not have my great-grandmother, or even Adah's great-grandfather, maligned. If you willfully defy me, I will burn your scroll."

"Then my life will be burned along with it," she said pitifully, but elicited nothing but a skeptical smile from him, as he took hold of the empty parchment.

Once, when Pninah and Samuel came for a visit, Osnath appealed to her uncle, but obtained no succor from him.

"Eliab speaks rightly, my niece," he ruled. "You will write a scroll depicting only those parts of Ruth's life that it is proper for the people to know about. But for this you will be richly rewarded. Because it will deal with the life of the great-grandmother of the man who one day will be a glorious king in Israel, I shall see to it that it is preserved for posterity.

"I will arrange it so that in due course it will be deposited in the House of the Lord, wherever he may choose to have his name dwell in the future. I will ensure that it is copied hundreds of times over and sent to scroll rooms around the land of Israel, and then copied again and again in those scroll rooms as well. Thus will it be passed down from ancestors to descendants for as long as the sun shines over the earth."

If Osnath had only Eliab to contend with, she would have stood up to him. She was sure that in his love for her, he would have relented. But since both her husband and her uncle were aligned against her, she gave in and wrote only what they permitted her to write.

Thus, one day, she sat down and began writing:

Long ago, in the time of the judges, there was a famine in the land . . .

And it came to pass that the scroll she wrote, *The Scroll of Ruth*, was preserved and copied countless times and passed down from generation to generation. Because Ruth had met Boaz at the time of the harvest, the scroll was read on high places at the festival of the wheat harvest, and so also until this very day.

HISTORICAL NOTE

This novel consists of two interlaced stories set in ancient Israel, an agricultural-pastoral society, in separate time periods three generations apart.

One tale, that of Ruth, is set in the era of the judges, which, by biblical account, followed the initial occupation of the land of Canaan by the Israelites. This period (widely dated as spanning from the twelfth to the mid-eleventh centuries BCE), described in the book of *Judges*, was marked by domestic turbulence and bloody battles with various enemies, including the Canaanites, the Philistines, and the Moabites.

The story of Ruth, as rendered in the biblical *Scroll of Ruth*, on the other hand, though also set at the time of the judges, depicts a state of peace between the Israelites and the Moabites. For that reason, some critical biblical scholars have branded *Ruth* as a piece of fiction. In their view, this literary work was written centuries later, with the didactic purpose of fostering tolerance toward marriage with foreigners who become a part of the people of Israel, in contravention to another tradition, which shunned such intermarriage.

However, although the period of the judges was fraught with warfare, hostilities were intermittent: The book of *Judges* mentions that the sporadic battles were interspersed with periods of peace. In one such period, for instance, peace lasted for no less than eighty years (*Judges* 3:30). The tale of Ruth must have taken place during one of those spells of peace. Thus, there is no reason to doubt that the book of Ruth sprang from an account of actual rather than fictitious events.

At the time of the judges, the tribes of Israel were in the nature of a loose confederacy, with a large degree of tribal autonomy, under the traditional patriarchal authority of the "elders." In moments of crisis all or some of the tribes rallied behind sporadic charismatic leaders, referred to as judges, most of whom served as judges and military leaders at one and the same time. During the latter part of this period, the tribes were beginning to aspire to a national leader and a central administration, that is, to a king, to confront the menace of old and new enemies.

But this aspiration came to fruition only in the later years of the prophet Samuel (widely dated to the late eleventh century BCE), in which the second of this book's stories is set. Apart from being a prophet, Samuel was also the last of the great judges, and the "king-maker," who anointed both King Saul and King David in his lifetime.

His ability to do so apparently did not derive from any coercive power he might have wielded. Rather, it stemmed from his widely renowned charismatic leadership and from the high esteem he enjoyed among the people. It was also based on the fact that the political structure was close to what today we would refer to as a "theocracy," which rendered it legitimate for the prophet, the representative of the Almighty, to designate the king.

In both the periods described in the novel, literacy was not yet widespread, and scribes acted as teachers to limited circles. Even so, there is indirect, circumstantial evidence for some literacy among women, especially those of high social standing: the Bible ascribes important literary works—the Song of Deborah, the Song of Hannah—to prominent women.

Women's literacy is also attested to by archeological evidence: A few seals belonging to women were discovered, with their owners' names inscribed on them in Moabite and Hebrew (among other ancient languages). Since seals were used to attest to the authenticity of written documents, it may be presumed that the owners could read the documents on which they pressed their seals. The seals discovered are mainly from the ninth to the seventh centuries BCE. But it is conceivable that similar seals existed in the twelfth and the eleventh centuries, but were not discovered. Hence it is quite feasible that the two heroines of this novel, one Moabite and the other Israelite, both of high social stature, were well versed in the art of reading and writing.

There is no substantial evidence as to who wrote the various books of the Bible that followed the Torah, the Five Books of Moses. Some commentators have raised the possibility that women participated in writing those books, a possibility I have also taken up in this novel.

ACKNOWLEDGMENTS

I would like to express my deepest gratitude to the people who have devoted time and effort to reading this book, each of whom made an invaluable contribution to its improvement. They are (in the chronological order of reading it): Tamar Fox, Yaara Zeidman, Nitza Keren, Liora Bernstein, Olivia Marks-Woldman, Maria Antoniou, Tamar Halevy, Pauline Douglas, Ruth Etzioni, and Jane Cavolina (who corrected numerous flaws in both content and style).

I also owe a debt of gratitude to Itzhak Jamitovsky for his well-taken professional comments on the historical note.

Special thanks go to my agent Judith Riven, whose excellent comments on the manuscript and whose support and encouragement have been far above and beyond the call of duty.

I am deeply indebted to Ali Bothwell Mancini, the book's editor, for her brilliant comments, which saved me from many pitfalls, helped guide me through the final stages of writing, and greatly improved the book's quality.

Finally, hearty thanks to my husband, Zvi; my sons, Ethan and Oren; my daughter, Tamar; and my daughters-in-law, Hedva and Ruth for their unfailing patience and support, without which this book would not have seen the light of day.